Desert Wind

Books by Betty Webb

Lena Jones Mysteries
Desert Noir
Desert Wives
Desert Shadows
Desert Run
Desert Cut
Desert Lost
Desert Wind

Gunn Zoo Mysteries
The Anteater of Death
The Koala of Death

Desert Wind

A Lena Jones Mystery

Betty Webb

Poisoned Pen Press

Copyright © 2012 by Betty Webb

First Edition 2012

10 9 8 7 6 5 4 3 2 1

Library of Congress Catalog Card Number: 2011933445

ISBN: 9781590589793   Hardcover
            9781590589816   Trade Paperback

Poisoned Pen Press
6962 E. First Ave., Ste. 103
Scottsdale, AZ 85251
www.poisonedpenpress.com
info@poisonedpenpress.com

Printed in the United States of America

For the Downwinders

Acknowledgments

No author works alone. Of particular service this time around were the excellent Robert C. Kezer, Marge Purcell, Debra McCarthy, and the Sheridan Street Irregulars—especially Scott Andrews, who explained the differences between carbines and rifles. Additional thanks to Cowboy Dave, whose wisdom guided this book, and Police Chief (ret.) James Webb for his advice. My eternal gratitude to all those good folks. Any mistakes that appear in this book are down to me, not them.

"The past is never dead. It is not even past."

—William Faulkner

Chapter One

August 1954: Snow Canyon, Utah

From his vantage point with the horses on a small hillock, Gabe Boone watched the cameras track the actor across the simmering desert floor toward the skin-draped yurt. Even with the heavy makeup around the man's eyes, no one would have mistaken him for Genghis Khan. His height, his build, his long-legged stride—they could only have belonged to one man: John Wayne.

"He sure is something to see, ain't he?" drawled Curly, another wrangler on the film set.

They'd been standing there holding the horse's reins going on two hours now. Curly was twice Gabe's age, but because of a life spent mainly on ranches and in too many bars, he looked sixty. His face had been burned saddle-brown by the sun and wind, his tobacco-stained teeth almost the same color.

Gabe, only twenty-two and a non-drinker, non-chewer, flashed pearly whites. "He is that. But he don't look like no Mongol."

"Seen a lot of Mongols, whatever those be?"

Gabe walked over to a big bay, straightened its saddle, and tried to look knowing. "Cowboys like us is what they are, from somewhere out in China."

"Commies." Curly spit a disdainful wad of tobacco on the ground, barely missing his own boot.

Gabe sighed. There Curly went again, seeing a Commie behind every rock and cactus. You'd think *he* was the one left

Korea minus a finger. Gabe stared down at the stump where his left forefinger had been. Curly could rave on, but as for himself, after what he'd been through over there, he didn't want to think about war, politics, or what-have-you, didn't want to think about anything except settling down and raising a family. Abby wanted kids, lots of them. He did, too. The sound of kids laughing, well, wasn't that what life was all about?

Curly wasn't through griping. After spitting again, this time a little further away, he said, "Damned Commies, them Chinese, them Ruskies and all their stinking friends, think they can come over here and take away our horses and saddles and make us call 'em Comrade. Well, we got a big ol' answer for 'em, don't we?"

Gabe didn't want to hear about *that*, either. He was sick of it. "All right, all right. The Commies is devils and the rest of us is angels. Have at it, I don't care. But that Mongol emperor Wayne's playing lived hundreds of years ago, long before Red China or that Korea mess, and I'm betting you dollars to dough-nuts ol' Genghis wasn't no Commie. What I was trying to tell you is that Abby and me, when we drove her dad's truck over to Los Angeles last year, we went to this Chinese restaurant on Hollywood Boulevard and met a guy who was actually born in Mongolia, and believe me, he didn't look nothing like John Wayne. Not that it matters. With the big man in the movie, it's sure to be a hit."

Mood soothed, Curly jerked his head toward the actress below, a porcelain-skinned redhead who looked even less Asian than Wayne. "Miss Hayward should sell a few tickets, too. Wonder if I can get Harriet to dress up like that."

At the thought of Curly's wife, with her doughy arms and massive belly, dressed in a see-through harem outfit, Gabe laughed so hard it spooked Steel, Wayne's favorite horse. Once he settled the animal down, he said, "Can't hurt to ask."

Curly grunted. "There's inexperience talking."

Gabe didn't bother to argue. Now that Wayne was out of sight of the cameras and his own worshipful eyes, he turned his attention elsewhere. While Steel and the other horses pawed at the hot earth in irritated boredom, he studied the scene spread out below. A mile of dusty flatland stretched out before him, encircled by tall red and white sandstone formations. Here and there black lava boulders dappled a renegade patch of green, while above, the cloudless blue sky almost seemed to glow. Normally deserted, Snow Canyon swarmed with more than two hundred Hollywood types, a dozen or so wranglers, and upwards of three hundred Paiute Indians outfitted to look like Mongols. Because of their high cheekbones and weathered faces, the Paiute looked a lot more Asian than the high-priced actors.

But they were all—wranglers and Indians—grateful that in the two months working on this movie they'd earned more than they usually saw in a year. Enough for Gabe to finish the down payment on that little ranch he and Abby had been saving up for. God bless Hollywood. It had made her smile for the first time in...

"How is Abby these days?"

Curly's question, coming right on top of Gabe's thoughts, startled him. "Uh, fine, I guess."

"That blue-eyed pup I brought over cheer her up any?"

Gabe believed that if there was any trait worse than being mean to horses, it was lying to a friend, so he was careful in his answer. "She's been feeling some better, has that pup sleeping in a box right next to the bed. But it takes a woman hard, losing a baby like that."

"Men, too, maybe."

Refusing to let Curly see him flush, Gabe turned away from the other man's watchful eyes and fiddled with Steel's bridle. The night before he'd polished the leather until it gleamed, but by mid-morning it had already been coated by red dust. Not just the bridle, either. Yesterday, Curly had joked that all the wranglers were red by the end of the day. "Red as them Paiutes," he'd finished.

The old wrangler hadn't exaggerated much. The red dust covered every man and woman in the canyon, darkening their faces, hennaing their hair, even creeping into their underclothes.

The wranglers didn't mind. Dust and heat, it was all the same to them, part of the pattern of the day. It was different for the actors. They made their money from their faces, so a crowd of make-up artists kept fussing around to keep them pretty.

Except for Wayne. The dirtier he got, the better he liked it. Now, *there* was a man, Gabe thought. The real deal. No wonder he was called "The Duke." Unlike most of those Hollywood actors, Wayne could ride with the roughest of them, damned be the dust, damned be the scorpions, damned be the snakes and the cactus and damned be all the hell Snow Canyon threw at him. Sometimes at night the Duke even came over to the chuck wagon and shared a bottle or two—or three or four—with the wranglers, matching them drink for drink, slapping them on their backs, telling dirty stories that made you laugh in spite of yourself. And that wasn't all. Despite his movie reputation as an Indian-killer, Wayne didn't ignore the Paiutes, either. The fact that some of them couldn't speak English didn't faze him none; he had the gift of making himself understood. Many was the night Gabe heard the Duke's deep laugh boom over the Paiutes' own, carried on the wind from the Indian encampment.

"A man's man," Gabe whispered to the horse. "Tough as need be."

"What's that you mumbling?"

Before Gabe could give another carefully considered answer, Curly doubled over and began to cough. He coughed so long and hard that Gabe feared he'd cough up his lungs.

"You okay there, pardner?"

Between coughs, Curly waved Gabe's concern away. "Never… been…better. Damned…dust."

There had been a lot of coughing lately, from the wranglers, the Paiutes, the Hollywood people—even the horses. That red dust oiled its way out of the air and down into a man's lungs, settling there to make trouble until he coughed it back out. But men could take care of themselves. It was the horses Gabe worried about. He didn't know which was worse on the animals, the dust that gave them so much trouble breathing or the blisters that formed on their mouths after they'd grazed on the puny straggles of buffalo grass poking from the parched red earth. Come to think of it, some of those Paiutes suffered from the same blisters. Maybe that was because they ate the rabbits and ground squirrels that had been eating the bad grass. Used to hunt the antelope, the Indians did, brought down deer and elk. But lately, the larger animals had been dying off, covered with sores all over their bodies. Sometimes their coats and muzzles looked so scary the Paiutes wouldn't touch them, made do with smaller game and whatever else they could forage. Desert plants, pine nuts, spindly stuff that would hardly keep a chicken alive.

This canyon country was a hard country. Men and horses had to be hard to endure it.

When Curly's coughs died away, Gabe turned his eyes to the film set, where the Duke was swaggering toward Susan Hayward, his hand on the huge knife at his waist. The cameras—one of them mounted on a small metal track—moved back as he approached her.

The scalding wind, blowing down from the canyon and toward the small hillock where Gabe and Curly waited, lifted the actor's words to them. "What Temujin wants, he takes, Bortai!"

The beautiful redhead clutched her skimpy costume close to her breasts. Defiance lit her eyes. "No dog of a Mongol…"

She began to cough.

Chapter Two

Present day: Scottsdale, Arizona

Monday, 9 a.m.

It had been a rough weekend, but the new week wasn't looking much better. When I unlocked the door to Desert Investigations, Jimmy wasn't there.

The very fact that I'd had to unlock my office should have been warning enough. Even though I lived in the apartment upstairs and Jimmy lived three miles away on the Salt River Pima/Maricopa Indian Reservation, my partner always beat me to the office by at least an hour. Nothing pleased him more in the early mornings than to raise the blinds, turn on the computer, and while it was warming up, grind some Starbucks while he sang a Pima prayer. By the time I made it downstairs, the hour-old coffee would be thickened to perfection.

Not today. Shut blinds. Cold computer. No coffee.

Jimmy's desk being closest to the door, I grabbed his phone and punched in his cell number. After four rings, it switched over to voice mail. "Ya-ta-hey, hola, and hello! I'll be out of reach for a week or two, but if you leave the standard message, you'll receive the standard reciprocal phone call as soon as I get back." Beep.

Out of reach for a week or two? "Hey, Jimmy. Lena here. Call me. I'm at the office, it's Monday morning and, well, I expected you to be in. Why aren't you?"

Then I tried his landline.

Same message.

Deciding that coffee would help me think, I went over to the fancy Krups he'd bought for the office last Christmas, dumped in a handful of Guatemalan Antigua beans, hit EXPRESS BREW, and waited while the machine made grinding, then gurgling, noises. Sixty seconds later I poured the steaming cup and sipped at it as fast as my scalded taste buds would let me. Once the caffeine hit, I opened the office blinds, hoping that more light would chase away my growing sense of unease. It didn't.

At nine on Mondays, there is little pedestrian traffic in Old Town Scottsdale. Most art galleries don't open until ten, and given the August heat, few tourists braved the ninety-five-degrees-and-rapidly-climbing temperature. As I watched, one perspiring couple shuffled along the pavement, wiping sweat in unison from their brows. Not far behind, a lone woman wearing a dangerously bare sundress—melanoma, anyone?—peered into the window of an Indian jewelry store, then moved past my sightline, leaving the sidewalk empty and me alone in a growing silence.

By now I should be listening to the tap-tap of Jimmy's fingers on his keyboard, his soft chuckles whenever he uncovered the old crimes prospective employees of Southwest MicroSystems believed were long-erased. We should be discussing how the past eventually caught up to everyone, trailing after them like the stink of dog shit on new shoes. Instead, all I could hear was the discreet hiss of our new air conditioner. Unnerved, I walked over to my own desk and turned on my computer. Seconds later I called up my favorite blues station, and the haunting wail of Blind Willie McTell on "Statesboro Blues" killed the silence.

Now I could think.

Jimmy Sisiwan had been a full partner ever since Desert Investigations had opened several years back, and we had so much in common that I sometimes called him "Almost Brother." Like me, he was an orphan, his Pima parents having died not long after his birth from the diabetes that ravaged the tribe. Unlike me, he'd been adopted by people who loved him, whereas I—deemed unadoptable because of certain behavioral issues resulting from a gunshot wound to the head—had made the rough rounds of Arizona's foster care system. Jimmy was even-tempered, but as for me, let's just say that ongoing anger management therapy kept me out of jail. The point is, Jimmy calms my chaos. No matter what kind of crazy messed with my mind, he always has my back. Without that big Indian, I feel naked.

"Jimmy, where the hell are you?"

I hadn't realized I'd spoken aloud, and the sound of my voice echoing around the sharp corners of the room startled me. Furnished in mauve and bleached pine, the office had all the personality of a furniture showroom, but it worked for our high-roller clientele. By the time they came to see us, life—in the form of predatory gold-diggers, missing teenagers, and various and sundry con artists—had kicked them around so much they needed soothing, not stimulation. But now all that Yuppie Bland unnerved me. Something was wrong.

As Blind Willie finished the last few bars of "Statesboro" and started on "Broke Down Engine Blues," I finished the last of the Guatemalan Antigua. That's when I noticed the message light blinking on my phone. I entered my PIN number and hit the speaker button.

Jimmy's voice floated out.

"Hi, Lena. Sorry about the short notice, but something's come up and I have to leave town. At least it's August and not much is going on. In the unlikely event that Southwest MicroSystems sends over a new batch of background checks for us to run, which is doubtful because as you'll remember, they're in the middle of a hiring freeze, call Jean Begay. I checked with her before I left town, and she said she'd be happy to help with backgrounders or anything else computer-wise. See you in a week." Pause. "Or two."

Click.

When the relief that he hadn't been mangled in a car accident faded away, I replayed his message and listened all the way to the end. A week or two? If he'd had time to contact Jean Begay, why hadn't he bothered to phone me? Swallowing my annoyance, I muted Blind Willie in mid-yowl and called Jean. She answered immediately, but our conversation proved something I already knew: Navajos aren't chatty.

"Good morning, Jean. Lena Jones here."

"Hi."

"Um, I just called to ask, well, do you know where Jimmy is?"

"Nope."

"But…"

"Other phone's ringing. Have a nice day."

Jean rang off, leaving me staring at the receiver as the silence closed in again. When I turned the radio station back up, Blind Willie had finished and Big Joe Williams was carrying on about his "Little Leg Woman." I listened to that for a while and pretended I wasn't worried. Jimmy was a grownup. If he'd wanted me to know where he was, he would have told me.

Big Joe Williams gave way to Mississippi John Hurt, who morphed into Elmore James, who later stepped aside for John Lee Hooker—who reminded me of my murdered father…

I cut the Internet radio off and tried to find something to do. Not easy, today.

The television series that had hired me as a consultant remained on hiatus while industry gossip hinted that it might not be renewed for the next season. Fortunately, Desert Investigations had thrived for years before Hollywood came a-knocking and would continue to thrive after the program was cancelled. But as Jimmy had been careful to point out, it was August, and our clients had fled for cooler climes. Nonetheless, I called up our case files on the computer and started going through those that remained open.

DI-CASE:4109/Stallworth. Elizabeth and Douglas Stallworth had hired us to track down their twenty-one-year-old daughter, Jennifer. When last seen, Jennifer was part of the inner circle surrounding a New Age minister who fleeced his flock out of millions. Upon his release from prison, his shorn flock welcomed him back with open arms.

Forgiveness is a wonderful thing, but stupidity isn't quite as wonderful, especially when the combination of the two made it possible for victims to be re-victimized. Although aware that her parents had lost more than two hundred thousand dollars to Father Felon, Jennifer signed over to him the deed to the Paradise Valley condo her parents had given her, along with the title to her new BMW 335i convertible. When I pointed out to the Stallworths that Jennifer was an adult and thus enjoyed the legal right to ruin her life, they had not been happy. After much discussion, I'd given in to their pleas to keep an eye out for her, but so far, she and Father Felon remained off the grid.

I scrolled down to DI-CASE:3867/Bryce. For the past two years, Richard Bryce IV had been searching for his third wife, Chrissie, who had run off with her stepson—fifteen-year-old Richard Bryce V. The trail had grown stale, but the cops and I were still looking.

Then there was DI-CASE:4218/Haggerty. Stephen Haggerty, owner of Haggerty and Sons Jewelers, had loaned a boatload of diamonds to adorn the spindly limbs of five socialites for their appearance at the Helping Hearts Charity Ball. The next morning, their chauffeur was found at Sky Harbor International Airport, passed out across the front seat of their rented limo, his blood filled with orange juice and Rohypnol. The phony socialites were gone, along with the diamonds. Rumor had it that they were now working Florida, but so far, I'd found nothing concrete.

After an hour spent going through other open cases and making a few phone calls, I found nothing that called for my immediate attention. None of the cases involved violence, just the usual frustration and heartbreak. I was halfway tempted to shut down the office and drive to the gym when the phone rang. The caller identified herself as Amy Flanagan, the new Human Resources Supervisor at Genesis Cable. She sounded tense.

"Ms. Jones, Beth over at Southwest MicroSystems—she's a friend of mine —recommended Desert Investigations to me. Here's my problem. Genesis has a new contract for the West

Valley, so we have to bring some new hires aboard, and quick, too. I have thirty job applications sitting on my desk right now. Five of them are for high level positions, so you see that, uh…"

I helped her out of her discomfort. "You need them checked fast and you need them checked deep, right?"

She expelled her breath. "Exactly."

Problem was, although I could play around with Google and Dogpile, I didn't have Jimmy's more advanced computer skills. With the realization that we were probably losing a new client for good, I apologized and offered Jean Begay's phone number. Flanagan thanked me and hung up, leaving me glaring at Jimmy's empty chair.

Irresponsible rat!

Then I caught myself.

Being a foundling, I had no known living relatives, and because intimacy had always been difficult for me, I also had few friends. The old saw counseled, "Keep your friends close and your enemies closer," but Jimmy's friendship had taught me the flaw in that philosophy. Whenever I began tipping over into the shadow side of life, his steadiness always brought me back. He would say at such times: *Love your friends, forget your enemies.* Yet here I was, angry at the most decent man I'd ever known over something as insignificant as one lost client.

Another thing Jimmy had taught me: When anger blooms, search for the seed. Knowledge being prequel to understanding, I placed a call to Michael Sisiwan, Jimmy's uncle. If anyone knew Jimmy's whereabouts, Michael did.

"Pima Paint and Collision," Michael Sisiwan chirped into the phone. "You wreck 'em, we fix 'em."

I forced myself to sound casual. "It's Lena, Michael. Jimmy wasn't in the office when I came in but he left me a message saying something about being out of reach for a couple of weeks. At least that's what I think the message said. You know how landlines are. Talk to somebody in China and the connection's so clear it sounds like you're talking to someone across the street, but try to get a message from someone who lives down the road and all you get is static. If my guess is right and he is out of town, out of curiosity, where'd he go?"

Unlike me, Pimas never lie, but they can evade. Trying to get information from one could be like navigating a minefield of politeness.

"Jimmy? Sorry, Lena, but that man does not give me every detail of his schedule."

"Understood. I'm simply asking if you know where he is."

"Hmmm. Do I know where the man is." A statement, not a question. Michael knew and wasn't going to tell me.

"Michael, I'm getting worried. Jimmy has never disappeared like this before, so stop playing games."

Another long pause. A laid-back tribe, Pimas like the subtleties of conversation, the slow dance around the word room. But because of his collision business, Michael was used to dealing with anxiety-ridden white folks, and a little directness had rubbed off.

"Since you put it like that, if Jimmy wanted you to know where he was and what he was doing, he would have told you. I am very sorry, but…Oh, look. Here comes a messed-up Ranchero. Think I will mosey over there and check the damage. Always liked Rancheros. Prettiest thing Detroit ever produced—a car that looks like a pickup. Or a pickup that looks like a car. This one is turquoise, too, my favorite color, not that other colors are not nice. Red. Yellow. Even gray, which is under-appreciated, seeing how it is the color of rain clouds, which in the desert is always good news. You think the fellow might be interested in selling that pretty thing?" He didn't wait for my answer. "You take care now, Lena."

Click.

Shut down for the second time, I sat there and thought for a while, but the more I thought, the more uneasy I became. Jimmy had always taken the financial success of Desert Investigations as seriously as I did. He was hyper-dependable. In the past, whenever something necessitated an abrupt leave of absence on his part, he had always contacted me first. On the two occasions he couldn't reach me—I was sometimes called out of town, too—he'd left detailed messages on both my cell and my landline. One week last spring he hadn't made it to the office at all, but his phone message informed me he'd been called to testify in federal court about a disputed Indian water rights claim. The winter before, he received a last-minute offer from a friend to go dog-sledding through the Alaskan tundra, but before he said yes, he wanted to check in with me. After I told him he was nuts if he didn't go, he detailed the route they would take, adding that he'd carry along both his cell and his laptop. Yet now, he'd shrouded his whereabouts in mystery.

Looking back, I realized I'd sensed the wrongness of things before I'd walked downstairs to an empty office. Maybe even three nights earlier.

The nightmares began on Friday night, with my usual flight through a dark forest, determined men not far behind, blinding flashes of gunfire, screams…Three nights in a row, a new record, even for me. Once I'd woken up murmuring Jimmy's name.

Scientists say you can't see into the future, and to that, I say baloney. Oh, you might not be able to "see" it like you can see pictures on a television screen, but you can often sense it. Warnings ripple through time like the strings of a harp, their vibrations audible to any attuned listener. Label this ability "precognition" or "sixth sense," the terminology didn't matter. What did matter is that all weekend long I'd known that something was amiss. Wherever Jimmy was, whomever he was with, he needed me.

After shutting down my computer, I locked up the office and headed out to my Jeep. Telephones and computers are all very well, but when it comes to investigation, there's nothing like boots on the ground. I fired up the engine and peeled out of the parking lot.

One of the more interesting facts about Old Town Scottsdale is that despite its art-and-nightlife-friendly reputation, it abuts the western edge of the Salt River Pima/Maricopa Indian Reservation. Now that Casino Arizona had brought some much-needed income to the tribe, my drive east on McDowell Road took me past a flurry of new homes and Pima-run businesses.

Indian poverty, at least in this area of the state, was becoming eradicated. Unlike the white folks who subdivided their portion of the Sonoran Desert with look-alike houses and look-alike yards, the Pimas left the desert alone to do its wild thing. Their widely spaced new homes, most of them clean-lined stucco ranches, sat surrounded by unmanicured creosote bushes, mesquite trees, and stately saguaro cacti. The Indians hadn't decimated the wildlife, either. You could still see families of javelina and wild-eyed coyotes slipping through the wide spaces between the houses.

When it comes to living in harmony with Nature, we could learn a few things from the Pima. But of course, we won't.

Within minutes I had turned off McDowell onto the dirt road that led to Jimmy's trailer. The busy cross-reservation highway lay only a few hundred yards behind me, but his Airstream was located within a grove of ancient mesquite with limbs so heavy they scraped the ground. No one would see what I was about to do.

Unless you're a professional thief, picking locks isn't all that easy, but I've learned from the pros. Once inside, I paused a moment to get my bearings, feeling the hot, still air of the trailer sucking the breath right out of my lungs. Ever eco-conscious, Jimmy had turned off the air-conditioner before he'd left town. Not wanting to fry, I fumbled for the switch and flipped it back on. After a few moments, I could breathe again.

Once my eyes became accustomed to the dim light, I gave a brief glance around. I'd been here before, but was amazed anew at Jimmy's unique style of decorating, so different than that of our bland office. The carpet was a deep burnt orange, the same color as the sandstone mesas that surrounded the reservation. Pima-patterned pillows were scattered artfully across a brown leather sofa. A hand-made coffee table comprised of saguaro cactus spines studded with tiny bits of turquoise held up two Hopi kachinas; they looked like they were about to leap into battle. But it was Jimmy's cabinetry I admired most. The oak cabinets above the kitchen sink were covered with paintings of

Pima gods: Earth Doctor, the father-god who had created the world; Elder Brother, who after defeating Earth Doctor in battle, had sent him into hiding in a labyrinth beneath the desert; and Spider Woman, who'd tried in vain to make peace between the two. Jimmy's factory-built Airstream had become a holy place, and I hoped his gods would forgive my intrusion.

Knowing my partner's habits, I went straight to the telephone stand, another piece of furniture-as-art. The only thing on top was a blank notepad, with a pencil next to it.

Resorting to one of the oldest tricks of the trade, I rubbed the top sheet with the soft-leaded pencil, and little by little, block letters began to appear. 928-555-7535. Below that, 928-555-7400. Telephone numbers with a far northwest Arizona area code, the double-zero number probably a business. All I had to do was call, but that created a slight problem. If I used Jimmy's phone and he answered, caller I.D. would show I'd broken into his trailer. If I used one of my own phones, there was a good chance he wouldn't pick up.

Fortunately, there was another way to gain the needed information. After stuffing the sheet of paper into my carry-all, I headed out.

As soon as I arrived back at the office, I turned my computer on again and logged onto the reverse phone directory. The 535 number turned out to be the reservations office at Sunset Trails Guest Ranch. The name looked vaguely familiar, but I couldn't quite place it. The next number startled me: the Walapai County Jail.

I stared at the screen for a while, thinking.

Guest ranch. Jail.

Jail. Guest ranch.

Bingo.

Ted Olmstead, Jimmy's adoptive brother, was assistant manager at Sunset Trails Guest Ranch, which was owned by Hank Olmstead, their father. A full blooded Paiute and the older member of Olmstead's large adoptive brood, Ted had been visiting the Pima Rez several months earlier for an Inter-Tribal pow-wow when Jimmy introduced us. Less than a week later, Ted's wife Kimama had been shot to death, but to my knowledge, her killer had never been identified. Although the husband is usually the first suspect in such cases, Ted had never fallen under suspicion. At the time his wife was shot, he'd been more than an hour's drive away, leading twenty-five dudes on a long trail ride.

But now, had there been new developments in the case that necessitated Jimmy's presence?

Hoping for an answer, I ran WALAPAI COUNTY JAIL+ THEODORE OLMSTEAD through Google. The first item that popped up was from the Saturday issue of the *Walapai Flats Journal-Gazette.*

> **WALAPAI FLATS, ARIZONA**—Friday night, sheriff's deputies picked up Theodore Olmstead and are holding him as a material witness on suspicion of having information about the shooting death of Ike Donohue, a resident of Sunset Canyon Lakes. Donohue's body was found by tourists at Sunset Point early Friday morning. His car was parked nearby.
>
> According to witnesses, Olmstead, the assistant manager of Sunset Trails Guest Ranch, was involved in an altercation Thursday with Donohue at a service station in Walapai Flats, where both had stopped for gas.
>
> "Mr. Donohue said something to the Indian, like, 'I'm sorry, but I got to the pump first,' and the next thing you know, he was on the ground," said Mia Tosches, of Sunset Canyon Lakes. "He must have got hit pretty hard, poor guy."
>
> A second witness disputes Tosches' story.
>
> "Donohue just slipped on an oil spill and made a big fuss about it," said Earl Two Horses, owner of the

service station. "Ted didn't touch
him."

A source who didn't want his name
released said there had been bad blood
between Olmstead and Donohue ever
since Olmstead's wife, Dr. Kimama Olmstead, 36, a local veterinarian known
for her political activism, was killed
in a drive-by shooting this past May.
Her murder remains unsolved, but the
source said that Olmstead blamed Donohue for creating the hostile environment that led to her death.

"Mr. Olmstead has not yet been
charged with any crime," said Walapai
County Sheriff Wiley Alcott. "He is
merely being detained to prevent a
failure of justice. Comments he made
after Mr. Donohue's body was found led
our detectives to believe that Mr.
Olmstead might have some knowledge as
to the perpetrator or perpetrators of
the crime. I would also like to point
out that Mr. Olmstead, having relatives and friends on various Indian
reservations throughout the U.S.,
presents a serious flight risk."

Ike Donohue, the press spokesman
for the Black Basin Uranium Mine,
which is due to open next week, was
formerly in charge of public relations
at Cook & Creighton Tobacco, located
in Durham, North Carolina. He leaves
behind a wife, two sons, a daughter,
and four grandchildren, all residents
of North Carolina, where he lived
before his retirement five years ago.

It is not yet known if Theodore
Olmstead has obtained counsel.

Illustrating the article was a head shot of Donohue, a handsome, thin-faced man in his early sixties. His smile was movie-star-broad but didn't reach his eyes.

Jimmy being Jimmy, he'd ridden to his brother's rescue. Again, this brought up the obvious question: why hadn't he wanted me working with him? Despite my partner's considerable computer skills, I knew more about the ins and outs of criminal investigation than he did. Ted's situation called for an experienced detective, not a desk jockey.

That "material witness" thing worried me, too. Since 9/11, it had become easier for law enforcement officials to hold someone indefinitely without filing charges. All the authorities needed was to hint to a sympathetic judge that pubic safety might be at risk, and the judge would comply. In this case, the victim being employed as the spokesman for a nearby uranium mine made a good argument. Given the ongoing oil crisis, the country's nuclear power plants needed all the enriched uranium they could get. Hell, Ted was lucky he hadn't been sent to Gitmo.

Further piquing my curiosity was the mention of Ted's wife being a political activist. That was news to me, but when I Googled her name, she popped up in more than six thousand hits. Reading through the more reliable sites, I discovered that she and the group she headed—Victims of Uranium Mining (V.U.M.)—had raised legal hell over the proposed opening of the Black Basin Uranium Mine outside Walapai Flats, less than twenty miles from the Grand Canyon. V.U.M. pointed out that Roger Tosches, the mine's owner, had at one time operated the Moccasin Peak Uranium Mine, located on the Navajo Reservation. Scores of Navajo miners had died of lung and kidney cancer, V.U.M. said, caused by the ingestion of the mine's radioactive dust. But the damage hadn't ended there. Moccasin Peaks' mine tailings—leftover rocks from which the uranium had been extracted—continued to pollute the reservation. According to V.U.M., the Navajos were suffering from highly increased rates of various cancers due to not only working in the mine, but because of the poisonous tailings, which contained radioactive material and high amounts of arsenic.

The same poisoning would happen to the nearby Grand Canyon, V.U.M. warned. Did Americans want one of the world's most magnificent places turned into a radiation hot spot?

An opposing press release—most probably penned by public relations flak Ike Donohue—had disputed V.U.M.'s claims, saying that the Black Basin would meet all federal safety standards. Ignoring the problems at the Moccasin Peak Mine, the release added that the new mine would provide jobs for approximately four hundred and fifty workers.

More curious now, I Googled Donohue and discovered in press conference after press conference, he had repeated that the Black Basin and its planned waste disposal methods were well within Federal guidelines. Ecofriendly, too, kind to the birds and bees and green leafy trees. Donohue never once addressed V.U.M.s concerns that the new mine would be operated by the same man who had so despoiled the Navajo community.

As for the possible despoiling of the Grand Canyon, he never brought it up.

In a lengthy interview on the front page of the *Walapai Flats Journal-Gazette* a week before Kimama's death, Donohue was vicious in his portrayal of Kimama Olmstead, decrying what he called her "insensitivity" to the local economy, reliant for decades on the mining of various minerals, including silver, gold, and copper—as well as uranium.

"Mrs. Olmstead and the other hysterics in V.U.M. don't care about the common working man," Donohue sniped in the article. "Mrs. Olmstead's own lucrative business won't be affected, because Fluffy will always need a vet, and barring tort reform, V.U.M.'s high-roller attorneys will continue to chase ambulances. The people who will be hurt if the Black Basin doesn't open are the honest, hard-working miners who need those jobs to feed their families."

With that quote, Donohue had managed to hint that not only were Kimama and V.U.M. hypocritical, but lazy, too. His work for Cook & Creighton Tobacco had taught him well: don't address the argument, smear the other guys. The problem with smears, though, is that they so often rebound on the person who created them. Had someone killed Donohue because of his work on behalf of the Black Basin Uranium Mine?

Not that I'd ever find out. For some reason, Jimmy had decided that the case wasn't my problem. It stung, I'll admit. I'd helped members of Jimmy's Pima family out of trouble before, and he'd always been grateful. In this case, though, I had no choice other than to respect his autonomy.

Heaving a sigh of relief, I gave in to Google's siren call and spent the next half-hour surfing the web. Eventually I landed on a Southwestern gardening site that informed me that, yes, cigarettes will most definitely rot your lungs, but on the upside, they make a dandy pesticide. The hyperlink under that sentence sent me to another site devoted to the eradication of sewer roaches.

Huh! A few days ago, after finding and squashing one of those two-inch-long monsters in the office's rest room, I'd briefly considered calling in the exterminators, then backed off because of the strong chemicals they sometimes used. Nicotine, though…Apparently, all you did was stir a cup of loose tobacco into a gallon of warm water, add one tablespoon of dishwashing liquid, then cover and let the mess brew overnight. The next day you poured the brownish liquid into a sprayer, then spritzed any remaining roaches back into the hell from whence they came.

Too bad I hadn't known about tobacco's one redeeming quality while breaking into Jimmy's trailer. Because of the lack of Federal tax, the price of tobacco in all its forms remained low on the rez. I decided to drive out there again for lunch, enjoy a nice bowl of mutton stew at Peg's Pima Cafe, and on my way back, purchase a month's supply of the killer weed at Chief Lloyd's Peace Pipe.

Thinking about Jimmy again sent me off on another Google hunt. To find out if he had any luck yet in getting Ted out of jail, I logged onto the *Walapai Flats Journal-Gazette* home page to see if anything further was mentioned about Donohue's murder.

What I found canceled my cockroach-killing plans. "Arrest Made In Donohue Case," screamed the headline.

WALAPAI FLATS, ARIZONA—Sunday afternoon sheriff's deputies arrested James Sisiwan, brother of Theodore Olmstead, who is being held as a material witness in the murder of Ike Donohue.

Tipped off by a local resident who claimed that Sisiwan, a resident of the Salt River Pima/Maricopa Indian Reservation near Phoenix, was suborning perjury, the arrest was made at the Desert View Motel, where Sisiwan was staying.

"You know how it is, these Indians all stick up for one another," a source, who asked not to be identified, told reporters. "This Sisiwan guy was driving all over, telling people they'd better think twice before they linked his brother to Mr. Donohue's murder."

When asked if Sisiwan had behaved in a threatening manner, the source said, "He was too smart for that. He just hinted."

The sheriff's office had no comment.

Sisiwan has been booked into the Walapai County Jail pending formal charges.

Autonomy be damned. Jimmy needed my help.

I shut down the computer, locked the office, and ran upstairs to pack.

Chapter Three

Walapai Flats was easy to find on a map, but hard to get to. A few miles north of Flagstaff, the highway dwindled into a two-lane blacktop that ran along the edge of the Navajo Reservation, and after that, my rented Chevy Trailblazer had to slow for sheep, wild horses, and the errant coyote.

Once I left Navajoland, my trip got truly hinky. Because the Grand Canyon was in the way, I had to veer miles around it and drive all the way into Utah before cutting west again on Route 9. Still in Utah, I hooked over to I-15, which hustled me south through the mountains that lined the massive Virgin River Gorge, and ultimately, back into Arizona. Having made a massive half-loop around the Grand Canyon, I exited the freeway at the picturesque old mining town of Silver Ridge and drove a few more miles east to Walapai Flats.

More than six hours to travel a lousy two hundred as-the-crow-flies miles.

But as I had discovered earlier that morning, the once-a-day commuter hop from Phoenix Sky Harbor into the Walapai County Airport was booked for the next three days. God only knows what would happened to Jimmy by then.

I finally rolled into Walapai Flats as the sun was setting. Situated along a long narrow plain but surrounded by high red-and-orange mesas, the area was spectacular. Because of the town's geographic isolation, it had remained populated only by Paiute Indians and miners until Hollywood discovered it in the Fifties. A couple of decades later, the land developers began cashing in. Now retirement communities and lavish resorts were sprinkled across the high desert.

When I turned onto John Wayne Boulevard, I was met by two billboards. One proclaimed, WELCOME TO WALAPAI FLATS—JOHN WAYNE LOVED IT AND YOU WILL TOO! The other announced, JOIN GOVERNOR EVELYN HASKER AND LOCAL DIGNITARIES TO CELEBRATE THE OPENING OF THE BLACK BASIN URANIUM MINE. 8 A.M. SUNDAY. FREE HOT DOGS & POPCORN! From atop the billboard, red, white and blue balloons waved in the breeze.

As I drove along, streetlights shaped like nineteenth-century gas lamps began to flicker on, casting a seductive golden glow over what at first looked like a town untouched by time. From the information I'd pulled down from the Internet before leaving Scottsdale, I'd learned that the town was originally little more than a general store and a gas station. Thanks to the real estate boom and the new airport, its amenities now included an RV park, two motels, a supermarket, several restaurants, an espresso café, a bookstore, and a sprinkling of gift shops and the usual small businesses. Everything, even the entrance to the RV park, mimicked the Old West architecture made famous by oater films and television shows. Raised wooden sidewalks covered by deep overhangs. False storefronts with the proprietors' names emblazoned in gilt lettering. Watering troughs for horses. The town's 1880's disguise worked so well that the herd of Escalades and Hummers parked in front of the Walapai Flats Saloon came as a shock.

Since I wasn't here to sightsee, I ignored the town's picturesque charms and headed straight for the county government offices across the street from the city park.

To the average person, the modern concrete-and-steel construction of the Walapai County government complex might contrast oddly with its ersatz Old West neighbors, but for an ex-Scottsdale cop like myself, it was the same old, same old.

Facilities like this were meant to be secure, not cute. Pushing open the heavy exterior door, I found myself in a large lobby lined with metal benches. Straight ahead stood a set of double doors labeled COURTROOMS; to my left the sign above a long hallways said SHERIFF'S OFFICES; to my right was a narrower door, flanked on one side by a metal detector and on the other side, a bulked-up detention officer. The sign above that door said COUNTY JAIL ANNEX.

Talk about one-stop shopping.

A bored-looking deputy just south of retirement age manned the desk at the far end of the lobby.

"I'd like to see James Sisiwan," I told him, eyeing the metal detector, thankful I'd locked my snub-nose .38 up in the Trail-blazer's glove compartment.

"You can't see him because his father bonded him out this morning." The deputy didn't bother looking up from the magazine he was reading.

Jimmy and his adoptive father had been estranged for years, partially because Jimmy had taken back his tribal name, but while a family crisis doesn't necessarily heal old wounds, it often numbed the pain. Could Jimmy now be staying at his father's guest ranch, standing hand in hand with the rest of the Olmstead clan, singing "Kumbaya?"

"I drove all the way up here from Scottsdale, officer, so how about letting me see Ted Olmstead?"

Wrong thing to say. Scottsdale had a reputation for snobbery, which the rest of the state found less than endearing, and from the sour expression on the deputy's face, he was no exception.

"Visiting hours are over," he said, slowly turning the pages of his magazine. I craned my neck forward and saw it was *Better Homes & Gardens*.

"Already?" I checked my watch. Fifteen minutes to eight.

"Yep."

This was no time to make a fuss. "Does Ted have an attorney yet?"

"I have no clue." He pretended to study a two-page spread on decorating a Soho loft.

Defeated, I said in my most polite voice, "Well, thank you for your time, officer."

"No problem."

I turned on my heel and headed for the door. Before I got there, he called out, "Visiting hours start at nine tomorrow. Better be here early. It's always a mob scene."

I waved my thanks and stepped out onto the still-warm pavement.

What to do now? The GPS unit in my Trailblazer showed the location of Sunset Trails Guest Ranch, but it was almost dark and the idea of getting lost in the Arizona badlands spooked me. Instead, I decided to check into the motel I'd spotted on my drive through town. It had a decent-looking restaurant attached, and my stomach was rumbling.

When I entered the reception area of the Covered Wagons Inn, I would have sworn I'd entered a particularly lush ranch house. Faux Navajo blankets draped casually across leather sofas. Cowhide rugs hunkered down on the saltillo tile floor. An old wagon wheel pretended to be a chandelier. And a life-sized cardboard cutout of John Wayne—the kind you used to see in theater lobbies—stood guard over it all. The actor was wearing an old-fashioned red, double-breasted shirt.

Yippy-ki-yay, pardner.

The cowboy-clad man at the counter welcomed me with a hearty "Howdy, ma'am," and explained he only had one room left. "A single king, I hope that'll work for you."

After I assured him it was fine and filled out the necessary paperwork, he handed me the key card to my room, adding, "You missed the complementary hors d'oeuvres and wine-tasting in the Duke's Saloon, but we're still serving dinner in the Stage-coach. The special tonight is tournedos of beef simmered slowly in a merlot reduction sauce with potatoes Lyonnais as side. Our vegetarian selection is penne pasta served in a Romano sauce sprinkled with fresh basil from our very own herb garden."

Nothing like good ol' chuck wagon fare to make a cowgirl feel like ropin' a few steers.

My room was pretty much what I expected. Wild West Redux—setting aside the Internet hookup, wide-screen TV, digital radio/alarm clock, Sleep Number mattress, hair dryer, botanical bath products and all the other accoutrements that went along with indoor plumbing. Cozy, too, with ankle-deep carpeting, distressed pine furniture, a down comforter dyed the colors of the Grand Canyon, and café au lait walls decorated with historic photographs of cowhands, miners, and Indians. Studying the prints more closely, I determined that the Indians were Paiutes, whose reservation was situated nearby.

After showering, I walked over to the Stagecoach Restaurant and took a seat at a deuce that offered an unobstructed view of the room. The room was decorated to remind patrons they were in the West, in case they'd forgotten. Lariats and branding irons hung on weathered wood paneling that looked like it had been stripped off a barn. However, the aroma of mesquite-grilled beef made my mouth water. A good meal would ease my mind. Jimmy might have bonded out, but if he was mixed up in a murder case, he was still in trouble.

The gray-haired waitress acted disappointed when I ordered a hamburger instead of the tournedos of beef, and iced tea instead of the suggested burgundy, but she recovered enough to serve the burger with a smile. As I ate, I studied the other diners. Among them were an unusual number of May/December match-ups, the men averaging twice the age of the women. Sitting at the table not far from mine was a particularly interesting couple. The man, a prosperous-looking sixty-something, seemed entranced by his dining partner, a deeply tanned blonde wearing a diamond solitaire so massive that it was a wonder she could lift her manicured hand.

When the waitress refilled my iced tea, I asked, "Do you get a lot of business from the resorts?"

She smiled, revealing a mouth full of silver inlays. "All the resorts have their own restaurants, but the Angus beef we serve here is locally raised on our owner's ranch. His son's our chef. Eric graduated last year from the Scottsdale Culinary Institute and was offered a job at one of the Vegas casinos, but he turned it down to work for his father."

I motioned toward the couple across the way. "Are they regulars?"

Here voice held a reverential note when she answered. "Every Monday. That's Mr. and Mrs. Tosches. He owns the Black Basin Mine and Mrs. Tosches adores our tournedos."

The article I'd read about Donohue's murder had mentioned Mia Tosches as a witness to the dispute between Ted Olmstead and the murder victim. Risking another question, I asked, "Did Ike Donohue eat here? The man who, er, got killed?" The word "murder" seemed too rough for such a nice restaurant.

"Mr. Donohue worked for Mr. Tosches." With that, her chattiness ended and after asking me if I wanted dessert, either crème brûlée or strawberry crêpes, to which I answered no, she handed me my check and walked away.

Once I returned to my room, I took a leisurely soak in the tub, then threw on an oversized tee shirt and started work. I plugged my laptop into the Internet jack and Googled Donohue+Tosches. After a few false hits due to my error-prone typing of last names, a couple of interesting items popped up. From an article in the *Arizona Business Journal* I learned that Roger Tosches not only owned the Black Basin Mine, but was the lone developer of Sunset Canyon Lakes Resort, too. The resort appeared to be his only solo business effort, though, because a man named Cole Laveen was named as partner in his current mine holdings. No mention was made of Tosches' wife, Mia, but I did find an article about Ike Donohue's widow. A photograph in *Arizona Gamesman* showed Nancy Donohue in full hunting regalia standing over a dead elk, her foot on its bloody side, triumph on her face.

Call me a cynic, since I couldn't help but wonder how much she inherited upon her husband's death.

Two more hours of surfing turned up little else. This was where Jimmy's expertise would have come in handy. He knew how to hack into sites that mere mortals couldn't access. Irritated by my limited computer skills, I snapped the laptop shut and went to bed.

I'd brought along a Sue Grafton novel to get me through the lonely nights, but somewhere in the middle of the fourth chapter, I fell into a dream-plagued sleep.

I stood at the entrance to a mine. A wooden barrier had been erected in front of the dark opening, with a sign saying, DANGER! NO ADMITTANCE! I started knocking back the slats with a large rock when Jimmy emerged from the moon's shadows and pushed me away.

"Don't go in there, Lena."

"But there's something I need to find out!"

"What you don't know can't hurt you."

"That doesn't make sense, Jimmy, so step aside."

He didn't move, but the moment I raised my hands to push him out of my way, he vanished.

I stepped over the remaining wooden slats and entered the mine.

Deeper shadows now surrounded me, but for some reason, I could still see the moon above. As I stared in amazement, I realized that I was no longer in the mine, but in a forest. Enveloping rock walls had transformed themselves into tall pine trees, their hanging branches creating a tunnel-like pathway. Fearless, I walked along, listening to the sounds of crickets, nightbirds…

Gunshots.

Children screaming.

In the magical way of dreams, my long-lost mother appeared beside me. Frightened, I took her hand. "I want to go home," I whispered.

"It's too late," she said.

Other children gathered around us. One, a girl of around six, whimpered. "Don't let them catch us, Auntie Helen."

"You'll be safe with me," my mother answered, but I knew she was lying, that our pursuers were only yards behind.

It was our turn to die.

When I screamed myself awake, I had to wipe away tears from my face. Nightmares are worse when they're not dreams—they're memories.

Chapter Four

July, 1959: Northwestern Arizona

As Abby watched from atop the fence rail, Gabe eased the saddle onto the young gelding so gently it didn't even flinch. He tightened the cinch slowly, like he'd been doing all week to get the horse used to it.

"Yeah, that's it, Star," he whispered. "We're pals, always gonna be pals. Just gotta get this first ride over with."

Star, a rangy sorrel with a quarter-size splash of white on its forehead, twitched its ears, but its eyes remained calm. Only a couple of months before Curly died, the old wrangler had trailered the animal over to Gabe's spread. With Curly's wife dead the year before, there was no one else to leave it to.

"I'd a brought you my roping horse but he got sick on me with all them boils livestock been getting these days, so I had to put him down," Curly had explained, then took time off to cough. Finished, he lit up another cigarette. "Only wisht I had more to give you."

"You gave me plenty, and I mighty appreciate it," Gabe had answered, with no exaggeration. There'd been the blue-eyed pup, grown these past five years into a gray and black heeler Abby named Blue. Now added to that first fine gift were the gelding, a lived-in saddle, a halter, a many-times-mended bridle with a gone-green bit, two coils of rope, and a rusting Ford pickup held together with baling wire. The sum total of a man's life.

Looking into Curly's yellowed eyes, Gabe had said, "Once the hospital fixes you up, you'll be good as new. Then you come by and I'll give 'em back. Loans is all they are."

Whistling past the graveyard that had been, and both knew it. Sure enough, a week later Curly shot himself.

"You be careful," Abby called to Gabe from her perch on the top rail as Blue waited loyally below. "That Star, he's a big one. Don't you go pulling a John Wayne, now."

Every time Gabe took a chance with a horse, Abby teased him like that. She knew how he felt about Wayne and tolerated it, had even framed the autographed photo the Duke had given him, hanging it right above the center of the sofa so everyone who walked into the ranch house could see how important Gabe was. "To my good friend, Gabe Boone. Ride 'em, cowboy! An admiring John Wayne," it said.

"You're the one oughta be careful, Abby. A five-months pregnant woman's got no business sitting on a top rail like that. What if you fall off?"

"I'll sit where I want, cowboy."

Gabe hid his grin. Losing their first baby had hurt her spirit something terrible, but with a new baby on the way, the old Abby was back. She sang at her work during the day and held him tight at night, singing a different song. "Women got no sense," he whispered to Star. "None at all. Why, that girl actually loves me."

"What're you telling that horse?"

Gabe grinned at his boots. "Just that he's gonna be a good 'un."

Abby's laugh was as pretty as a breeze playing through mesquite. "Sure you were, cowboy."

Gabe put his foot in the stirrup and swung himself into the saddle.

Star splayed out his feet. Humped his back.

Oh, here we go. Gabe waited for a thousand pounds of horse to explode underneath him, but nothing happened. The animal just turned his head and gazed quizzically at him.

Gabe tugged gently on the right rein to straighten the gelding's head, tapped its flanks with spurless boots, and shifted his weight forward. "Move along now."

Star walked three steps forward, then stopped and looked back at him again. Gabe straightened its head and tapped its flanks. The horse obeyed, moving three more steps. Stopped. Looked back. Gabe tapped its flanks and got more steps. Stop. More steps. Stop. More steps. Repeating that three-step-stop-three-step dance, man and horse eventually made a complete circuit of the corral.

Abby opened her mouth in a theatrical yawn. "My, this is exciting."

"Yeah, I'm thrilled to death."

Gabe was secretly pleased. Bucking broncs might be fine for a rodeo, but they were a pain in the neck for ranch work. Better to have a steady horse, one that didn't try to out-wild its rider. A no-nonsense horse that got the job done.

"Gabe!"

Concentrating as he was on the gelding's step-stop-step progress, Gabe at first missed the strained note in his wife's voice.

"Gabe. Something's wrong!"

Gabe jerked his head up, saw Abby climbing down from the fence rail toward a worried-looking Blue, her jeans darkened with blood.

Oh, Abby.

Chapter Five

First thing the next morning I placed a call to Sunset Trails Guest Ranch and asked to be connected to Jimmy's room. To my surprise, the young woman who answered informed me he wasn't staying there. After identifying myself as Jimmy's business partner, I asked where he might be staying.

"He's at the Desert View Motel. By the way, Lena, I'm Leilani, his sister."

Sister. I wondered how many more of Jimmy's siblings worked at the ranch.

When I told her it was nice to meet her, as it were, she replied, "Jimmy's told us a lot about you and what a good detective you are, so I'm really glad you're here. Ted's in a lot of trouble, and as much as I love Jimmy, him being my older brother and all, I'm afraid he's made things worse than they already are. Did you know he even got himself arrested? The way he looks, his long hair, that tattoo on his face, gosh, he really scares people."

Not women, I thought. The number of women who'd taken advantage of Jimmy's sweet nature was long and growing ever longer. There had been the divorcee who'd talked him into buying her a house full of furniture, then dumped him; the topless dancer whose full tuition he'd paid for cosmetology school but who dropped out the second week; the ex-con who stole his truck…But had he ever retaliated? Nope. He took his lumps and moved on to the next user. Compared to Jimmy's messes, my love life, which included a serial cheater and a hard-drinking cowboy who'd almost got me killed, wasn't all that bad.

Leilani sounded too young to hear the truth about her gullible brother, so I merely said, "Yeah, I heard about the arrest."

With that, I gave her my cell number and told her to call me if she learned anything new, then rang off and looked around my room. On the bottom shelf of the nightstand, I spotted a copy of the Walapai County Yellow Pages, where I found the listing for Jimmy's motel. It was still early, so there was a good chance I might catch him in his room. But when the Desert View clerk transferred me to his extension, he didn't answer. Figuring that he had left for breakfast before visiting Ted at the jail, I decided to grab some breakfast myself.

The morning was relatively cool and a slight overcast promised to keep it that way. As I walked to my Trailblazer, the scent of frying bacon wafted to me from the Stagecoach, but I gave it a pass. Walapai Flats being such a small town, there was a good chance I might find Jimmy at one of the other local eateries. A few minutes later, I was proven right. Halfway down John Wayne Boulevard, I spotted Jimmy's Toyota pickup in front of Cowboy Cal's Espresso & Smoothies.

Entering, I saw my partner on a corner stool underneath an old movie poster of John Wayne that advertised *The Searchers*. Jimmy was so busy slurping down a pink smoothie he didn't see me.

I walked over and tapped him on the shoulder. "Couldn't find a Starbucks?"

"What the…?" Turning around with a scowl, Jimmy found himself facing several alarmed faces. He lowered his voice. "Lena. Why am I not surprised?"

I slid onto the stool next to him. Leilani was right. Jimmy was a big man, and with his waist-length black hair and the curved tribal tattoo across his temple, he could look pretty fierce. Especially when scowling.

Smiling, I said, "You're not surprised because state-licensed investigators like myself are good at finding people, even when they don't want to be found. I drove up last night to bail you out, but was informed that your dad already took care of that. What's all this about you 'suborning perjury'?"

He shifted uncomfortably on the stool. "I was merely trying to get people to open up, to tell me what they knew about Donohue's murder."

I thought about that. "How close were you standing when you questioned them?"

"Close. I read in *Investigator's Monthly* that to get information from people that's what you should do. Stand close. What difference does it make?"

Did the man never look in a mirror? I motioned to the plastic cup in front of him. "What are you drinking?"

"Apple Cherry Soynami with wheat germ."

"Good?"

An exasperated sigh. "Lena, if I'd wanted you up here, I'd have invited you along."

"Judging from the pink moustache you've sprouted, it's at least drinkable, so I'll have one, too. And, Jimmy, I'm just here to help."

He wiped his upper lip. "Don't need your help."

"I disagree. There's that suborning perjury business hanging over your head, and your brother's still in jail. Your dad couldn't get him released, too?"

His scowl intensified, turning the tattoo even darker. "He tried. It didn't work."

"Then you both need my help."

Leaving him to mull that over, I went to the counter and ordered an Apple Cherry Soynami without wheat germ from a pretty redhead. In homage to the place's cowboy theme, she wore a Western shirt and cowgirl hat, but her makeup was pure L'Oréal. By the time I returned to my stool, Jimmy had calmed down.

"Why'd you leave out the wheat germ?" he asked, looking at the cup.

"Tastes like sawdust."

"It's good for you."

"I'm healthy enough."

His scowl disappeared into a grin that softened even my own crusty heart. "You are so self-destructive."

"Am not."

"Are too. Listen, there's nothing going on here that I can't handle myself, so why don't you drive back to Scottsdale and take care of business."

"Murder *is* my business." The minute I said it, I realized how melodramatic it sounded, so I added, "And so is bailing my partner out of the pokey."

"That's all well and good, but who's taking care of the office?"

Now he worries. "You know as well as I do that nothing much happens this time of year. But the calls are being transferred over to Jean Begay. As for walk-ins, we never get them."

"We did one time."

"Remember how that turned out?"

His grin widened. "That lawsuit was fun, wasn't it?"

"Not to mention the money we wound up collecting."

"Bought me a new truck."

"Bought me a new wardrobe."

He laughed out loud, making heads turn again. "Oh, yeah. More black jeans, black tee shirts, and two pair of black Reeboks. You're some fashion plate, Lena."

From the counter, the redhead threw him a flirtatious look. The girl's clear eyes and perky step hinted that she wasn't dysfunctional enough for him, so I resisted the urge to play Cupid and plunged back into business.

"I'm not going away, Jimmy, so you might as well fill me in on what you've learned so far."

"Outside." With a sigh, he stood up and tossed his empty cup into the trash container. I took a final chug at my smoothie and did the same. The thing had been too sweet for me, anyway.

As we left the shop, two customers I recognized from the restaurant last night exited several paces behind us. Mr. and Mrs. Tosches. He sported an especially vulgar Rolex and his child bride's diamond ear studs had to be at least a carat each. They moved down the sidewalk a few paces, where the man pretended to be fascinated by a display in the hardware store window next door, and the woman kept batting her eyelashes at Jimmy.

"Let's go someplace less crowded," I murmured to Jimmy. "We've got an hour to go before we can see Ted."

After a pause long enough to make me nervous, he finally said, "You staying at the Covered Wagons?"

At my nod, he told me he'd meet me there.

Ten minutes later we were sitting at the card table in my motel room, where it was considerably more private. From Jimmy's body language, he didn't think much of the decor, especially not the framed photographs of Paiute Indians. Their faces bore a trapped look, as if they'd knew their life had irrevocably changed, and not for the better.

To get his mind off racial memories that had to be humiliating, I said, "That couple who followed us outside seemed pretty interested in our conversation. Mr. and Mrs. Tosches, right?"

He turned away from the photographs. "Apparently you've already been busy snooping around, but yeah, Ike Donohue—the man Ted's accused of killing—he worked for Tosches."

"Could there have been some sort of disagreement between them?"

"Anything's possible except Ted's guilt."

From past experience, I knew that given the right motivation, anyone was capable of killing. Mothers killed to protect their children, husbands to protect their families. Even children killed. When I was nine, I'd tried to kill the foster father who raped me. Unfortunately, my knife hadn't gone deep enough.

Skipping the pop psychology lecture, I said, "We both know that this 'material witness' thing is a precursor to an arrest. The authorities must have a strong suspicion that Ted killed Donohue, but haven't collected enough evidence yet. Why are you so certain he didn't do it?"

Jimmy shook his head. "Because he told me he didn't."

"Oh, well, that proves it."

He glared at me, but said nothing.

"You're going on your feelings, is that it?"

The glare didn't go away.

"Okay, then, Jimmy. Maybe you can tell me what Ted said he was doing at the time of the murder. That's if he told you anything at all, other than protest his innocence."

Grudgingly, he said, "He said he was driving around, thinking."

"About what?"

"Things."

"Is there any chance someone saw his car? With him in it?"

"Truck, not car. A blue half-ton Silverado. If anyone saw him, they haven't come forward."

"What a great alibi." The minute the words were out of my mouth, I wanted to call them back. My partner didn't need wisecracks, he needed help. "Sorry. I'm still cranky from the drive up here. But if we're going to get Ted out of jail, we need to come up with something more concrete than a 'just driving around' kind of story."

His glare finally faded, replaced by a look of despair. Whoever said Indians didn't show emotion never knew an Indian. "I know, Lena, I know. I tried to get him to say more, but he's not talking. He won't even talk to Dad. Dad tried to get him to open up, and when Dad tries to…"

Jimmy had seldom discussed his adoptive family other than to say his parents were good people who had given him and his likewise adopted siblings every opportunity, including college educations. I knew he and his adoptive mother had been close, but she'd died some years earlier. I also knew Jimmy and his father didn't get along.

"Speaking of your father, what's the deal with staying at the Desert View Motel instead of the guest ranch? Even though you two are estranged, surely he'd be more than happy to let you bunk there so you can spend time with your brothers and sisters. They must be upset about Ted's situation, too."

Jimmy didn't answer right away. Instead, he looked up at the largest of the framed photographs on the motel room wall. It showed a large Paiute family, the mother wrapped in a shawl, the father holding a bow. One of the half-dozen children clutched a puppy. Instead of smiling for the birdie, they looked guarded. Perhaps they already knew that soon their children would be taken from them and shipped off to boarding schools, and that for the rest of their lives, they would be treated like aliens in their own land. Did I detect a gleam of sympathy in my partner's eyes? Or was it anger?

When he turned back to me, he'd wiped all emotion away and his voice was level. "No point in staying at the ranch. Besides the disabled kids, Leilani's the only one still living there, and even she's headed back to college in a couple of weeks. As for the others, time marches on, right? Some started their own businesses; some are married and busy with their own families. As for Dad, the less said about him the better."

"So you two are still having problems."

"Nothing you need to worry about."

In other words, his relationship with his father was none of my business. "Then I'm glad to hear the situation isn't all that dire. If I'm going to be of any use to Ted, I need to find out as much about his situation as possible, so why don't the both of us visit him at the jail, then drive over to the ranch together. Maybe one of the wranglers knows something."

"No!" As if shocked by his reaction, he cleared his throat and modulated his voice. "What I mean to say is, morning's are bad because everyone's busy with the guests. There's no need for you to go out there at all, it'd be a waste of your time."

"But…"

"I've already interviewed everyone at the ranch, wranglers included. There's nothing left for you to find out."

Here again is an area where trained investigators have skills the average person doesn't. We can tell when someone's being evasive.

I tried to remember what Jimmy had told me about his early childhood in Salt Lake City. He'd described a veritable Garden of Eden, with happy school days, camping excursions in summer, ski weekends in winter, all the happy-happy any child could wish for. His adoptive parents had been non-drinking, non-smoking church-goers, but a healthy lifestyle didn't always guarantee a long life. Five years after the family bought the guest ranch and moved to Walapai Flats from Salt Lake, Jimmy's mother died from a sudden heart attack.

There is no Eden, no matter how much we long for one.

Given Jimmy's evasive behavior, I fleetingly wondered if all those old tales of good times were merely attempts to cover up a family secret, then immediately hated myself for thinking it. Still, the possibility sent my thoughts scurrying along an interesting path.

I studied the photograph of the Indian family. Jimmy's skin was almost as dark as theirs. Born red, raised by Whites. If push came to shove, which side would he choose? Nature or nurture, that was the question. We aren't only ourselves, we are our ancestors—our grandfather's grandfather and our grandmother's grandmother, back through countless generations until ancient genes rumbled underneath modern mindsets. If a crisis arose and Jimmy felt he had to sacrifice one side of his family to save the other, which side he would wind up on?

I leaned forward over the card table and took his hand. "Is there something you need to tell me?"

"Nothing's going on." He wouldn't look at me.

"You think I can't tell when you're holding back? Look, I'm worried about you, and I'm worried about Ted, but I can't help either of you if I don't have all the facts." When he still wouldn't meet my eyes, I added, "Oh, well. You're probably right about the time. Later would be better. I'll drive out to the ranch by myself after lunch. Who knows? Maybe I'll discover something you missed."

"Stay away from the ranch!" He grabbed my wrist hard enough to leave a red mark.

"Have you lost your mind?" I snapped, twisting out of his grip.

Horrified by his own actions, he looked down at his hands. They were shaking. "I…I…Oh, God, Lena. I'm so sorry!"

He stood up from the table so quickly it toppled over. Then, before I could stop him, he rushed out the door.

As I was mounting the steps to the Walapai Flats government complex, Jimmy's pickup rolled into the parking space behind mine. The morning sun was in his eyes as he approached, so he didn't see me until the last moment. When he did, he halted and made a half turn back toward his truck. I'd seen more cheerful faces on men about to be executed.

"Jimmy!" I called. "Don't walk away. Please!"

Shoulders hunched, he stopped mid-turn. Was he still angry, or just embarrassed by his outburst at the motel?

I held out my hand. "Are we still friends, Almost Brother?"

He came toward me slowly, his face a study in pain. When he took my hand, he held it longer than he would a mere handshake. "For life, Almost Sister."

The lobby was noisier than the night before, only partially because of a loudspeaker reeling off names. Against the wall, a long row of benches held groupings of men, women, and crying children, each adult clutching either a blue, yellow, or green slip of paper. To our right, a line of people were handing yellow slips to an armed deputy before making their way through the security checkpoint that led to the jail annex. The longest line was in front of the reception desk, which I now realized was the complex's clearing station. A female deputy manning the station was handing out yellow paper for jail business, blue for the sheriff's offices, and green for admission to the courthouse. She looked bored, as if she'd rather be tracking down serial killers.

"Sheriff's offices, courthouse, or jail?" she asked, when our turn finally came. Her eyes were too dulled over to focus on us.

"Jail," Jimmy said. "We're here to see Ted Olmstead."

Upon hearing his voice, her eyes cleared and a smile transformed her dour face. "Ah, Mr. James Sisiwan in the flesh. How nice to see you again. It's not all that common to have a former prisoner voluntarily return a couple of days later. Miss us?"

He smiled back. Jimmy had never met a woman he didn't like, even when they were cops. "Just visiting my brother, Terry."

"And the lady with you is?"

"My partner."

"Partner?" Deputy Terry frowned at me.

Aware that with my long blond hair and less than stocky build I didn't look like anyone's idea of a private investigator, I handed over my state ID card. "Lena Jones, Desert Investigations."

She studied my ID as if hoping to find an error.

I tried not to let my irritation show. "It's all in order. If you have questions, you can call the state licensing board. Need the phone number?"

Jimmy's voice was more soothing than mine. "Lena's good people, Terry."

The deputy handed my ID back. "If Jimmy says you're good people, then you're good people." She wrote something down on one of the yellow slips and handed it to Jimmy. "Take your seats, if any are left. I'd get you taken care of right away, but first I need to call over and see if your brother is allowed to see anyone who's out on bond. I'm not sure how that works."

Jimmy and I dutifully sat down on one of the long benches. The building, being relatively new, hadn't yet accumulated the worst odors that could permeate such places: vomit, urine, fear. The only smell I noticed, besides a blending of deodorants, was the tea rose cologne emanating from a woman sitting across from us. One of her eyes was bruised and a long scab marred her jaw. It looked like someone had worked her over. The toddler on her lap, a little girl, wore a cast on her left arm. On the bench next to them was a large metal lunchbox, nothing a woman or child would use. Maybe she was dropping it off for someone at the complex. I wondered who the thug was.

I could hear Jimmy grinding his teeth. "Are you thinking what I'm thinking?" he whispered.

"Maybe it was a car accident."

"Not with that…"

"This is neither the time nor the place, Jimmy. We're here to see Ted, nothing else." For the rest of our wait, I kept my eyes averted, otherwise I'd wind up grinding my teeth, too.

A few minutes later, the loudspeaker belched out our names. Before we joined the line in front of the jail's security station, I hurried over to the bruised woman and handed her my business card. "If you're having a problem with a domestic partner, give me a call."

She snatched up the card, but kept her eyes down.

"Fifteen minutes, that's all you get today," an elderly detention officer said, as he greeted us by name once we'd entered the jail's visiting room. "Mr. Olmstead's attorney is due any minute and he'll want privacy."

The room proved as bland as the lobby. Small plastic cubbies offered a modicum of privacy, and reinforced Plexiglas separated visitor from prisoner. Small holes in the barrier allowed them to communicate, however poorly.

When another detention officer brought Ted in, I was shocked by how much he'd changed in the months since I'd met him. His weight was down and his eyes had settled deeper into his gaunt brown face. Understandable, really. In that time, his wife had been shot to death, and now he was involved in another homicide case.

We couldn't touch him but before sitting down, Jimmy raised his open hand and pressed it against the Plexiglas. Ted leaned forward and did the same, covering the shape of Jimmy's hand with his own.

"My brother," Jimmy whispered.

"My brother," Ted repeated.

To some Easterners all Native Americans look the same, but in reality, each tribe has its own culture and physical attributes. Jimmy, a Pima, had a big, muscular build that sometimes got him mistaken for Polynesian. Ted, a Paiute, was shorter and darker, with a distinct Asian cast to his features. Despite their differences, they didn't need to speak to communicate. For the longest time the two stood there silently, their hands separated by a quarter-inch of Plexiglas, their eyes saying everything that needed to be said.

Finally, Ted—more for my benefit than Jimmy's, I suspect—said, "I didn't do it."

"I know," Jimmy and I chorused.

We took our seats while Ted told his side of the story.

Yes, he admitted, he had been involved in an argument with Ike Donohue, but the other man had started it. Donohue arrived at the gas station first, and was filling up his Mercury Sable at the gas pump on the opposite side of the island. When Ted got there, he pulled alongside the diesel pump needed for the ranch's big truck, but as soon as he lifted the handle, Donohue rushed across the island and jerked it out of his hand, splashing fuel on Ted's pants.

"Donohue's car used regular, so what was the big deal?" Jimmy asked.

I suspected their set-to wasn't about gas at all. "The newspaper account I read before driving up here said a woman named Mia Tosches witnessed the altercation. I saw her at a restaurant last night, and she's pretty attractive."

Ted shrugged. "If you like the type." His own Kimama had been a raven-haired Paiute beauty.

"Where was Mrs. Tosches standing when Donohue challenged you for the diesel pump?" I asked.

"She was coming out of the gas station with a Coke. She'd parked that big Mercedes of her husband's at the pump ahead of mine."

"Was it a diesel pump?"

Light dawned on Ted's face. "No, it wasn't. And the Mercedes needed diesel, which meant she'd have to back up to use the same pump I was using. But I didn't realize it then, and because of the way Donohue was carrying on, he wasn't making any sense. Mrs. Tosches stood there giggling, like she was enjoying the whole scene. Next thing I knew, Donohue stumbled and began to fall. I tried grabbing onto him, but he went down anyway. You mean to tell me that's what all the fuss was about, Donohue wanting to look good in front of Mrs. Tosches? Bully me away from the diesel pump so she could have first dibs?"

"Sounds like it."

"But that guy has to be forty years older than her!" Ted sounded like he couldn't fathom such disparity.

I could. "No fool like an old fool."

Small events can have big consequences. If Ted hadn't arrived at the gas station at the same time as Donohue, none of us would be sitting in the jail visitor's room. Unless the sheriff knew something Ted had neglected to tell us about.

"Ted, other than the Black Basin Mine disagreement, which we'll get to in a minute, was there anything else that connects you with Donohue? For instance, did he or his wife ever take part in activities at the ranch?"

He shook his head. "Not Mr. Donohue himself, but his wife came along on several of our trail rides. Pretty good in the saddle, too, doesn't need any babysitting like some of the others." He managed his first smile. "You know how dudes are."

I remembered that photograph of Nancy Donohue, rifle in hand, foot on a dead elk. No dude, she.

"How about the murder weapon? Any word yet on the ballistics tests?"

"Not that I know of," Ted said. "Does it matter?"

"Maybe." Arizona being Arizona, there were would be plenty of firearms at the ranch, ranging from handguns to hunting rifles. Since the issue of firearms was a moot point until we saw the ballistics report, I decided to delve further into the personalities involved. Ballistics tests might provide proof, but personalities provided motive. "The newspaper account I read said you, let's see, how did the reporter put it, 'blamed Donohue for creating the hostile environment that led to Kimama's death.' Could you go into detail about that?"

Ted's face grew guarded. "Mr. Donohue was the public relations flak for the Black Basin Mine, which meant that it was his business to make V.U.M.—the Victims of Uranium Mining—look bad. Some of the things he said about Kimama bordered on slander."

"Such as?"

He looked at Jimmy as if pleading for help, but Jimmy remained silent. After taking a deep breath, Ted finally answered. "Lots of reasons. Apparently, before Donohue moved here, he was some big deal PR guy back east, and when Roger Tosches, the owner of the Black Basin, needed a little help, he hired Donohue. Well, Donohue set out to convince everyone the mine would be safe, which is just about the biggest crock of... Well, it wasn't true, and Kimama knew it."

After mentioning his murdered wife's name, he had to swallow before he could continue, and when he did, his voice was bitter. "Kimama knew all about Tosches' history with the Moccasin Peak mine on the Navajo rez, and how the thing killed the miners and how the tailings are still contaminating the drinking water. She called a press conference at the school auditorium, got the newspapers in, the TV crews, plus all the local bigwigs, and blasted his treatment of the Navajos. Cancer, arsenic poisoning, the whole deal. So what did Donohue do? He charged the stage, grabbed the mike, and called Kimama a gullible dupe of false research. Since he was a PR pro and a lot slicker speaker than she was, at least half the people bought into his version."

He cleared his throat. "Look, Lena, I know darned well how much this town relies on the tourist trade, but not everyone works at a resort or guest ranch. With so many of the mine closings—yep, the gold, silver and copper are all gone—a quarter of the people up here are unemployed, and they're desperate. Once Donohue got through slandering Kimama, he pointed out that the Black Basin Mine would bring in more than four hundred jobs. In a town this size, that's a lot."

"So Kimama's warning about the safety issues was ignored?"

"That's exactly what I'm saying. But she didn't give up. V.U.M. filed a petition in federal court, and using the disaster at Moccasin Peak as an example of what could go wrong when a uranium mine was operated by the wrong people, she got the

Black Basin's opening date put on hold. When the mine didn't open when it was supposed to, everyone blamed her. She got threatening phone calls and hate mail, unbelievably creepy stuff. She ignored it, and for a while there, it looked like V.U.M. might get the opening put off indefinitely, or at least until the mine management was transferred to someone with a better reputation, but then…"

"But then she was killed."

His eyes flashed with hate. "But then she was murdered! And I'm telling you that Donohue's responsible!"

I hoped Ted's attorney would counsel him not to speak ill of the dead. Especially not to a cellmate, who might be tempted to turn state's evidence in exchange for a lighter sentence for his own crimes.

After cautioning Ted against loose talk, I said, "One of the unusual things about your situation is that you're being held as a material witness, not an actual suspect. What do you know about that?"

Disgust replaced the rage in his eyes. "The sheriff told me it was partially for my own protection."

"Because of the Black Basin Uranium Mine business?"

Ted looked like he was ready to spit. "Don't forget, I'm a long-time member of V.U.M., too, and I wasn't exactly being quiet about the mine, either. From what I hear, once Donohue was killed, the sheriff was worried—he says—that the same people who went after Kimama might come after me out of some sense of revenge. But if you believe that tall tale, I've got a three-legged horse I'd like to sell you."

Ted's disbelief notwithstanding, the scenario did make sense. The sooner I sat down for a confab with the sheriff, the better.

Before I could tell Ted what I planned to do, the visiting room door opened and the elderly detention officer shuffled back in. Behind him waddled a short man in a wrinkled gabardine suit, carrying a briefcase almost as fat as he was.

"Your attorney's here, Mr. Olmstead," the officer announced, motioning for us to leave.

We did.

On the way back to the lobby, Jimmy told me he'd wait behind to alert the attorney that his father had hired Desert Investigations to help with the case.

"Officially?" Handshakes seldom impress lawyers.

He fished in his shirt pocket and drew out a piece of paper. It was a hand-written note on Desert Investigation letterhead. "Dad gave me a dollar and I wrote out a receipt."

Oh, that Jimmy, always a step ahead, sometimes in the wrong direction. When he asked if I'd wait with him, I shook my head, saying I had several errands to run, but first, I was going to try and see Sheriff Alcott.

"Tell you what, Jimmy. It's ten now. How about we meet for lunch around one at that restaurant down the street from the park? Ma's Kitchen. That'll give me time to take care of a few things. Don't try to interview anyone, you hear? It would be a shame if your father had to bail you out again."

"Don't worry, I've learned my lesson. Next time I talk to anyone, I'll stand well back." With that, he settled himself down on the same bench we'd been sitting on earlier.

The lobby was still crowded, but the bruised woman and her child were gone.

Chapter Six

Sheriff Alcott's secretary informed me that he was too busy to see me, but penciled me in for the next afternoon. "Better call and confirm," she said. "His schedule has been pretty fluid for the past few weeks."

In Scottsdale, "a fluid schedule" would have meant the sheriff was working on something big, but here in the boonies, it could have been either a reflection of understaffing or incompetence. Frustrated, I decided to pay a visit to Sunset Trails Guest Ranch, but was careful not to let Jimmy know. There was no point in risking another freak-out.

Ten miles out of town, a gravel road split off Route 47, heralded by a sign announcing that the Sunset Trails Guest Ranch was located one mile down "one of the most scenic drives in Arizona." The sign didn't exaggerate. Enraptured, I rolled down the Trailblazer's tinted windows, the better to see the true colors of red and orange mesas and the yellow-gold sun chasing purple shadows from the beige desert floor. Only a few hundred feet away, the Virgin River—no longer encased by the steep cliffs of the Virgin River Gorge to the north—burbled merrily along, shaded by tall cottonwoods and silver-green sage. Adding to the road's unearthly beauty, a nearby coyote yipped a farewell aria before turning in for the day.

Too soon I was parking my Trailblazer in the ranch's visitor's lot. Near the guest ranch's main building—a two-story log lodge pretending to be a pioneer structure—people dressed in riding gear waited to be mounted on the horses being led from the corral. As I approached the lodge, a large dog ran out to meet me. Not certain of the animal's intentions I froze, but my concern proved unnecessary. The moment the blue-eyed heeler reached me, it flopped down on the ground, bared its belly, and grinned.

Pet me, pet me, he begged.

Never one to snub a friendly dog, I complied.

A few tummy-rubs later, my new friend escorted me to the lodge's front steps, then ran off to join the horses.

I had never met Hank Olmstead, Jimmy's adoptive father, but as I entered the pine paneled lounge area decorated in leather and wood, I recognized him from a photograph Jimmy had once shown me. Tall and lean with a sun-roughened complexion, he stood in front of a massive stone fireplace, gray head bent solicitously while he listened to a young couple's complaints.

"…wasn't as good as usual," the woman said, sounding annoyed. The combination of professionally streaked hair and perfectly applied makeup with designer shirt and jeans made her look like a dressed-down fashion model.

Olmstead nodded. "My apologies about breakfast, Mrs. Arden. Because of a death in his family, our regular cook had to leave town suddenly. We expect him back day after tomorrow."

"You're saying we have to wait for another two days to have decent food?" snapped her husband, who with his vulture-beaked nose and acne-scarred skin, was nowhere as pretty as his wife. To make up for his physical shortcomings, he'd strapped onto his ostrich-skin boots a pair of sharp-roweled spurs that might have belonged in a silversmith's showroom but nowhere near a horse.

Olmstead smiled wearily. "I'm truly sorry about this, Mr. Arden, because we've always enjoyed having you as guests. Why don't you let me comp you this morning's trail ride? And tomorrow's?"

Some of the irritation disappeared from the ugly man's face. "That's big of you."

"Sunset Trails always tries to accommodate." Olmstead shook the man's hand. "Let me personally escort you nice folks out to the wranglers so I can be certain they give you two of our best horses. By the way, you might want to take off those spurs. They tend to annoy the horses, and we don't want any accidents, do we?"

He waited until Arden reluctantly unbuckled his equine torture devices and handed them over. "Wonderful quality," Olmstead said. "I'll put them in our safe, okay? Now, let's get you mounted up. You're about to take in some of Mother Nature's most glorious scenery."

As the trio clomped past me, I pretended to be engrossed in the Sunset Trails brochure I'd lifted off a table shaped like a wagon wheel. It highlighted the ranch's Old West amenities: nearby airport, spa, heated pool, satellite TV.

Moments later, Olmstead returned looking thunderous but he feigned pleasure as soon as he spotted me. "Good morning, young lady. Here to inquire about Sunset Trails? We offer wonderful vacation packages…"

I raised my hand to halt the sales pitch. "I'm Lena Jones, Jimmy's partner."

The bonhomie disappeared. "Then we'll need privacy." He turned on his heel.

I followed him down the hall and into a small office that paid more attention to utility than theme. Mismatched gray and white file cabinets lined the room, surrounding a battered desk that could have been rescued from the town dump. The only decoration on the wall behind the desk was a cross, which did little to break up the room's starkness, but on the opposite wall hung a large studio photograph of the entire clan. In the center sat Hank Olmstead and Jeanette, his deceased wife, a thin but kind-faced woman. Jimmy had told me that the Olmsteads had no biological children, but made up for the lack by adopting eleven kids. The photograph was testimony to the Olmsteads' open hearts. Among the children grouped around Hank and his wife, I counted five Whites with what appeared to be Down syndrome; three frail-looking Asian girls; a Hispanic boy in thick glasses; and a girl with possible Polynesian ancestry who wore a brace on one leg. Standing together in the back were Ted Olmstead and a teenaged Jimmy who hadn't yet obtained his tribal tattoo.

"Beautiful family." I gestured toward the photo as I settled into a chair. "Quite the United Nations."

After closing the office door, Olmstead took a seat in the big leather chair behind the desk. I realized, then, the importance of the photo's placement across the room. This way he could look at his family all the time.

His hard face softened. "We are very proud of our children. Now, what can I do for you, Miss Jones? I must say it's a surprise to see you. James said he was going to handle Theodore's situation himself, but here you are. Not that your kind visit is necessary. I've called in one of the best attorneys I know, and he will be consulting with Theodore first thing this morning."

I inclined my head. "We saw the attorney at the jail. Attorneys are great for handling the legal end of things, but Ted'll need a good investigator, too."

"Of course. That's why James drove up here. To lend his expertise."

James. Not Jimmy. You can tell a lot about people from the way they refer to others. For instance, I was "Miss Jones." He also used the formal version of both his sons' names. Had Hank Olmstead always been like this, or had catering to ranch guests for so long made him this way?

I smiled, hoping to lighten the atmosphere. "Jimmy and I are a team. He handles the Internet investigations, while I take care of the field work."

"A division of labor makes sense."

"Exactly." I reached into my carry-all and pulled out my digital recorder. Setting it on his desk, I said, "I hope you don't mind if I tape this conversation?" I'd displayed the recorder merely out of courtesy, because in Arizona, anyone is allowed to tape a conversation without the other's knowledge. A strange law, but one private investigators love.

Olmstead appeared comfortable with the recorder's presence. "Anything that will help Theodore."

I pressed the RECORD button. "Mr. Olmstead, how well did you know Ike Donohue?"

"Only to say hello to on those rare occasions we ran into each other in town. Mr. Donohue was no horseman."

At my show of puzzlement, he explained, "None of the resorts around here have stables, too expensive to keep up, so some of them have standing arrangements for us to furnish horses whenever any of their residents want to ride. Mr. Donohue owns one of those condos at Sunset Canyon Lakes, but as I have stated, riding was never his sport. He preferred golf, and there's a championship course over there."

"Ever hear anything negative about him?"

"Nothing comes to mind."

His answer had come too quickly, but this wasn't the time to push. The longer Olmstead felt comfortable, the smoother the interview would go. "Tell me what you can remember about last Thursday, the day Donohue was killed."

A frown. "I thought he was killed Friday."

"His body was found Friday morning, but I haven't yet learned the exact time of death. It might have occurred as early as Thursday night. We'll find out for certain when Ted's attorney gets a copy of the autopsy. The newspaper account hinted that Ted's altercation with Donohue on Thursday had something to do with his getting picked up, if not actually arrested, so I need to know everything that happened on Thursday, what you saw, what you heard. More importantly, tell me what you know about anyone around here who might have been carrying a grudge against Donohue. Surely Ted wasn't the only person who'd had a problem with him."

Olmstead glanced at the family photograph again, but this time his face gave away nothing. When he spoke, his tone was cautious. "As far as I can remember, last Thursday was like any other day except that I spent much of the morning calling around to find a substitute cook. After breakfast was squared away—Theodore, my daughter Leilani, and I wound up cooking it ourselves, much to the dissatisfaction of our guests—Theodore went outside and helped the wranglers saddle up the horses. When he came back in, he said we needed to get the vet out, that one of the horses had a nasty gash on its flank. Coyote, probably, we're plagued with them. Until the vet arrived, Theodore busied himself talking to guests. After the horse was taken care of he drove the van over to the airport to pick up a few more guests, settled them into their rooms, then…"

"Those guests. What were their names?"

Olmstead flipped a few pages over on his desk calendar, then read, "Bill and Evelyn Nash, Minnesota. Sol and Thelma Bernstein, Ohio."

"Are they regulars here?"

"It's their first visit, so I'd appreciate it if you don't alarm them. Returns make up more than 60 percent of Sunset Trails' business, and we hope they come back."

This explained why he'd been so accommodating with the Ardens. "To your knowledge, did any of your guests run into Ike Donohue on Thursday?"

"Miss Jones, you must understand that our guests are free to come and go as they please. Some of them even rent cars as soon as they arrive so they can drive down to the Grand Canyon, over to Las Vegas…"

I broke into his travelogue. "And a lovely time they have, I'm sure, but to get back on track, tell me what you know about Ted's altercation with Donohue."

Another frown, either because he didn't like being interrupted or because he didn't like the subject matter. "The newspaper blew that all out of proportion, and I can guarantee you that Theodore didn't start the argument. It's my understanding that Mr. Donohue could be a difficult man to deal with on a personal level. Arrogant. Abrasive. Regardless, he was quite successful as spokesman for the uranium mine. Most resort owners, myself included, don't like the fact that the open pit operation will be so close to the Grand Canyon, but he was able to sweep our objections under the rug by stressing that the mine would furnish much-needed uranium to the state's nuclear plants. With gas and oil prices as high as they are around here, he convinced just about everyone that nuclear power was America's only alternative. What do you think about nuclear power, Miss Jones?"

He was trying to deflect my attention away from that gas station altercation again, but I gave him the courtesy of an answer. "Considering the tragedy in Japan, I'm not sure I see nuclear power as the best answer to our energy woes, but that's for the experts to decide. What I'm concerned with is Ted's situation. How did the authorities find out about his fight with Donohue?"

"It wasn't a fight!" He took a few deep breaths, then with difficulty, leveled his voice. "Mr. Donohue may have reported it. Or Mrs. Tosches. Like many young people, she can be over-imaginative. Afterwards, a deputy went out and talked to Earl Two Horses, who runs Walapai Gas-N-Go. Mr. Two Horses is an excellent mechanic and has been taking care of all the ranch's vehicles since we opened. Paiute mother, Navajo father. Lots of good blood there."

"Is Earl a close friend of Ted's?"

"Their wives were close, but Theodore and Mr. Two Horses were too busy for much socialization, other than attending pow-wows together from time to time. Once Theodore's wife died…"

"Kimama."

A nod. "Yes, Kimama. After my daughter-in-law's death, Theodore stuck closer to the ranch, so I guess you could say his friendship with Mr. and Mrs. Two Horses faded some." Another pause, another look at the family photograph.

If Ted was always taking the ranch's cars in for service at Two Horse's gas station, there was no reason the two men couldn't remain close. "Did something happen between them?"

Olmstead shrugged. "Theodore stopped attending the, ah, activist gatherings, too. He was still a supporter, but I think the meetings reminded him too much of his wife, so he stayed away. It might have disappointed Mr. Two Horses."

"Are you talking about the Victims of Uranium Mining meetings?"

Olmstead looked pained. "Yes. Mr. Two Horses remains quite active in V.U.M. His father was one of the Navajos who worked at a uranium mine on the Navajo Reservation. Do you know anything about what happened, and is still happening, at the Moccasin Peak Mine?"

"Enough to know that V.U.M. is afraid the same thing might happen in Walapai Flats."

Another nod. "I imagine Mr. Two Horses expected Theodore to become even more involved in the protests after Kimama's death. But losing a wife can make a man draw into himself." He looked at the family photograph, then down at his wedding ring. For a moment, I thought he might break down. He didn't.

"You said Earl Two Horses' father worked at the old Moccasin Peak. Was he one of the casualties, by any chance?"

"Lung cancer. The company never issued the proper masks to the Navajo miners."

"Then I take it that most of the Indians around here are against the opening of the Black Basin."

"And you'd be wrong. Many of the local tribes look forward to getting jobs once it opens. Shoshones, Paiutes, even some Navajos. Indians have to buy groceries and toys for their children, too, Miss Jones."

Stung, I was about to inform him that since I live next door to a reservation myself, I was well acquainted with tribal shopping habits, thank you very much, but at that moment the door opened and a tall wrangler, his face hidden by the battered Stetson he wore, leaned in through the open door, and said, "We're about to head out, Mr. Olmstead. Want us to take the canyon trail, or the one along the river?"

His back was angled away from me but I didn't have to see the man's face to recognize him. I'd heard that voice almost every day for years.

Dusty.

The cowboy who'd almost gotten me killed.

Dusty had been working at a Scottsdale area dude ranch when I met him. I was a police officer then, still patrolling the streets. One day I clocked Dusty driving sixty-two miles an hour in a forty-five mile zone, and while writing him a ticket, couldn't help but notice his uncanny resemblance to the young Clint Eastwood. Cops were discouraged from turning traffic stops into romantic encounters, so after handing him the summons I climbed back into my patrol car and regretfully watched him drive away. Back then, Scottsdale wasn't as large as it is now, and we soon ran into each other again under less official circumstances. When he asked me out, I accepted.

The problem was this: Dusty drank. A lot. While on benders, he would disappear for weeks, then reappear in my life as if nothing had happened. Hobbled by commitment issues of my own—what survivor of multiple foster homes doesn't have them?—our on-again, off-again relationship worked for me until a woman he married during a blackout found out where I lived. She shot up my apartment, almost killing me in the process.

Appalled, Dusty entered rehab and swore off the sauce.

I swore off Dusty.

Now my bad penny had turned up again, and I was faced with a decision. Should I continue sitting quietly behind him, hidden by the open door, or should I announce my presence and get the discomfort out of the way.

Remembering what one of my kinder foster fathers, a Baptist minister, once said, "Sufficient unto the day is the evil thereof," I remained quiet while Olmstead told Dusty to take the dudes along the river trail. When the conversation ended and the door shut, I began breathing again.

"Are you all right, Miss Jones? You look pale."

Olmstead's voice roused me from my shock. "I'm fine, thanks. It's this higher elevation, I guess. Walapai Flats is about a thousand feet higher that Scottsdale."

"One thousand, two hundred and eight feet, to be exact. It's not like we're Denver."

"Another nice town." Olmstead wasn't the only person who could deflect.

"If you don't mind the traffic."

Small talk can be pleasant, especially after Olmstead's previous formality, but it's a waste of time during a murder investigation, so I picked up where we'd left off. "You've told me that your relationship with Ike Donohue was slight, but is it possible you or your guests might have heard something negative about him, something that might provide a motive for his murder?"

"Miss Jones, I have better things to do with my time than listen to idle gossip. Same with my guests."

If there had been gossip about Donohue, I'd ferret it out whether he liked it or not. "I'm sure you're a busy man, Mr. Olmstead, and I understand your not wanting to worry the guests, but if I'm going to help Ted, I need considerably more information than I have now. So please. Who disliked Donohue?"

"Enough to kill him?"

"Over time, even the smallest disagreement can fester."

He looked at the family photograph again. "Jesus counseled us to forgive the sins of others."

"Jesus isn't involved in this case, though, so would you mind answering my question?"

Olmstead didn't like that, but in accordance with his beliefs, he forgave me instead of slapping me upside the head. "Perhaps some of the people involved in V.U.M. get fairly emotional, but never to the point of shooting anyone. They're responsible people. But since you're determined to dwell on the negative, drive over to Sunset Canyon Lakes and talk to Mrs. Donohue. Like you, she never misses a chance to speak her mind. As for me, I hardly knew the man. Nor, as far as I know, did anyone else on this ranch, whether wrangler or guest."

"What about your other children? The ones who still live at home."

"They know nothing."

"I need to hear that for myself."

He pursed his lips. "I'm not letting you anywhere near them. Aren't you aware of their condition?"

I turned around the look at the family photograph. "I take it, then, that your Down syndrome children are the only ones left at home."

"Other than Theodore and Leilani, of course. As for the others, even if they did see something, which I doubt because they spend almost all their time in the family home out back, their language skills are so limited they won't be able to convey that information to you in any meaningful way."

"I've known numerous people with Down syndrome, and most have no trouble conversing. Some live independently and even hold down jobs."

"The ones Jeanette and I adopted are not high-functioning, Miss Jones. Now ask me something else and leave my children alone."

After that, the interview degenerated. Every question I asked was answered with a noncommittal. Olmstead knew no evil, heard no evil, saw no evil, and certainly wouldn't speak any evil. Several frustrating minutes later, I thanked him for his time and left.

Pulling out of the parking lot, I thought back to the family photograph he'd continued looking at throughout our conversation.

Husband. Wife. Children. Everyone smiling. Everyone happy.

But pictures could lie.

As I neared the part of the highway that paralleled the Virgin River, I had to slow for a long line of horseback riders ambling along at dude speed. Dusty and the blue-eyed dog led the group, while another wrangler took up the rear. Not yet ready to face the unpleasantness that was certain to come, I kept my face averted.

Chapter Seven

April, 1966: Northwestern Arizona

The funeral for Abby's mother was a short one, but as soon as they arrived home, Gabe insisted his wife go straight to bed. "Edna's at peace now, girl. As for you, you need your rest."

Abby argued for a while, insisting she stay up and get the roast started, but she eventually gave in and let him lead her to the bedroom, old Blue trailing behind. "I know I'm letting you down, Gabe," she said. "Half the time I can't garden, can't clean house, can't even cook. What good am I?"

As he tucked the bedspread around his hollow-eyed wife, Gabe said, "You don't never let me down, Abby. Just having you with me is enough. You give the smile to the day."

The depression had hit Abby last month, right after her sixth miscarriage ended in a hysterectomy. Now she spent more days in bed than out. To everyone's surprise, Gabe had stepped up. In addition to his already considerable ranch chores, he'd learned to garden, mop, and wash dishes. Sometimes he even put on Abby's strawberry-patterned apron and cooked. Hell, making a roast was easy. You rubbed the meat with garlic, sprinkled on the narrow leaves of that green plant Abby grew in what she called her herb garden, and shoved it all into the oven at three hundred-fifty degrees for, say, two hours, more if it was a bigger piece of meat. Wondering how much the roast weighed, Gabe tilted his head toward the kitchen.

"Oh, Gabe, so much death."

The roast could wait. Turning back to Abby, Gabe took her hand. "Your mama's at peace now, Abby. Remember how bad she was hurting."

Abby squeezed his hand. "I remember."

Who could forget? It had maddened Gabe, seeing Edna suffer. That tough ranch woman, popping out twelve kids as if it'd been nothing, once even limping through her housework with a leg fresh broke by an ornery horse. Cancer-reduced to a moaning ragbone wreck. Ten days ago, when the pain made her scream, Gabe had knocked down her doctor when he refused to give her more drugs, claiming he didn't want her to "become an addict."

"I'll *addict* your ass!" Gabe had yelled, as his fist connected with the doctor's nose.

It took two nurses and several orderlies to pull Gabe off him, but the upshot of the deal was that Edna got her morphine. Compared to that, having to spend a couple nights in jail was a bargain. A woman like Edna, she deserved defending. Why, hadn't she given him his Abby?

With callused hands, he stroked his wife's cheek. "You get some sleep, girl. I'll take care of things around here."

When he started to pull his hand away, she hung on.

"Not just Mama, Gabe. It's everybody." She started reciting what Gabe called her Death List, beginning with their own lost babies, moving on to two sisters, a brother—all dead in the past few years. When she started on her dying nieces and nephews, Gabe decided it was time to pull her mind out of the graveyard.

"Say, girl, maybe over the weekend I'll drive us up to Silver Ridge to see that new Doris Day movie, *Do Not Disturb*? I can't wait to see it, I surely can't." Truth be told, the thought of sitting through another Doris Day movie made him want to puke, but Abby loved the actress, had even bleached her sorrel-colored hair blond so she'd look like her.

Gabe's plans for the weekend didn't interest his wife. She started talking about the past, before her mama got so sick. "Remember last winter, when we saw that John Wayne movie?"

He smoothed her Doris Day hair, wishing she'd go back to natural. But whatever she wanted, he'd accept. His fine girl could do no wrong. "Which movie was that? *In Harm's Way* or *The Sons of Katie Elder?*"

"*In Harm's Way.* Remember what I said then, that in thirty years, you'll look like him?"

Gabe chuckled. "Yeah, soon's I grow four inches and my brown eyes turn blue."

She kissed the stump where his left forefinger used to be. "Don't know why you worship him so, Gabe. You're the real war hero. Wayne's just an actor."

He pulled a play-frown. "Now don't go saying anything bad about the Duke, girl, or I'll write and tell him. You make that man mad and he'll come out here and mess you up something awful."

Abby gave him a smile, the first in a long while. "Oh, I do love you, Gabe, I do."

Gabe said nothing. He didn't have to.

.

Chapter Eight

Before I left the guest ranch, Olmstead called Sunset Canyon Lakes to grease the wheels for me.

"Katherine Dysart is the leasing agent," he explained. "She and her husband do business with us, and they've offered to help. At the very least, Katherine can steer you in the right direction. But be careful. Other than Mrs. Donohue, the residents tend to be very private people."

No surprise there, since that was why they'd bought into a gated community in the first place.

For most newcomers to Arizona, the idea of living in the desert sounds like a dream come true and the reality isn't far off. But for others, once the grandeur of the scenery begins to pall, they discover the desert is a vast expanse of rock and cactus, heat and dust. These disgruntled souls then attempt to transmogrify the landscape into something more reminiscent of rural Minnesota. In the case of land developers with unlimited pocketbooks, they often succeed, just as they had with Sunset Canyon Lakes.

A few miles north of the guest ranch, I spotted a flash of green on the horizon. As I drove toward it, the green gnawed away all those subtle beiges and browns I so loved until the only color left was a spreading landscape of gaudy green. Lording over this unnatural sight was a sign that boasted, SUNSET CANYON LAKES—THE OASIS IN THE DESERT.

Ah, the miracles of irrigation.

My eyes were so dazzled by all that greenness I almost failed to notice a smaller sign directing visitors to park their vehicles in the large lot to the west of the main gate. SUNSET CANYON LAKES IS A CAR-LIMITED COMMUNITY. VISITORS MUST PARK THEIR CARS AND WAIT FOR SERVICE, it demanded. Filled with foreboding, I drove up to the gatehouse and asked the security guard for better instructions, then learned why Hank Olmstead had insisted on calling ahead. Getting into a nuclear power plant would have been easier than getting into Sunset Canyon Lakes.

After showing the guard my ID and answering a series of questions designed to weed out Islamic terrorists and Mexican illegals, I was told that once I parked my car in the visitor's lot, someone would come by to pick me up. Oh, and did I carry a firearm? Very nice, Miss Jones, but leave it locked in your car. Only uniformed police officers carry in Sunset Canyon Lakes. I grudgingly complied, and five minutes later, I was being chauffeured via golf cart onto the resort's hallowed grounds.

"You'll need a map to find your way around, and you can pick one up at the leasing office, which is where we're headed," said my handsome young escort, whose nametag identified him as DEREK. He swung his left arm around in an arc, taking in the scene before us. "The resort is so big newcomers are always getting lost. If that happens to you, simply hop on one of the trolleys. It'll eventually wind up wherever you need to go. One comes along every five minutes so that even people who live here year round rarely need to use their cars."

Derek hadn't exaggerated the resort's size. Straight ahead lay the five-hundred-acre Sunset Canyon Lake, upon which windsurfers and kayaks bobbed on the water. To our right flowed the neatly trimmed fairway of an eighteen-hole golf course. Separating these nondesert attractions was a broad stretch of green parkland shaded by lofty eucalyptus and Aleppo pine, theoretically planted to keep the desert sun from zapping the residents with skin cancer.

Amazed and aghast at the waste of Arizona's meager water resources, I asked Derek, "Where does all that water come from?"

"The Virgin River," he answered. "The lake is actually a reservoir."

As we zipped along toward the leasing office, the sun emerged from its cloud cover. I shaded my eyes as we passed several swimming pools, tennis courts, a clubhouse, two restaurants, and a spa. Located in a small complex off the main thoroughfare, boutiques offered tennis rackets, golf clubs, sports attire, evening wear, exotic cheeses and fine wines. The resort's architecture differed dramatically from that of Walapai Flats. Instead of the town's self-conscious Old West knockoffs, the buildings here formed a mélange of concrete and glass with a smattering of wood thrown in to soften the edges. I could see why the place would appeal to city dwellers; they'd feel like they'd never left home.

Sunset Canyon Lakes was broken into separate neighborhoods, my guide informed me. The Lakes, arcing around the western end of the big lake, were individually owned condos. The Fairways, on the southeastern side of the resort, were timeshares. All were glass-fronted, offering spectacular views of either lake or golf course.

"No single-family homes?" I wondered aloud.

"Oh, yes." Derek waved his hand again, this time toward the golf course. "We can't see them from here because they're hidden in the trees on the other side of the golf course. Very exclusive. To get in there, you have to go through another gate."

"A gated community within a gated community?"

"Cool, huh?" He rattled off the names of several film and music stars, some of whom I'd actually heard of. "The celebrities have their own private pools, of course. Private planes, too."

By the time we arrived at the leasing office, my desert-dweller eyes had gone into shock from all that green. It was a relief when a thirty-something brunette wearing a nametag identifying her as KATHERINE ushered me into a reception area as sleek as she was. But my eyes continued to be dazzled because the large picture window overlooking the pool area let in harsh sunlight that bounced off the room's chrome and leather furniture. Scattered here and there were steel sculptures resembling crashed space satellites. A large abstract painted in somber tones of gray and black sneered at me from the wall. The room's only homey touch came from a silver laptop humming away on a chrome and glass desk.

"Welcome to Sunset Canyon Lakes, Miss Jones," Katherine said, her Boston accent modulated into a soft purr. "How do you like our little resort?"

"Impressive, but I'm here on business." I handed her my card. "I understand Hank Olmstead called you about my visit?"

An elegant nod. "Re the matter of Mr. Donohue's death and the problems Ted subsequently encountered. Very unfortunate. We're fond of Hank. And of his son, too, of course. My husband and I consider them both friends." Her face, which had assumed a tragic mask, switched to brisk business mode. "How may I be of help?"

"A map would be nice."

"Certainly. Sunset Canyon Lakes is labyrinthine enough that newcomers frequently get turned around. Most of our units are owned by their occupants, but we always have a few available for lease. As well as the timeshares, of course"

Her elocution was so superb she made me feel like a hayseed. "On my way here, I didn't see any children. Is this an age-restricted community?"

"Correct. Anyone wishing to buy a unit here must be fifty-five or older. You can, however, arrange for a one-time rental of a timeshare, as long as you do not bring children. A nice summer camp is located within driving distance, and most parents are happy for the respite."

"She's one of the timeshare people then?" I pointed out the window toward a bikinied and familiar-looking beauty basking on a chaise by the Olympic sized pool. Mia Tosches, the woman who'd accused Ted of roughing up Ike Donohue, was surrounded by a phalanx of young men who looked as good as she did. "Surely she can't be more than twenty."

This time Katherine's smile revealed a feline gleam. "Mrs. Tosches is older than she looks."

Feigning ignorance, I said, "Really! Then does Mrs. Tosches' husband fulfill the age requirement to live here?"

"Most certainly, but his age is irrelevant since he's the man who developed Sunset Canyon Lakes."

As owner of the Black Basin Mine *and* the developer of a high-roller resort, Roger Tosches had to be quite the moneybags. "Good point," I conceded. "What about those body-builder types Mrs. Tosches is talking to? They don't look like senior citizens to me."

"They work here," she said dismissively. "And they're on their lunch break. Well, a couple of them are timeshare people, and as you noticed, they're fitness-oriented." She paused, then added, "Mrs. Tosches does admire fit men."

Meow. "The Tosches don't have their own pool?"

"Of course they do."

"Pardon me if I seem dense, but then why is Mrs. Tosches using this one?"

"She likes young company. She also likes horseback riding, and spends a great deal of time over at the guest ranch."

I wondered why Olmstead hadn't shared that information with me. "Mr. Tosches doesn't ride with her, I take it."

"With his varied business interests he has little free time, but when he gets the chance, he plays golf with his friends." She gestured toward the young men talking to Mia. "*Her* friends see to it that she's never lonely."

Young woman, older husband, possible different sexual interests, and Katherine Dysart wanted me to know all about it. This made me curious about Katherine herself. Given her demeanor, she'd once led a different life than the one she led now: ushering prospective renters around someone else's money-maker.

"Where do you live?" I asked her, apropos of nothing other than that *Nosy* is every PI's middle name. "In Walapai Flats?"

The question amused her. "Where my domicile of choice would be either a trailer or tract home? Hardly. My husband Trent, who also isn't fifty-five, is the recreation director here, and as such, he is required to live on the property. Trent organizes various entertainments—book clubs, wine tastings, trips to Las Vegas, the Grand Canyon, Zion National Park, that sort of thing. For the horsy outings, Ted has been of invaluable help to Trent, and that is only one of the two reasons we want to see him out of that vile jail and back at the ranch. The other reason, well, we simply like him. He's an honest, straightforward man, and those qualities are in short shrift these days."

Leaning over the chrome and glass desk, she picked up several brochures along with the promised map. "Perhaps you could pass these out to your friends? They highlight the ownership portion of the resort and are perfect for those who are more, ah, mature, and no longer have children cluttering up the house. As I'm certain you've noticed, Sunset Canyon Lakes is a marvelous place to retire for anyone who wishes to escape from the hustle and bustle of the city."

When she glanced down at the business card I handed her in return, her voice took on a wistful tone. "I see you're from Scottsdale. It used to be so lovely. But now..."

She didn't need to finish because we both knew the end of that sentence: "But now it's just another traffic-clogged city."

Because of its car-control philosophy, Sunset Canyon Lakes certainly wasn't traffic-clogged, not unless you counted the myriad golf carts scooting along its paths or the open-air trolleys shuttling residents back and forth. The resort, Katherine informed me, was not the ecological nightmare it first appeared. Fewer cars meant fewer gas omissions, and the golf carts and trolleys were all electric. The lake, where motor craft were also banned, provided the water for the golf course, trees, and the greenbelts lining every pathway.

"So you see, Sunset Canyon Lakes is not simply a pretty face," she finished, smiling at her own witticism. "We're an eco-friendly community that contributes to the environment, not subtracts."

Not quite won over, because most of the irrigation would evaporate into the hot desert air, not settle into the water table, I said, "Hey, if I had the money, I'd buy a unit right now."

Her intimidating elegance fell away when she winked. "To purchase, you'd have to scrounge up an older partner, Miss Jones. But we do have some wealthy widowers in residence if you're in the market."

"I'll give it some thought. Let me ask, do you know the Donohues very well yourself? I'm wondering how Mrs. Donohue is bearing up, and frankly, if she'll even talk to me."

"I had only a passing acquaintance with Mr. Donohue. As for Mrs. Donohue, yesterday, while I was showing a prospective lessee one of our better properties, I saw her and her friends on their way to the golf course, which leads me to believe she's bearing up quite well." That feline gleam again. Katherine didn't like Nancy Donohue any more than she liked Mia Tosches.

Having gathered as much information as possible, I headed out, wondering again how a woman like Katherine Dysart had wound up in a leasing office. Her accent was Boston, her demeanor Old Money. But since the recent economic collapse had claimed some surprising victims, I temporarily pushed my curiosity aside.

Catching a trolley to the Donohue's condo on the other side of the resort turned out to be easy. All you did was stand at the curb looking lost, and within seconds, one of the things trundled along and scooped you up. I showed the map Katherine had given me to the handsome young driver, who identified the Donohue's neighborhood as The Lakes, and promised to call out my stop. Feeling less adrift, I walked past several rows of gray-haired seniors and took a seat in the back.

My comfort proved short-lived. As we bumped along through the ever-present greenery, I found myself growing unsettled again. The whole resort seemed "off." Too many lined faces, too few young ones. With its perfectly clean streets, perfectly neat condos, and perfectly groomed landscaping, Sunset Canyon Lakes was a childless Disneyland. While I did admire the almost car-less streets, I balked at the childfree yards. In some ways, they seemed even more unnatural than a green desert.

Don't get me wrong—I don't crave kids, and my biological clock has long since forgotten to tick. I'm closing in on forty, have no children, and don't yearn for any. There's a reason for that. My own early years had been so miserable that I've never been able to equate childhood with anything other than pain. But childless streets? To me, other people's children were visible proof that despite life's frequent grotesqueries, most people still had faith in the future. Sunset Canyon Lakes was all about the past, about money already made, marriages accomplished or lost, travels finished, hunters home from the hills and kicking back for their remaining time on Earth.

"The Lakes!" the bus driver suddenly announced.

Relieved to be pulled out of my philosophical funk, I clambered off the trolley and onto a wide pathway that meandered through a spindly forest of palm trees. As I trod the path to the Donohue's concrete and glass condo, I saw the lake glimmering in the distance. Behind it, red and purple mesas reached up to the sky. Chez Donohue had a killer view.

At my knock, the big oak door opened immediately, but instead of being confronted by a grieving widow, I saw a strong-jawed woman holding a martini in her hand. I'm five foot-eight, yet she topped me by almost four inches.

"Mrs. Donohue?"

She waved the martini at me. "That's me, kiddo. You must be Cassie, Arnie Brinkman's new wife. Welcome to the Book Bitches. Food and drinks are on the sideboard, courtesy of the other Bitches."

"Actually, I'm…"

But she was already headed into the living room, where six carefully groomed women had gathered. None of those hothouse roses held anything resembling a book, and judging from the slurred bits of conversation that drifted toward me, they were well on their way to getting soused.

Grief takes people different ways. In my days as a police officer, I'd often delivered bad news, standing close to the next-of-kin in case they began to crumple to the floor. Some erupted into hysterics. Others stood there blank-eyed, unable to take in the fact that their lives had changed forever. A few even laughed. Experience had taught me that none of those early reactions meant a thing. One of the laughers slit his jugular within minutes of my leaving his house. Two criers turned out to be wife-killers. So I didn't judge this widow. For all I knew, Nancy Donohue deeply loved her husband and had organized this drink-a-thon to keep from throwing herself into Sunset Canyon Lake with a cinder block tied around her neck.

However, I couldn't forget that newspaper photograph of her holding a rifle, her foot triumphantly placed on the neck of a dead elk.

Before trailing after Mrs. Donohue, I took a moment to study the sunken living room ahead. The decor was Southwest Standard: pale earth tones relieved here and there by Indian-print toss pillows. A collection of dusty woven baskets and Kachina dolls were spread along the half-wall that divided the living and dining areas. The double doors off the entry hall stood open to reveal a den with a more idiosyncratic personality. In this very male room I saw a bookcase stuffed with what appeared to be manuals, a plain wooden desk, and an ancient recliner held together by duct tape. Arranged in a haphazard pattern on the walls were a series of black and white photographs of various men shaking hands, but I was too far away to make out their faces. The only spot of color among the photographs was one depicting something red and gold and blurry.

"Don't stand there gawking, Cassie! Come join us!" Mrs. Donohue called.

Deciding to let the mistaken identity situation play itself out, I followed her orders. Stepping away from the den and down into the living room, I noticed that one of the overstuffed chairs had begun to fray along the seams. The wooden coffee table sported a deep gouge, as if something sharp had fallen across it. No attempt had been made to repair the flaw, which made me suspect a lack of domesticity on Nancy Donohue's part, as well as the absence of household help. Maybe she was difficult to get along with?

As I sank into an elderly chair, I spotted a possible thorn in Donohue's collection of hothouse roses, a thin woman in her late thirties whose Goth appearance separated her from the others. Black tee shirt, baggy cargo pants, Doc Marten boots, spiky black hair, nose ring, Celtic tattoos marching up her spindly arm, black-polished fingernails bitten to the quick. No trophy wife, she.

"Tell us more about your exciting life in New York, Olivia, and don't leave out a thing," a face-lifted redhead somewhere between fifty and seventy, demanded of the Goth. "Especially the newspaper part. Is it true you once interviewed Osama bin Ladin?"

"His cousin," Olivia answered, her voice as spiky as her hair.

"Was he as crazy as Osama?" another woman asked.

"There's a difference between crazy and evil," Olivia said. "From all accounts, Osama was perfectly sane. His cousin, however…"

"Oh, God, let's not start in on that again," Mrs. Donohue interrupted. "I've heard all about 9/11 I care to. It's water under the bridge, anyway."

At that casual dismissal of so much suffering, I stiffened. So did black-clad Olivia, although her face didn't change.

"The most interesting interview I ever conducted was with the actor Leif Noble," she said. "He chugged Chivas all the way through and when I asked him if the rumors about him and that thirteen-year-old girl were true, he threw his drink in my face and called me a whore."

"Well, are you?"

The other women gasped at Mrs. Donohue's ghastly question, but Olivia merely smiled. "Unfortunately, no. Whores make more money than reporters."

Mrs. Donohue bared her big horsy teeth. "Too bad you're merely a time-sharer, dear. At least you're honest, which is more than I can say about the rest of my friends." With that dig, she turned to me. "Now it's your turn to tell us all about yourself,

Cassie. We're all dying to know how you managed to lure Arnie away from Roberta. She clung like a cocklebur, that one."

Time to break up the party. "Actually, Mrs. Donohue, I'm…"

"Nancy, dear. I hold no truck with formality."

"Well, Nancy, I'm not Cassie Brinkman. My name's Lena Jones and I'm a private investigator. I was hoping to talk to you about your husband's murder."

Glasses stopped clinking. Women stopped talking.

The great killer of elk, however, didn't bat an eye. "What do you want to know?"

Most of the other women leaned forward in anticipation, but Olivia remained unnaturally still.

"Perhaps we should speak in private?"

Nancy Donohue waved her martini glass. "There are no secrets here."

In my years as an investigator, I've heard that statement many times, and each time it had preceded a lie. But a good investigator can learn as much from lies as from the truth. Once again grateful for Arizona's liberal taping laws, I reached into my carry-all and switched on my digital recorder.

"Where were you the night your husband was shot?" I asked, determined to shock the arrogance out of her.

She wasn't fazed. "Irrelevant, since that Indian ranch hand has already been arrested for his murder."

"If you mean Theodore Olmstead, the *assistant manager* of Sunset Trails Guest Ranch, he's merely being held as a material witness, not charged with anything."

"There's a difference?"

"Quite a big one, actually, because it means he hasn't been accused of any crime. Now that he has a good attorney, there could even be a chance he can get released. Unless, of course, the authorities gather enough evidence to bind him over for trial."

"My, my, how complicated," piped up one of the other women, a tipsy dowager with lavender hair.

Ignoring her, Mrs. Donohue said, "If there's a chance he might get released, which quite frankly comes as a surprise to me, then perhaps some privacy is called for." Addressing the Book Bitches as a whole, she added, "If you ladies will excuse us for a few minutes, I need to step into the den with this investigator creature. In the meantime, besides gossiping about me behind my back, perhaps you can come up with some ideas for this fall's book list. Remember, anything having to do with politics and religion is out."

"That just leaves mysteries, cookbooks, and romance novels," one Book Bitch grumbled before Mrs. Donohue shut the den's thick double doors behind us. For the first time, I became aware of a faint smell of cigarettes.

My nose must have twitched, because Nancy Donohue said, "Ike smoked, the awful man, but I made certain he did it only outside the house. The stench clung to his clothes, though, and settled in here. I'll have to fumigate everything he ever touched."

She plopped onto a straight-back chair, leaving the duct-taped recliner for me. Perhaps she thought it had germs. "Ask your questions, Jones, but make it snappy, because as you can see, I have company."

Much closer now to the photograph wall, I saw that Ike Donohue was the common denominator in all the black and white photos. Tall, lean, and clean-featured, only a slight stoop to his shoulders kept him from being movie-star handsome. In each photograph, he was smiling his phony smile as he shook hands with an assortment of military and business types. In three of the pictures, a benevolent-looking man who looked like everyone's favorite uncle, stood next to him. The sole color photograph, which had been too blurry from out in the hall for me to discern its subject matter, was of a mushroom cloud exploding over the desert.

Mrs. Donohue had said to make it snappy, so I did. "From what I've been able to find out, the last time your husband was seen alive was at the Walapai Gas-N-Go early Thursday morning. Where were you that day?" As an afterthought, I added, "And that night."

"Home."

"Was anyone with you during any part of that time?" One of those good-looking pool boys, for instance?

Oblivious to my thoughts, she answered, "Elizabeth Waide dropped by around dinner time. She's the old bat with the purple hair."

"How long did she stay?"

"Until all the Beefeaters was gone. The bottle was almost full when she got here, and considering the speed with which she was knocking back martinis, it might have been a couple of hours. She could still walk when she left, I'll give her that."

A drunk witness makes a bad witness, but I asked the next question anyway. "This would have been at what time?"

Her eyes tracked up and to the left, something that often happens when people are about to tell a lie. "About an hour before dinner. I was roasting a chicken. By the time the blabbermouth shut up and hit the road, it'd burned. Ike, who had absolutely no taste buds thanks to all those cigarettes, would have eaten it anyway. If he'd lived. Since he didn't, I threw it out. What a waste."

Her comment was so outrageous that Olivia's observation about the difference between crazy and evil flashed into my mind. Then I reminded myself about the danger of passing judgment so early in an investigation, and forced myself to focus. Nancy Donohue had rolled out an alibi that would be easy enough to check. Neighbors snoop, and someone might have been watching as the purple-haired Elizabeth Waide visited. Come to think of it, the woman might not have been as drunk as Nancy wanted me to believe. Whatever the case, Ted's attorney would have access to the police report giving the estimated time of Donohue's death. The autopsy would zero in on it.

"You said Mrs. Waide visited before dinner,'" I asked. "What time do you usually eat?"

"There's no 'usually' to it. We kept to a strict schedule. Ike is, *was*, diabetic and he had to eat his dinner promptly at six every day or his blood sugar went wild. You have no idea how much trouble that caused me."

If the chicken had burned, then Mrs. Waide left somewhere between six-thirty and seven. "What did you do when he didn't show up for dinner?"

"I finished reading *White Hunter, Black Heart* and went to bed."

"You never noticed that your husband didn't come home?"

She shrugged. "It wouldn't have been the first time. I wasn't aware somebody had stopped his clock until two deputies showed up at the door. I had to cancel my tennis date. Very annoying."

Oh, what a happy marriage those two must have had. "You and Mr. Donohue were married for how many years?"

"Fifteen."

Recalling the newspaper article, I said, "I was under the impression you have grandchildren."

"They're not mine, thank God. I'm Ike's second wife."

"What happened to the first Mrs. Donohue?"

A quick bark of laughter. "You mean, did I murder her to get him? Hardly. That dullard is still alive and kicking. She was one of those 'stay-at-home-moms,' as housewives like to call themselves these days. Always cooking and cleaning, absolutely no interest in anything outside the home. Ike was bored stiff. Unlike her, I do things. I'm not the domestic type and never have been. Or at least I wasn't until Ike had to go and develop diabetes."

As self-involved and pathologically insensitive as Nancy Donohue was, living with a diabetic must have been frustrating, so my next question was a given. "Did Mr. Donohue carry life insurance?"

"Not enough to kill for." With that, she stood up. "Interview's over, Jones."

"One more question."

She made a big show of looking at her watch, which like mine, was a cheap Timex. The solitaire nestled next to her wedding band didn't have a diamond's usual brilliance, either. Were the Donohues having financial problems? If so, a nice insurance payoff would come in handy. I'd ask Jimmy to check.

Oblivious to the way my mind was tracking, she said, "One more question then I go back to the Bitches. Just because Ike was stupid enough to get himself killed doesn't mean I have to stop living my own life."

"Who do you think killed your husband?"

"If neither I nor that Indian did it, you mean? Offhand, I'd say Roger Tosches. The man's a complete scoundrel."

With that, she escorted me to the front door and shut it behind me so quickly it slammed me in the ass.

Chapter Nine

Tuesday noon

In some ways, Nancy Donohue reminded me of one of my least favorite foster mothers. Brisk. Unfeeling. Oblivious to the needs of others. When the social worker had turned me over to Mrs. and Mr. Putney, I was only nine years old and already in serious emotional trouble. But for some reason, no one seemed aware of that, especially not Mrs. Putney.

Maybe my obvious physical disabilities just kept people from noticing the rest. The bullet that had entered my brain left me with a dragging left leg and a weak left arm. To give credit where due, Mrs. Putney saw to it that I continued my rehabilitation program until the left side of my body was as strong as my right. For that, I'll always be grateful. But she didn't handle my fragile emotional state nearly as well. When I cried, she told me to shut up. When I couldn't eat, she forced me to until I threw up. When I begged for my bedroom light to be left on at night, she called me a baby.

Had the social workers told her what had happened to me? That I'd been shot in the face by my mother, then left for dead on a Phoenix street? That when I regained consciousness in the hospital two months later, I could tell the social workers little— just that I remembered my mother screaming, "I'll shoot her, I'll shoot her now!" That my father was already gone, shot to death in the forest that haunted my nightmares? Whether Mrs. Putney knew or not, she wouldn't leave a light on.

I had no way of knowing that the next foster home would be much, much worse.

Pushing the memory of Mrs. Putney out of my mind—and hating Nancy Donohue for resurrecting her in the first place— I called Katherine Dysart to get black-clad Olivia's last name. Eames, Katherine told me. Olivia Eames. Mission accomplished, I sat in my rental car outside the gate of Sunset Canyon Lakes for a few minutes, digesting what I'd learned.

The fact that Nancy Donohue hadn't bothered to act the grieving widow was actually a point in her favor, since I'd never met a homicidal wife who didn't wail like a banshee over her husband's murder. Still, her almost pathological coldness unsettled me enough to want Jimmy to delve into her background. Olivia Eames' and Katherine Dysart's past, too, and not merely out of curiosity. Both women were fish out of water in Sunset Canyon Lakes, and I wanted to know what they were doing there. One of the first things I'd learned when conducting murder investigations was to look for any object that seemed out of place, especially when that object was human.

I checked my watch again. Although not yet noon, it felt as if hours had passed since I arrived at the resort's gate. It was time to leave the Emerald City and return to the real world, so I pulled out of the parking lot and headed for Sunset Point, where Donohue's body had been found. If I arrived a few minutes late for my lunch with Jimmy, he'd understand.

After all that unnatural green, it was a relief to drive through a more subtle landscape, the desert's stark beauty softened by the enormous blue sky. Above, red-tailed hawks soared along the updrafts. I even spotted a condor, one of the few that had been released into the Arizona wilderness in hopes of bringing the birds back from near-extinction. Condors are scavengers. They eat anything dead, including road kill. I wondered if one had been among the birds found snacking on what was left of Donohue's body.

As it turned out, Sunset Point was easy to find but difficult to reach. Situated at the top of Walapai Mountain, the highest point in the mountain range that created the Virgin River Gorge, the scenic viewpoint was only available to people with four-wheel-drive vehicles or hikers who had the stamina for the steep climb. It was all up and around, switchback after dizzying switchback, as my SUV hugged the inside of a poorly maintained gravel road. Heaven help any sight-seer who suffered from vertigo.

Just as I thought the winding road would continue forever, it dead-ended at a metal barrier that kept me from driving straight into the canyon. After setting my emergency brake I stepped out and looked into the distance. Grand Canyon National Park lay twenty miles to the south. A million or so years ago the Virgin River Gorge had been formed by the seasonal runoff that fed into the Colorado, but while the gorge itself was no Grand Canyon, it was no mere arroyo, either. The sides presented a sheer drop of more than twelve hundred feet. At the bottom, the river surged along the rock walls like a silver snake, carving the canyon ever larger and deeper.

What a great place to dispose of a body.

However, as the fluttering remains of yellow police tape proved, Donohue had become snagged on a cactus-studded outcrop ten feet below the ledge I stood on. Easy pickings for scavengers, not so easy for law enforcement. The bad news was that the sheriff had been forced to call for an expert rock-climbing team to retrieve the body. The good news was that whoever dumped Donohue hadn't been able to climb down to tumble him off the outcropping into the river below. Otherwise, the victim might have floated all the way to the Gulf of California and then onto the shoreline of Mexico.

A mishmash of tire tracks criss-crossed the ground. Somewhere among them would be the tread of the killer's tires, now covered by dozens of others: SUVs, sheriff's office vehicles, and looky-loos who were always attracted to scenes of violent death. No matter. I'd already learned what I needed to know. It wouldn't have taken a strong man to heave Donohue off Sunset Point. The spot where he'd gone over was less than three yards from the metal safety barrier, and the ground sloped sharply toward the drop-off. A woman could easily have rolled his body in, no problem.

Satisfied, I climbed back into my rental and headed to Walapai Flats.

The drive was uneventful until I neared the cutoff to Sunset Trails Guest Ranch, where I spotted the same line of horseback riders I'd seen earlier in the morning. Morning trail ride completed, they were headed back to the ranch. This time, Dusty and the blue-eyed dog brought up the rear, watching out for stragglers.

We don't always love the right people. By "right people," I mean the people who are good for us, who even as they encourage us to grow, watch our backs as we stumble and fall through life. Loving the unlovable can be a saintly thing—Mother Teresa thought so, anyway—but for most of us mortals, loving the dysfunctional can be dangerous.

Dusty's love affair with alcohol had almost killed me. True, I'd almost been killed before: as a child, as a cop, as a private investigator. Three strikes and you're out, right? Not in my case, but I was no fool and knew my lucky streak wouldn't last forever. Walking away from a man I still loved had been painful, but at least I remained alive to tell the tale. The nights, though…

Those long, lonely nights without Dusty lying next to me, nights without the feel of his hands, his lips…Even now, watching his easy sway in the saddle, I wanted to open the car door and run after him, screaming his name. I imagined my hands on his back, pulling him closer to me, smelling his sweat…

Jesus, Lena, what the hell are you thinking?

As Dusty rode by, I turned my head away, but he was so busy riding herd on the dudes that he didn't once glance into my car.

Despite my concern about being late, I arrived at Ma's Kitchen five minutes early. A wall of sound enveloped me as I opened the door. Customers chatting and laughing, cutlery clinking, meat sizzling on a grill somewhere. The restaurant's decor furthered its homey name via wooden chairs, scarred wooden tables, and little pink doilies decorating every available surface. I stood in the reception area for a moment, worrying that we might not find a seat, but then I spotted Jimmy waiting for me in a back booth. A waitress was flirting with him: another moth attracted to his flame.

He waved. "Hey, Lena! Meet my new friend Tara."

Tara, a waifish brunette with eyes that took up half her face, scowled when she saw me. She probably thought Jimmy and I were on a "date" date.

"Nice to meet you, Tara," I said, as I slid into the booth across from him. "What's today's special?"

"Liver and onions," Tara said, trying hard to smile at me. "Or spaghetti marinara."

Interviews with possible suspects were tough enough without adding onion breath into the mix, so I chose the spaghetti, hoping it wouldn't be too garlicky. Jimmy followed suit. Once Tara disappeared with our orders, he informed me that Anderson Behar, Ted's attorney, had not only officially brought Desert Investigations on board, but that he had already begun to share information. The nice thing about busy restaurants, especially when you're sitting in a back booth, is that your own conversation disappears into the rest of the noise.

"I drove over to your dad's ranch this morning," I said, studying Jimmy's face for his reaction.

"Really?" He pretended to be fascinated by the pink doily on our table. "Learn anything interesting?"

"Very much so."

He caressed the doily, rubbing the fabric between his thumb and forefinger. "My mother used to make things like this. My adoptive mother, that is. Crocheting can be time consuming, but she said it relaxed her. Ranch living…"

"I saw Dusty."

His fingers froze.

"On the way over here, I figured everything out. Your disappearing act. The scene at the motel. When Dusty left rehab, you got him the job at your father's ranch, didn't you? That's why you didn't want me involved in this case, because you knew I'd come up here and see him. You were forgiving enough to get him a job, but you didn't want me to start up with him again, did you?"

When his eyes met mine, I saw a depth of anger I didn't know my peaceful partner was capable of. "He almost got you killed, Lena."

I wanted to argue that the woman who shot up my apartment wasn't Dusty's fault, but my commitment to the truth wouldn't let me. It *had* been Dusty's fault. If he hadn't disappeared to Vegas on a week-long bender, he wouldn't have wound up married to the crazy bitch, and she wouldn't have followed him back to Scottsdale toting a loaded gun. I was alive only because she was a lousy shot.

"You could have told me Dusty was here, you know." Giving up the blame game, I added, "Oh, Jimmy, did you really think I would allow him back into my life?"

"Stranger things have happened."

I started to protest, then stopped. Jimmy was right. Warren Quinn had happened, a Hollywood film director every bit as wrong for me as Dusty had been. But Warren was now in my past, too. For better or for worse, I was alone and would always be alone. Better lonely than dead.

Noticing my hesitation, Jimmy began to relax. "Can we talk about the case, instead?"

Safer territory, to be sure. "Sounds good to me. I recorded a couple of interesting conversations today. You want to transcribe them or should I?"

"I'll let you do the honors."

Although I typed thirty words a minute and Jimmy something like eighty, I agreed as a peace offering. "Fine. What did Ted's attorney have to say."

Over the restaurant's din, I learned that Anderson Behar had already received a copy of the preliminary autopsy report on Donohue, which estimated the time of death between nine and midnight last Thursday night. Ballistics tests revealed the murder weapon to be a .38. A handgun, then. He'd been shot

from approximately five feet away, and the angle of the wound—
a straight-on projectory—further proved suicide unlikely.

"Jimmy, did you ever find out what kind of firearm killed
Kimama?"

"The slug they dug out of her was a thirty-ought-six. Ballistics never matched it to anything, but they suspect it was fired
from a low-velocity carbine. Anything larger would have gone
right through her and the car she was sitting in. And kept on
going after that."

Two different murder weapons: a carbine and a pistol. It didn't
necessarily mean two different killers. "What else?"

"Ted's fingerprints were on Donohue's belt and watch.
Considering that, I'm surprised the prosecuting attorney hasn't
already filed charges."

"Not really, Jimmy. Remember, when Donohue started to
fall, Ted tried to catch him." As they say, no good deed goes
unpunished.

"But Behar also said that Mia Tosches told a sheriff's deputy
that Ted threatened to kill the guy."

"Does that sound like your brother to you?"

He shrugged. "Ted always had a temper, but whether he
would threaten to kill someone, I don't see it. He's been working
at the guest ranch too long. Dad impressed on all us kids that
the ranch would lose business if we went around saying what
we were thinking. Especially about the guests."

Learning to control your mouth was a prerequisite for working with the public, especially the wealthy or semi-wealthy
public. If you insulted guests, they would never return, and
neither would their friends. My own experience had taught me
that workplace guardedness tended to bleed into other areas
of life as well, so I found it inconceivable that Ted would run
around town shouting threats at people, especially cash cows
from Sunset Canyon Lakes.

"Let's see if I have this right," I said, thinking aloud. "So far,
the only thing the sheriff has to go on is based on his altercation
with Donohue, a fingerprint match, and some threat he may or

may not have uttered at the Walapai Gas-N-Go. Pretty weak, if you ask me. A good attorney should make mincemeat out of it. How sharp did Behar seem to you?"

Jimmy waggled his hand, a gesture that usually means so-so. "The guy's not even a criminal defense attorney. Dad hired him because he used him in a real estate transaction a few years ago over in Silver Ridge. The guy's licensed in three states."

Which Behar would almost have to be in this area, where cases frequently slopped across the state lines of Arizona, Nevada, and Utah. But a real estate attorney? "Are he and your dad friends from way back?"

"Since dinosaurs walked the earth."

Friendship is all well and good, but when faced with a criminal case, it accounted for little. Ted needed an experienced criminal attorney, not a buddy.

"Check Behar out, just to be safe. The last thing Ted wants now is a real estate attorney who's in over his head, so try to talk your dad into hiring someone who knows what he's doing. Oh, and check out V.U.M., Victims of…"

"Victims of Uranium Mining," he finished for me. "They've been giving the Black Basin Mine advocates a lot of grief."

"Rightly so, from what I hear about what happened with that other uranium mine Roger Tosches used to run." I recounted everything I'd learned during my visit to Sunset Canyon Lakes.

When I finished, Jimmy gave me an admiring look. "Consider me impressed. The Nancy Donohue woman would never have let me in her house, let alone talked to me. I'll start working up backgrounders on her, Katherine Dysart, and Olivia what's-her-face…How do you spell that reporter's last name?"

"E-A-M-E-S. She works on a New York newspaper, but I'm not sure which one. *The Village Voice*, probably. She's vacationing—she says—at a timeshare over there, but I can't help but wonder why. Doesn't look the type, if you know what I mean. Tattoos. Black nail polish. Less than eighty years old. I want to know more about Ike Donohue, too. Before he moved here, he did PR for some tobacco company in North Carolina, and at the time of death, was doing the same for the Black Basin Mine. His choice of employers sorta piques my interest."

Jimmy made a face. "First the guy fronts for tobacco, claims it doesn't have anything to do with lung cancer, emphysema, strokes, or heart attacks, then he fronts for a man whose other uranium mine killed dozens of people. How could he do that?"

"No conscience, no problem. Which leads me to something else. Check into the first Mrs. Donohue. The current Mrs. Donohue said her predecessor is alive and kicking, but I'd like to make sure."

"You don't trust anyone, do you?"

"In this business, trusting people can get you killed. Another heads up. Nancy Donohue is a hunter." As well as being a cold-hearted bitch. "See whatever firearms are registered under her name. Make sure you do a down-and-dirty on Roger Tosches, who as it turns out not only owns uranium mines, but Sunset Canyon Lakes as well. Look into Mia Tosches, too. I'm curious as to why she was so quick to point the finger at Ted. See if there are any skeletons doing the funky chicken in her closet. If there are, I want their names and addresses."

"Are we talking a May-December marriage?" he asked.

"In spades."

He winked. "Girl's gotta make a living, Lena."

"Don't we all."

Our lunches arrived, and for a while we ate silently. I decided that Ma was Italian, because the marinara sauce was spiked with enough fresh basil to start a basil ranch. Ma hadn't gone easy on the garlic, either. So much for my concerns about the liver and onions special.

When Tara collected our empty plates, Jimmy ordered apple pie à la mode. I went for the pie, too, but virtuously skipped the ice cream. While Tara fetched our dessert, I brought up another sore subject. "Why aren't you staying at Sunset Trails? Why the Desert View Motel? I saw the place when I passed through town and it looked pretty seedy."

"Where I stay is my own business." He fingered the pink doily again.

I wasn't going to let him off the hook that easily. "This case is starting to look hinky, and if I'm going to help Ted, I need to know everything, even stuff you'd rather I didn't."

"My problems with Dad have nothing to do with this case."

"Let me be the judge of that."

Ma's apple pie arrived, letting Jimmy off the interrogatory hook for a while, but as soon as the pie disappeared down our respective gullets, I brought up the subject again. "Does the problem have anything to do with your moving down to the Pima reservation and taking back your birth name?"

"Kind of." His answer was grudging, but at least it was an answer.

"Explain *kind of.*"

"Dad wanted me to help run the ranch with Ted. But I wanted to find out who I was, and I couldn't do that while leading someone else's life."

"What do you mean, 'someone else's'?"

Brown eyes regarded me steadily. "In case you haven't noticed, Lena, I'm not white."

I thought back to the family portrait in Olmstead's office and the Technicolor children. "Your brothers and sisters weren't white, either, so what does color have to do with anything?"

He looked down at his pie plate, as if hoping another slice would magically appear. "Considering your own background, I thought you of all people would understand."

How often in life we miss the obvious. While I'd been scrambling around for the past few years trying to find my birth parents, Jimmy had been doing the same thing. The fact that he, unlike in my own situation, knew his birth parents' names and where they'd lived didn't make his job easier. Names are just words, phonics written on air. It's the meaning behind a name that matters, the centuries of genetic loading the word represents. For good or ill, when you're cut off from your birth name, you're cut off from your past. Like most adoptive parents, the Olmsteads had given their children new first and last names, saying in effect, "Now you are one of us." This was true and commendable. But the new name only told part of the story.

Take mine, for example: Lena Jones.

A couple of years ago, in a brief thunderclap of memory, I had remembered that my mother called me "Tina," but after being shot, my wounded four-year-old mouth slurred the "T," and I was temporarily given the name Lena Doe. When I was fostered out, an unimaginative social worker turned "Doe" into "Jones," and Lena Jones was born. Neither first nor last name had anything to do with my biological life; my real identity had been shot away along with a piece of my brain.

Did Jimmy feel like that?

I bore a scar on my forehead where the bullet had entered. By odd coincidence, Jimmy bore a tribal tattoo in the same place. Maybe it wasn't coincidence. Maybe, as he once told me, we had always been connected in spirit.

"I'm sorry, Almost Brother," I said. "I didn't think."

His face softened. "Sometimes you forget to, Lena. You've always been…" He paused, then started again. "Anyway, my birth parents died so early that I don't remember them, but that doesn't mean I can't feel their pull. As soon as I graduated from ASU, I moved over to the reservation to learn how to be Pima again, and that's when the problems with Dad started. We'd gotten along fine before."

I didn't have to ask if moving onto the reservation had worked, because I already knew the answer. Jimmy was the most peaceful soul I had ever met. Olmstead, however, was like the sharp edge of a knife. "Your dad felt betrayed, didn't he?"

Jimmy nodded. "None of the other kids, not even Ted, did anything like me."

"But Ted married another Paiute. Attended pow-wows. Remained Indian."

"He didn't leave the family. Or the church."

There it was: faith. Like many people in this part of the state, the Olmsteads were conservative Christians. In accordance with their fundamentalist beliefs, they led lives that glorified home, family, and healthy living. They didn't drink, smoke, or use anything that contained caffeine. Whenever possible, they even raised their own food. Ted was still a member of his father's denomination, but Jimmy, having embraced the ancient polytheistic faith of his tribe, was not.

Oh, religion—the great divider.

"Couldn't your mother have done something to mediate the situation? From what you've told me she had a soothing effect on your father. And was more broad-minded."

He started fingering the doily again, his face suddenly sad. "She was dead by the time I left for college. She'd been sick for a while—cancer, like so many around here—but just as we thought she was getting better, she had a heart attack. Afterwards, Dad became even more stubborn. That's partially the reason I chose ASU; it was as far away as I could get from here without leaving the state. It was also right next door to the Pima Reservation, and I started going over there and, well, I found my people. You know the rest."

What must it have been like for him, finding his extended family after so many years? Would it be like that for me if I ever found mine? "Jimmy, do you think…?"

Before I could finish, Tara returned with the check in a pink plastic tray. Slapping down some bills, I told her to keep the change, then added, "Tell Ma her food's delicious."

"Tell him yourself." She pointed toward the lunch counter, where a big hairy man wearing bib overalls and a chef's toque stood chatting with a customer.

When he looked over at me, I blew him a kiss.

Ma blew one back.

After that, Jimmy returned to the Desert View Motel and his trusty laptop, while I drove to the Walapai Gas-N-Go, scene of the infamous altercation between Ike Donohue and Ted Olmstead. Time to talk to an actual witness.

Like most of the town's buildings, at first glance Walapai Gas-N-Go looked like it had been built in the late eighteen-hundreds, but on closer inspection, I saw two islands of gas pumps half hidden by a wall of plastic designed to look like logs. Since my rented Trailblazer was jonesing for some high-octane, I pulled alongside a full-service pump and waited, my digital recorder already turned on. Within seconds, a rangy, dark-skinned Indian strode out of the building and over to me. The script above his left pocket identified him as EARL.

"Fill her up, Ma'am?"

"Yes, please." Indians value good manners, and since I'd already irritated one Indian this week, I introduced myself politely and eased into conversation while the Trailblazer drank deep of Saudi Arabia's finest.

"Sure is pretty country up here, isn't it?"

"Yes."

"Hot, though."

"Yes."

"Worked here long?"

"Yes."

"I understand that you know Ted Olmstead."

"Yes."

Gee, we were getting along like a house afire. "How well do you know him?"

Two Horses stared at the gas pump. He hadn't yet looked me in the eye, a habit Anglos consider essential for polite conversation but many Indians construe as rude. Then he surprised me by volunteering, "Ted Olmstead did not kill Ike Donohue."

"But he hit him, right?"

"No, he did not. Mr. Donohue was so busy looking at Mrs. Tosches that he did not see some spilled oil on the ground and he slipped."

Before I could ask anything else, a silver minivan pulled up to the pump behind me. In it were several yelling children and two young women who looked like they'd rather be anywhere other than where they were. Without another word, Two Horses walked toward the van, but halted midway when one of the women jumped out and said, "Let me get it, Earl. Anything to get out of this damned van."

He came back, smiling faintly at the ground.

I hated to intrude upon his Laugh of the Day, but I had a job to do. "The newspaper article said Mia Tosches saw the whole thing, and that Ted most definitely hit him."

"Ted grabbed at him, trying to keep Mr. Donohue from falling, but Mr. Donohue fell anyway. That is what Mrs. Tosches saw."

"She was confused, then?"

His eyes flickered. "Maybe confused, maybe not."

Well, well. Another person who didn't like Mia Tosches. "Do you know of any reason she would make up that story?"

After a silence long enough to grow uncomfortable, he finally answered, "You need to talk to Ted Olmstead about that."

I was about to ask another question when the silver minivan's pump gave a loud click and the sound of gushing gas stopped. The second woman in the van climbed out. Her hair was awry and she looked even more crazed than the first.

"Hey, Earl!" she called. "You got any Valium in that store?"

"We did not receive our regular shipment of mind-altering drugs this week," he answered with an Indian-straight face.

"Aw, shit."

Pump Woman reattached the hose to the pump while the other fiddled with the gas cap. "We have to get back in that van," Pump Woman said.

"Aw, shit." Gas Cap Woman repeated.

When they left, their kids were still yelling and fighting.

"Was something going on between Ted and Mia Tosches?" I asked Earl.

His eyes still on the departing van, he answered, "Not that I am aware of. In the meantime, Miss Jones, you have a nice day." With that, he walked away.

When an Indian signals that he's through talking, he's through talking. With nothing else to be gained at the Walapai Gas-N-Go, I drove off thinking about young Indian men and blondes with elderly husbands.

Chapter Ten

July, 1975: Northwestern Arizona

After saluting the autographed photograph of John Wayne hanging over the sofa, as he did every time he entered the house, Gabe locked up his rifle in the gun cabinet. He'd clean it later, but right now he smelled sausage frying. As upset as it made him, he had to admit he was starved.

Black nose twitching, Blue Two followed him into the kitchen.

Abby was sick again, not just sad over all the dying, but sick in a way that scared Gabe half to death. Tired all the time, bones hurting, throat swole up so bad she could hardly swallow, ignoring everything the doctor said about taking things easy. Yet she paid no mind to her pain and worked as hard as any ranch hand, spent the cool mornings milking the cow, feeding the chickens, tending her garden—growing fat tomatoes, red-tipped lettuce, onions the size of a man's fist—then, when the sun began to sizzle the day, she'd come in and start cooking.

Made him furious, it did.

"Girl, you sit down! I'll finish cooking, do the dishes, too."

Mule-like, she shook her head. "Don't you tell me what to do, cowboy. You need to be minding your own store. Wasn't you and Blue Two supposed to go look for that heifer disappeared yesterday?"

"Already found her. While you was messing around in the garden."

When Abby smiled, she looked almost well. "Don't keep me in suspense. Where was she and what was she doing?"

"Dying in that cottonwood grove by the river, that's what she was doing. I put her down. Coyotes gonna be happy tonight."

The smile disappeared. "That's the third one lost in a month. If this keeps up…" She didn't finish. A rancher's granddaughter, daughter, and wife, she knew dead cattle meant money trouble. Their little herd, once a hundred and climbing, now stood at sixty-three, and half of them didn't look much better than the dead heifer.

Bad news delivered, Gabe decided this was a good time to tell her what he'd been thinking. "Uh, Abby, I thought I'd drive over to Miller's spread this afternoon, see if he could use an extra ranch hand."

Her face crumpled. "Miller's? Surely he has all the help he needs! Besides, if you start working for him, how are you going to get anything done around here? Not unless you can figure out a way to make two of you, like they do in them crazy science fiction movies. Oh, it's my fault, all my fault. If I'd been able to give you babies, they'd be old enough now to help and…" She trailed off again.

Gabe fixed a smile, pretended he was happy about the way things had worked out. "Why, they'd do nothing but take my mind off you, girl. Can't have that, can we? You're all I want, and haven't I told you a thousand-plus-times how much I…"

"Love don't mend fences or milk the cow."

She'd braced herself on a chair back to stay upright, so Gabe decided it was time to lay down the law. "Worry-wart, that's what you are, Abby, and worrying never got nothing done. Now I don't want no arguing, 'cause you're going back to bed whether you like it or not. Can't have you fall on your pretty face, can I?"

He followed his tough talk with a grip around her ever-narrowing waist and shepherded her down the hall toward the bedroom, with Blue Two close behind. Abby was too weak to struggle, just leaned against him and whispered, "I'm so sorry I let you down."

At that, he halted their march and turned her to face him. She looked ten years older than she should have, lines trenching her face, gray growing through lusterless hair, shoulders hunched from pain. But still his Abby.

He pressed his lips to her hair, smelling sausage and Evening in Paris. "Ain't nothing you could do would let a man down. Don't know what I'd be without you."

"Happier, probably." But she managed a smile.

"My silly girl."

Chapter Eleven

The meeting with Earl Two Horses—unsatisfactory though it was—finished, I headed toward the Covered Wagons Inn to transcribe my interviews and make a few follow-up phone calls from the comfort of my motel room. Given what Ted Olmstead and Earl Two Horses told me about the altercation at the Gas-N-Go, Mia Tosches' version made me wonder if she held a personal grudge against Ted.

I would have given the disparity in their stories more thought, but as I neared my motel, something I saw made me pull my Trailblazer over to the side of the street. A large crowd had gathered in front of the billboard that announced the upcoming mine-opening celebration. The hand-painted picket signs proved that Victims of Uranium Mining weren't giving up their fight against the opening of the Black Basin Mine. BAN URANIUM MINING NOW! and DON'T POLLUTE NATURE'S MASTERPIECE—THE GRAND CANYON, screamed the signs lofted by a group of long-haired youths who wouldn't have been out of place on any college campus. YELLOW CAKE = DEATH said the sign carried by a middle-aged woman who appeared to be Navajo. REMEMBER FUKUSHIMA said one, carried by a little girl who looked to be around eight years old. An elderly woman in a wheelchair held a shaky sign that mysteriously asked, HASN'T WALAPAI COUNTY SUFFERED ENOUGH?

Olivia Eames stood at the edge of the group, scribbling in her reporter's notebook. Walapai Flats might have been a small town, but this was a big city-type demonstration, complete with bullhorns, the media, and gawkers on the sidewalk. The only thing missing was cops in riot gear.

I started to pull away from curb, but stopped again when I saw a counter-demonstration bearing down on them from the other end of the block. This new group's signs had been professionally printed. The majority proclaimed either MINES MEAN JOBS or SCREW THE ARABS! AMERICA NEEDS NUCLEAR POWER! These were carried by muscular young men—prospective miners, I supposed—as well as women in dresses accented by red, white, and blue sashes, and a few cowhand-clothed individuals who probably worked the town's souvenir shops. Among the latter I recognized the barrista from Cowboy Cal's Espresso and the clerk at my motel. Behind them marched a phalanx of middle-aged men in business suits. Their signs declared THE WALAPAI FLATS CHAMBER OF COMMERCE PROUDLY SUPPORTS THE BLACK BASIN URANIUM MINE.

I stepped out of my car to see what would happen when the opposing groups joined up. I didn't have long to wait. They met in the middle of the street, but other than the exchange of a few angry words, the encounter was peaceful enough. Gratified that civility still reigned in the wild, wild West, I started to climb back into the Trailblazer when a small group of men ran out from between a Colonel Sanders and a car wash. They were waving baseball bats.

I could have grabbed my .38 out of the glove compartment and fired a warning shot into the air, but what goes up must come down and I personally knew of two deaths resulting from falling bullets. Instead, I took a more conservative course of action: grabbed my cell phone from my carry-all and called the cops, wondering why none had been dispatched to monitor the demonstration in the first place.

The strongest anti-mining demonstrators quickly formed a human wall between their weaker numbers and the bat-wielders, but some of the thugs made end runs around them. Screams erupted as blows were struck. Despite the danger, I grabbed my .38 and rushed across the street to where I saw the elderly woman lying on the ground, the arm on her wheelchair smashed. But she still clutched her "Hasn't Walapai County Suffered Enough" sign.

"Get away from her!" I snapped to the goon who stood grinning down at her.

"Make me, bitch." He raised his bat again.

"That can be arranged." I aimed at his torso, always the best shot. Then I rethought the situation and aimed at his balls.

At that point, sirens sounded in the distance, and with a final curse, the man fled back in the direction he'd come from.

Some of the other bat-wielders weren't as swift. Within seconds sheriff's deputies were piling out of their cruisers. As they truncheoned some of the men and tasered others, I helped the woman back into her wheelchair. "Are you hurt?" I asked

"Not even my pride," she replied.

Before I could ask her the meaning of her sign, she and her chair were scooped up by several anti-mining women, and hustled into a van. They sped off, tailgated by Olivia Eames driving a black Ford Explorer.

I was left standing in the middle of the street, watching the final roundup of thugs next to one of the Chamber of Commerce marchers. A prosperous-looking man in his forties, he smiled at me benignly.

"That wasn't supposed to happen," he said, tsk-tsking. "Don't judge our town by this little dust-up. We're normally very peaceful folks."

"Oh, I'm sure of that. But do you know what that woman's sign meant: 'Hasn't Walapai County Suffered Enough?' Regardless of how a person feels about uranium mining, the Black Basin hasn't even opened yet, so I don't see how any suffering could have happened already."

"Enjoy your stay in Walapai Flats," he responded. Then he handed me a ten-percent-off coupon at Big Hoss' Western Emporium and walked away.

Back at the Covered Wagons Inn, I put the demonstration out of my mind and busied myself with phone calls. After several hours of frustration, I gave up. No one I called had answered, including Mia Tosches, Nancy Donohue, the purple-haired Elizabeth Waide, and Olivia Eames. Determined to track Mia down, I tried Katherine Dysart at the Sunset Canyon Lakes leasing office and was transferred over to voice mail, which informed me that the office was closed for the day. Fortunately, she'd given me her cell number, which she answered on the first ring. No joy there, either.

"Sorry, Lena," Katherine said, "Mia left the pool hours ago and I have not seen her since. She might be playing golf. Or tennis." A long pause. "Or something. If she drops by again, I'll tell her you want to get in touch. She's on the curious side, so she might be intrigued. Now if you'll excuse me, Trent and I must finish setting up for the wine and cheese mixer at the clubhouse tonight. It's mainly for the tenants, but if you want to attend, you'll be my guest. I'll leave word at the gate. Come to think of it, Mia will be there, too. Some of our recent hires are going to attend, and she never misses the chance to check out new talent."

After accepting the invitation, I hung up. Katherine couldn't have signaled more strongly that Mia Tosches fooled around on her husband, which increased my curiosity about Katherine and what had inspired her antipathy toward Mia. Maybe she had a good-looking husband. Whatever the reason, I'd soon find out. While I wasn't looking forward to a return to the Emerald City, alcohol did loosen lips.

I spent the rest of the afternoon transcribing my interviews and surfing the Net, but in the end, learned little more than I already knew. Health experts attributed the spike in cancer among the Navajos to the Moccasin Peak Mine, and the federal government had subsequently awarded a hundred thousand dollars to some of its victims. As for the contaminated water supply, the Feds levied only a minimal fine against Tosches, and the poisonous runoff from the Moccasin Peak continued. Because fines for environmental crimes were so low, the Feds had actually made it cheaper to ruin the nation's water than keep it clean in the first place. Did Tosches plan to handle the

Black Basin runoff in the same manner? If so, no wonder the locals were pissed.

I finally pushed myself away from my laptop and called Jimmy. As expected, he was still working. "Hey, guy, how's the hacking coming along? Hope you're having better luck today than I am."

"I prefer the term 'research,'" he said, reproof in his voice. "Actually, it's going fairly well, considering. Several hits, several surprises. For starters…"

Glancing at my watch, I said, "That background noise you hear is my stomach growling. After being stuck in this motel room for so long, I'm desperate for fresh air, so why don't I pick us up a bucket of chicken and we can have ourselves a little picnic in the park across from the government complex. Once you've filled me in on everything, we can walk over and visit Ted."

"*Fried* chicken?"

"Okay, Mr. Clean Living. Fried for me, grilled for you."

"Bring napkins."

By the time I arrived at Walapai Flats City Park with my arms full of take-out, the sun was thinking seriously about setting. It hung low in the sky, flirting with the streaky red, orange, and yellow clouds that puffed around it. What appeared to be half the town's population had turned out for the show. I recognized a few bandaged survivors of the demonstration. The bat-wielders were a no-show: they were somewhere else, torturing puppies.

A flock of screeching starlings had taken roost in the mesquite trees. I waded through the sunset-gawkers and piles of bird crap to the picnic table where Jimmy was tapping busily on his laptop.

"Still working, partner?"

He turned the laptop around so I could see the screen. Two kittens on pawnation.com were playing with a guinea pig large enough to eat them both. "Busman's holiday."

When the kittens grew bored, I handed Jimmy a bag. "Grilled with side of slaw. Large iced tea, no sugar. Other than the revelation that kittens are cute, what'd you find out?"

"First things first," he mumbled, fishing out a thigh.

While we ate, I told him about the demonstration and how it had ended. "Can you believe there were no cops there to begin with? Is law enforcement in this town completely lacking in common sense?"

"Budget cuts," he explained. "Terry, that deputy you met this morning, told me all about it. Late last year the town council laid off the town's entire police force, including the police chief. Now the sheriff's department not only has to cover the outlying county but the town as well. Frankly, I'm surprised the place is as law-abiding as it is."

With the town being that financially strapped, no wonder the opening of the Black Basin was such a hot-button issue. Not that it excused taking a baseball bat to an old lady.

For the next few minutes we ate silently, watching the action in the park. The day cooled faster than in Scottsdale's low desert, and in addition to the protestors nursing their wounds, entire families were taking advantage of the lower temps. Some lounged on blankets on the park's grassy berm while others barbequed dinner, every now and then sneaking looks at the Technicolor sky. Most families had taken up residence at the picnic tables nearest the crowded children's playground, outfitted with the standard attractions: slide, swings, monkey bars, and several big metal animals mounted on springs. All were being swarmed over by a collection of children ranging from toddlers to tweens. The presence of the middle-schoolers surprised me until I remembered that, due to its lack of size, the town had no mall.

At the table nearest the sandbox, a young Hispanic couple watched their identical toddlers digging away like miniature archeologists in search of dinosaur bones. A small girl with a cast on her arm approached the twins. She said something—we were too far away to hear—and the two moved far enough to the side to let the girl in, whereupon she joined the dig with her uninjured arm.

"Isn't that the kid we saw at the police station?" Jimmy asked. I nodded.

"Where's her mother?"

Squinting across the playground, I saw a woman sitting alone at a picnic table, watching the girl. She was so far away from us I couldn't tell whether she'd collected another bruise. "She's over there. By the…"

Before I could finish, a large, sandy-haired man hurried down the grass berm straight toward her. The setting sun was in his eyes, making it difficult to interpret his expression. He was either grimacing from the light or was in a rage. As he approached the woman, he pointed to the little girl. His mouth moved, but his words were indistinct.

The woman shrank back. Her voice was lower, so I couldn't hear her reply.

Whatever she'd said, the man didn't like it. He grabbed her arm and yanked her to her feet. Jimmy and I both stood up, but the father of the sandbox twins was already walking toward the couple.

"That's one big man," Jimmy said. "Let's wait and see what happens."

The Hispanic had a couple of inches and about forty pounds on the other. At his approach, the bully drew the woman to him in what now looked like an embrace. With one eye on the Hispanic, he kissed the woman quickly, then let her go. Clapping his hands cheerfully, he offered up a shit-eating grin to the Hispanic. The woman tried a wobbly smile. Words were exchanged, nothing else. After a few seconds, the bully walked up the berm alone, the splendor of sunset at his back. The Hispanic watched him go, then scooped up his twins and returned to his own wife. He stroked her hair and murmured something I couldn't hear. She shook her head, but the tension left her face.

By the time this played out, the bruised woman and her daughter had left the park in the opposite direction the bully had taken.

"What did we just see?" Jimmy asked.

"An abuser caught in the act. From his reaction when the Hispanic guy broke it up, it looks like he doesn't want people to know about his home life. Wonder why? Most abusers don't

bother disguising their behavior. Nothing we can do about it
now, though. I gave the woman my card. Maybe she'll call." I
forced a note of optimism into my voice.

"I'm not hungry any more," Jimmy said, pushing away his
grilled chicken with an expression of distaste. "Ready to hear
what I found out?"

No longer hungry myself, I tossed our uneaten dinner into
a nearby waste can, where three starlings flew down and began
fighting over it.

I pointed to the laptop. "Start with Mia Tosches."

"I was going to, anyway. She's quite the bad girl, our Mia,
or at least she used to be." He tapped a few keys, bringing up a
newspaper article from *The Apache Junction Gazette*, dated fifteen
years earlier. Daylight was fading, but I had no trouble reading
the headline on the laptop's bright screen.

TEEN GANG APPREHENDED

Friday afternoon six teens, ages ranging from 13 to 17, were apprehended
at the Superstition Springs Mall for
allegedly shoplifting from a J.C.
Penny's store. Several of the teens,
including the 17-year-old girl suspected of being the group's leader,
had been arrested at the same mall
last month and are already facing
trial in juvenile court. Because
they are minors, the *Gazette* will not
release their names.

The stolen items included makeup,
scarves, costume jewelry, and a fur-
trimmed jacket valued at $345. The
older girl was allegedly wearing it
when apprehended.

"My daughter's a good girl," the
teen's mother, a widow, protested when
interviewed at her Apache Junction
home. "She would never do anything
like this. She's very popular, and

the other kids at school have always
been jealous of her, so I think she
was set up."

When asked to explain her statement, the teen's mother said she'd
heard it on good authority that store
security had been tipped off to the
group's actions by two of the 17-year-
old's classmates who were shopping in
the store at the time as the alleged
shoplifters.

I turned to Jimmy. "What makes you think Miss Teenage Thief was Mia Tosches? There aren't any names here."

"I have the police report."

"Those kids were minors, Jimmy. That report would have been sealed, along with every court document concerning the case."

He looked at me with pity. "Oh ye of little faith. Trust me, I have the report. Mia's maiden name was Albright, as stated on her first Las Vegas marriage license."

First? "Maybe it's another Albright."

"Living at the same home address as listed on the police report?"

Jimmy's computer talents being varied and mysterious, I stopped arguing. "Okay, so it's Mia. But she was seventeen. Kids can turn around." After all, I had.

"That was her first run-in with the law, at least the first where she was caught. I've only studied about half the information on her, and I've already uncovered several other incidents. She and her cohorts—you'll have noticed she was referred to as the group's leader—received suspended sentences. But, yes, you're right about some kids turning around. The others have stayed out of trouble, at least from what I could tell. But Mia was arrested again two years later for walking out of a jewelry store in Scottsdale with an eighteen-thousand-dollar ring. Her excuse was that she'd been trying it on when she remembered that she was supposed to meet a friend for lunch at Applebee's, said she forgot all about the ring when she left the store with it on her finger."

Behind me, the starlings were arguing so loudly that I had to raise my voice. "Was she ever convicted?"

"Charges dropped after her mother paid for the ring."

"*Paid* for it? That's a lot of cash."

"Her mother took out a second mortgage on her house. It got foreclosed on a couple of years later after she had to hire another criminal defense lawyer, who got Mia off by the skin of her teeth in a second jewelry store heist."

I sighed. "What'd her precious darling daughter steal that time?"

"Another ring. A bigger one this time. Apparently she likes bright, glittery things."

I remembered the huge solitaire I'd seen Mia wearing. The light bouncing off it had almost blinded me. "Did she ever do time?"

"Never."

"Must be nice to have a mother who bails your crooked ass out of jail."

"Not really. It means you never learn your lesson."

True enough, given the fact that Mia's crimes had escalated. "Did any of her crimes involve violence?"

"None I've found so far. Like I said, I still have a lot of work to do."

"A minute ago you said something about Mia's *first* Las Vegas marriage license? *First*? She married there twice? Come to think of it, that newspaper article, it's dated fifteen years back. If she was a high school senior then, she'd be thirty-one or thirty-two now." Silly me, mistaking a grownup for a child bride.

"Thirty-two and a half. And yeah, each of her three marriages took place in Las Vegas. She moved there after barely graduating from high school. Before you ask, yes, you have to be twenty-one to work at a Vegas casino, but that's not what she did. In fact, there's no record of her ever working anywhere under any name. She fell off the radar for a couple of years, and who knows what she was doing to support herself, but we can guess. Then the marriages started. Jardine, her first, was a Baccarat dealer at Caesar's Palace. Graumann, the second, owned Sweet Rides, a car dealership. She finally hit the big time with Tosches."

A loud squawk made me turn my head. Two starlings had grabbed opposite ends of a chicken breast; neither wanted to let go. As they jerked it back and forth, a cactus wren swooped down, picked off a small piece of fried skin, and departed with it. The starlings dropped the breast in shock and flew off after the wren. Greedy bastards.

"Any financial settlements after the divorces?" I asked Jimmy.

He shook his head. "Not from the Baccarat dealer. When she split from Graumann, she cashed in to the tune of a little more than two hundred thousand in property, plus spousal support until she remarried. Comfy, but no fortune. She took care of that quickly enough, though. Six months after her divorce, she snagged Tosches, who was in town for a golf tournament. It was one of those gimmicky charity deals where all the caddies were babes in bikinis. Did I mention that our girl was once Miss Bikini Las Vegas? And knew a three-wood from a driver?"

Vegas golf courses are great places to meet men, especially when you're spilling out of your bikini. I wondered if Tosches had run a background check on his darling bride. Probably not. When it came to bikinied hotties, most men thought with Mister Friendly.

"Nice to see a woman move up in the world. Have you come up with anything concrete between her and Ted?"

Jimmy's usually open face closed down, signaling a forbidden subject. "Ted would never have an affair with someone like Mia Tosches."

It was all I could do not to harrumph. In my experience, women who married for money were like tigers prowling the jungle on the lookout for vulnerable prey. Once they'd slaked their appetite for bright shiny things, they turned their attention to the more sensuous pleasures. Handsome Ted, still grieving over his wife's death, would certainly have been vulnerable enough.

"How about Tosches himself? Any dirt there, besides the dirty uranium mine on the Navajo rez?"

"Some," he said. "But not as much as you'd expect, considering everything he's been involved in. Then again, he's a local, and this town tends to protect its own."

Tosches, the only progeny of a wealthy copper mining couple whose private holdings included the land the Black Basin was on, had increased his inheritance tenfold by judicious investments that remained unaffected by the current economic downturn. He'd used some of his fortune to develop Sunset Canyon Lakes, and had already doubled his investment.

"He was born with a silver spoon in his mouth and he turned it into gold, metaphorically speaking," Jimmy said. "On the civic responsibility side, not much, other than being the president of the Walapai Flats Chamber of Commerce and a member of the National Mining Association. Oh, and he's an avowed enemy of the Sierra Club, as well as V.U.M. No surprise there, since he believes land is meant to be developed, not looked at."

"Nothing at all suspicious?"

"No wants, no warrants, no record of drunken nights at bordellos or associations with mob figures. But I couldn't find any record of large bequests to any charity, either, and given the amount of money the guy has, that's surprising. And…" He turned the laptop around again, letting me scroll through newspaper accounts of OSHA investigations regarding injuries incurred during the building of Sunset Canyon Lakes. One man had fallen to his death while working on the six-story timeshare building; another had his leg amputated after a similar fall. Both victims' families accepted settlements so miniscule I found them shocking.

"Tosches has good attorneys, doesn't he?"

"The best."

"I'll bet he has an iron-clad pre-nup with Mia."

Jimmy's mouth tugged at the corners. "No pre-nup at all, Lena. The guy was crazy in love. Or lust."

Oh, Mr. Friendly. How foolish you can be.

"Don't worry, I'm not giving up on the Tosches," Jimmy said. "I already have so much material it'll take days to sift through. Moving on, you also asked about Olivia Eames."

"The reporter. I saw her covering the demonstration today, so I guess she's the real deal."

Renewed squawking signaled the return of the starlings. This time there were seven of them, and they busied themselves in the trashcan so deeply that I could only see their tail feathers sticking out. As they bitched and fought over the chicken dinners' remains, a crumpled napkin flew out of the trash and bounced toward me. I picked it up and returned it to the trash. Unfazed, the starlings continued gorging.

When I sat myself back down at the picnic table, Jimmy said, "Olivia got her start at the Silver Ridge newspaper."

"Silver Ridge? That old mining town over by the freeway?"

"Correctomundo, kemosabe. When she graduated from Silver Ridge High, where she was editor of the school paper, she received a scholarship to the University of Missouri's School of Journalism. After getting her bachelor's, she lit out for the East Coast, served an internship at the *Boston Globe*, and from there, moved on to—surprise, surprise—the *New York Times* and some pretty meaty stories."

Apparently the *Times* had a more relaxed dress policy than I would have guessed. "What kind of meaty stories are you talking about? Political stuff?"

"Not exactly. An investigative piece on an outbreak of *E.coli* she managed to trace to an upstate packing house. She wrote another piece on defective pacemakers that wound up putting one of the manufacturer, another New York company, out of business. She's quite respected in the journalism community, won several awards."

"Pulitzer?"

"Not yet, but I'd say she's on her way. She did snag a George Polk Award for the meatpacking story. I wonder why she's hanging around Sunset Canyon Lakes and not in Silver Ridge, where she's from? Maybe she didn't come out here to renew familial ties.

I mean, if she did, she'd have bunked with her folks, wouldn't she? Or if they were full up, she could have found a closer place to stay. There are two motels in Silver Ridge, and both look nice. I checked them out online."

"She's working a story, Jimmy." I was willing to bet Olivia had wrangled her way into Nancy Donohue's book club not so much for her love of books, but because of the Black Basin Mine connection. Nancy was, after all, married to the mine's public relations expert. Or was, until he was snuffed. The only question was, considering the fact that the East Coast had plenty of scandals of its own to investigate, why had she come all the way out here to dig up Arizona dirt? Maybe she thought the Black Basin flap was Pulitzer-worthy and couldn't pass it up; journalists could be obsessive that way. But if the mine was the reason for her visit, why now? Why not a year earlier, when Ted's wife was murdered?

But maybe she did. "Jimmy, did you find anything to indicate that Olivia came out here after Kimama Olmstead was shot?"

"Nope. She didn't. I checked."

"What about her personal life?" Not that reporters had much time for one.

An expression I couldn't read flickered across Jimmy's face. "What?"

"Well, I did do a little light digging, and…Sure you want to hear?"

"Stop being coy."

"It's sad, Lena."

Jimmy's continued hesitation, combined with the stiffening breeze and the lowering light, was beginning to annoy me. "How sad?"

"Sad as in being gang-raped. Sad as in losing her fiancé in the World Trade Center."

Mercifully, he only gave a brief summation of both horrors. While Olivia was covering a story in the East Village one night, a group of men dragged her into an abandoned warehouse and raped her over a six-hour period. The men were never caught. Four months later—on 9/11—her fiancé, a policeman, was killed at the World Trade Center while attempting to rescue a woman in a wheelchair.

As soon as I could speak, I asked, "And she's still sane?" more rhetorically than anything else.

"Two-day stay in the hospital following the rape, then back to job, she even wrote about the rape, campaigned for better lighting and a heavier police presence in the neighborhood. She got what she wanted and the instance of sexual assaults dropped. During the terrorist attacks, she continued to work that story, too, even after she found out her fiancé had been killed. She filed an article a day for twelve days, and didn't take a day off for two months. At Christmas, she took a week's vacation and came back to Silver Ridge for a week, stayed with a distant cousin."

"But she's not staying with her family now." I frowned, thinking hard. Olivia was working the Black Basin Mine story; I'd already seen evidence of that.

Misreading my expression again, Jimmy said, "Families are odd creatures, Lena. They can hold tight during a crisis, then split apart over something minor."

Like Jimmy's.

Time to change the subject. "I was thinking about the mine, not families. Did you get any info on Nancy Donohue?"

It was his turn to frown. "I'm haven't gotten to her yet, but I will."

"See if you can find out what kind of insurance policy her husband carried." I described Nancy's threadbare furniture and the duct-taped recliner in the den." I left out her cold heart.

"Sounds promising," he said. "She wouldn't be the first woman to kill for money."

Due to the darkening sky, most people had deserted the park. I checked my watch. Visiting hours at the jail began in twenty minutes.

"Let's go," I said. "Can't wait to start standing in line."

After I'd stowed my .38 and my digital recorder in the Trailblazer's glove compartment, we climbed the stairs to the government complex, where my joking premonition proved true. Because most people visited their loved ones after dinner rather than mid-morning, the check-in process took much longer than it had this morning, and by the time we reached the actual visitor's area, visiting hours were almost over. Also thanks to the later hour, I saw more family visitors—spouses, grandparents, and children—visiting their loved ones. Children being children, some loudly voiced their displeasure at being told to sit down and shut up while Mommy visited Daddy. Fortunately, no screamers sat next to us, just an elderly couple on one side, and a weeping woman on the other.

I'd already warned Jimmy that I had some hard questions for Ted, so conscious of the time constraints, I kept the greetings to a minimum and started right in. Keeping my voice low enough that the kiddies wouldn't hear, I said, "Ted, did you have an affair with Mia Tosches?"

Behind the Plexiglas barrier that separated us, his eyes flickered from me to Jimmy, who kept his eyes down. I could tell from my partner's posture he was unhappy with my directness, but the fact that he kept his mouth shut meant that he knew more frankness was called for.

Ignoring my question, Ted asked Jimmy, "Been to see Dad lately? He seemed stressed when he visited this morning."

"Oh, he's…"

I cut in. "Ted, look at the clock. We don't have time for idle chit chat."

He ignored me again, asking Jimmy how well the head wrangler, in this case, Dusty, was handling the tourists in his absence. Jimmy neither reframed my question or changed the subject. No expert in interrogation, he simply reminded Ted that he hadn't yet visited the ranch, but planned to do so tomorrow.

All this deflection was to be expected. Indians, even those raised in non-Indian families, weren't big on discussing their sex lives; they felt it was the height of vulgarity. Squirming with impatience—the clock in the visitor's room was ticking down—I asked my question again. Again Ted ignored me. Keeping his eyes on Jimmy, he said his attorney had told him there was a possibility that this "material witness stuff" might be made to go away.

"Ted, please," I pleaded. "We've only got ten minutes left."

For all the good that did me, I could have been turning somersaults on the moon. Ted continued pretending I wasn't there, kept yakking at his brother about the ranch, the horses, the dudes, the weather.

Until I'd had enough. "Hey! Look at me and tell me the truth. Did you screw, fuck, or whatever, Mia Tosches?" This time I didn't bother lowering my voice.

Ted, who like most Indians, never used vulgarities, finally looked at me. "Lena, please!"

"Cut the crap. I'm going to sit here and recite every synonym for 'fuck' I can think of until you tell me the truth. Bone, hump, schtup…"

Jimmy, another clean-mouther, lowered his head and moaned softly.

"Did you play hide the kielbasa, respond to her booty call, screw…"

Ted raised his hands, as if to ward off demons. "Lena! Watch your…Oh, heavens, your language. There are children present!"

"Knock boots, do the wild thing, the mattress mambo, get lucky, grab some ass…"

"We only did it once!" Ted yelled so loudly that most people in the visitor's room turned to see what was going on. The older kids looked thrilled.

When I smiled and waved, everyone except for the teenagers went back to minding their own sad business, and I returned to mine: questioning a reluctant client. Lowering my voice, I said, "Good thing you fessed up before your brother here fainted. Now that we've got the schtupping out in the open, tell me, why just once?"

"Because she was married!" Ted hissed.

"She was married the first time you screwed her."

"You don't understand. She…she…"

I could see where this was headed, so I cut him off at the pass. "If I hear one more man whine about some woman whose evil wiles overcame his own innate purity I'm going to puke. As soon as I've finished puking, I'll resume my list of synonyms. Look, Ted, I'm not asking for a detailed account of who did what to whom, however entertaining that might be, but I want to know how the situation started and how it ended. I especially want to know why after your romantic interlude, Mia Tosches now hates you enough to lie to the cops about that altercation at the Gas-N-Go, which is what got you locked up in the first place."

Admission finally made, Ted explained what led to their encounter, but the tale he told wasn't much different than those I've heard before. After several weeks of group riding lessons at the ranch, Mia requested a private tutorial. Since giving private lessons to the folks living in Sunset Canyon Lakes was nothing new, Ted hadn't given this a second thought.

"I should have been more alert when she said she wanted to work on her trail riding skills," he admitted. "Most private lessons are given in the ring."

"So you took her out on the trail. Then what?"

He tensed again, then lowered his head and mumbled, "Well, you know that bend by the river, where the trail veers away from the road and there's a bunch of cottonwoods that…?"

"Don't know it, don't want to. Hurry this along. I still have a few synonyms left."

A deep inhale. "When we reached the cottonwoods, Mia said she was feeling dizzy and needed to dismount and could I help her. So I…" He swallowed.

"You jumped down, helped her dismount, I get it. And you stayed real close, so you could catch her if she fainted, right?" I wasn't being sarcastic. When I'd first met him at that pow wow, Ted carried an air of gallantry that I'd found refreshing in this jaded age.

"Something like that. She kinda slumped against me so I put my arms around her, you know, to hold her up, but…"

"But things progressed from there. Because she's really hot."

"Yes." He stared at the floor as if something fascinating was going on down there.

"Okay, so after the 'Hallelujah Chorus' what happened?"

"We, uh, we got back on the horses and rode back to the ranch."

I could imagine the conversation they'd had along the way, but I had him repeat it as well as he could remember. It was always possible that she could have been so het up by his wonderfulness that she'd confessed all her sins.

Still staring at the floor, he said, "She told me she wanted another, uh, private lesson next week, well, that would be this week, wouldn't it, but I said I was busy. She didn't want to hear that, kept pushing and pushing, so I finally had to tell her that, um, what happened had been a mistake, that she was a wonderful person and under other different circumstances I'd want to see her again, take her someplace nice like she deserved, but since she was married that our, uh, that this had better be the end of the, um, private lessons."

"Her response was?"

"She said I'd be sorry."

Mia told the truth there. Ted was sorry. Sorry for his moral lapse, sorry for the clumsy way he'd handled the aftermath, and especially sorry he'd wound up in jail separated from his family and his job. Regardless of all that sorry, he still sat on the other side of a thick Plexiglas partition, waiting to be hustled back to his cell. Not that I was being judgmental. I'd done plenty of stupid things in my own life. Everyone has, and most of us get by with it—at least on this wicked Earth—but Ted's fall from grace had resulted in consequences that hardly fit his crime.

"This happened on what day, Ted?"

He finally looked up at me, but it took an effort. "Last Wednesday. I was so worried about what she might do to get back at me that I drove around all night, thinking. The next night, too. That's the real reason I don't have an alibi."

"Did you drive up to Sunset Point, by any chance?"

"No. Basically, I just drove around in the desert. There are some roads out there you can handle if you're in a big truck or a four-wheel drive vehicle. I remember being out by Mitten Mesa for a while."

"Anything else?"

"Sorry. That's about it."

Jimmy, tired of letting me do all the talking, said, "Didn't you say Dad visited you this morning?"

Ted nodded. "And every morning, regardless of what's going on at the ranch."

An expression of sorrow briefly crossed Jimmy's face. Ted was the favored son; Jimmy only tolerated. Their conversation returned to small talk and remained that way until an announcement came over the loudspeaker that visiting hours were over. With relief I headed out the door, leaving Jimmy behind to say an extended farewell. While the other visitors surged through the lobby, I sat down on a bench and waited.

People with the rare good fortune to never have had a loved one or friend incarcerated tend to type those families as knuckle-dragging Neanderthals or, during their more compassionate moments, victims of downward genetic drift. But that's hardly the case. Besides committing murder, thievery, and mayhem, everyday men and women could wind up in jail for sundry non-violent crimes—failure to pay parking tickets, lewd language in public places (here's looking at you, kid), even mouthing off to a police officer who was having a bad day. None of these encroachments against the public good said anything about the quality of the offenders' families, all of whom were swept along with them for the bumpy ride through the justice system. This included spouses, children, parents, extended families, friends, and employers. Passing by me were red-eyed women; elderly folk in wheelchairs, their hands shaking with palsy; children asking why Daddy couldn't come home with them; and morose parents wondering where they'd gone wrong.

Another reason I hated jails was because by their very pre-trial nature, the innocent bunked with the guilty, addicts were incarcerated instead of treated, and the scum of the earth mingled with folks who'd merely been in the wrong place at the wrong time.

As the glum horde passed by, I noted a sheriff's deputy in the hallway ushering them into the night. Tall, sandy-haired, big smile. Friendly and outgoing, he nodded to the elderly and chucked the children under their chins. He looked familiar, but at first I couldn't figure out where I'd seen him. He wasn't one of the officers I'd dealt with on my earlier trips to the jail. Then, when he grasped a wobbly senior by the arm to steady him, it clicked. Officer Smiley Face was the bully in the park.

While I was still assimilating this, Jimmy appeared beside me. "Did anyone ever tell you you've got a dirty mouth?"

"Look at that cop," I whispered. "The one by the door."

Jimmy's back stiffened. "Oh, no."

"Let's get out of here, but don't catch his eye. In case his wife does wind up asking for help, we don't want him to know we're connected to Ted."

We separated before approaching the door. Solitary blonde, solitary Indian, nothing but the old same old. Blonde with Indian, memorable. Our caution paid off, because at the door, the deputy winked and said to me, "Pretty night, isn't it, ma'am? Almost as pretty as you."

I nodded and said to a well-dressed woman beside me, "Hope it cools off soon, don't you?" I hoped he'd think I was with her.

"Damned desert never lets up." The woman blotted her face with a lace-bordered hanky. "I miss Oregon."

I continued our casual comments as we walked down the steps. At the curb, too late for the bully cop to notice our separation, she headed for the parking lot while I found a place in the shadows and waited for Jimmy.

"That poor woman," he said, after arriving at my side.

Yes. That poor woman. Few cops are batterers, but those that are can find themselves protected by fellow officers who in other instances are admirably quick to enforce antibattering laws. In the first place, cops are good at covering up their own violence because they've learned from the pros. But even when cop buddies can't help but notice, other factors can come into play. As a former cop myself, I know how much we have to rely on our partners, because we so often battle life-and-death situations together. It's the us-against-them mentality, and when you're that close, you can ignore an instance or two of bruised knuckles. The person riding with you in the squad car is the same person watching your back when you enter a drug den where shots are being fired.

My own partner had saved my life in just such an instance. Regardless of the danger to himself, he'd stayed beside me the day I was shot, using his own body to shield me from continuing gunfire. If I'd found out later that he beat his wife, would I have reported it to the higher-ups? I might first have urged him to get anger management counseling. If he'd shown up at work one more time with bruised knuckles, then, yeah, I'd have reported him.

Even if one officer filed a report against another, sometimes nothing came of it other than a ruined partnership. In all domestic abuse situations, there was an inequity of power, but in cop-against-spouse matters, that inequity strutted on steroids. A wife complaining of abuse was complaining about a man who not only carried a gun and knew how to use it, but someone who also knew how to sanitize a crime scene. Let's say she looked past the possibility that the next crime scene might be her cooling body, and lodged a complaint, anyway. Not only would she have to testify against her husband in court, she would also have to go up against his cop friends, most of whom would empathize with the stress he endured on a daily basis. Their testimony would be slanted accordingly.

In spousal abuse situations, finances needed to be factored in, too. In many cases, the cop was the major bread-winner, and if convicted of battering, he would lose his job. His spouse knew that, which was another reason so many battered wives kept their mouths shut; they needed their husband's paycheck to buy formula for the baby.

Barring a direct complaint from his wife against Officer Smiley Face, there was little either Jimmy or I could do to help her or her daughter, other than to tip off CPS to a possible child abuse case, which I'd do the moment I got back to my motel. Not that I thought much would come of it. Smiley Face's genial "Sure-love-ya-folks-but-it's-closin'-time" routine at the station house proved he was adept at disguising his dark heart.

As Jimmy and I walked through the shadows toward our cars, I thought of an often-used phrase, which when once used as a book title, rocketed the author onto the best-seller list. "Speaking truth to power," sure sounded nice, but power almost always won.

Chapter Twelve

It's easy to get lost in the desert at night. No lights, only a pale moon and even paler stars, no familiar landmarks, nothing to guide me other than the Trailblazer's GPS unit. As I drove along the two-lane blacktop, wildlife dramas played themselves out in front of me. Why does the coyote cross the road? To chase the jackrabbit on the other side. I witnessed several of these chases, rooting, in turn, for the rabbit, then the coyote. One had to die in order that the other would live. My musings about Nature red in tooth and claw ended when I saw, standing in the middle of the road ahead, a particularly scrawny coyote looking down at a flattened rabbit. Road kill. As my rental approached, she turned toward me, eyes yellow-bright. Although I was quick on the brake, my car slid almost into the coyote's side before it stopped. The coyote merely sat there. Didn't move. Kept looking at me.

We long-time Arizonans know to beware of wildlife exhibiting atypical behavior. Coyotes are clever beasts who instinctively know humans aren't their friends. Upon spotting us or even our vehicles, they usually make tracks into the brush, especially when carrying a kill. Another thing about coyotes: they don't share. Except, of course, when it comes to their pups. As I stared at the coyote and she stared back, I saw her swollen teats. Another reason she shouldn't be standing in the middle of the road watching cars drive by. She should grab that road kill and run on home.

But she didn't. We watched each other for a few more moments before I figured out what was wrong. She was salivating, and not from hunger. Foam rimmed her mouth, dripping onto the rabbit. When I studied her eyes more carefully, I realized how dazed they were. Flat, irises dilated, glowing with pain.

Rabies.

With one hand I lowered the automatic window six inches— she still didn't move—while I reached into my carry-all with my other hand for my .38. Better a quick death than days of suffering. As for her pups, tomorrow I would search for them and deliver the same harsh mercy. They were doomed because they'd been drinking her milk.

"Over here, Mama," I called. I poked the .38's short barrel out the window. I hoped my voice would make her shift her position but she remained stationary. Knowing better than to step out of the car, I turned the steering wheel hard right and rolled the SUV to a position broadside to her thin flank. She still didn't move, which was testament to how sick she was.

I aimed carefully, then fired.

The bullet hit her behind the left foreleg, a clean heart shot. She dropped straight down, her frothy muzzle resting on the road kill. A hind leg jerked twice, then stilled.

It would be irresponsible to leave a rabid animal on the road, lest some soul with more compassion than caution came blundering along and attempted to help, perhaps even rendering mouth-to-snout resuscitation. Such things have happened out here in the tourist-visited West, so I had to get her off the road. Trying to figure out how to keep my own hands untainted by her blood and saliva, I exited the car. A glance back at the coyote's rapidly-filming eyes assured me she was dead, which made me feel both sad and safe, but I couldn't see a way out of my quandary. If I'd been driving my Jeep, I would have everything I needed, from tool chest to tarp. But the rental had nothing, other than a….

…a jack.

It was an ugly business, but the jack worked. Once I'd used it to scoot the coyote's body off the road, I performed the same task with the rabbit, then covered them both in dirt, brush and rocks. To make certain I could find the same spot the next morning—in daylight everything looked different—I stacked the rocks into a triangular cairn. The thought of going out to kill a litter of pups depressed me, but leaving them to die of rabies or slow starvation depressed me even more.

On that grim note, I climbed back into my rental and headed for the Emerald City.

Katherine had informed me that the mixer's theme was One Night in the Wild West, so I wasn't surprised when I entered the resort's cavernous party room and saw scores of senior citizens dressed in Western drag: designer jeans, cowboy boots handmade in Italy, elaborately fringed shirts no real cowboy would be caught dead in, and an assortment of Stetsons sporting hatbands made of silver, turquoise, and feathers. At the far end of the room, ersatz cowboys and saloon girls were attempting to do the funky chicken to Old Sons of the Pioneers tunes played by a similarly dressed band.

The booze had been flowing for a couple of hours, and lips were already loose, which was good for me, since I'd already taken the precaution of slipping my digital recorder into my carry-all. Stray bits of gossip trailed after me as I hurried into the lady's room to wash the dirt off my hands. When I emerged, Katherine was the first person I recognized. She and a handsome man were standing near a pair of sliding glass doors that opened onto a patio lit by Japanese lanterns. Clad in a high-necked Victorian dress with an enormous bustle, she should have looked ridiculous instead of more elegant than ever.

"Trent and I are delighted you could come," she said, after introducing me to her husband. "We'll do anything to help Ted."

Standing approximately six-feet-two, Trent was black-haired, blue-eyed, with film star features, a blinding smile, and well developed pecs that strained against his tight gunfighter's shirt. His handshake was firm without being aggressive, and his deep voice sounded as modulated as a diction coach's. The only off-note was the crudely inked tattoo that edged out of his high collar. Mostly hidden, the visible black lines resembled the top half of a spider's web. The last time I'd seen a similar tattoo had been on a lifer at Arizona State Prison.

"No costume?" Katherine said, interrupting my thoughts, as she handed me a nametag that already had my name printed on it. So much for anonymity.

"I see enough Western garb trolling the malls in Scottsdale." Trent smiled at my quip. Questionable tattoo aside, he really was dazzling, and it was easy to guess Katherine's animus toward the voracious Mia Tosches. "Last week's Mystery Night might have been more your style, Katherine tells me," he said. "You could have come as Sherlock Holmes and figured out who killed our volunteer corpse. That was before Ike Donohue was killed, of course. If we'd known what was going to happen, we'd, uh, have picked a, uh, different theme. I mean…"

I rescued him from his discomfort. "Of course. Anyone figure out whodunit? At Mystery Night, I mean."

"The successful detective came as quite a surprise," Katherine said. "Mia Tosches, if you can believe it. She pegged the killer right away."

"Maybe she watches TV mysteries in her spare time."

Katherine gave me a pained smile. "Apparently so. After her big win, she told us she's a big fan of *Law & Order*. And *Monk* and *Murder She Wrote* reruns. She reads, too. Even has a large collection of signed Agatha Christies. Made her husband buy them for Christmas."

My, my. Quite the intellectual. After a few more pleasantries, I lowered my voice and told them about the rabid coyote. "You might want to warn the residents to avoid any animal acting strangely. You know how people are. They'll bring home anything cute."

"Animals are off limits at Sunset Canyon Lake," Katherine said.

"The animals don't know that," her husband admonished. "Squirrels are always coming over the walls, and rabbits, well, they're everywhere, aren't they? They and the gophers play hell with the golf course. I've heard the maintenance men complaining."

"Point taken," Katherine said. "Trent, here's what I suggest we do." Giving me a quick nod, she ushered him away, leaving me alone to scan the room.

Mia Tosches, the youngest person in the room by far, flaunted her youth in a red saloon girl outfit, or part of one, anyway. Her dress' neckline plunged almost to her navel and its hemline gave up the ghost a mere inch below her crotch, allowing her to show almost as much skin as she had earlier in her microscopic bikini. Roger Tosches, a paunchy Wyatt Earp with an age-spotted face and thinning hair, didn't appear to mind his wife's efforts to bare all. In fact, the Beast to his wife's Beauty appeared to revel in the lusty glances several "cowboys" threw toward her. After all, she was his, wasn't she? At least in a contemporary, loosey-goosey kind of way.

Attempting to look casual, I moved through the crowd until I found a close spot near them. Mia was discussing their last trip to Monaco, where they'd had a great time in the casino. Every now and then she threw in a dig about the huge amount of money he'd lost, and he kept changing the subject back to the upcoming mine opening.

"I know you're bored by the whole thing, honey, but I've arranged for a very nice actual ribbon-cutting ceremony," Tosches said. "You'll be doing the honors instead of me. Photographers will be there, and your picture will run all over the state, maybe even nationally."

Mia made a face. "I've never trusted the press. One day you're best buddies, next day they're snooping under your bed."

"Not the *Journal-Gazette*. I've got them eating out of my hand."

"Better watch it, Rog. You're liable to wake up some morning and find your hand bit off. You seem to forget that the hag from the *Times* will be there, too. God knows what she might dig up on you. Or already has."

"I can handle her."

"Like you handled the mess in town today? Thugs with baseball bats?"

That Roger Tosches had sponsored the riot didn't surprise me at all, but that his wife would discuss it so openly did. Cursing myself for not having it on already, I reached down into my carry-all and pressed the RECORD button on my digital recorder. I moved closer to the couple, but by then it was too late. Mia's attention had been caught by a new arrival.

"Speak of the devil," Mia said, her well-manicured finger pointing at Olivia Eames. "She looks like an Old West vampire."

Not an unfair description. The reporter, who'd made straight for the drinks table, was a vision in black gunslinger attire, sporting two plastic six-guns slung from black holsters, black hat, black jeans, and a black Western shirt. Instead of black Reeboks like my own, her feet were shod in black pointy-toed boots with silver tips—the only non-black note on her costume. The get-up provided a shocking counterpoint to her papery white skin, which made her look as if she'd spent her entire life indoors with shades drawn against the sun.

Hoping Tosches and his wife would resume their conversation about the mine opening, I hovered nearby for a few more minutes but the topic had played itself out. Tosches began complaining about the numerous plumbing problems the condos at the Lakes had recently experienced.

"What're they doing over there, flushing gophers down the toilets?" he grumped to his wife.

"They probably catch them on the fairway. By the way, when are you going to do something about that? I'm sick and tired of having my game disrupted by those filthy rodents."

Her husband shot her an annoyed look. "I'm doing the best I can."

"Maybe your best isn't good en…" Mia cut off her barb with a gasp. "What the hell is Nancy doing here? Shouldn't she be home crying over Ike?"

Following her eyes, I saw Nancy Donohue dressed in a rhinestone cowgirl outfit. She was whooping it up by the drinks table with the rest of the Book Bitches. Momentarily giving up on the Tosches, I moved toward them.

The closeness of the crowded room had given me a headache, and even though someone had opened the sliding doors leading to the patio, I could still smell the sweat emanating from the dance floor. Smoking in public places was illegal in Arizona, but I smelled cigarette smoke. Die-hards on the patio were sneaking a few. And for God's sake, was that a note of marijuana sweetening the more acrid stench of tobacco? I remembered, then, that although these folks looked old to me, many were young enough to be members of the Woodstock generation. If the sheriff ever raided Sunset Canyon Lakes, they would be dragged into the cop cars, trailing their bongs behind them.

"Well, if it isn't the big city detective!" Nancy Donohue bayed, interrupting my train of thought. "Catch my husband's killer yet?"

"Not yet." I reminded myself that despite their resemblance, Nancy wasn't the foster mother who'd so neglected my frail emotional state. Carrying that old ghost around could cloud my investigative judgment, so I pushed Mrs. Putney back into the bitter past where she belonged, and smiled.

"Are you still convinced Ted Olmstead didn't do it?" she asked.

"Absolutely." Although that may have been an exaggeration.

"Where's your proof?"

"You can't prove a negative. How well did you know Ted?"

"I've ridden with him many times. On a horse, not a bed," she smirked and cast a glance in Mia Tosches' direction.

Knowing her well, the other women in the book group—all of them in saloon girl garb—didn't bother to look shocked. Neither did I. "The last time we talked, you named Rog…"

She put up her hand. "No names. We're in public. Lawsuits, you know."

It was hard to keep from laughing at this sudden display of discretion, but I managed. "Nancy, when we spoke earlier today, you said it wasn't unusual for your husband to stay out late, sometimes even all night. Had your husband's behavior changed in any other way in the last few days before he was killed?"

At first I thought she wasn't going to answer, but after taking a hefty swig of whatever she was drinking, she answered, "Funny you should ask. Starting a couple of months ago, it was like living with a different person. I put it down to the fact that he'd stopped smoking, which always makes people edgy, and I even asked Elizabeth here about it. When her husband stopped, she almost had to have him carted off to the giggle factory, but Ike wasn't acting anything like Jim."

"Jim was a mess," Elizabeth piped up. Her purple saloon girl dress perfectly matched her hair. "He kept pacing back and forth, yelling all the time at every little thing, really unpleasant. I finally told him that if he was going to continue acting like that, I'd rather he went back to smoking. He…"

Mrs. Donohue shot her a look. "We're talking about *my* husband, not that lout you live with." Then, to me, "As I was saying before we were so rudely interrupted, Ike's behavior changed. He wasn't acting as nuts as Jim did, only distracted, like he had something on his mind."

"Any idea what it might have been?"

She shrugged her rhinestoned shoulders. "Haven't the foggiest. But here's something for you. The other day I opened his cell phone bill and saw a slew of long-distance charges, some to phone numbers in Durham, North Carolina, where we used to live. When I asked him about it, he told me it was none of my business, something he'd never said to me before. We had one hell of an argument over it, too, but he still wouldn't explain, walked right out the door leaving me standing there with my mouth open. Well! You can imagine that I wasn't about to let something like that hang, so I called one of the numbers, and guess what?"

"I'm all ears." So was my digital recorder.

"His ex-wife Claudia answered the phone!"

Behind her, one of the Book Bitches tittered.

Mrs. Donohue ignored her. "Now why would he call that woman? I mean, it wasn't like he was thinking about going back to her, because she'd long since remarried some oaf who used to work for the same company he'd worked for, which I happen to think is pretty suspicious in itself, for the obvious reason."

"I'm afraid I don't understand."

"Do I have to paint you a picture? Ike's children always hated me because they thought I'd taken him away from their mother, but seeing as how Claudia remarried right away—and to somebody she must have already known, no less—there must have been some hanky-panky going on, and not only on Ike's side. So why the hell would he call that cheating whore?"

Talk about the pot calling the kettle black. "Did you ask her?"

"Oh, I asked her plenty, that's for sure, and she told me it was none of my business and hung up before I could give her a piece of my mind. When I went after Ike again, he told me the same thing!" She took another swig of her drink, then continued. "Look, Jones, if that really *is* your name, Ike knew better than to keep secrets from me because he knew I'd find out everything anyway and God help him then. Him staying out all night, that didn't surprise me because all men are sluts, aren't they? But those strange phone calls, yeah, that was new. The fact that he didn't want to discuss any of it with me, well, you asked about behavior changes, that was *big time* new. Oh, and some of those other calls? They were to his kids, but I can't imagine why. At my suggestion, he'd written those losers out of his life years ago."

Not only had she broken up her husband's first marriage, she'd alienated him from his children, too. But I was a detective, not a priest, so I didn't tell her to recite a thousand Hail Marys and change her heartless ways. "Did you track down the other calls?"

"Of course I did, what do you take me for? Some were to people he knew when he was married to Claudia, like that troll Gerald Heber. I wound up talking to the granddaughter because old Heber'd been dead for years."

"Did she say why he'd called?"

"Once he found out Heber was dead, he didn't say why. But one funny thing. Before he hung up, he asked her if she smoked. When she said she did, he told her to stop immediately. Coming from him, that's quite the advice, eh? I had better luck with the Arizona area codes—more people were still alive!" She cackled like a mad thing.

I pushed the memories of Mrs. Putney back down. "Did anyone tell you why he was calling?"

"Most wouldn't talk to me, just hung up, people are so rude these days. But one woman, our former cleaning lady, of all people, said he'd called to apologize for docking her pay $139.49 when she broke a serving platter. She said he told her he was sending out a check to make amends."

"Make amends," a phrase used by people involved in Twelve Step programs. One of the steps, I'd never been clear on which one, involved making amends to the people you'd hurt in your drinking or drugging days.

"Did Ike drink?" I asked.

"No more than anyone else. Less than most, actually. Being in public relations, he needed to keep his wits about him."

"Did he use drugs?"

A scowl vicious enough to scare Dracula. "You fool. This conversation is over." She turned her sequined back to me.

As I walked away, my head was buzzing. What was the meaning behind those phone calls? If Nancy Donohue was to be believed, her husband hadn't been an addict of any kind, unless you counted his addiction to nicotine. But maybe the merry widow didn't know as much about her husband's problems as she thought she did. Some alcoholics managed to hide their drinking for years before getting caught. The fact that Ike had been going out at night, sometimes not returning until morning, was odd in and of itself. Nancy obviously suspected an affair, but he could have been visiting a Walapai Flats crack house. At his age such a possibility was unlikely, but neither age nor social status proved barriers to addiction. Just ask those pot smokers out on the patio.

Then I remembered that Las Vegas, Sin City itself, was less than three hours away. The condition of Nancy Donohue's living room, the scuffed and threadbare furniture, could have been put down to Vegas-lost money, not poor housekeeping. Perhaps Donohue had developed a gambling problem, and spent those late nights at the casinos. But if so, wouldn't Nancy have noticed a sudden shortage of funds?

Neither Jimmy nor myself had yet seen a copy of Donohue's autopsy. If he had been currently addicted to any sort of drug, it would eventually show up on the tox screen, but that report wouldn't come in for weeks. Even if he'd recently kicked his habit, the damage—such as old track marks—might still be present. A history of alcohol abuse, of course, could be determined by a fatty liver. I made a mental note to obtain a copy of the autopsy from Anderson Behar, Ted's attorney, first thing in the morning. Thinking of that attorney, I experienced a flash of irritation. If anything had been out of line on that autopsy, Behar should have already disclosed it to Desert Investigations. Then again, he was a real estate attorney who had never tried a murder case in his life. What had Hank Olmstead been thinking, hiring him? But I couldn't let myself off the hook about the autopsy, either, when all I'd been concerned with was the murder weapon. Why hadn't I thought about…

"Get any good quotes on that recorder in your tote bag?"

Olivia Eames' voice startled me out of my funk. Of course a reporter would notice what I'd been doing.

I gave her a rueful smile. "I'm not sure."

She smiled back. "Take anything Nancy says with a grain of salt. She's not nearly as heartless as she'd like people to believe."

"And Satan runs a rescue mission for homeless vets."

Olivia laughed, revealing two small sores on the inside of her bottom lip. Given her gauntness and pale complexion, I transferred my suspicions about senior druggies to her. Crystal meth? Or merely a visit from herpes simplex, the virus that causes cold sores?

Unaware of the way my mind tracked, she asked, "How's the investigation going? From what I've been able to ascertain, Ted Olmstead's still being held."

"Unfortunately, that's true, but I'm following up on some promising leads." My second lie of the day. "Did you know Ted?"

"Never met the man. If he's innocent, the truth will come out. Maybe not today, maybe not tomorrow, but soon enough."

"That sounds awfully trusting coming from a journalist."

She shrugged her bony shoulders. "The American justice system isn't entirely corrupt."

"Just partially?"

That raspy laugh again. "You've got me there. Seriously, though, the guy has a good lawyer, doesn't he?"

"Ted? He should be so lucky. His father hired a real estate attorney."

Her black-rimmed eyes widened. "For a *homicide* case?"

"I'm afraid so."

She didn't say anything else for a moment, only smiled faintly at the group of cowboys and saloon girls forming themselves into a line to dance to the twang and thump of "Cotton-Eyed Joe." After one chaps-wearing man stomped on his partner's boot-clad foot and she stormed off the dance floor, Olivia finally spoke again.

"Enjoying the mixer?"

The abrupt change of subject threw me. "I'm not a fan of theme parties. They kill every bit of spontaneity the human animal has left in its over-regimented soul. Nice outfit you're wearing, though."

"Like you, I'm partial to black." She fell silent again, watching the dancers. As soon as the music clomped to a halt, the fiddle-player told them to form up for "Turkey In the Straw." Obediently, they gave it a try, and after a few missteps and collisions, managed a passable square dance.

"They're sure having a good time," Olivia said.

Her wistful tone made me ask, "Aren't you?"

"Too much work to do."

I decided not to mention seeing her at the demonstration earlier. "I take it you're not here on vacation."

"Can't put anything over on a detective, can I? If I were vacationing, it certainly wouldn't be here. It would be someplace less crowded, like the Arctic Circle. I'm here to cover the reopening of the Black Basin Mine."

"Why does the *New York Times* care about an Arizona uranium mine?"

"'Ask not for whom the bell tolls; it tolls for thee,' John Donne wrote," she said. "That's something the EPA, OSHA, and the U.S. House and Senate should take more seriously. Pollution, especially the radioactive kind, has a nasty way of not staying put. It blows where the wind blows, and in this part of the country, that means from the west to the east. Particulates in Arizona air become particulates in Nebraska, Pennsylvania, and even New York. Ergo, the environmental bell tolls for us all. Besides, even New Yorkers admire the Grand Canyon."

Well, she was the journalist, not me. "But I was under the impression that uranium mines themselves aren't radioactive enough to bother anyone. Isn't the real problem the runoff from the mine tailings? I hear it contains arsenic, radon, and other crap, which is why environmental folks are raising so much hell."

Her face shut down. "You're only partially correct. Arsenic does show up in the mine tailings, which pollutes anyone or anything living downstream. But while raw uranium may not be all that dangerous in and of itself, the first step of processing, which is done right at the mine, intensifies the radioactivity by turning the ore into something called yellow cake. When the workers breathe the yellow cake dust, their lungs rot. Those Navajos that worked on the Moccasin Peak Mine have a lung cancer rate that's five times higher than the Navajos that didn't work there. Their bones and kidneys aren't doing so well, either."

I remembered one of the picket signs that puzzled me at the demonstration: YELLOW CAKE = DEATH. Now I understood. "Considering that you're writing about all this, Olivia, I'm surprised Roger Tosches let you lease a time share."

"He doesn't keep tabs on who's living at this abortion he calls a resort. Katherine took care of the lease. We're old friends."

I should have made the connection before. "Ah, from the days you worked at the *Boston Globe*."

"You've done your homework. Yes, I met her when we worked on a couple of stories together."

"She was a journalist?"

"A source. Listen, I've already done all the background work I need on the Black Basin and nothing much will be shaking in that area until the opening ceremonies on Sunday. If you're still in town day after tomorrow, I'm driving over Silver Ridge to finish up some research on a story that's even more interesting than the mine. It's another environmental issue that impacts—or, more correctly, impacted—Arizona and points east. Want to come along?"

Intriguing though it sounded, I explained that I was here to help Ted, not tour old mining towns.

She pulled a business card from her pocket. "Here's my cell number. We'd only be gone about three hours. If you get a break in your schedule, give me a call."

As I took the card from her, I saw a small spot of blood on her lower lip. I pointed. "Your mouth is bleeding."

She wiped the blood away with a black-painted fingernail. "Damned cold sores are driving me nuts. Look, I've pretty much had it with this party and its damned Western music, so I'm going back to the timeshare. Like I said, give me a call if you change your mind. I promise the trip will be illuminating, and who knows? You might even find another case to work on. Maybe several."

On that mysterious note, she left.

As I stood there pondering the unlikely coincidence of Olivia and Katherine knowing each other in Boston, someone bumped into me from behind.

"Oops, guess I'd better look where I'm going." Mia Tosches, on her way to the drinks table.

I gave her my best smile. "It's crowded in here, isn't it? But it's a nice party."

Mia halted her progress and looked me up and down, noting my jeans, tee shirt, and scuffed Reeboks. "You're not in costume, but my, my, you still look good. Did anyone ever tell you you're a very striking woman?"

She moved closer to me, close enough that I suspected sexual interest on her part. Up until this moment, I'd been under the impression that she confined her extramarital activities to the male gender. Live and learn, right?

"Thanks for the compliment. I'm only a guest this evening and didn't have a costume handy," I explained. "But I'm thinking about buying one of the condos. Sunset Canyon Lakes is such a beautiful place, and the no-children rule is brilliant. Speaking of brilliant, I love your saloon girl outfit. You look pretty good, yourself." You can never stroke a narcissist too much.

"My husband said the same thing. He's Roger Tosches, the man who built Sunset Canyon Lakes."

"A man of rare taste." As the extended version of "Turkey In the Straw" ended and "Tumbling Tumbleweeds" began, the dancers slowed their dosey-doeing into a waltz. Using her sexual interest in me—all's fair in love, war, and criminal investigation—I continued my raves about Sunset Canyon Lakes. After the butter-up, I zeroed in. "Yes, the way the streets are laid out, the electric shuttles instead of gassy traffic jams, looks to me like your husband's built the perfect community. Well, except for that business about the murder."

The gleam in her eye disappeared. "The Indian who did it's already in jail, so you don't have anything to worry about."

Big of her to consider my peace of mind. "He works over at Sunset Trails Guest Ranch, doesn't he?"

"Wrangler or something. Say, would you like to go out some time? My husband doesn't mind. You and I, I think we have chemistry."

"How flattering." I moved slightly away from her. "Do you know the guy? Ted, I think his name is."

"I took a couple of riding lessons from him, is all. Why do you care?"

Sometimes honesty really is the best policy, but this wasn't it. Every good detective knows that the best way to interview reluctant people is to start with something they're interested in, and by a good stroke of fortune, Katherine had provided me with that information.

"Ever since I started watching *Law & Order*, I've been interested in the whole crime and punishment thing."

Her eyes lit up. "You like *Law & Order* too? Too bad you didn't attend the Mystery Night mixer last week. One of the groundsmen volunteered to be murdered, and we were supposed to figure out who did it, with what weapon, and why. I won."

"Really?"

"Really. Roger hadn't wanted me to take part, but I insisted. I've always been good at that kind of game, even used to play Clue with my mother and her friends. I beat her every time."

Oh, yes, the mother who'd lost her home paying her thieving daughter's attorney's fees. "Well, then, since you're so good at mystery games, why don't we try one now?"

"Can't. It's only you and me. Or do you want to rope in a few more players? The Book Bitches might be interested. Especially Nancy. She has a devious mind."

"Just us. Here's how we can do it. We can pretend that Ted isn't the guy who murdered Ike Donohue and that we've decided to solve the case ourselves." Remembering her collection of Agatha Christies, I added, "You know, like Hercule Poirot and his friend Hastings. You can be Poirot. Who among the people here tonight would you choose as the killer? And why'd he or she do it?"

"But I told you, that ranch hand…"

"Have some fun with it, Mia. Pretend the case isn't solved."

The slight glazing across Mia's eyes hinted that I hadn't yet hooked her. Like most criminals, she had been gifted with cunning, but little true curiosity. I needed to put the focus back on her Achilles heel: her ego. "I guess you got lucky last week when you solved the 'pretend' case. Not so easy in real life, is it?"

The direct challenge worked. "I can win any game when I put my mind to it."

Was it my imagination, or had she decreased the distance between us again? "Then prove it, Poirot. They say the spouse is always the first suspect. What do you think?"

"Game on. If we're basing this game on real people, then you're talking about Nancy Donohue."

"I hear she's good with a gun."

"A regular Annie Oakley. And from all the nasty things she's said about her husband, I don't think she liked him much. As for motive, she's probably up for a big life insurance payout. Everyone's insured for at least a mill these days, aren't they?"

"Oh, at least." I nodded sagely. "You *are* good at this. You've already come up with a suspect and a motive. Who else might have done it? For pretend, of course."

"How about that Two Horses guy who runs the Gas-N-Go? Yeah, I know, he's not here in the room, but everybody's always talking about what friends he and that ranch hand were, which I'll bet's a bunch of crap, seeing as how they're from different tribes. Ted's a Paiute and the gas station guy, Earl, is half Navajo. Navajos were, what's the phrase, the Paiute's hereditary enemies."

Who would have thought that Mia Tosches could tell the difference from one tribe and the other, let alone be knowledgeable about ancient tribal grudges. Maybe at some point in her life, she'd had an Indian friend. Or an Indian lover. That possibility might bear looking into.

"Sounds good, Mia, if the Gas-N-Go guy had killed the ranch hand, but aren't you losing track of something here? Ike Donohue was the person who was murdered, not Ted."

With a chuckle, she said, "I didn't lose track. The way I see it is this: Two Horses killed Ike Donohue so Ted, his ancient enemy, would be blamed. You know the old saying, revenge is a dish best served cold."

It would never do to underestimate Mia Tosches, because she was smarter and more well read than she appeared. "That's pretty Machiavellian."

She preened. "It is, isn't it?"

Since she hadn't asked what 'Machiavellian' meant, it was quite possible that she kept an underlined copy of *The Prince* tucked underneath her pillow. Well, I shouldn't have been surprised. Like most larceny-minded folk, Mia probably spent much of her day accumulating information that might prove useful in the future.

As if to prove my point, she continued her recital of possible suspects. "See that man my husband's talking to? Roger's the one in the cute Wyatt Earp outfit."

Standing next to Tosches was a bland-faced man whose only outstanding physical attribute was his Bozo the Clown hairstyle, a ruffed orange-ish ridge that not only ringed his bald pate but perfectly matched his orange cowboy shirt.

"That's Cole Laveen, my husband's new partner in the Black Basin Mine," Mia said. "He could have killed Donohue. Awhile back, when that Kimama woman managed to halt the mine's opening, Roger let him buy in. Since Laveen wasn't connected to the problems Roger had at the mine on the Navajo rez, he got this bright idea that someone with a clean history looked better for the regulatory agencies, and God knows old Laveen has a clean history. Regardless of how comical he looks, he's the dullest human being who ever walked the face of the earth. But appearances always lie in those detective shows, don't they? He could have killed Kimama to get the mine started up again, then turned around and killed Donohue because Donohue was blackmailing him."

"Mia, that's amazing." I meant it, too.

She winked. "Or, we can say Roger did it."

"Your husband?"

"Men like that don't make a fortune without doing an evil deed here and there."

For a moment, I pitied Roger Tosches, who slept every night with a scorpion in his bed. One day she'd turn around and sting him. "Money's always a prime motive, so I can see why he'd kill Kimama Olmstead, but what would be his motive for killing Donohue?"

"The same reason the Laveen couple might kill him. Blackmail. It would be even more understandable in Roger's case, because Donohue worked for him and knew where all the bodies were buried."

I pretended ignorance again. "Donohue only did public relations work for your husband. He wouldn't have access to any dangerous information like that."

"That's what PR people are for, to cover up scandal. But if you don't like blackmail as a motive, then how about this? The murder could have been a simple case of jealousy. Donohue wanted me and Roger got jealous."

Despite myself, I began to laugh.

Mia did, too. "Motives don't always have to be subtle, Lena." Her arm brushed mine, not accidentally.

I stepped back again. "Ah, but they have to be believable, and from what I've heard, your husband is very open-minded."

She gave me a look so intent it spooked me. "For someone who doesn't even live in Sunset Canyon Lakes, you sure know a lot. But you're right about that open-minded bit. That's something Roger and I agreed on before we got married. I mean, girls will be girls, right?" She closed the distance between us again.

And boys will be boys, I thought, remembering Warren and Dusty. After silently reaffirming my vow to stay away from anything that smacked of romance, I asked one final question. "How about you, Mia? We can't count you out, either, because you're part of this mystery game. What would be your motive for killing Ike Donohue?"

With an evil smile, she leaned forward and patted my rump. "I'd do it just for the thrill."

Chapter Thirteen

November 1979: Northwestern Arizona

That was it, then.

Gabe walked into his ranch house for the last time, went into the cold kitchen, and slipped Abby's strawberry-patterned apron off its hook. He pressed his nose against it, smelled her Evening in Paris perfume and the lingering scents of thousands of meals. Then he folded it carefully and tucked it into his saddlebag. Memories safely stowed, he went back into the living room and saluted the autographed picture of John Wayne. He started to walk away, then changed his mind and put the picture into his saddlebag, right next to Abby's apron.

"Nothing to stay here for no more."

Blue Four, standing sentinel by his left heel, cocked his head quizzically.

"Now that Abby's dead, the bank can have it all and we don't care, do we, Blue?"

Hearing his name, the dog grinned.

Abby had had such a hard time dying that only the guard catching Gabe trying to sneak his rifle into the hospital had kept him from putting her down like he'd do to any grievously suffering animal. And she was his wife, for God's sake, his one dear thing in all this world. Later that day, after he'd promised not to do anything stupid, he pushed the IV stand aside and crawled into the bed with her despite the guard's disapproving glare.

"That's my good girl," he'd murmured, not caring what the man, any man, thought. Abby's skin felt like paper, her bones like matchsticks. Her Evening in Paris had long since faded; now she smelled like death. He bundled her to him. "You go to sleep now."

She'd managed a smile, breathed out hard. Then her eyes went dull.

It was over.

It was over for so many of them. Abby's mother, father, sisters, nieces and nephews.

Not only family.

Friends.

Curly. Karlene Hafen. Sheldon Nisson. Lenn McKenney. John Crabtree. Delsa Bradshaw. Geraldine Thompson. Arthur Bruhn. Irma Wilson. Daisy Lou Prince. Donna Jean Berry.

Over, too, for half the people he'd met on that lifetime-ago movie: John Wayne, Susan Hayward, Agnes Moorehead, Dick Powell, Pedro Armendariz, the Paiute extras, the wranglers…

And the animals. Oh, Lord, the deer, the sheep, the cattle, the horses, Blue One, Blue Two, Blue Three—even Star. All dead too soon because of the disease the wind blew through the desert, like that Middle Ages thing Abby had raved about when she was hopped up on morphine. Only this wasn't no Black Plague, this was American Plague, and the dying wasn't as merciful.

Gabe looked down at his dog, into the face of its great-great-grandfather. "You about set, Blue?"

Blue Four wagged his tail.

"Then let's get the fuck out of here."

Chapter Fourteen

As soon as the sun rose the next morning, I left the motel and drove back to the area where I'd shot the coyote. Everything looks different in the daytime, especially in the early morning when shadows are long. Although I'd placed a rock cairn over her body it took several passes along the blacktop to locate the right spot. During the fourth pass, I found her.

She had picked a peaceful place to die. Near the cairn, a jackrabbit—more fortunate than the road kill last night—hopped through a miniature forest of cholla cacti. On the west side of the road, silver-green cottonwoods trembled in the breeze that whispered along the Virgin River. Not far away, a mitten-shaped mesa glowed red and purple in the new light, a brilliant contrast against the softer lavender hues of its sister mesas that stretched for miles behind it. Providing a soundtrack to this otherworldly scene, a flock of sparrows sang as they darted through the pink-streaked sky.

When a less musical sound, a cross between a sneeze and a cough, caught my attention, I looked toward the river and glimpsed something increasingly rare in Arizona: a small band of pronghorn antelope grazing in the brush. Hunters had decimated the animals in the southern part of the state, but in these wild northern badlands they were making a comeback. Under ordinary circumstances, I would have watched their slow progress along the riverbank, but I wasn't here to sightsee.

The day promised to be a hot one, so after exiting the Trail-blazer I attached a filled canteen to my gun belt. Through no fault of my own, I'd once been caught out in the desert without water, and I'd never let that happen again. I patted my jeans pocket to make certain my cell phone hadn't slipped out while I'd been rustling around inside the car. It was there, but remembering those big mesas and their tendency to block signals, I doubted the phone would work. Still, the tenuous connection to civilization made me feel more secure.

Steeling myself, I set out to follow the coyote's paw prints to her den.

The ground was so strewn with boulders and rocks that tracking was difficult but not impossible. Stretches of soft sand revealed that the coyote had crossed the road mere feet in front of my rental. She appeared to have come from the east, in the direction of the mitten-shaped mesa. I struggled up the loose shale of the graded incline bracketing the road until I reached a hard granite ridge at the top. Squinting my eyes against the sun, I made out a tumble of boulders at the base of the mesa. The perfect place for a wild animal's den. Ever alert for the rattlesnakes endemic to this part of the country, I wove my way through the rock-strewn ground toward it.

A few minutes later I found the coyote's den, cunningly hidden in a depression between two massive boulders and further disguised by a dense stand of brittlebrush. Cautiously, I looked in.

Out of a litter of four pups, three were already dead.

I helped the last one die.

The desert was populated by scavengers that might spread the disease, so I holstered my .38 and sealed the tomb with rocks. Heavy-hearted, I started back toward the Trailblazer. As soon as I was in calling range, I would alert the Walapai County Department of Health Services. The coyote hadn't developed rabies on her own; she'd contracted it somewhere. Maybe from a skunk, a bat, or even a brush with a rabid mountain lion. The outbreak needed to be eradicated before a human came into contact with a rabid animal.

I was so deep in thought that at first I didn't respond to the shower of sand that suddenly kicked up from the desert floor nearby. But when it was followed a millisecond later by the sharp report of a rifle, I dove for cover behind a rock outcropping.

Some fool city hunter out for pronghorn, amateur enough to shoot at anything that moved?

"Hey!" I yelled. "Hold your…"

Before the word "fire" left my mouth, another shot rang out. This time the bullet pinged off the outcropping, scattering stone chips everywhere.

"Asshole!"

Another shot. A hit even closer than the last.

No amateur, then. Whoever the shooter was, he was zeroing in. On purpose.

Someone was trying to kill me.

The "why" being irrelevant right now, I slipped my .38 out of its holster and waited. During my running and ducking, I hadn't been able to get a definite fix on the source of the shots, but I thought they'd come from an area fifty yards to my east. The next shot, illuminated by a brief flash, proved it.

Now that I knew where my assailant was hiding, I could take appropriate defensive action. One quick look behind revealed the long, safe barrier of the rock ridge I'd originally clambered up. A few yards beyond that, my Trailblazer waited on the side of the road. Enough large boulders lay between my present position and the ridge that I might be able to make it, but once the land fell away on the shale slope, there was no cover at all. When I started down, I'd be totally exposed.

Often the best defense is a good offense, so I aimed in the general area where I thought the shooter had taken cover and snapped off a shot. I was rewarded by a grunt of surprise.

Good. Now he knew I was armed.

Simply returning fire was no solution. My snub-nose .38 might be a nice weapon for close work, but it performed poorly at distances. From the sound of my assailant's gunfire, he had a rifle, maybe even one with a sight, so he was better armed for our desert shootout. A quick check of my cell phone revealed that my earlier concerns were true: no signal. At least I'd had enough sense to bring along a canteen. I had only taken a couple of sips while searching for the coyote's den, so there was a chance I could simply wait the shooter out. But from a better spot, one visible from the road.

Gauging the distance to a boulder nearer the Trailblazer, I fired two more times, then ducked and ran. I reached cover before he had time to react, and paused to regain my breath. Only one more sprint and I would reach the rock ridge.

Better to act now before he realized what I was doing.

I ran again but this time he was ready for me and his next shot hit my canteen. At least a half cup of precious water spilled down my leg before I managed to fling myself over the ridge. After landing hard on the loose shale, I caught my breath again, then put my thumb over the hole to still the flow. Scrabbling around on the desert floor, I found a pebble that looked to be the right size. When I jammed it into the hole water still trickled out. Desperate to stop the flow I ripped a piece off my tee shirt, wrapped it around the pebble and jammed it in again. Success.

I took a short sip from the canteen, then placed another pebble in my mouth, an old Indian trick used as a stopgap from thirst. As the sun rose higher, the day would heat up even more. No point in going to all this trouble just to ultimately pass out from dehydration.

I reloaded my .38. There was no way of knowing whether this would end in a face-to-face shootout but if it did, I wanted to be ready. My situation wasn't good, but it could have been worse. I was within sight of the blacktop, and soon cleaning ladies would begin their commute to Sunset Canyon Lakes. Or maybe I'd be seen by some early-bird shopper heading toward Walapai Flats to buy more fancy Western duds. All that increased activity might scare the shooter away. Then again, maybe not, because what good would a Walapai cleaning lady or an Eastern dude do me? Threaten the shooter with a mop or a Mont Blanc pen? With no reasonable alternative in sight, I settled in and waited for the shooter to make the next move.

Twenty minutes passed, then thirty. The morning breeze stilled as the sun climbed higher. Birds that had ceased their calls when the shooting started began to sing again. Warmed from the sun, a gopher snake slithered toward a gnarled mesquite where a woodrat sat nibbling on a seedpod. Sympathizing with the prey, I whistled a warning, and the woodrat scurried away.

A while later—I'd stopped checking my watch—a grouping of four cars sped along the road toward the resort. None slowed to look at the parked Trailblazer. Maybe they thought some tourist was having a look-see at the pretty scenery. As soon as the last car disappeared over the horizon, the shooter tried his luck again but I was well hunkered down now and his shots did little more than kick up sand.

One of the worst things about holding a crouching position for a length of time is that your body rebels. My weak left leg, scarred from a bullet wound during my days on the Scottsdale police force, began to cramp. I twisted it first one way, then the other, but what little relief I could find was momentary. As soon as I reversed it to the original position, it cramped again and the right leg began cramping in sympathy. The pain increased, making me realize that my plan of waiting out my attacker out wouldn't work. I needed to end this stalemate before I became so crippled up that I couldn't move at all, let alone run for cover. But try as I might, I couldn't think of a sensible and safe alternative. Not even a semi-sensible, semi-safe one.

I was still racking my brain for a possible solution when Fate, that arbitrary dame, intervened. In the distance I heard music. A choir of angels singing me up to Heaven? Given my past, doubtful. The music drifted closer, revealing the rich tenor of Garth Brooks bragging about friends in low places. Barreling toward me was a battered red pickup, an American flag flapping from its big CB antenna. Seconds before the truck reached my Trailblazer, I saw printed on its side, MONTY CARSON, FARRIER. The windows were down and the driver, a male, was blasting his stereo at top volume. Unless I was wrong, that long dark shape in the rear window was a loaded gun rack.

Angels don't always wear wings; sometimes they wear leather aprons.

I knew what to do. When the driver slowed to check out the Trailblazer I fired my .38 at the truck's hood. The resulting clang was testament to the hours I'd spent at the firing range. Braking, the truck slewed sideways along the asphalt, leaving behind two curls of rubber. Oh, yeah, I'd caught the driver's attention, all right.

As the truck came to a complete halt, I fired twice more, this time in the air. Garth Brooks yelped a final note and stopped singing.

Within seconds, a bowlegged little man wearing a farriers' leather apron and carrying a big shotgun, came hurrying toward me.

"You shot my truck!" he howled. "Drop that gun, you stupid bitch, and get your reckless ass down here before I shoot it off!"

Never had bad temper sounded so sweet.

"Radio for help!" I yelled down to him. "But don't come any closer. Someone's shooting at me, and I'm pinned down here!"

From the next ridge over, I could hear rocks sliding in the distance. When I peeked above my own ridge, I saw a trail of dust rising from the desert floor, testament that my outgunned assailant was hoofing it out of there. It was over.

I holstered my .38 and walked downhill toward him with my hands in the air, wondering how my insurance company would react when the farrier submitted his claim.

"People are always shooting something up around here, Miss Jones," the deputy said, handing me back my ID after I'd explained my situation for the third time. "This is Arizona. But you'd be better off minding your own business, not wandering around causing trouble."

It was Officer Smiley Face. The wife-beating deputy, now revealed as Deputy Ronald Stark, had arrived less than five minutes after the farrier saved my ass, explaining that he'd been checking on a report of a dead pronghorn in the road.

"I haven't caused any 'trouble,' as you so incorrectly put it." I was growing more uncomfortable by the minute, partially because Stark's eyes were hidden behind a pair of mirrored sunglasses, the kind that make people look like Martians or hit men.

A cold smile. "Walapai Flats is a small town and I've heard about the questions you've been asking. We keep an eye on people who poke their noses into things that don't concern them." Turning away from me as if I didn't matter, he said to the farrier, "You did right radioing this in, Monty. For all you knew, there was an emergency. But you know how women are, excitable, always imagining things that aren't there."

Monty frowned. "Lena don't seem all that excitable to me."

Although from a distance the farrier had appeared to be much older, up close I could see that he was no more than fifty, but his face was deeply creased and burned by the desert sun. After I'd explained my situation, his temper had cooled to the extent that he'd even volunteered to walk back out into the desert with me to look for shell casings to back up my claim of attempted murder. Deputy Stark, however, was reluctant. And his comment about people poking their noses into unwanted places worried me. Was he talking about my connection to the Ike Donohue case, or could he have found the business card I'd given his battered wife? Adding to my discomfort was the fact that his cruiser looked dusty enough to have been driving across surfaces a lot rougher than blacktop.

Stark pasted on his insincere smile again. "Monty, Monty, Monty. If you think you're a judge of women, you've been standing out in the sun too long."

"Maybe so, but people in glass houses, eh, Ronnie?"

Something passed between them that hinted of past trouble. More concerned about the present, I let it go. "Officer Stark, it's less than a two-minute walk to that ridge where the shooter was holed up. I counted four shots, which pretty much negates a mere slip of the trigger finger, not to mention the fact that he refused to stop shooting when I identified myself as non-pronghorn. If we find more than one shell casing, it'll go a long way toward proving I'm right. Otherwise, go ahead and call me hysterical, be my guest. But if I wind up dead on your beat, Monty here might mention to your superiors that a serious crime was reported to you and you did nothing about it, didn't even fill out a report. Are you ready to shoulder the blame for that?"

Stark shifted his feet. "I'll take a quick look and fill out that little report you're putting so much emphasis on, but I'm gonna want you folks to stay with your vehicles."

"Bullshit to that, Ronnie," Monty snapped. "I'll be right on your heels."

I wanted to kiss the banty-legged little guy. "Me, too, Deputy. As a trained officer of the law myself, which I'm sure you've also found out, I can help spot possible evidence."

Stark looked like he wanted to gun whip us both, but when he started up the shale slope with us right behind him, he didn't chase us away. Once we reached the top of the ridge where I'd holed up until Monty came alone, I pointed to a scar where a bullet had chipped the granite. When I began digging in the sand in front of it, where the first bullet had hit, the deputy remained silent.

Within seconds I'd managed to unearth an almost-pristine copper slug: while I was no ballistics expert, it looked to me like a thirty-ought six from a low-velocity carbine. Not unusual, maybe, but it was the same type of ammo that had killed Kimama Olmstead. I figured that the sheriff, busy though he was, would be interested in seeing it.

"Are you carrying an evidence bag, officer?" I already knew the answer. No.

Monty volunteered that he had baggies in his truck. While I stood guard over the bullet with a reluctant deputy acting as witness, the farrier hotfooted it back to his truck, then returned with two baggies that smelled faintly of tuna fish.

"Here ya go," he said, holding them out with one hand while transferring his sandwiches to the other. "Might as well have me an early brunch" With that, he began wolfing them down.

Both men watched as I rolled the bullet into the baggie and sealed it. A ballistics test would identify the caliber more accurately. Then I stabbed the stick upright into the ground to make the spot easier to find if further investigation proved advisable.

We had more luck when we reached the rock fall where my assailant had hidden out. Four ejected cartridges lay scattered across the ground. Yep, he'd been using a carbine. As I cooed over my finds, Monty gave me the other baggie, and I scooped them in with a rock chip. There was more than an even chance that the shooter's fingerprints were on them.

Deputy Stark accepted the baggies reluctantly. "I don't know what you think these will prove, because this entire incident was caused by some deer hunter a little too eager to fire at anything that moves."

Monty snorted. "A deer hunter using a carbine? Nobody around here's that stupid, not even the dudes. Far as that goes, Lena don't look like no deer, neither, and we ain't exactly standing in the middle of the woods. In clear country like this, any man that can't tell she's a woman 'stead of a pronghorn needs to be walking around with a white cane, not a rifle. Have you forgot that we had us a gunshot death a few months ago that nobody's answered for yet? I wouldn't mislay those evidence bags if I was you, Ronnie. That woman's killer could be the same careless deer hunter." His emphasis on the last two words revealed what he thought of the deputy's theory. "Maybe even the same deer hunter who killed that Donohue fellow."

Stark frowned. "From what I hear, no carbine took Mr. Donohue out. As for the other one, you talking about that Indian woman?"

"How many other gunshot women we got us in Walapai County?"

The deputy wasn't giving up yet. "We do have one unsolved killing on the books, but I'm talking about Mr. Donohue. Unlike you, I'm not certain the Indian woman's death was murder. I'm guessing she came between a hunter and a pronghorn like Miss Jones here did, and he took off when he realized what he'd done."

"Nobody in town believes that but you, Ronnie."

"Maybe you paranoid V.U.M. types don't, but I'm speaking for the sheriff's office."

I sincerely doubted that. I didn't trust Officer Smiley Face, so to hammer home the fact that Monty and I had witnessed him accepting the two baggies into evidence, I said, "Unsolved murders tend to make a police department look bad, officer, and I'm betting the sheriff will be curious to see if the rifling on that carbine slug matches up to the one that killed Kimama Olmstead. He might even be curious enough to put a rush on it at the crime lab."

The cold smile made its reappearance. "We're done here. You folks have yourselves a nice day." Without another word, he walked back to his dusty cruiser.

As we watched the cruiser disappear down the road, Monty said, "I got me a police scanner in my truck. Wasn't no report of a downed pronghorn."

The news didn't surprise me. "You know him well, the deputy?"

"Knew his mama. Sweet woman, dead now. Didn't have no better sense than he does, but that still wasn't no reason for his daddy to treat her like he did. 'Course, none of them Starks is exactly burstin' with brains. Ronnie's the smartest of the bunch, which says a lot about the rest of them."

He finished his second tuna fish sandwich, then rubbed his hands against his leather apron. "Well, like the boy said, you have yourself a nice day, Miss Lena Jones. There's some horses waitin' on me need shoes." He winked. "And I'll be talking to your insurance company soon's I'm done."

After gulping down some water from my canteen, I called the Walapai County Board of Health Services and alerted them to a possible rabies outbreak. Then, I decided that as long as I was in the same general area, I'd stop by Sunset Trails Guest Ranch and talk to Hank Olmstead again. Now that I'd spent some time in Walapai Flats a new question had arisen. Where did his employees stand on the new mine? Did any of them have feelings strong enough about the issue to resort to violence? I hadn't seen anyone from the ranch at the demonstration, but that meant nothing. Most of the wranglers and lodge workers would have been working. But I also wanted to know more about the guest ranch's agreement to provide equine activities with Sunset Canyon Lakes. Had Katherine brokered it or had her husband Trent? In a murder investigation no stone should ever go unturned because something ugly might be hiding under it.

Not wanting to show up at the ranch unannounced, I drove until the mitten-shaped mesa lay two miles behind me, then pulled over to the side of the road and checked my cell phone for bars. Three. I was back in business.

"Sunset Tails Guest Ranch, Leilani speaking." Jimmy's sister.

After identifying myself, I asked if it would be all right if I dropped by to speak to her father.

"Oh, Lena, this isn't a good time because one of our guests was thrown from a horse and we're waiting for the ambulance and Dad's beside himself and he's…" She stopped and took a deep breath. "…snapping at everyone."

"Are the injuries serious?"

"A broken leg, for sure. We're worried about a couple of ribs, too." Leilani lowered her voice. "Mr. Arden, that's the guest, he's been a bit of a problem ever since he got here, and, well, he demanded a better horse than he was given yesterday. So for some crazy reason Dusty let him ride Cisco. Well! Mr. Arden didn't last five minutes. Not that Cisco is difficult, he's not, but he used to be a cutting horse and can turn pretty fast. Apparently that's what happened. They were all out on the trail and a rabbit ran right in front of Cisco so he swerved. Mr. Arden didn't swerve with him, went right over the side. Not only that, but he got his foot tangled up in the stirrup. He's lucky the horse didn't bolt with him hanging upside down like that. I can't imagine Dusty putting him on that Cisco."

A not uncommon riding accident, but Leilani was right. Dusty had wrangled at guest ranches for two decades and should have known better. Dudes, especially the testosterone-fueled male version, often exaggerated their riding skills. Why hadn't Dusty seen through the man's lies? Maybe he had something on his mind. Or someone. Mia Tosches, perhaps? That cowboy had always liked the ladies, something which had caused no end of trouble between us.

"Lena, you there?" Leilani's voice interrupted my train of thought.

"Uh, sorry. What were you saying?"

"I was saying that tomorrow would be a better day for you to come out. Dad should have settled down by then, along with the rest of us. Ten o'clock, say?"

I agreed, then rang off. Next, I called Anderson Behar's office and asked his secretary to email me a copy of Ike Donohue's autopsy report as soon as it came in. But there I hit a wall.

"I'm sorry, Miss Jones, but the only person of record allowed to receive information like that is James Sisiwan," she told me.

"He's my partner at Desert Investigations," I argued.

"I said I'm sorry."

If she was sorry, why did she sound so damn happy? Biting back the snarky comment I wanted to make, I told her as politely as possible to email the autopsy report to Jimmy and gave her his email address.

"I can only do that with Mr. Sisiwan's permission," she said.

Bitch! "Then I'll tell him to call you." I hung up before I totally lost my temper, certain that when the world finally ended, it would be because some officious secretary refused to push the SAVE OUR ASSES button until she received permission from her boss.

It took me a few minutes to calm down, but when I did, I fished Olivia Eames' card out of my carry-all and placed another call. The reporter picked up right away. Not wanting to keep the air conditioner running while we talked, I opened the Trailblazer's windows to let in fresh air. At this particular bend in the road, I was close enough to the Virgin River to smell water.

"Lena Jones here, Olivia. Hey, what do you know about Mia Tosches?"

She began to laugh. "Girl, you just provided a bright spot in a shitty day! I love to gossip about that woman. What do you want to know? Who she and her turd of a husband have been sleeping with?"

"They both fool around?"

"Separately and together. The Thoroughly Modern Tosches, as they're known in Walapai Flats."

"She hit on me last night at the mixer."

"Don't brag. She hit on me, too. So'd he, as a matter of fact, but ewww!"

"Other than that, do you know anything that might tie either of them to Kimama Olmstead's death? Or Ike Donohue's?"

The laughter disappeared from her voice. "Only suspicions, Lena. And you know what they say, suspicions and a dollar won't even buy you a cup of coffee."

It occurred to me that if she did know something, she wouldn't share, at least not until she broke the story. So I asked her about something else that had been bothering me. "Last night you mentioned that Katherine Dysart acted as a source for one of your stories at the *Boston Globe*," I asked. "Which story would that be?"

"Why do you want to know?" Now she sounded cautious.

"It might be important. If you don't tell me, my partner will find out anyway." I kept my voice light.

The caution vanished from her voice. "That big Sisiwan guy? Long black hair? Tribal tat on his temple? A real cutie?"

Oh, lord, not her, too. "Yeah, the cutie."

"I hear he's Ted's brother. That's an interesting family, isn't it, all those adopted kids. Tell me what you thought of Hank."

Olivia was a pro, leading me down the garden path while ignoring my question. But I knew how to play the game, too. "Hank Olmstead? I couldn't get a fix on him, other than that he's worried enough about Ted to hire an attorney, however limited that attorney's skills may prove to be. Nice segue, by the way, Olivia. Answer my question about Katherine."

She chuckled, but still played it coy. "Katherine was an unnamed source in the story, and no matter how good your partner is, he can't find what's not in print."

"I thought newspapers like the *Boston Globe* frowned on using unnamed sources."

"It's verboten if they're the only source in the story, but I used six other sources and named each one. Katherine gave me some useful background info, that's all. And you don't segue so bad yourself."

"Was the article about women whose husbands were imprisoned?"

The silence was so long that I began to think the call had been dropped. Before I punched in her number again, she said, "That's one hell of a wild guess, Lena."

"Not so wild. I spotted one of those home-made prison tattoos on Trent's neck. A pretty unusual accessory for an Ivy Leaguer. Nothing like walking around with your rap sheet hanging out for God and the whole world to see."

"He's in the process of having it removed."

"But in the meantime, there it is. If Dysart is his real last name, and even if it isn't, Jimmy will find out all about him."

She sighed. "You're right. And since it's all on record anyway, I might as well give you the sordid details. Yes, Trent served time. He and Katherine were at the Brae Burn Country Club one afternoon and for some reason, maybe he'd had too many celebratory cocktails after coming in two under par, he wound up in an argument with one of the Kennedy cousins. It got physical. Long story short, Trent socked him one, and on the way down the guy's head slammed into the corner of a table. He never regained consciousness. Trent was contrite, but that didn't count for much during his trial. He was convicted of second-degree manslaughter and was sentenced to ten years in a medium-security prison. Turns out, there wasn't much *medium* about it. The place was so rough that he had to join a prison gang just to survive; hence the tattoo."

"Ten years? He must have been released early on good behavior."

"That and over-crowding. But Boston being Boston, and with neither of their families speaking to them, Katherine convinced him that it might be best to start all over someplace else. Not easy to do with a prison record, so when a job search turned up dual openings at Sunset Canyon Lakes, they jumped at it. Satisfied now?"

"Roger Tosches didn't mind hiring an ex-con?"

"Roger Tosches believes the only good Kennedy is a dead Kennedy."

Chapter Fifteen

Jimmy and I arrivedat the same time at the jail, where a friendly but firm deputy told us that visiting hours were cancelled. Drugs had been found in one of the inmate's cells, and the jail was on lock-down for the next twenty-four hours. And sorry, the sheriff was even busier today than yesterday, but I was welcome to call back later in the day when things calmed down. The sheriff was aware of my need to discuss the Ted Olmstead case, and yes, but for now I had to be patient.

"Lunch at Ma's Kitchen, then?" I asked Jimmy, as we walked down the steps in disappointment.

He looked glum. "Might as well."

Ma's being so close, we left our vehicles in the county lot and walked over. We were early enough that the restaurant wasn't yet crowded yet, so we had our choice of booths. The scent of garlic in the air announced that pasta was on the menu again. Once Jimmy's little friend Tara took our orders—we both chose the linguini in clam sauce special—I lowered my voice and told him what had happened that morning.

Alarm leapt into his eyes. "You need to stop driving around alone in the desert."

"Hard to do, since this is Arizona."

"You know what I mean, Lena. There's a lot of hostility floating around this little town. Remember that riot you ran into yesterday?"

"Who could forget?" The vision of the elderly woman and her smashed wheelchair would remain with me for a long time. Jimmy was right. For all its homey charm, Walapai Flats played house with a surprising streak of meanness, but if I'd been the timid sort, I wouldn't have driven up from Scottsdale in the first place. Hell, I'd never leave my office at all, just remain anchored to my desk, merely answering phones. Private investigation was a dangerous business, because you never knew what kind of violence lurked around the corner. And God help me, I loved the game.

To get Jimmy off the subject of my safety, I told him about last night's mixer and my conversations with Mia Tosches and Olivia Eames. "According to Olivia, Tosches doesn't mind his wife's extracurricular activities."

Jimmy grunted. "Maybe, like that guy in the movie, he likes to watch."

"*Being There*, with Peter Sellers."

"Totally overrated, too," he said with a sour look. "Give me a good Western any time as long as it's the Indians who win."

"That keeps your movie selection down to a bare minimum."

He smiled. "Apparently you didn't see my DVD collection when you broke into my trailer."

Time to change the subject. "I almost forgot to tell you. Trent Dysart, Katherine's husband? He's an ex-con."

"Based on your female intuition?"

"Don't be sexist." I described Trent's prison tat and my conversation with Olivia Eames. "Look into him and see what other kinds of dirt you can dig up. Prison can make a man violent, even if he wasn't violent before. And since Trent actually did kill that guy, supposedly by accident, I'm curious. He and Donohue both lived in Sunset Canyon Lakes. Who knows what kind of confrontation they might have had."

"Sounds promising. I'll check out Katherine, too."

"That mixer, by the way…"

I was interrupted by Tara delivering our linguini, which looked and smelled delicious. She served Jimmy with great flair;

me, perfunctorily. "Pie comes with the special," she told Jimmy, batting her long lashes. "We'll be getting busy in a couple of minutes, so I suggest you make your choice now. I'll keep an eye on your booth and when you're about finished with your entree, I'll bring it over. So what do you prefer, apple, peach, lemon meringue, or banana cream?"

Jimmy gave her a gentle smile. "Surprise me, Tara. I trust your judgment."

She flushed with pleasure then turned to me. "You?"

My own smile had no effect on her. "Apple. With a scoop of vanilla ice cream."

After she walked away, I said to Jimmy, "I don't know how you do it."

"Do what?"

"That thing you have with women."

He gave me a long look. "I like people, even women. Or more accurately, especially women. Unlike men, most women take the time to delve beneath a person's surface and aren't blinded by an artificial exterior."

If I hadn't known Jimmy better, I might have interpreted his comment as a dig at my own track record. Warren, the sophisticated film director; Dusty, the handsome wrangler. Had I looked beyond their slick surfaces when I met them? I tried to convince myself that my attractions ran deeper than that, but a small voice inside me whispered, *Liar!*

We busied ourselves with our linguini. After finishing the last oily morsel, I said, "Just so you know, on my way back into town I called Ted's attorney's office and asked his secretary to email you a copy of Donohue's autopsy report. She said she won't do it without vocal confirmation from you, so call the bitch."

"Language. We're in public." Jimmy pushed his plate away. "He was shot to death. We already know that."

"But him calling around, apologizing for past behavior, that sounds like Twelve Step work to me. I want to know more about that. Now are you going to call or not, dammit?"

"I'll call her if you stop cursing."

"Deal. And Donohue…"

Cutting me off, Tara arrived at the table bearing two huge slices of pie; banana cream for Jimmy, apple à la mode for me.

"I've always admired a woman who's not afraid of food," Jimmy said a few minutes later, as I attacked my dessert. "But back to Ike Donohue. So you think some Twelve Step program might have played into his death?"

"I can't think of another reason for those 'I'm sorry' phone calls, especially since he took the time to tell the granddaughter of an old friend to stop smoking. Considering the fact he used to do PR for a tobacco company, that sounds like an 'amend.'"

"Maybe we should have looked for a drug connection in the very beginning. The lockdown at the jail proves there's a problem in this town."

"There's a drug problem in every town."

"On every reservation, too."

We sat in silence for a moment. Jimmy had lost cousins to overdoses; I'd lost friends. The drug epidemic in America had become so widespread that few families remained untouched.

Then I remembered something I'd meant to ask earlier. "By any chance have you run across Donohue's insurance policies? I've been wondering how much his wife will get."

"Donohue left his wife a million and a half. These days, that wouldn't be considered astronomical, but we've run into plenty of people who would kill for much less."

"Nancy needs new furniture."

He grinned. "Well, there you go."

As soon as I finished my apple pie, I glanced over at Jimmy's banana cream. "Boy, that looks good. I reached over and helped myself to a forkful. "Mmmm. It's as good as it looks."

"Say, did you call the Board of Health about that rabid coyote?"

"Even before I called Anderson Behar's insufferable secretary." I gestured with my fork toward his pie. "Do you want the rest of that? If not, I'm eating it."

He shoved it toward me. "Knock yourself out."

I left Jimmy to flirt with Tara, but instead of returning to my car, took a stroll through town. A good PI can glean information in the unlikeliest of places.

Although the day was too hot to be pleasurable, the overhangs that shaded the raised wooden sidewalks kept the temperature tolerable. Tourists were out in full force, strolling along John Wayne Boulevard, peeking into shop windows offering John Wayne tee shirts, John Wayne key chains, John Wayne DVDs. Each store sported a sticker on its door proclaiming the proprietor was a proud member of the Walapai Flats Chamber of Commerce. Spotting a familiar face inside Big Hoss' Western Emporium—also a proud member of the Walapai Flats Chamber of Commerce—I walked in. The prosperous-looking gentleman who'd handed me a 10 percent off coupon at the demonstration yesterday was building a small pyramid of John Wayne coffee mugs on a table.

I pulled the coupon out of my carry-all and said, "I'll take the mug that says, 'Don't say it's a fine morning or I'll shoot ya.'" On that issue, Wayne and I were in accordance; mornings weren't my favorite time of day, either.

"Excellent choice," the man said. "The quote's from *McLintock*. We carry the film in DVD or VHS, whichever you prefer."

"Was the movie made around here?"

"Nope, down by Tucson." He reeled off a list of movies filmed in Walapai County and then tried to get me to buy one. Or two. Or three. When I declined, he walked over to a nearby shelf and brought back an obviously phony Indian headdress no real Indian would be caught dead in. "How about this? The green feathers match your eyes perfectly."

"Just the mug, thanks."

Recognizing that I wasn't in a shopping spree mood, he led me to the counter, where I handed him my American Express card and 10 percent off coupon. As he picked up my card, I said, "Say, didn't I see you at the demonstration?"

A furrow appeared between his eyebrows. "That was a very rare and unfortunate situation. We Walapai Flatians are actually very peaceful people."

"That's what you said yesterday, too. But if a little thing like a demonstration can get those peaceful people riled up enough to whack each other with baseball bats, what's the problem with uranium mining? Is it radioactive or something?"

"Of course not!" Toning it down, he added, "Uranium mining is a perfectly safe enterprise when it's handled responsibly. Those demonstrators you saw are nothing but radical environmentalists. If they had their way, we'd be back burning candles for light and riding bicycles to work."

It didn't sound that bad to me, though it would play hell with Desert Investigations' website and Facebook page. "There was something else that puzzled me at the demonstration, an elderly woman carrying a sign that said 'Hasn't Walapai County suffered enough?' What did that mean?"

"I have no idea." He handed me my mug and my receipt. "Have a nice day."

I ran into the same polite brush-off at Cowboy Clem's Western Wear, where I purchased a white Stetson; Tumbleweed Books, coming away with a copy of *Arizona in the Movies*; and at Kalico Karen's Koffee Kup, the special of the day being Iced Caramel Mocha Frappuccino. While I lapped up the calorie-laden thing, I perused a copy of the *Las Vegas Sun* someone had so kindly left on the reading rack. A story on B-2 informed me that a new casino had opened in Vegas, this one with a Wild West theme; it featured daily reenactments of the shootout at the OK Corral at two, Indian attacks at six.

The Vegas newspaper reminded me of Ike Donohue's odd phone calls. Since Donohue had remained successfully employed by the Black Basin Mine right up until the day of his murder, I decided he probably wasn't addicted to booze or drugs. Maybe he gambled.

After finishing my Frappuccino I resumed questioning the proud members of the Walapai Flats Chamber of Commerce, but my luck never improved. Everyone assured me the uranium mine wouldn't make the town or the Grand Canyon radioactive, and tsk tsk, wasn't that fuss at the demonstration a shame? It was all the fault of those nasty environmentalists. The old woman's picket sign? Sorry, no clue. By three I gave up. I walked back to my Trailblazer and headed for the Gas-N-Go, where I caught Earl Two Horses clearing away litter by one of the pumps.

I rolled my window down. "Hey, Earl. Got a minute?"

"If you're a customer."

My gas tank remained three-quarters full, so while Earl dumped the litter into a trash receptacle, then walked toward the store, I pulled the Traiblazer over to the parking area. Steeling myself for more obstruction, I followed him. Except for the clerk at the cash register, a middle-aged woman with harlequin eyeglasses and old-fashioned beehive, the store was empty. When Earl said something to her I couldn't hear, she smiled and grabbed her purse.

"See you tomorrow, then," she said, getting up. "Oh, I forgot to tell you earlier, the Hostess delivery guy called and…"

They discussed a delayed shipment of Twinkies as I wandered through the store. It was a lot like the Circle K's in Phoenix, with a little of this, a little of that. I picked up a Diet Coke, a bag of vinegar potato chips, and two Slim Jims to tide me over until dinner. When the clerk finally left, I took my purchases to the counter.

"There was an anti-mining demonstration in town yesterday," I said. "Why didn't you go over to root for your side, whichever side that is?"

"Too busy working." He made a big show of counting the money in the till.

"Good turnout, even the New York media was there."

"New York's a big city." More counting.

"Eight million people, I hear. Did you know one of their reporters is covering the Black Basin Mine opening?"

"No such thing as bad publicity."

"Even when it's about opening a uranium mine near a town that relies so heavily on tourism? Please, Earl. All I want to do is help Ted, but no one will tell me anything. I was hoping that since he's your friend…"

My groveling opened him up somewhat. "The only thing I know about Mr. Donohue is that he bought his gas here, and sometimes milk and eggs. He used to buy cigarettes, but he stopped doing that last month."

"You know anything about his wife Nancy?"

"Fine woman, that."

"What!?"

A hint of a smile. "Do not pay so much attention to people's mouths, Miss Jones. Sometimes they just like the sounds that come out. The only real measure of a man or a woman is their actions. Now, please excuse me because I must balance my books and that is a difficult enough task in itself without holding a conversation at the same time." He started fussing with the till again.

I held my ground. "What do you know about Roger Tosches?"

"Rich. Owns the Black Basin. Sunset Canyon Lakes, too."

"That's all you know? You haven't heard any rumors about him?"

"Don't listen to rumors."

Getting a cat to sing an a cappella version of "Stairway To Heaven" was easier than getting Earl to talk, but I kept at it. "How about Mia, Tosches' wife? Know anything about her?"

"She caused trouble for Ted Olmstead."

"I heard she plays around and that her husband doesn't mind."

"You through buying stuff?"

"Why? You going to throw me out?"

"I'm thinking about it."

Gratified by the half-smile he gave me, I said, "Earl, we both want to get Ted out of the mess he's in, so tell me anything you know about the people over at Sunset Canyon Lakes." I had a sudden thought. "Or about Deputy Ronald Stark."

With that, he lost interest in the money. Framing his next words carefully, he said, "People he arrests sometimes have accidents on the way to jail."

Gee, what a surprise. "Did anyone ever lodge a complaint against him?"

"No one in Walapai Flats is that foolish."

"Do you know anything about his wife?"

"She has many accidents."

"How about the daughter?"

"The one accident's all I know of, her arm. Heard she broke it falling off a swing."

My temper rose. At him, at a town that purposely knew nothing about nothing. "Dammit, Earl, hasn't anyone around here done anything to help her and that poor kid out?"

Frustration clouded his normally stolid face. "She will not leave him. As for the little girl, someone called Child Protective Services last week and they came out and checked the home. They found no reason to investigate further."

"How do you know this happened?"

When he didn't answer, I guessed he either had contacts at the local CPS office or that he'd made the call himself. I would have pursued it further but the door opened and two teenagers came in and headed straight for the soft drinks cooler. Relief was in Earl's voice when he said, "I must get back to work now, Miss Jones. Have a nice day."

People sure were polite in Walapai Flats, even when they're telling you to get lost.

I was halfway to my Trailblazer when I remembered a statement Mia Tosches had made in passing, but that I'd taken little note of at the time. Turning on my heel, I walked back into the store and waited until Earl finished ringing up the teenagers' sales.

As soon as they left, I said, "I was told you're half Navajo on your father's side."

He didn't look up. "My father was Chester Two Horses of the Bitter Water People."

"I was also told your father worked at the Moccasin Peak Mine."

"It is an honorable thing for a man to support his family."

"He died there, didn't he?"

Earl's silence lasted so long I thought he wasn't going to answer, but after he finished counting the money in the till and making a note in the record book next to it, he closed the cash drawer and looked at my right ear. That as was close as a Navajo would come to looking you in the eye.

"Yes, Miss Jones. And yes, he died of lung cancer."

Once back in my SUV, I sat there digesting what I'd learned. Earl was bitter, and rightly so, because the man who was at least partially responsible for his father's death was now opening another mine. True, Roger Tosches had brought a new partner on board, a man who on the surface, at least, was of shining reputation, but what difference did it make when Tosches would still call the shots?

It was time to take a look at the root cause of so much dissention. From the descriptions I'd been given, the Black Basin Uranium Mine was located fifteen miles southeast of town, tucked between a series of rocky crags pretending to be mountains. It could have been a rough trip, but a series of signs provided directions, and the wide, smooth road to the mine was a miracle of modern engineering, the better to move heavy equipment. When at last I crested a double-humped hill and saw the activity below me, I was astounded.

A fence ringing the entire valley floor enclosed a collection of massive earth-moving machines, each sporting red, white, and blue streamers attached to various appendages. One vehicle was like something out of a nightmare, a monstrous edifice the size of a three-story building. It had a crane-like extension from which jutted a circular series of blades, making the thing resemble a pinwheel designed in Hell. This was the bucket wheel excavator, the bane of ecologists everywhere. Even the American flag waving atop its roof couldn't lessen its terror.

An army of men wearing hard hats swarmed around the machines like acolytes attending to pagan gods. Less nightmarish were the workers nearest me. They were building the stage for the opening day ceremony and setting up big, stadium-style grandstands. As I drove closer to them with the windows of the Trailblazer rolled down, I heard whistling and singing. It sounded like they were happy to have jobs.

Somewhere in the midst of all this hustle and bustle would be the original mine shaft, the exploratory hole dug months earlier that proved the uranium deposit was rich enough to make this enormous expense worthwhile. I thought I saw the entrance peeking out from behind the bucket wheel excavator, but couldn't be certain. In a few months, the shaft, the surrounding hills, and most of the valley would have disappeared, replaced by a crater at least a hundred feet deep. Whatever witches brew lay hidden below would be accessed by roads spiraling down from the valley floor, making the resulting configuration resemble an upside-down wedding cake—if the cake was a half-mile across.

How much would all this cost? Millions? Roger Tosches had already spared no expense in getting ready to dig his big hole in the ground, hoping that the return would far eclipse the start-up costs. No wonder he'd hired PR slickster Ike Donohue to refute the claims of Kimama Olmstead and the members of Victims of Uranium Mining. His entire fortune must be riding on the mine's success.

After responding to a few friendly waves from the workers, I followed the road away from the party planners around to the opposite side of the valley, where I came to a closed gate that warned, URANIUM MINE: DANGER. So much for the assurances of the Walapai County Chamber of Commerce. In case visitors couldn't read, two black-clad guards armed with assault rifles stood in front of the gate. To their side lurked a matching black Hummer. When I stepped out of the Trailblazer, one guard raised his rifle and the other—the larger of the two—walked toward me looking no less dangerous. His AR-15 was pointed at the ground.

"This area is closed to visitors," he said. "Move along."

In my best dither, I said, "Oh, I was just out for a drive and decided it would be nice to see everything before it gets too crowded, officer." I'd added the title merely to flatter him. Most rent-a-cops wanted to be police officers but a large number of them couldn't pass the physical and mental requirements, let alone the background checks.

Big-and-Mean was impervious to flattery. "This ain't no museum."

Behind him, Almost-As-Big-and-Mean laughed. At least he had a sense of humor.

"I know, I know. It's going to be a uranium mine, but I've heard so much about the Black Basin, can't I take a peek?" Little Miss Blonde, that was me, driving around, admiring the scenery, totally harmless.

"How'd you like a rifle barrel up your ass?" Big-and-Mean shifted his assault rifle into ramming position.

Almost-As-Big-and-Mean laughed again.

My charms having failed, I said, "Well, it's sure been nice meeting you fellas."

I got the hell out of there.

Having spent much of the afternoon running around in the heat, it was a relief to get back to my air-conditioned motel room. Toweling off after a quick shower, I remembered that I still hadn't discovered the meaning of that mysterious picket sign: *Hasn't Walapai County suffered enough?* Not knowing the elderly woman's name, I couldn't ask her, but I could ask the person who'd chased after her when the demonstration turned into a riot. Olivia Eames.

As I picked up the nightstand phone to punch in the reporter's number, I noticed the message light blinking.

"Ted's attorney emailed me a copy of Ike Donohue's autopsy, and we need to talk," Jimmy's voice alerted me. "It includes a big surprise, something I'd prefer not to discuss over the phone, so why don't you swing by here as soon as you get back? I'm still following up on that other information you asked for, too."

Since the conversation with Olivia would be the shorter one, I called her first. Her phone rang six times before she picked up, and when she did, her voice sounded fogged

When I told her what I wanted, she said, "The elderly woman who got knocked down? Yeah, I interviewed her, but girl, you've…you've picked a…a crappy time to call. I've got one of my damned migraines and the medication's just now ki… kicking in. Jesus, here it comes. Wow, this is some s…serious shit. Call me b-back tomorrow and I'll give you her name and phone number. Bye, 'til…whatever."

The rattle and bang on the other side of the line told me she'd dropped her cell. I waited to make certain she was all right, heard her mutter to herself, then another rattle as she picked it up with a final imprecation.

Dial tone.

Jimmy's motel was within walking distance, especially if you're as fit as I am, but when I opened the door, the afternoon remained so hot I elected to drive over in my lovely air-conditioned rental. When I arrived, he took his own sweet time answering my knock, leaving me broiling on his doorstep. When he did finally make it to the door, he was barefoot and shirtless, and his shoulder-length black hair was wet. Good lord, no wonder the man was a chick magnet. With his perfectly formed pecs and abs, he looked like something on the cover of a romance novel.

Startled at the bronze expanse of chest set off by low-slung jeans, I blurted, "When did you start working out?"

"About fifteen years ago," he answered wryly. "Don't tell me this is the first time you've noticed."

Face flaming, I entered his room. It was damp and smelled like soap. "So what's the big surprise with Donohue's autopsy? And would you please put on some clothes?"

Without a word, he padded over to the closet and grabbed a rust-colored tee shirt that proclaimed ILLEGAL IMMIGRATION BEGAN IN 1492. When he slipped it on, he was damp enough from his shower that it clung to his torso. He still looked half-naked.

"Better?"

"Infinitesimally." Averting my eyes from his gloriousness, I studied the room.

It was no Covered Wagons. The walls were green-colored cement blocks, and neither the orange tweed carpeting nor the rose-and-purple paisley bedspread matched them. Given Jimmy's usual sensitivity to his surroundings, I wondered how he could stand it. He'd made the best of the situation, though, placing his laptop on a spindly table. It was in "rest" mode, and the screen-saver, a portrait of Sitting Bull, drifted peacefully by.

"So what's the big news you couldn't tell me over the phone?" I asked.

He sat down next to me, tapped a couple of keys, and Sitting Bull vanished. "Ted's attorney emailed me the autopsy report on Ike Donohue, and it turns out that his killer did him a favor. The poor guy had advanced lung cancer and it'd metastasized to his spine. He must have been in horrific pain."

This changed everything. "Is there a possibility he committed suicide?"

"Nope. The killer was standing at least five feet away, as much as eight."

In Nancy Donohue's conversation with me, she had attributed her husband's behavior to the effects of nicotine withdrawal on a body already stressed by Type 2 diabetes, not the pain of end-stage lung cancer. By the time Donohue had sworn off cigarettes, it had been nothing more than a futile attempt to stave off the inevitable. The autopsy explained something else that had been bothering me, too. Like some terminally ill people, Donohue had tried to right his wrongs in order to die with a clear conscience, thus the advice to a friend's granddaughter to stop smoking.

This line of thought brought about two intriguing possibilities. Donohue, in his attempt to make peace with his Maker, might have reopened one too many old wounds and gotten killed for it. On the other hand, maybe his wife, who knew her way around firearms, had played Jack Kevorkian. Was the "murder" actually a mercy killing? One that might even garner her a higher insurance settlement than death by natural causes?

"Lena? You've got a strange look on your face."

"I'm thinking this case just got a lot more complicated."

"You can see why I didn't want to discuss this over a phone. Well, I still have more research to do, so…" Having delivered the polite Pima version of *Get lost!* he bent over his laptop and started typing.

Before driving back to my own motel, I sat in the Desert View's parking lot for a few minutes, thinking about the peculiar relationships between husbands and wives as the Trailblazer's air conditioning chased away the heat. At what point did married people share moral responsibility for their spouse's immoral lives? If you knew you were married to a war criminal, did that make you guilty by association? If you knew you were married to a child rapist and kept quiet about it—as my sixth foster mother had done—were you a criminal too? Or because you loved him, did you get a Get Out of Jail Free card?

At what point does love become a crime?

Because Ike Donohue had been the mouthpiece for a tobacco company, some moral sticklers might claim he'd led a wicked life, but to give the devil his due, Donohue was a smoker himself. Near the end, he was at least trying to play catch-up in the ethics arena. Nancy, however…

When I pondered this conundrum, a rust-eaten 1997 Chevy with Utah plates pulled up next to my Trailblazer. It disgorged three screaming children and a careworn woman with a lit cigarette hanging from her mouth. She looked old enough to be the children's grandmother, but judging from her twenty-something leggings and ultra-short skirt, she was probably their mother. Her mouse-colored hair was faded but not gray, and as yet no wrinkles had appeared around her stunned-looking eyes. An old man, his face liver-spotted and gaunt, remained in the front passenger's seat. He was smoking, too.

The results of Ike Donohue's public relations efforts?

Before Parking Lot Woman reached the motel office, the smallest of her children, a girl wearing a lacy pink dress, tripped and fell over a curbing. Instead of getting up, she simply lay on her side howling. With an expression of infinite patience, the woman picked the child up and nuzzled her hair. Because my window was rolled up to keep the heat at bay, I couldn't make out what she said, but the child stopped sobbing, gulped once, and gave her mother a kiss on the cheek. Parking Lot Woman kissed back, and with that, the quartet vanished into the motel office.

Once the Trailblazer had cooled to a comfortable tempera- ture, I began backing out of my space. Before I made it, two of the children I'd seen earlier burst from the motel office followed by their haggard mother, who was still carrying the little girl. She waved a single key at the elderly man; the entire gang was going to share one room. With two adults puffing away, I didn't want to think about those children's lungs. Balancing the girl on her hip, the woman unlocked the door next to Jimmy's room and ushered her rambunctious brood inside, then returned to the car and tenderly helped the old man out of his seat and into the room. Before closing the door behind them, she tossed the stub of her still-lit cigarette out onto the pavement. Then she put the little girl down and lit another cigarette, inhaling deeply while she watched the traffic go by on John Wayne Boulevard.

If I live to be a hundred and twenty, I'll never understand people.

That thought reminded me to make a phone call, so I pulled forward back into my parking space and punched a number on my cell phone. Nancy Donohue picked up immediately. She didn't sound pleased.

"You again, Jones. This is getting tiresome."

"I'm sure it is, so I'll be as brief as possible. Did you know your husband was ill?"

"I told you, you ninny. Ike was a Type 2 diabetic, and Lord, was that man a whiner. You'd think he was the only person in the world to ever come down with something. Me, my arthritis is flaring up but I don't go around whining about it."

Instead, you take out your discomfort on everyone you know. Aloud, I said, "I'm talking about the other thing."

"Oh, for heaven's sake, what other thing, Jones? Make it snappy, because I have places to go and people to see."

Maybe she didn't know the truth about her husband's health. Nancy wasn't the type of person a dying man would open his heart to, so he might have kept her in the dark while he scurried around, trying to right his wrongs.

In case I was wrong about everything, I said with as much compassion as I could muster, "Nancy, the autopsy results on your husband have come back, and the medical examiner found something you should know about."

"Like what? Syphilis?" The old harridan actually laughed. "Wouldn't surprise me, given those times Ike stayed out all night. VD, or STD, or whatever PC bullshit they're calling the wages of sin these days. Serves him right. If it was the clap or whatever, I'll dance on the cheating bastard's grave. Then I'll get my own ass checked."

There was no gentle way to say it. "Your husband didn't have a sexually transmitted disease, Nancy. He had end-stage lung cancer."

Now her laughter sounded forced. "Don't be ridiculous. Granted, the fool huffed and puffed all the time like the big bad wolf, but that was because he was dumb enough to smoke three packs a day. His problem, not mine. But dying? What kind of fool do you take me for?"

"No fool, Nancy, just a woman whose husband didn't tell her everything. Look, if you want to talk to the medical examiner yourself, I have his phone number. It's…"

She slammed the phone down, almost deafening me.

A couple of hours later, when I called Jimmy to see if he wanted to meet for dinner at Ma's Kitchen, he declined, saying that he was still working.

"It doesn't help, having the family from Hell bunked down next door. The kids have been screaming nonstop. The noise is so bad I knocked on their door to see if someone was getting killed, but they were simply running around, shooting off cap guns. Happy as clams, if clams are happy. The mother invited me in for a game of Monopoly, but I declined. Say, if you want, you can come over here and share some pizza. I've already ordered out, but there's probably enough for two."

"What kind of pizza?"

"Cheese, ham, onions, pineapple, and anchovies."

Pineapple, anchovies, and screaming kids: not a good combination. "I'll pass, but tomorrow morning, say, around seven, let's meet at Ma's for breakfast. Afterwards we can see if the jail's still on lockdown because I have more questions for Ted. I want to see the sheriff, too, and make certain Deputy Smiley Face turned in his report on that shooting. Along with the bullets and cartridges."

He made a disgusted sound. "Sure would be bad if it got lost in the system, wouldn't it? In the meantime, promise me you won't go driving around alone in the desert."

"See you at breakfast, partner. Eight sharp."

"Lena! You didn't pro…"

"No, I didn't, did I?" With that, I hung up.

After a quick steak dinner at The Stagecoach, I returned to my room and tried to read the Sue Grafton novel I'd begun, but my mind refused to focus. Unbidden, it harkened back to my conversation with Earl Two Horses about Detective Smiley Face's abused wife and daughter. In a perfect world, a loving mother would have long ago rescued both herself and her child, but past experience with battered women told me she'd stay until someone got killed. Maybe her, maybe the child, maybe…You can't expect common sense from abused women. They were like battle-weary soldiers suffering from post traumatic stress syndrome: they either let the beatings continue or went crazy themselves.

Not feeling hopeful, I picked up the Sue Grafton novel again, but a half hour later I was still on the page I'd started. I gave up on the literary world and clicked on the TV. A few rounds of channel surfing turned up little more than news accounts of the latest terrorist attacks or so-called reality shows that featured snotty, over-dressed, overly made-up women pretending they were Beverly Hills housewives. After opting for pay-for-view, I watched a cadre of zombies sweep across the White House lawn. One wore a straw hat emblazoned with a red, white, and blue hatband that read DONALD TRUMP FOR PRESIDENT. As they staggered up the steps, I finally drifted off.

The pine-scented night air closed around me as I became aware of pain in my hands. My four-year-old self was back at the mine entrance, clawing away the last board that covered it.

Behind me, my mother said, "Oh, honey, look at your hands. They're bleeding."

When I turned around, I saw she was bleeding, too, but her wound was in her right temple where the bullet had struck her.

"Does it hurt?" I asked.

She didn't answer, just drew me to her in a hug. "Shhhh, now. We must be quiet or Abraham will find us. And you know what Abraham does to children."

At the name, I clutched her tighter. "Will he hurt me like he did the other kids?"

She started to answer, but then I heard more gunshots.

"They're closer," my mother said. "Do you trust me?"

I nodded. Of course I trusted my mother. Didn't every little girl?

She kissed me on the forehead, and said, "I'll always love you, Tina." With that, she shot me in the face, then kicked me in the stomach. I fell backwards into the mineshaft to join the other dead children.

I was still falling when the sound of my own moans woke me. I didn't get back to sleep until around three, but even then I tossed and turned. When the phone at my bedside rang at six forty-five, I was almost glad for an excuse to crawl out of bed.

"'Lo?" I mumbled, still half-asleep.

It was Jimmy. "Ted's getting released!"

That happy news worked better than a good night's sleep. "What happened? I asked, fully alert.

"Dad called, said he was going down to the police station this morning to turn himself in."

"Your dad confessed to killing Ike Donohue!?"

"No, no, the other guy, he confessed everything. I'm only telling you what Dad told me when he called."

"What other guy? I'm confused, Jimmy. Take a deep breath, slow down, and begin at the beginning."

He tried, but he was so excited he made little sense. "It was the cook who killed him. The cook at Dad's ranch. He'd been out of town for a funeral and didn't get back until late last night, didn't even know anybody was in custody until he started making breakfast this morning. That's when Dad told him about Ted and the whole murder thing, while he was chopping up potatoes for the home fries. I mean, the cook was chopping up the potatoes, not Dad. As soon as he, the cook, heard Ted was in jail, he put the knife down and told Dad everything, that he shot Donohue. Then he went and finished making breakfast, can you believe it? He's on his way to the police station to confess. Dad called Ted's attorney, and he's driving in from Silver Ridge right now to file some legal papers. I don't know exactly what they are, but they're supposed to be able to help get Ted released and Dad said…"

I listened while he babbled on in a stream-of-consciousness that would have made James Joyce proud. When he finally ran down, I said, "Let's see if I've got this right. The cook at Sunset Trails killed Ike Donohue and he's turning himself in."

"Isn't that what I said?"

"In a roundabout way. Why did the cook kill Donohue?"

"Didn't I say?"

"No, Jimmy, you didn't."

"He said he murdered his wife."

Damn the English language. "Who killed who's wife?"

Speaking more slowly, Jimmy said, "The cook said Donohue killed his—the cook's—wife."

Ran her down in his car, maybe, when he was lit to the gills? Strange, because the background check Jimmy had run on Donohue hadn't revealed any brushes with the law.

"Tell you what," I said. "I'll meet you at the jail in an hour. By the way, what's his name?"

"The cook's?"

I laughed. The brightness of Jimmy's joy had chased away the dark terrors of my night. "Yes, Jimmy, the cook. Donohue's murderer. What's his name?"

"Oh. It's Boone. Gabe Boone."

Chapter Sixteen

No one was thrilled to see us at the county complex. The jail's lockdown had been lifted the night before, but the fact that Hank Olmstead brought in a man who confessed to killing Ike Donohue left the harried deputies little time to schmooze. After announcing ourselves to the officer manning the front desk, we joined Olmstead on a bench in the lobby. Now that freedom for Ted was at hand, his adoptive father looked ten years younger. The worry had disappeared from his eyes, and the slump that had detracted from his six-foot-plus height was gone. He sat close to Jimmy, and for once, didn't speak to his son with an edge in his voice. Joy was as strong a bonding agent as grief.

"Shouldn't Ted's attorney already be here?" I asked. "I'd hate to think…"

The sound of doors slamming down the hall drew our attention. From the direction of the sheriff's offices, voices shouted back and forth. At the same time, phones began ringing non-stop.

"What's happening?" Jimmy asked, rising from his seat.

"Wait here!" Olmstead ordered. He walked over to a group of deputies assembled near the information desk. After a brief conversation, he returned shaking his head. "Something's up, but they're being tight-lipped about it."

I hoped it didn't have anything to do with Ted. Terrible things could happen to a man in jail. My concern faded when seconds later the deputies charged out the door so fast they almost knocked over portly Anderson Behar, who was entering the complex with his over-stuffed briefcase.

"Wow, where's the fire?" the attorney asked.

Olmstead shook Behar's hand. "No fire that I know of, Anderson, but it was very kind of you to drive here so early."

"Glad to do it since I'm double-billing you for it." At the look on Olmstead's face, Behar winked. "Joke, Hank. Joke."

Behar rested his heavy briefcase on the bench, opened it, and rifled through his paper collection. After pulling out a blue-covered packet, he took it to the duty officer, who picked up his phone and punched in a number. The deputy said a few words to the person on the other end, then waved the attorney down the corridor toward the sheriff's office. Olmstead attempted to follow but the deputy told him to sit down.

"Theodore's my son," Olmstead grumbled, returning to the bench. "I can't imagine why the sheriff won't see me, too."

I could. Over the past few days, I'd learned that if there was any possible way to complicate a situation, Olmstead would find it. Given his prickly personality, how he managed to run a successful tourism business was beyond me. But his behavior did explain why Jimmy had such a talent for getting along with problem people; he'd had plenty of practice.

Less than ten minutes later, Behar was back, a strange expression on his face.

"What's wrong?" Olmstead asked.

Behar shook his head. "Nothing, as far as Ted's concerned. I found out what that commotion was all about, though. It'll speed up his release, since he has an iron-clad alibi for this one. As soon as the courthouse opens up, I'll deliver these papers to the clerk, get an emergency hearing, and that'll do 'er. Ted should be released by the end of the day, if not earlier. Relax, Hank. It's a good news day. For some people, anyway."

"I don't want to wait that long before I see him," Olmstead carped.

"You won't have to. A detention officer will be out here any minute to take us in. But only you and I were cleared."

Jimmy looked disappointed at not being able to see his brother right away, but settled back down on the bench without a fuss. I was less sanguine. "Mr. Behar, you said something about Ted having an iron-clad alibi for 'this one.' What did you mean 'this one'?"

Behar glanced around to see if anyone was listening, but the only deputy remaining in the lobby was the man at the front desk, who was leafing through a magazine. "Well, the sheriff didn't swear me to silence, so I guess I can tell you. The whole town will know soon enough, anyway. It appears there's been another high-profile death."

I immediately thought of Officer Smiley Face's battered wife and child. "A domestic?"

"No, no." To Olmstead, he said, "Hank, I'm pretty sure you know the dead man. It's Roger Tosches, the man who owns the new mine and that big resort."

The color drained from Olmstead's face, but his voice betrayed no emotion. "We were acquainted, yes."

"What happened?" I asked Behar.

"The sheriff told me that Mr. Tosches' body was found on that long gravel road leading to Sunset Trails." He frowned. "Hank, you saw nothing, ah, unusual on your way here?"

"If I had, I would have reported it," Olmstead answered.

Behar got that look lawyers get when they're not certain their clients are telling the truth. "Maybe you were distracted."

Olmstead frowned.

The attorney pretended not to notice. "Anyway, that's where all those deputies are headed, to your ranch. If you ask me, it seems like a pretty heavy response to something that might have been an accident, but maybe that's the way they handle things around here. I asked the sheriff if it was a car accident and he said no, that the cause of death had not been determined."

That's what law officials always say, even if a big butcher knife is sticking out of the corpse's chest.

"And Hank?" Behar continued, sounding worried. "Considering that whatever it was happened on ranch property, prepare yourself to be questioned. Make sure you don't talk to them unless I'm with you, understand?" Spoken like a halfway decent criminal attorney.

Olmstead looked affronted. "Why would they want to talk to me?"

His determined obtuseness made me want to shake him. Olmstead would have driven down that road on the way to the jail this morning. How could he have failed to see a dead man lying in the road? Perhaps the attorney had confused the word "near" with the word "on" and Tosches' body wasn't actually on the road. Maybe it was off to the side, hidden in a creosote thicket.

"Mr. Behar, did the sheriff give any indication of when the body was found or how long it might have been lying there?"

When the attorney shook his head, Olmstead began to look worried. For his sake, I hoped Tosches had dropped dead of a simple heart attack—after Olmstead had walked through the county complex doors.

Making my excuses, I left them waiting to see Ted and took off for Sunset Trails Ranch.

When I pulled to the shoulder of the blacktop, I saw wooden sawhorses and crime tape blocking the turnoff to the ranch. If lookey-loos didn't get the message, a sheriff's cruiser, blue lights flashing, was parked behind them. Several more cruisers, an ambulance, and a farrier's truck were parked about a hundred yards further down. Just beyond was a black Mercedes, nose pointed toward the distant lodge. A dark lump lay near next to the car. If Tosches had been there when Olmstead and the cook left for the jail, they'd need to swerve around him before continuing on. There was no way, simply no way, they could have missed him.

As I exited the Trailblazer, a deputy emerged from the nearest cruiser and swaggered up to me. Officer Smiley Face, wearing those spooky mirrored sunglasses. He wasn't smiling today. In fact, Deputy Stark looked downright tense.

"Move along, Miss Jones. There's nothing to see here." A tic pulled at the corner of his mouth.

"What happened?"

"Nothing to do with you. Get into your car and go on back to town before I arrest you for interfering with a crime scene."

Crime scene. *Thanks for the information, you dim bulb.* I tried for another slipup. "I was at the jail when the call came in that Tosches had been shot. Anybody know the caliber of the bullet?"

"Being a hot-shot former police officer, you should know we have to wait for ballistics testing on that."

So he was shot. "Not if any shell casings were left lying around, like when someone shot at me."

The nervous tic disappeared, replaced by a sneer as he spread his legs and put his hands on his hips in the "I dare you" position. Inching his right hand down to the top of his holster, he growled, "Return to your car!"

Realizing he'd like nothing more than to whack me across the face with his Glock, I backed off. When I drove away, I saw in my rear view mirror that he was still watching me through those mirrored sunglasses.

Several hundred yards from the barricade, the blacktop curved around a rock ridge. The second I was out of the deputy's sightline, I pulled to the side of the road and called Jimmy. "Is your dad near by?" I asked when he answered.

"Sure is. Why?"

"Move away so he can't hear you."

When he spoke next, he'd lowered his voice. "Okay, I'm on the other side of the room. Dad's really worried about the Tosches thing. Behar told him…"

I cut him off. "Is there another way to reach the lodge or is that gravel road the only way in?"

"Lena, Dad says…"

I interrupted again. "Whatever kind of meltdown he's having, fill me in when we meet up later because right now I need to get to the ranch before the detectives do. Tosches was shot to death on ranch property, so answer my question." I hated to talk to my partner like that, but time was a-wasting.

A grunt. "I know what I'm getting you for Christmas: a course in etiquette. But since you're acting like a jackrabbit with its tail on fire, there's a dirt trail along the river where the wranglers take the guests riding. It crosses the highway about two miles west of the road to the ranch. The terrain's pretty rough, better for horses than cars, but your Trailblazer should be able to navigate the worst spots. Frankly, I don't understand the rush. Shooting or not, the lodge is a whole mile from the turnoff, so I doubt if anyone there knows anything."

"If they do, I want to find out before the cops tell them to keep their mouths shut." I ended the call.

The river trail wasn't hard to find, and Jimmy hadn't exaggerated its difficulty. So many big rocks were scattered along it that the average vehicle would have bottomed out, but with the Trailblazer's high clearance I bumped over most of them with no trouble. Once I had to veer off-road and onto a steep incline to skirt a Volkswagen-sized boulder that turned the trail into a one-horse lane, but the Trailblazer handled the incline with dispatch. Past the boulder, the trail widened again, and within minutes I was pulling into the ranch's parking area.

There's nothing more wonderful than a ranch in the morning. A rooster crowed, hens clucked, and cactus wrens sang their tiny hearts out. Over in the corral, horses whinnied while the wranglers tacked them up. As I stepped away from the Trailblazer, the same blue-eyed heeler I'd met the other day came barking up to me, eyes sparkling, tail wagging.

"Hello there, big fella," I said, stooping to pat his head.

He gifted me with a wet slurp across the face.

"Don't kiss and tell," I warned. With the dog at my heels, I walked toward the lodge. As luck would have it, the first person I ran into was Dusty. The handsome devil stood near the steps, looking great in his ass-hugging Levis.

I hardened my heart. "Good morning, Dusty. If you're expecting customers, you can forget it."

"Lena?!" He stared at me in shock. A master of the quick recovery, he walked toward me, arms spread wide.

I took three steps back. Not far enough back, however, that I couldn't smell soap and Brut. "Has anyone other than Hank Olmstead and the cook left the ranch this morning?"

"Lena, honey…"

"I'm not your honey. Did you hear what I asked?"

He shook his Stetson-hatted head. It was old and ragged, but he made it look good. "I don't know because I've spent most of my time in the corral getting the horses ready for a trail ride. I can't see anyone driving off into town yet, it's too early. Leilani doesn't do the shopping until around ten. But Lena, honey…" He started toward me again.

I held up my hand to keep him away. "If you're thinking of picking up where we left off, cowboy, forget it. You cheated on me, your new wife shot up my apartment, our relationship tanked, end of story."

Responding to my harsh tone, the blue-eyed dog began to whine. So did Dusty.

"But Lena, babe, I got an annulment, and you know how much I lo…"

"Don't call me babe, either. Roger Tosches was shot to death on the ranch road, right at the highway turnoff. The road is crawling with cops."

It was Dusty's turn to take a couple of steps back. In the silence that followed, the dog, apparently deciding that he no longer wanted to be part of the conversation, took off toward the corral and the sweeter company of horses.

Dusty found his voice again. "Tosches? Shot to death? You can't be serious."

"Very much so. Can you prove you didn't leave the ranch this morning? The sheriff's detectives are going to come screeching up that road any minute, Dusty, and with your background, you know they'll want to talk to you." Speeding tickets, bar fights, even one shooting. The other man had shot at him first, but it still looked bad on a police report.

He swallowed. "I got up with the rest of the wranglers—we sleep in the bunkhouse, you know—took leaks with them, showered with them, ate breakfast with them, saddled up with them…Hell, I haven't spent a damned second alone."

The relief I felt made me wonder if my feelings for him were as dead as I'd hoped. "Anyone else disappear during that time? One of the other wranglers? A maid? Maybe a ranch guest?"

"The other guys were as busy as me. The maids don't show until ten, and none of them's arrived early that I know of. As for the guests, we wranglers don't eat with them so I have no way of knowing where they were or whatever the hell they were doing. Most of the time, I don't even see them until they show up for their morning ride, which is now. We've got twelve horses saddled up and ready to go, but so far only ten riders, all guests. The other two are supposed to be driving in from Sunset Canyon Lakes. Or were. With the road being blocked, I guess the ride count stays at ten. If the cops let us ride out at all, that is."

At Dusty's mention of a possibly cancelled ride, I realized that Tosches' murder, following so quickly after Donohue's, could be a financial disaster for the ranch. There was nothing I could do about that, so I continued my questioning. "What about the family? Did any of them besides Hank leave the ranch?"

"Forget the family. They all live in the house out back. Most of them can't drive, anyway, and they certainly don't have access to weapons. You do know that they're, ah, disabled, don't you? Joyce and Pat, Mr. Olmstead's sisters, help take care of them."

"Did either sister leave the ranch?"

"Jesus, Lena, I'm not a baby-sitter. How would I know? The house's location kind of limits spying, anyway. It's behind that rise, way back in the cottonwoods."

"Did you hear any gunshots this morning?"

He gave me a pitying look. "I hear gunshots every morning. In case you haven't noticed, this is big game country."

Deputy Smiley Face had said as much the day before. Studying Dusty's blue eyes for any sign of evasiveness, I asked, "How well did you know Mia Tosches? I hear she comes out here to ride."

Those wonderful blue eyes sidled, first to the left, then the right. "Only to say hi to, that's all."

"Ever ball her?"

"Lena, your language!"

Oh, these men, with their philandering ways and lying eyes, expecting their own wives and girlfriends to be ignorant, faithful, and clean-mouthed. But Dusty wasn't my boyfriend any more. That was a road long since traveled, and I wouldn't be taking the trip again.

"C'mon, Dusty, you've never let a piece like that—excuse me, a *woman* like that—walk by without making a run at it."

"You can be so crass." At least his eyeballs stopped twitching. "All right, all right. We had ourselves a fling, nothing more than that. Her husband sure as hell didn't mind."

"She told you that?"

He looked up at the sky, as if imploring the heavens to come to his aid. They didn't. "Kind of."

I enjoyed watching the son of a bitch squirm. "Out with it, cowboy."

"She, uh, she invited me up to her place to have dinner with her and her husband, said that she'd told him all about our, uh, liaison, and that he was interested in meeting me. Then she said that after dinner we could all, um, I believe the phrase she used was 'get to know each other better,' and it was damned clear what she meant." Seeing my face, he added, "Look, I may not be Percy Pureheart, but three-ways have never been my thing. I told her I wasn't interested and that was that. I never saw the little freak again."

It was seedy enough to be the truth. Tosches was kinky and so was Mia; two peas in a nasty little pod. Realizing there was nothing more I would get from Dusty—nothing I wanted, anyway—I decided to go in search of Leilani. Before starting up the lodge steps, I asked him another question. "What do you know about the cook?"

"Gabe? He's a real stand-up guy. There's gossip going around the ranch this morning that's he confessed to killing Ike

Donohue, but that can't be right. Gabe may have his eccentricities, but he wouldn't hurt a fly."

Every murderer I've known had been described by at least one person as possessing the inability to harm our winged friends. "How long's he been working here?"

"Can't help you there, 'cause he was here when I signed on last year. He's a damn fine cook, too."

I'd leave the cops to worry about the cook; he wasn't my problem. Right now, Dusty was. But I hadn't taken my leave from him quickly enough. Before I could duck out of the way, he crossed the space between us and slithered his cheating arms around me.

"Honey, I've done a lot of thinking and I realize how badly I treated you and I think we should…"

"No, we shouldn't." I disentangled myself and bounded up the steps to the lodge.

The smell of breakfast bacon lingered in the air as I walked through the dining area and down the hall to the office, where I found an attractive Polynesian woman sitting at Olmstead's desk, working on a laptop covered with daisy stickers. She was around twenty, with her long black hair gathered into a perky ponytail by a yellow ribbon. Her Western-style blouse was the same yellow. Even the nametag spelling out LEILANI had been printed on a yellow background. When she saw me, her smile became as sunny as her outfit.

"Hi, there," I said, smiling back. "I'm Lena Jones. We've talked on the phone."

When she stood up to extend her hand, the brace on her left leg clanked. "Oh, Miss Jones, we are so grateful for the help you've given Ted. You and Jimmy kept his hopes alive until poor old Gabe confessed."

In the face of such cheer I hated to bring her down but it was necessary. "The police haven't been here yet, have they?"

That beautiful smile vanished. "What's wrong? Did Gabe change his mind about confessing? I can't believe he could kill anyone, but Dad said…"

"Leilani, this isn't about your cook. Roger Tosches was found shot to death this morning on the road to your ranch."

Stunned, she sat back down. "First Mr. Donohue, then Mr. Tosches. What in the world is going on?"

"I don't know, but that's why I'm here, to find out as much as I can." I almost added *So Tosches' murder doesn't blow back on your family like Donohue's did. If your Dad goes to prison, Jimmy might never return to Desert Investigations. With his strong sense of loyalty, he might feel obligated to stay and help run the ranch, and Leilani, I can't let that happen.* I kept my fears to myself. After bringing her up to date on the morning's events, I asked, "Did any of the guests or anyone else you know of leave the ranch after your Dad drove Mr. Boone into town?"

"I…I…" She took a deep breath. "As soon as Dad and Gabe left for the sheriff's office, I came over here to check the inventory so I could figure out what supplies to pick up in town and what to order online, so I have no idea who was here or not. Dusty might. Did you ask him?" At my nod, she continued. "He's the head wrangler and is pretty good at keeping tabs on who is where. We can't have our guests wandering off into the desert by themselves. City folks, they think there's a drinking fountain next to every cactus."

"How well did you know Mr. Tosches?"

"Hardly at all. Dad knew him better, and didn't much like him. As for me, I'm sorry Mr. Tosches is dead, and in such a horrible way, but he was a pest."

This was the first time I'd ever heard a gazillionaire referred to as a pest. "In what way?"

"Mr. Tosches was always trying to get Dad to sell him the ranch so he could build another one of those awful resorts. At first he simply called on the phone, but recently he'd begun dropping by in the mornings, probably hoping he'd catch Dad at a weak moment. Maybe that's what he was doing when…" She gulped. "When he got shot. Not that Dad had anything to do with it, of course."

"Of course he didn't." The thought of another Emerald City gobbling up more of the desert's natural terrain disgusted even a city dweller like me, so I could imagine Olmstead's ire. "I take it your dad refused to sell."

"Well…" She bit her lip. "The tourist business is dependent on the economy, and when the economy crashes, so do we. Things were pretty tight around here, which is what gave Mr. Tosches the idea. A couple of years ago Dad made some investments that on the surface seemed secure, but they tanked with the economy. Then our usual guests started canceling their reservations because they were in financial difficulties, too. Things were so bad, for a while I suspected Dad was giving Mr. Tosches' offer some serious thought. Ranch problems aside, medical costs were eating us up."

I glanced over my shoulder at the family photo hanging on the rear wall. Several Down syndrome kids, others with different disabilities. No wonder Olmstead had been financially strapped. "But in the end your father decided against selling?"

"Yes, thank God. Not that Mr. Tosches accepted his refusal. He just kept coming by, pestering and pestering. He finally got so pushy with Dad they had a big fight." Realizing what she'd said, she tried again. "Well, not an actual fight, an argument, that's all. Nothing violent. A couple of weeks ago I was in the kitchen talking to Gabe about breakfast supplies, and I heard Dad and Mr. Tosches shouting at each other. Then the office door slammed shut. I guess Dad was afraid the guests might overhear."

Knowing that the authorities had fingered Ted because of a simple argument, I had to wonder what they'd do if they found out about a brawl between Olmstead and Tosches. "Leilani, it might be a good idea if you don't mention any of this to the cops."

"About Mr. Tosches and Dad arguing? No chance of that!"

Given Walapai Flats' small size, I wondered how long it would take before the cops got wind of the tension between Tosches and Olmstead. "Can you tell me anything about what happened this morning, how the cook came to confess to killing Ike Donohue?"

Leilani must have been fond of Boone, because sadness draped her pretty face like a cowl. "Poor old guy, what will he do? I mean…" When she wiped at her eyes, I realized she'd begun to cry. "He…Dad…I'm not sure because it was all over before I walked over from the house this morning. I was setting up the dining room for breakfast when Dad called me into the office and told me Gabe confessed to shooting Mr. Donohue. I couldn't believe it, and I'm not sure I really do now. But Dad said it was true, that while Gabe was just about to start cooking breakfast, he—Dad—told him about Mr. Donohue getting murdered and that Ted was being held on that material witness thing. Gabe was so upset he cut himself with the knife he was holding. After he stopped the bleeding, he went back to chopping the potatoes for the home fries. While he did, he told Dad that after breakfast was over, he'd drive into Walapai Flats and confess."

"I thought Mr. Olmstead drove him in."

"Dad talked him into accepting the ride. Maybe he was afraid Gabe might change his mind at the last minute and make a run for it in that old pickup truck of his." A worry line, almost the duplicate of her adopted father's, appeared between her tear-filled eyes. "You know what? I would never have thought Gabe was the type to kill anyone. He's never raised a hand in anger, not toward anyone, not even an animal. Especially not animals. You should see him with the horses and that goofy dog of his."

Hitler was supposed to have been an animal-lover, too, and a fat lot of good that did millions of humans. Out of curiosity, I asked, "What do you know about his personal life?"

She shook her head. "He never talked about it. Dad said he used to be a wrangler, and I know he was married once because there's a picture of his wife on his bedside table. She died a long time ago and he never got over it. I think her name was Abby."

"Losing a spouse takes some men that way." I was thinking about Reverend Giblin, the best foster father I'd ever had. Thirty years after his wife's death, he still mourned her.

"There's one more thing I can tell you about Gabe and it's really cute," Leilani continued. "He's a big John Wayne fan, calls him 'the Duke,' and he knows everything there is to know about him. He even has an autographed picture of him hanging in his room. Want to see?"

Before I could say that I wasn't a fan so I'd give the show-and-tell a pass, she was clanking to the door. "Did you know Wayne made a few films right around here? Several up by St. George, Utah, too. Because of the scenery."

"Doesn't surprise me in the least," I said, following her down the hall. "Mesas, canyons, cacti—it is spectacular. By the way, when I was talking to your head wrangler he told me that your cook had his, ah, I think he called them 'eccentricities.' Is the John Wayne thing what he meant?"

The hallway was a long one, and I counted eight doors, four on each side. Each had a name plate, giving the room's name. As we passed HIGH SIERRA, Leilani said, "Eccentricities? I guess that's what…"

She let it trail off, as if she'd regretted saying anything. Then she moved lowered her voice. "It's only that, well, considering all the trouble Gabe's in now, I don't want to say anything that might make it worse. I mean, it's not like he's crazy or anything. It's…It's…Oh, heck, I might as well tell you since you'll find out about it anyway. Gabe says John Wayne's ghost visits him."

"John Wayne's ghost?" I started to laugh, but her glower stopped me.

"Usually he keeps quite about it, but every now and then he decides to quote something Wayne just told him."

"Such as?"

"Once he said, 'I like grumpy old cusses. Hope to live long enough to be one myself.' Dad said it was a quote from *Tall in the Saddle*."

A cook who talked to John Wayne. "Sounds creepy."

She shrugged. "Being in the tourist business like we are, we see creepier things than that."

Up ahead, a man and woman emerged from their room. Among their other Western accoutrements, the man's leather chaps most likely had never brushed against a horse, and the woman sparkled in rhinestone-studded designer jeans that would dig into her fanny if she ever saddled up.

"Howdy, pardners," Leilani chirped, giving them a cheery wave.

The guests howdied back.

When they were out of earshot, I asked, "Who'll cook for you now?"

"Salvador Carola, the same guy who subbed for Gabe when he was in Salt Lake City. Sal used to run a small restaurant in Walapai Flats. He's okay, but nowhere near Gabe's level. Gabe's cooking is special. He once told me his wife taught him, and that she'd been the best cook in Walapai County."

Boone's room was Spartan, fitted with a narrow bed, a night table, a rocking chair, and chest of drawers. A small VCR player rested on top of the chest, surrounded by stacks of old VHS tapes, each one a John Wayne film. The only other personal effects were the fading picture of a young woman—a pretty blonde, photographed holding a pale-eyed puppy—and an old publicity shot of the actor on the wall over the bed.

"Nice picture," I said politely. "The inscription's nice, too. 'To my good friend, Gabe Boone. Ride 'em, cowboy! An admiring John Wayne.' Impressive. They actually met?"

"Gabe was one of the wranglers on the set of *The Conqueror*. I tried watching it once, and it was awful. I mean, John Wayne as Genghis Khan? Give me a break."

"Never saw it."

Men have been known to retract their confessions. If word of Olmstead's argument with Tosches leaked out and Olmstead fell under suspicion, knowing how many firearms Gabe Boone owned and where he kept them would be more important than movie trivia. And I'd seldom seen a rural Arizonan who didn't have his personal arsenal.

"Leilani, as long as we're already in here, would you mind if I poked around a bit?"

"I guess it wouldn't hurt. But don't mess up his things."

Given how few items were in the room, I saw little chance of that. A brief look in the small closet revealed that the cook held the same Spartan attitude toward clothing as he did in decor. His entire wardrobe consisted of one thick jacket, two pairs of jeans, three shirts, an old apron with a faded strawberry print, and a pair of boots ancient enough to have been worn by John Wayne himself. Only one drawer in the chest was in use, and it contained several pairs of bleached-thin boxer shorts and mismatched socks. I saw no photo albums, no letters. Leilani had mentioned that Gabe was getting on in years, which made the lack of personal items unusual. Most elderly people were weighed down with mementos, some almost to the hoarding stage. Nearing the end of their days, they wanted reminders of how much they had lived.

I squatted to look under the bed. Nothing there, not even John Wayne's ghost. "Not much on keepsakes, was he?"

"The only things Gabe owned were what you see here, plus his dog and pickup truck."

"Where's it parked?" I'd found no firearms in the room, no ammo, and no gun cleaning supplies, so it was possible he kept his armaments in his truck. In deference to the cops, I wouldn't touch, but I wanted to see.

"His truck's in back of the bunkhouse, where the wranglers keep their vehicles. You can't miss it. Sixty-seven Ford. It's red, or used to be. Probably hasn't been painted since it rolled off the assembly line."

"Does Boone have family nearby?"

"As far as I know, only that grandniece up in Salt Lake, the one who died of breast cancer. He and his wife never had any kids."

Supposedly, the cook had shot Donohue last Thursday night, left for the funeral the next morning, and didn't return until late last night. That was a full seven days, a long time to take off work.

When I pointed that out, Leilani said, "Traveling's rough on Gabe. He's eighty if he's a day. He drives into town, and sometimes around in the desert, but mainly he stays here on the ranch with his dog. That trip to Salt Lake, him driving that far—I've never seen him do it before. But he was really fond of his grandniece, talked about her almost as if she was his daughter. Maybe it's because he didn't have any kids of his own." Her eyes grew teary again. "I hope they're treating him right at the jail. I'm going to organize my schedule so I can visit him every day until I go back to school."

"That would be nice," I said. Even killers deserved visitors. I didn't relish the idea of an octogenarian in prison, but I knew all too well that anyone who's killed could kill again. Once you broke that ultimate barrier…"Leilani, do you know of any motive Boone would have for killing Donohue?"

"No, but whatever it was would have to be a pretty big reason, don't you think?"

"Not necessarily. In Phoenix awhile back, a ninety-three-year-old man living at a nursing home bashed in his roommate's head because he thought the guy's serving of apple sauce was bigger than his."

She looked appalled. "Not Gabe! He never argued with anyone. Just the opposite. He didn't talk much, so it was kind of hard to tell what he was thinking. After all these years I'm still not sure how he felt about working here because…" She shrugged. "Never mind. I guess it doesn't matter if he confessed."

Barring something unforeseen, the Donohue case was a closed book. The Tosches case, however, that was a different story. I'd stay in town until I was certain Olmstead was in the clear, but then I'd shake the Walapai Flats dust off my Reeboks and head home. I'd grown to dislike this town. Too many people with too many secrets, a town where even the cops and cooks were criminals. I was about to thank Leilani for her kindness in showing me around when a squawk of hip-hop seeped from the pocket in her denim skirt. Ludacris rapped "My Chick Bad" while she fished out her cell phone. Olmstead allowed his daughter to listen to that stuff? Maybe he was more broad-minded than I thought. Ludacris shut up when Leilani answered the phone.

As she listened to the person on the other end, the young girl disappeared, leaving in her place a competent businesswoman who wasn't afraid to make decisions. "Okay," she said briskly. "Certainly. We'd better get it over with, then, hadn't we? Send them to the office. I'm on my way there as we speak." After ending the call and tucking the phone into her pocket, she gave me a brisk smile. "That was our head wrangler telling me the police are here. They want to interview the entire staff about Mr. Tosches. They want to interview the guests, too. Looks like it's my turn to pour oil over troubled waters, so if you don't mind…"

In other words, we were done talking. I asked if it would be all right if I walked over to the house where the Olmstead family lived, since there was a possibility one of the aunts had seen something.

Still the firm young businesswoman, she shook her head. "That's impossible, I'm afraid. The Down syndrome kids—well, they're not really kids as far as their ages are concerned—they're not comfortable around strangers, so I'm going to keep the police away from them." She smiled. "You, too. Sorry.'"

I told her I understood and made my escape before she turned into her father.

The parking area for the wranglers' vehicles was large and some of the newer pickups had horse trailers attached to their bumpers. A gust of wind bearing the scent of horse manure blew over from the Virgin River as I wove my way through the Chevys, Nissans, and Toyotas to reach Boone's desiccated Ford. How the pickup had held together for a round trip to Salt Lake was a mystery, but its poor condition could explain why the cook had been gone for so long. Odds were, the truck had broken down, making him wait until the proper parts were shipped in. Looking the vehicle over, I noted that unlike most of the other vehicles in the lot, it didn't have a gun rack. When I peered through the driver's side window I saw no firearms on the floor, although a handgun could have been shoved under the seat or stowed in the glove compartment.

As I stood there thinking, another gust of wind, stronger this time, blew the sound of laughter to me. I looked toward the lodge, then at the rise that hid the Olmstead residence from view.

The few wranglers gathered around the corral were too engrossed in what they were doing to notice me. Ignoring Leilani's wishes, I walked up the rise.

When I reached the top I saw below me a ranch house surrounded by tall cottonwoods. Only the middle section appeared original. It was no more than thirty feet long and built of desert-colored adobe brick. Shaded by a veranda, it looked like one of those starter homes advertised in the real estate sections of the newspaper. To accommodate the Olmsteads' large brood, a newer wing had been added on each side, resulting in a not-unattractive U-shape. But the house, while pleasant enough, wasn't the property's main feature. The yard was.

In the Arizona badlands where properties are listed by the acreage, yards are seldom fenced. This one, which looked to be well over an acre in size, was completely enclosed by a chain link fence. It must have cost a small fortune, but I could see why the expense had been necessary. The Virgin River swept by less than five hundred yards away, and few Down syndrome people can swim.

I counted five of them playing on the most elaborate playground equipment I'd ever seen outside of a city park. Among the various toys were a swing set, two slides, some monkey bars, a foot-driven carousel, a couple of plastic wading pools, and a sandbox big enough to bury a horse in. Supervising the laughing brood were two jolly-looking women wearing jeans and tee shirts. Their faces bore a strong resemblance to Hank Olmstead's. The aunts.

As I watched, one of them jumped up and ran with arms outstretched to a young woman with an elfin face. Within seconds, everyone else joined her and began to sing and dance.

"Ring-around the rosie…"

The words of the centuries-old nursery rhyme floated to me on the river breeze. Regardless of their off-key rendition, the song lifted my heart.

Not only had Jeanette and Hank Olmstead adopted children who were too frequently passed over for adoption, they had created a veritable paradise for them. When Jeanette died, Olmstead took care their paradise didn't die with her.

As I returned to the Trailblazer, I decided it was time to reevaluate my opinion of Hank Olmstead.

Chapter Seventeen

Gabe had stayed in worse jails than the one in Walapai Flats. There'd been the jail over in Nevada, a building so old he could have kicked down his cell wall and walked away. He hadn't, though, because what difference would that make? In jail or out, he was still stuck in the same place.

Grieving for his Abby.

In his mind, she'd died only yesterday, snuggled up against him, her breath slowing, slowing, slowing, until it stopped altogether. He'd known then that his life was just as finished, even thought about going back to the ranch, picking up his rifle and sticking it in his mouth. Then he got to thinking about what John Wayne would say about that.

"A man who can't face livin' with hard times don't deserve to call himself a man," probably.

The Duke would have been right, too. Grief was something a man had to bear, no different than bearing what you were or weren't born with, just like them folks living on his and Abby's old ranch. They used to be called Mongoloids, but today the name for their condition was Down syndrome. Whatever they was called, he liked them. Hurt brains, big hearts. Funny how that worked. Sometimes the more hurt you were, the easier it was to be nice.

Looking back over all those years after Abby's death, Gabe knew he'd been the exception, because hurt as he was, he'd not been nice. Hell, he'd been downright mean there for a while, knocking over this man and that in whatever bar he happened to be drinking. Treatin' people like they was dirt. Except for women, of course, especially women who reminded him of his own sweet girl. Didn't ever do to treat a woman mean, no matter how drunk or hurt you were.

Then one day the meanness vanished. After almost twenty years of wrangling for other folks and being a guest of jails in Black Mesa, Sparks, Henderson, Hurricane, Tuba City, and God knows whereall, he and Blue Six had looped back to Walapai Flats for a visit with Abby. She lay sleeping beneath a coverlet of purple owl clover, serenaded by sparrows. Birds had always sung their sweetest around her.

That magic day he'd sat cross-legged at the foot of her grave for a couple of hours, telling her how much he missed her, saying that nothing seemed worth doing anymore without her around. He left out the part about Vegas and what he'd done there, left out the drinks and the fights and the jails because he didn't want to disappoint her, didn't want her to know how much he'd let his sweet girl down. Maybe she knew anyways. Some folks believed the dead looked down from Heaven, if there was such a place, and watched over those they left behind. The Heaven idea he liked, but not so much the watching business. It wouldn't a done for Abby to see the nasty drunk he'd become. Even most ranchers, and a tough crowd they tended to be, were scared to hire him.

After telling Abby for the ten-thousandth time how much he loved her and always would, he'd stood up to go back to his truck and the ever-patient Blue, but right then the Duke showed up for the very first time. The big man was ambling toward him up the graveyard path, wearing that red double-breasted shirt of his, trail-dirty jeans, and a hat that had seen an awful lot of bad weather.

"Yeah, you better get up off your rump, mister," the Duke growled. "What kind of a man passes his days crying over what's done and gone? Drink is fine, fights are fine—when there's good cause—but not when that's all you bother doin'. I'm mighty disappointed in you, Gabe, and that's a fact, because I always thought you had grit. Quit all this messing around and go home."

"Lost my home, Duke."

"I ain't been wrong before and I ain't wrong now. Go home, Gabe. You're needed."

So Gabe went home.

Sitting here now in the Walapai County Jail, he felt peace. With the Duke watching out for him, he could handle anything, prison bars or no.

"Doing what you did, that was a righteous thing," the Duke said. He was leaning against the gray concrete wall, still wearing the same red double-breasted shirt.

"Glad you think so, Duke."

"No thinking to it, Gabe. It's a matter of knowing. Your Abby would approve, too." Then the Duke vanished, leaving Gabe talking to the wall.

But that was fine. With the Duke gone away again, it was easier to see another face. Still looking at the gray concrete, Gabe said, "Your man's comin' to you soon, Abby. And then we'll have us a good ol' time."

Just thinking about that glorious day made his heart sing, and looking out toward the future he could see those heavy jailhouse walls falling down and his own sweet girl walking toward him.

Chapter Eighteen

The drive back to Walapai Flats from the ranch cemented my desire to leave town. While the place itself was pretty enough, all those dudes walking around in rhinestone cowboy get-ups depressed me. They brought in money, though, and kept the local businesses alive—especially the restaurants. While I was stopped at the town's only traffic light, I noticed that a line had formed in front of Ma's Kitchen. It was noon already.

Given that the sheriff's department was so understaffed, I idly wondered if Mia Tosches had been notified that she was a widow. Probably. Death notifications were something law enforcement officers normally performed as a matter of course, at least for the nearest and dearest. Then again, maybe his death wouldn't come as news to her. While I couldn't see her pulling a gun and messing up her manicure, it was easy to envision another scenario. Mia Tosches was no dumb blonde. As a teen she'd displayed an aptitude for organization and a talent for getting her friends to do her dirty work. Given her spectacular physical charms, it would have been easy for Mia to convince some naive pool boy or wrangler to get rid of a husband whose sell-by date had expired.

Dusty had admitted to having a fling with her. Surely he wouldn't have had anything to do with Tosches' death. The man was an amoral rascal, but I doubted he was murderous. Still…

Behind me, the blare of a car horn alerted me that the traffic light had turned green. Waving an apology at the cranky Volvo, I continued down John Wayne Boulevard to the county complex.

Jimmy, his father, and Ted's attorney were in deep conversation when I arrived. They sat on the same bench they'd occupied earlier that morning, but were now surrounded by a dozen visitors who hadn't been able to see their loved ones because of the previous day's lockdown.

"Ted's not released yet?" I asked, seeing him nowhere in evidence. "Please don't tell me the judge refused to cut him loose even after that Boone guy confessed."

"Everything's fine, only slow as molasses in January," Behar said, throwing me a triumphant smile. "The emergency hearing finished a few minutes ago, and the judge lifted the material witness hold. We're simply waiting for the paperwork to go through." Then he turned to Olmstead. "Resuming our conversation, Hank, are you sure you want to do this, pay for Mr. Boone's defense?"

Olmstead gave the attorney a stubborn look. "I owe Mr. Boone more than you can possibly imagine, Anderson. He's been with me going on two decades now, and as far as I'm concerned, he's family. Maybe you can get him released on bond so he can stay free until, well, you know. He doesn't have that many years left and I don't want them spent in a prison cell."

That was Olmstead—not necessarily likeable, but always admirable. His compassionate gesture would be wasted, though. If he'd been unsuccessful in springing his own son from jail, there was no reason to believe he'd have better chance with his cook, advanced years or no.

Behar voiced the same concern. "It's a lost cause, Hank. Given his confession, he'll surely be charged, and I can't see them letting a confessed murderer out on bond, regardless of his age."

Olmstead remained adamant. "He's never asked me for any favors, other than to take care of his dog when he had to drive up to Salt Lake. And now, of course. That dog's eating steak tonight. And always will."

So all's well that end's well, even for the dog. I pulled Jimmy aside and told him I'd be driving back to Scottsdale that afternoon. He wasn't happy, but he understood. When I left, Olmstead and Behar were discussing defense tactics.

I didn't make it down the steps before a voice called my name. "Lena, wait up!"

It was Olivia, recovered from her migraine. She hurried toward me, pale as a bone, dressed in black, her reporter's notebook at the ready. Planting herself firmly in my path, she fired off a series of questions.

"What's this I hear about someone confessing to Ike Donohue's murder? A cook, my sources tell me. Is that right? On my way here I saw a gaggle of sheriff's deputies swarming the road near Sunset Trails. Did some dude break his neck falling from a horse? There was an ambulance and someone was lying in the middle of the road. What the hell's going on around here?"

Staring pointedly at her notebook, I asked a question of my own. "I thought you were working on the mine story. You're going to take time out for a mere murder?

"Don't be sarcastic, Lena," she snapped. "It doesn't become you."

How little she knew me. "Sorry. I'm not used to getting up so early. Taking your questions in order, yes, someone confessed to Ike Donohue's murder, and, yes, it was the cook at Sunset Trails Ranch. He claims he killed Donohue, then took off to Salt Lake City to attend his grandniece's funeral, which is why he wasn't around to confess earlier. Question number two, re those cops on the road—Roger Tosches has been killed. Shot, like Donohue." I noted the stunned look on her face. And here I'd always believed reporters were unshockable. "As for question number three, 'What the hell's going on around here?' Olivia, I haven't a clue, but at least there's some good news. Ted Olmstead's getting released any minute now."

If her mouth opened any further, flies would swarm in, but her pen kept moving across her notebook. Shocked or not, she was still a reporter.

"I'm going in there," she said, already moving away from me and up the steps.

No wonder so many people hated reporters. Attorneys are accused of being ambulance chasers but they came in a distant second to journalists.

Packing finished, I was about to alert the Covered Wagons' front desk that I was checking out when my cell phone rang. I was tempted to ignore it, but seeing Jimmy's name on Caller ID changed my mind.

"Thank God I caught you," he said. "You'd better come back here. Dad got pulled into an interview room by a couple of detectives. They found out Tosches was putting pressure on him to sell the ranch."

Had Leilani blurted it out in an unguarded moment, or had Mia told them? I looked over at my closed suitcase and sighed. "Please tell me Behar's in there with him, Jimmy."

"Sure is. He insisted."

I was beginning to respect the pudgy real estate attorney. He'd truly risen to the occasion. "I'm on my way. In the meantime, see what you can find out. Say, is Olivia Eames still there?" Belatedly, I remembered that Jimmy had never met her. "Goth-looking reporter. Dressed in black."

"I saw a woman fitting that description trying to get in to see Mr. Boone. When they wouldn't let her, she turned around and started throwing questions at everyone, so the cops threw her out. Figuratively speaking, of course."

Too bad. Reporters could sometimes get information private detectives couldn't. I made a mental note to call her later.

As it turned out, the trip back to the jail was wasted because the detectives had let Hank Olmstead go right around the time his son was released. Mission accomplished, Behar had driven back to Silver Ridge to finish up a real estate transaction, while the two happy Olmsteads drove home, where Leilani was organizing a big Get Out of Jail party.

"The cook alibied Dad," Jimmy explained, as we stood in the lobby. "He told the investigator the same thing Dad did, that this morning, when they drove over here, there was no dead body in the middle of the road. No parked Mercedes, either."

That was a new one on me, cops taking a confessed killer's word, but I didn't want to rain on Jimmy's parade so I merely smiled and nodded.

"There's more," Jimmy continued. "While Dad was sitting in the interview room, some farrier named Monty-something called his cell phone and said he was the guy who found the body. He told Dad he'd been on his way to the ranch to shoe a couple of horses when he came across the scene, and said that Tosches was still alive when he got there. Unfortunately, Tosches died before the ambulance arrived. Being smarter than the average bear, the farrier realized he was looking at a possible murder, and jotted down the time—6:43 a.m. He was calling Dad in case there was any trouble, what with the ranch being so close and all. Dad handed his cell to one of the detectives, and the guy repeated the same story to him."

"That's all very nice, Jimmy, but…"

"Wait. The kicker is that Dad and Gabe Boone were clocked walking into the county complex at 6:55, and you know it's a half-hour drive from the ranch."

"Gunshot victims can take hours to die." It needed to be said.

"Not when they've been shot in the neck and blood's spurting from an artery. The farrier said he took off his shirt and tried to stop the bleeding. The police impounded his shirt because it was drenched in Tosches' blood."

I tried to picture the scene: a man bleeding out in the middle of a gravel road, a bare-chested farrier leaning over him, trying to chase away Death. "Did Monty say if Tosches was able to say anything before he died?"

"I'm not sure that came up."

No matter. The cops would certainly ask. If Tosches had been alive when Monty found him, there was a chance he'd lived long enough to ID his killer. Because the farrier had sense enough to check the time, Hank Olmstead was off the hook. Jimmy wouldn't be coerced into running the ranch, and he'd return to

Scottsdale and Desert Investigations. I wouldn't lose my partner. I felt like dancing a jig. Instead, I him asked how Ted was doing.

"He's lost a little weight, but Leilani's frying up some chicken and baking a big red velvet cake to remedy that. Oh, and she's found a replacement chef for the ranch, too. He'll be there in time to cook dinner for the guests. In the meantime, why don't you put off the drive back to Scottsdale and come to the ranch with me? Leilani's red velvet cake is the best. And we've got ice cream. The whole family will be there, including the aunts. You haven't met them yet."

The vision of a big, happy family reminded me of some unfinished business, so impulsively, I decided to put off my departure until tomorrow. The long drive back to Scottsdale would go easier with a good night's sleep.

"You go without me," I told him. "As long as I'm here, I want to talk to the sheriff about the Deputy Smiley Face situation."

The smile left Jimmy's face. "Good luck," he said, in a voice that revealed little hope, because we'd both traveled that road many times before to no avail.

With that he waved and left.

Steeling myself for another "He's too busy," I walked up to the deputy manning the front desk. I recognized him from an earlier visit to the jail, when he hadn't been all that helpful. His reading material today was *Loft Living*. Crossing my fingers, I said, "Is there any way I can have a brief word with the sheriff? I have some important information for him, but I've been trying to see him for days now without success."

"Sheriff's busy. Tell me and I'll pass it along to his secretary."

"It's confidential information, meant for the sheriff only." I pulled my ID out of my carry-all and held it in front of him.

He wasn't impressed. "You'll need to be more specific."

For all I knew, this man was bosom buddies with Officer Smiley Face, but I had to chance it. "It's about misconduct on the part of a Walapai County deputy."

"What kind of misconduct and by which deputy?" He looked as if he'd heard it all before; he probably had.

"I have good reason to suspect Deputy Stark beats his wife. And possibly his child."

To my surprise, he picked up his phone, punched in a number, and said to the person on the other end, "Elaine? There's a private investigator standing in front of me who wants to see the sheriff about that thing you and I were discussing yesterday." He waited. "Yeah. Him. Small world, huh?" He waited some more, then nodded. "I'll send her back." To me, he said, "Take the first left turn down the hall. Sheriff Alcott's office is three doors down on the right."

With that, he immersed himself in *Loft Living* again.

If you've seen one county sheriff's office, you've pretty much seen them all—U.S. and Arizona flags bracketing the piled-high desk, photographs of the sheriff shaking hands with politicians, a montage of criminal science degrees, civic awards, and I'm-a-Bigger-Deal-Than-You-Are plaques. Sheriff Wiley Alcott's office set itself apart by including several hunting trophies mounted on the walls: the heads of an elk, a sixteen-point buck, and two pronghorn antelope. On the long credenza behind his desk stood an entire stuffed mountain lion, its fangs bared. The lion looked like it wanted to bite someone—the sheriff, probably, for killing it. I'm no fan of using dead animals as decorations, but I tried my best to keep the distaste off my face. This was neither the time nor place for an animal rights discussion.

The sheriff was younger than I expected. Like most county sheriffs these days, he wore a suit and tie but there was no mistaking him for a civilian. Somewhere in his thirties, Alcott's face bore the studious expression of an academic, but with his bull neck, broad shoulders and Arnold Schwarzenegger build, the rest of him looked like a professional wrestler, albeit one that had taken time to get a professional manicure.

"I hear you have a complaint about one of my deputies," he said, as I settled myself into a leather visitor's chair.

"Deputy Ronald Stark beats his wife. And maybe his daughter."

He looked down at his desk, picked up a silver Montegrappa pen and began tapping it on the blotter. "Your proof?"

I described the scene in the park across the street. "My partner saw it, too. James Sisiwan, Hank Olmstead's son."

"Would that be the same James Sisiwan we recently charged with suborning perjury?"

"Jimmy's a big guy and with that facial tattoo of his he can look pretty scary. The entire suborning perjury thing is a misunderstanding."

The tapping stopped and he gave me a hint of a smile. "That's what they all say. But you can relax because we've dropped the charge. We're not Neanderthals here." The smile vanished and the pen-tapping began again. "Back to Deputy Stark. What makes you so certain you didn't misinterpret the events at the park? From the way you described what was going on, you didn't actually see Deputy Stark hit his wife or hear him threaten her in any way."

"No, but she looks beat up and her daughter has a broken arm." The minute the words were out of my mouth, I realized how flimsy they sounded.

"Both could have been the results of falls." Sheriff Alcott put his pen down, aligning it carefully with a six-inch high stack of blue-covered legal papers. "Here's how it works, Miss Jones. I've heard the rumors about Deputy Stark. Yes, that's right. Rumors. In the months since I was elected sheriff, there've been numerous people trooping in here with their suspicions about him, but every time I ask for proof of the abuse I get none, just different versions of 'I think' and 'I guess' and 'It sure looks like abuse to me.' Those aren't the kinds of statements that will hold up in court. He'll sue for reinstatement and damages if I fire him, and this county has neither the time or the funds to dick around in court for something like that. As for the alleged victim, yes, I have to say *alleged*, because when I brought her in here last week, she denied everything again. She may be walking around with a black eye now, but she still hasn't voiced one word of complaint to me, to CPS, or anyone else. Neither has the child. That might change when the little girl starts school next year and irregularities are noticed by a school counselor, but until then, what am I supposed to do, waterboard Deputy Stark to find out the truth?"

I understood his frustration because I'd felt it myself many times before. But that didn't mean he should simply sit there and fret. "There must be something you can do."

"I hear you're a former police officer. Scottsdale PD."

It came as no surprise to learn he'd checked me out. In his position, I'd have done the same. "That's right, for ten years."

"Tell me, former Officer Jones, while you were on the job how many times did you encounter a situation like ours, and what did you do about it when the woman refused to press charges?"

He already knew the answer: nothing. So I remained silent.

"The French have a phrase for it," he said. "*Plus ça change, plus c'est la même chose.* 'The more things change, the more they stay the same.' Understand?"

Unfortunately, I did.

"Just so you know," he added, "A couple of volunteers from a local group named Haven called on her, but they had no more luck than I did. She told them she was accident-prone."

With nothing more to be said on that topic, I switched gears. "I probably already know the answer to this, but why didn't you dispatch some deputies to oversee the anti-mining demonstration?"

"Good question, easy answer. Ten minutes before they were to be dispatched, there was a seven-car pileup on Route 47. Two fatalities. All this carnage caused by a couple of teenagers who out of high spirits tore down a stock fence and released forty-six steers onto the road, eight of which are now hamburger. Compared to that catastrophe, a demonstration by the heretofore non-violent members of Victims of Uranium Mining didn't make a blip on the Richter scale. I'm sure someone's told you about the budget cuts we've had around here. This town doesn't even have a police force anymore, so the sheriff's department is left covering everything that happens not only in the county—and it's a big county with a lot of runaway steers—but in town, too. Bar fights up the wazoo every weekend. Now, if that's all you wanted to talk about, I'm very busy and you have a nice day, hear?"

More Walapai Flats politeness. "One more thing. Why did your detectives question Hank Olmstead about the Roger Tosches killing?"

"Oh, for God's sa…. Standard procedure, Miss Jones, nothing to be alarmed about. But the killing did take place on his property and right around the time Mr. Olmstead was driving down the road where the death occurred. We'd be remiss if we didn't follow up."

Pointedly, he looked at his watch. From this angle, I couldn't see it all that well, but it appeared to be a Rolex. Arizona sheriffs made decent salaries, but nowhere in the Rolex range. He was also the first sheriff I'd met who spoke French, and unless I was mistaken, his suit was an Armani.

"Anything else, Miss Jones? I'm expected at a county commissioner's meeting in a few minutes."

"As a matter of fact, yes. What can you tell me about that cook who supposedly confessed to Donohue's murder?" I was curious as to why an eighty-year-old would kill someone.

His face closed in. "We're still looking into his story. Now, if you're finished…"

I held up my hand. "Another thing. Did Deputy Stark turn in an incident report on a shooting yesterday?"

"A report that identified you as the alleged target? Yes, he did. He also turned in a couple of Baggies that smelled like tuna fish. One had slugs in it, the other had casings. We sent then them to the crime lab."

"Anything back on them yet?"

He pointed his expensive Montegrappa pen at me accusingly. "Miss Jones, while we here in Walapai County may not be as backwards as you think we are, we're still not as slick as Scottsdale. Depending on the workload, ballistics testing can take days, maybe even weeks, especially on a random shooting that didn't hurt anyone. But rest assured that I'll be in contact if anything interesting pops up."

"Fair enough." I thanked him for his time and rose from my chair.

As I headed for the door, he called after me, "Oh, and these hunting trophies you're so pissed off about? They belonged to one of my predecessors, who just happened to be my grandfather. If I took them down, he'd rise up from his grave and shoot me."

Once back in the Trailblazer, I checked the gas gauge. It was still half-full, but since I planned to leave Walapai Flats tomorrow at sunrise, I decided to top off now. I pulled out of the parking lot and headed for the Gas-N-Go.

The temperatures had cooled. A merciful breeze blew in from California, rolling a vagrant tumbleweed down John Wayne Boulevard. In fact, the weather was so pleasant that for a moment I was tempted to drive one of the back roads leading out of town to the Grand Canyon. Whenever I'd visited the Canyon before, it had usually been to the more popular South Rim, so the opportunity to see it from the other side was tempting. But what point would there be in visiting the Grand Canyon for a mere couple of hours? It would only remind me of how fragmented my life had become.

The temptation was great, though, so I pulled to the side of the road, killed the engine, closed my eyes, and remembered. Canyons within canyons, mesas thrusting up from the mile-deep Abyss—Vishnu Temple, Wotan's Throne—the names of ancient gods superimposed upon rock formations that were here long before those gods were called into being, before the dinosaurs, even. A two hundred mile long gorge painted in red, pink, orange, yellow, purple, black, gray, white, impossible beauty in a place that couldn't possibly exist—but did.

I wanted to see it again, oh, how I wanted to. But I was here to work, not enjoy myself. Blinking the memory of beauty away, I fired up the ignition and headed for the Gas-N-Go.

The Trailblazer was still slurping down fuel when a familiar truck pulled up to the tank on the other side of the island. I waved hello when its driver hopped out. Monty looked somewhat worse for wear, with a fat lip and a scrape on his forehead. He was wearing a shirt so ancient and grease-stained the Salvation Army would have rejected it.

"My, my, if it isn't the truck killer," the farrier quipped, sliding a credit card into the pump.

"Unlike Roger Tosches, your truck's not dead."

The genial look left his face. "You heard about that?"

"Also that you were the one that found him. Do you mind filling me in?"

At first I thought he'd clam up, but he didn't. Even horseshoers talk to humans every now and then.

"Talk about your day from hell, and it's only half over. What's next? The plague? Locusts? First I find Tosches gurgling his life away, then the cops take my shirt and I have to wear my oil rag, then I get stomped by a twelve-year-old mare that should have known better. When I retire I'm goin' some place there ain't no horses. New York City, maybe. Nope, they've still got them police horses. My luck, one of them would bite me on the ass while I was crossin' the street. Anyways, I was supposed to shoe a coupla horses at Olmstead's, but when I turned down the ranch road, there was Tosches, sprawled out next to that big black Mercedes of his. Worst thing I seen since that poor colt over by…" He stopped. "Guess you don't need to hear 'bout that."

"I heard he was still alive when you found him," I prompted.

"More or less."

"Did he say anything?"

"Nothing you'd be interested in."

"Try me."

"Nothing but gobbledy-gook, mostly stuff I couldn't understand, except for one word, which might have been 'bitch.'"

As in, *Life's a bitch and then you die*? Or, *The damn bitch shot me*? "I take it he didn't name names."

"That would be awful nice for the sheriff, but naw, he didn't. He didn't recite no Gettysburg Address, neither. The man was too busy dying."

"Do you know anyone who might have wanted to kill him?"

A harsh laugh. "Better question would be, who didn't want to kill him? Tosches wasn't exactly loved around here, but if you want to play guessing games, I'd say maybe his wife. She's coming in for a pile of cash, and she's as nasty as a rattlesnake in heat, so I wouldn't put it past her. Half the people around here gonna be thankin' the Almighty when they find out he's dead, 'specially relatives of them men hurt in the Moccasin Peak Mine, and there's more of them around here than you'd think. They've been wantin' to pop him one for a long time. Even me. I lost a good friend over there before it shut down." He paused for a moment, then added, "Or it could a been one of them ecology folks shot Tosches. Talk about raping the desert! You been out to that mess they call Sunset Canyon Lakes?"

"I've had the dubious pleasure, yes."

"Then you know what I'm talkin' about."

"We're in agreement there. But back to the crime scene, Monty. Were any shell casings left lying around?"

"Like the ones we found when that asshole took potshots at you? No such luck."

"Tell me about the car. Were the doors open?"

"Driver's side was. And before you ask, nah, there wasn't any bullet holes in the windows, so I'd say he was outside standing next to his car when he got shot. Why the idiot would get out of that cushy thing to stand in the dust is anybody's guess. If it'd been someone else, I'd guess they stopped to admire the scenery, but not Tosches. He wouldn't know pretty if sat on his eyeballs."

"Sounds like he stopped to have a conversation with someone." I heard a click from the direction of the Trailblazer's gas tank, alerting me that the tank was full. As I returned the gas nozzle to the pump, I said, "By the way, Monty, I talked to the sheriff about Deputy Stark this morning."

"Didn't get anywhere, did you?"

"Nope."

He spat on the ground. "Sheriff Alcott is Ronnie's cousin on his momma's side."

Most small towns were seeped in nepotism, so I wasn't too surprised. "Is that why nothing's been done?"

Another spit. "Didn't say that. For all his fancy ways, Alcott's not a half-bad sheriff, and I'm guessin' he'd like to throw that little turd off the force. But knowin' Ronnie, he'd sue. These days with Granny Government breathin' down our necks, you can't fire some jerk-off just 'cause you suspect he beats the crap outta his wife."

"Too bad. I was thinking that Stark's wife might be more receptive with a woman. Maybe I could drive over to her place, talk to her woman to woman, convince her there's another way to live."

He gave me a level look. "There'll be hell to pay if Ronnie catches you talkin' to Connie."

"Stark's guarding the Tosches crime scene."

After Monty gave me the instructions to the house, I asked about the cars I might expect to see in the driveway.

"All they got is a silver 2006 Pathfinder. She don't have a car of her own. When she needs to do some shoppin', she drops Ronnie off at the police station and picks him back up in the evening, but this ain't the day she grocery shops. If there's a silver Pathfinder in the driveway, my advice is to drive on by. You get to tangling with him, he'll only take it out on her soon's you leave. Don't want that, do you?"

No, I didn't. I thanked him and drove off.

Ronald and Connie Stark lived in a dusty tract optimistically named Willow Brook Lane, located on the outskirts of town. Most of the one-story houses were unlandscaped, but a few brave homeowners had planted spindly bushes and even spindlier trees. The Starks hadn't made the effort, so their yard was nothing but dirt and rocks. Given that every blind in the house was closed, the whole setup looked depressing, but at least no silver Pathfinder snarled at me from the driveway. In case Deputy Smiley Face decided to drop in for a spot of face-thumping, I turned around and drove to the other end of the street, where I parked the Trailblazer behind a tractor-trailer. Then I walked back to the forlorn house and knocked on the door.

No answer.

I knocked again.

Still no answer.

I remembered what Monty told me about the Starks being a one-car family. There were no stores or businesses within walking distance; Connie Stark hadn't taken her four-year-old for a long hike to pick up toilet paper. Based on my experiences with battered women, almost all of them secretive and isolated, I figured she hadn't dropped in on a neighbor for a friendly chat, either.

I knocked again, harder this time, and yelled, "Connie, if you don't answer the door by the time I count ten, I'm calling the police!"

The door jerked open so quickly I knew she had been listening on the other side. Both her eyes had been blackened.

"Go away," she whispered in a voice as raw as a wound.

"Not until you talk to me." Pointing to her eyes, I said, "When did that happen, last night? Or this morning before he went to work?"

"Nothing happened."

"Right. You went to bed feeling perfectly fine, and when you woke up, you had two shiners. That must have been one hell of a dream. Did your daughter have a bad dream, too?"

"Annalee's fine. Go away."

"Not until I see her."

"One look, then you'll go away?" Fear leaped out of those terrible eyes.

"Hmmm." I hoped she'd take my noncommittal murmur for consent.

She did, and opened the door further. "Come in quick. I don't want anyone to see."

The house was clean, but at the same time, it was a shambles. As cheerless as an abattoir, almost every piece of furniture in the living room had been damaged in one way or another. Two seat cushions on the brown velveteen sofa had been slashed, and stuffing leaked like blood. A matching armchair with a broken foot tilted to one side. Head-sized dents decorated the off-white walls. The guilty air smelled like Pinesol and beer.

"Mrs. Stark, show me your daughter. Now!"

She was used to following orders. Shoulders hunched and arms crossed tightly against her chest, she hurried down a narrow hall, me right behind her.

Annalee's room looked nothing like the rest of the house. Painted shell pink, it was furnished with white-and-gold "princess" furniture—bed, chest, toy box—and not one piece had been broken. The little girl sat at a desk, drawing a picture of a dog. At least I thought it was a dog. Maybe it was a horse. Or an elephant. When she saw me, she said, "You're the lady at the jail. You gave Mama a card that made Daddy mad."

"I'm sorry it made your daddy mad. Did he hit you, too?"

She shook her head. "Daddy never hits me. He just hits Mama."

I pointed to her cast. "How did you break your arm?"

"I fell off the swings at the park. It hurt really, really awful and Daddy got so mad at Mama that he spanked her."

Deputy Smiley Face might beat the crap out of his wife, but I did believe that he hadn't touched his daughter. Not yet, anyway. Turning to Connie, I said, "We need to let Annalee finish her beautiful drawing. Shall we go back in the living room?"

"You said…"

"I know what I said." For emphasis, I took her by the elbow and guided her out of the room like you would a blind person, which in a way she was.

I nudged her over to the sofa, where she took a seat on the one cushion that hadn't been slashed. Settling myself on the lopsided armchair, I began my lecture, reeling out statistics on how many American women per year wound up in the morgue because of violent partners. I talked about safe houses and how they sheltered battered women and children. I told her how common it was for batterers to transfer their hostilities from their partners to their children, and how often the children wound up in the morgue, too. I told her everything I knew, said everything that could be said, and still she looked at me with unseeing eyes.

"You don't understand," she whispered. "Ronnie loves Annalee."

"He probably loved you once, too, and look how that turned out."

She shook her head so fiercely the sofa rocked. "He'd never touch her."

"If he kills you, she'll wind up in Child Protective Services."

"You don't understand," she repeated. "It's only that I, well, I do a lot of dumb things like burning dinner or not cleaning right or forgetting to make lunch and it frustrates him. If I was more careful, everything would be fine. I've promised to try harder. Ronnies' a good man. A good, good man. The absolute best. I'm lucky to have a man who cares enough to want his wife to be the best she can be."

She was quoting him.

"Connie, do you still have my card?"

Her silence was the answer.

I pulled another card from my carry-all. "Put this where he can't find it, under the rug, taped to the back of the toilet, wherever. When you decide you've had enough or when he graduates from you to Annalee—and he will—give me a call. I'll get you some help. And for God's sake, when help arrives, tell the truth!"

No response. Just that unchanging, unseeing stare.

Once I returned to my car, I had to sit there until I'd collected myself. Connie's numbed terror had stirred up my own past.

My sixth foster home.

Mrs. Putney had decided to pull out of the foster care system, so CPS sent me to live with Norma and Brian Wycoff. My sixth foster parents had been taking care of the state's unwanted children for years, and on paper they looked perfect. Mr. Wycoff owned a small printing company and was active in community affairs. Mrs. Wycoff, a full-time housewife, volunteered every Thursday afternoon at a nearby church.

Every Thursday afternoon Mr. Wycoff left work early and raped me.

I was nine years old.

Three decades later the memory of my own numbed terror still haunted me, so I sat in the Trailblazer until my breathing returned to normal and my hands stopped shaking. Forcing myself calm, I pulled away from the curb and headed back into town. Unless something changed, Connie Stark was doomed, but she was too damaged to realize it. Unable to protect herself, she wasn't strong enough to protect her daughter.

Just like Mrs. Wycoff.

While driving past the county complex, I remembered a person who might be able to do something about Deputy Smiley Face: Olivia Eames. Swerving at the last second, I pulled into the parking lot behind Ma's Kitchen and rummaged through my carry-all until I found her card.

A few seconds later I had her on the phone.

When I told her about Connie Stark, Olivia's response was mixed. Words of surprise, but delivered in a tone that made me wonder if something about Stark had already pinged her reporter's radar. "Are you talking about that big sandy-haired deputy, kind of good-looking? Smiles too much?"

"The same. Connie's covering up for him, and the sheriff says that unless she files a complaint, there's nothing he can do."

"She won't, though. Battered women almost never do. Psychologically speaking, they're too messed up. Every now and then one snaps out of her fog long enough to make the call, but even then she usually winds up dropping the charges, so the whole cycle starts all over again. You can't expect trauma victims to act sane."

I couldn't have summed up the situation better myself. Connie Stark's vicious husband had made her flat-out crazy, crazy enough to pretend her child was safe.

Olivia wasn't finished. "Here's the problem, Lena. I'm swamped. I've already got a couple of stories in the hopper, the mine opening and something else. Now I'll have to follow up on the Roger Tosches killing, too, because he owned the damned mine. The chances of my editor buying into a story about a

Walapai Flats cop who's only a suspected batterer are very, very slim. To sell it to him, I'd have to pitch it more as a feature, maybe even a series, with stats, quotes from local and national experts, the whole megilla. Organizing something like that takes time, and time's the one thing I don't have."

"When are you going back to New York?"

A pause. "I'll leave as soon as I've finished my articles."

"No firm date, then. Maybe you could tack on a few extra days. Don't they call those kinds of stories 'evergreens,' stories that are always worth reading?"

I heard a bitter laugh. "Not these days. In this economy most people are having such a hard time just making it that they don't want to read about domestic abuse. They'd rather read about some Hollywood star going to rehab for the eighth time."

"Please, Olivia."

A longer pause this time. "I'll see what I can do."

On that note, we said goodbye. For some reason—maybe it was hope alone—I believed that Olivia might succeed where I'd failed.

But her mention of the Black Basin Mine opening reminded me of all that mountain-moving equipment I'd seen and their probable cost. For Tosches to pay that much out of pocket months before he'd see any profit, the amount of money he expected to eventually make had to be enormous. Maybe it was time I found out how enormous.

Chapter Nineteen

In the desert, good air-conditioning can never be overrated. Neither can spa-quality bath salts semi-dissolved in cool water. As soon as I closed the motel room door behind me, I stripped, leaving a trail of dusty clothes from the door to the bathroom. I spent the next few minutes soaking in the tub, enveloped by the scent of lilacs. After washing away the day's accumulation of sweat and sadness I dried off and wrapped myself in the thick terry robe so kindly provided by the Covered Wagons management. Then I wandered over to the desk and opened my laptop.

I'm no Jimmy Sisiwan, so it took several false starts before I figured out which keywords would bring up the results I needed, but I finally got the hang of it. Typing in URANIUM+PRICE on Google landed me on a site that said high-grade uranium could sell for more than one hundred dollars per *pound*, and that uranium production from one mine alone could amount to as much as fifty thousand *tons* per year. And that, as they say in the 'hood, was one hulluvalot of Benjamins.

My success in coming up with uranium's cost-per-pound gave me confidence, so I typed in COLE LAVEEN. It would be interesting to find out how the Black Basin partnership would shake down now that Tosches was dead. Mia Tosches might inherit the entirety of her husband's share, but Laveen wouldn't be left empty-handed. I was under no illusion I'd be able to hack into legal documents like Jimmy could, but I might find out a few things about Laveen the man. Unfortunately, all I came up with was PR-type fluff. According to his bio, Cole Laveen had been born August 12, 1953, in Akron, Ohio. He graduated magna cum laude from Harvard Business School, married his high school sweetheart, and fathered six children. For two decades Laveen served as chief financial officer for a *Fortune* 500 company. He was an Episcopalian, a member of the Lions Club, Kiwanis and Rotary, and sat on the boards of several philanthropic organizations, including the Arizona Humane Society, Big Brothers and Sisters, and the Florence Crittenden Home. As for closet skeletons, if he'd ever received so much as a parking ticket, it didn't show up on any site I visited.

Failing with Laveen, I tried easier prey and was immediately rewarded with more colorful information on Nancy Donohue. At the age of nineteen she'd been ticketed for shooting her first husband, Dwight Bob Gleason, on the opening day of Deer Hunting Season, outside Billings, Montana. Her hunting partner survived, and a month later was granted an uncontested divorce. Exploring her new freedom, Nancy shot her way eastward, eventually winding up in Halifax County, North Carolina, where she bagged a final deer. Hunting season finished, she moved to Durham and took a job in the bookkeeping department of the Cook & Creighton Tobacco Company. Her next appearance on the Internet came in 1969 when she was named as co-respondent in an ugly divorce case between Ike Donohue and Evelyn Woodruff Donohue. Her civic and philanthropic activities were limited to membership in the National Rifle Association.

A crick in my neck hinted that I'd been hunched over the laptop for too long, so deciding I'd done enough research for one day, I stood up and stretched. Then I walked over to the window, opened the blinds, and looked out over the pool. Nothing but a gaggle of tourists wearing ill-advised bathing suits. I closed the blinds. I picked up the Sue Grafton novel, opened it. I read three paragraphs. I put the book down. I stretched again.

God, I was bored.

Not knowing what else to do, I turned on the television and flipped through the channels. TCM was running a John Wayne marathon, but after my poking around in Gabriel Boone's room, I was sick of the actor, so I kept flipping. For the next half hour, CNN's talking heads informed me about the collapse of the Euro, riots in the Middle East, reports of more radiation sickness in Japan, and the collapse of another Royal marriage. After a report about acid being thrown into little girls' faces in Afghanistan to punish them for attending school, I returned to Nickelodeon to watch cartoon penguins build a time machine. The penguins were cute, but I grew bored again, so I flipped back to the John Wayne marathon. With no TV guide in the room to tell me the name of the currently-running film, I had to guess. *True Grit?* Yeah, he was wearing an eye patch. I remembered hearing he'd received an Oscar for his performance, so deciding it couldn't be too bad, settled into watch.

Wayne was trading insults with a smart-mouthed teenage girl when my cell phone rang. Caller ID flashed the number of Sunset Trails Guest Ranch. Expecting Jimmy, I muted the TV and answered, eager to tell him what I'd learned about the price of uranium. Instead, it was Hank Olmstead with a proposition for me.

"Miss Jones, I'm grateful for everything you've done for us, and now I'd like to hire you—at Desert Investigations' standard rate, of course—to help Gabriel Boone. He did not, I repeat, did *not* kill Ike Donohue."

Confused, I said, "But he confessed."

"It was a false confession, of that I'm certain, and he only confessed after he learned that Theodore had been arrested."

"Ted was being held as material witness," I corrected. "Not arrested."

"Amounts to the same thing as far as I'm concerned. Look, Miss Jones, I'm convinced that Gabriel confessed merely to get Theodore released. If you can find out who really killed Ike Donohue, we can end all this foolishness and Mr. Boone can come back to the ranch where he belongs. Now, I'm not saying that he doesn't have it in him to shoot someone, and he just might if he caught them abusing a woman, a dog, or a horse, but he wouldn't do it in the dead of night and he wouldn't let someone else take the blame. Gabriel Boone is a man of utmost integrity."

It must be nice to trust another human being so implicitly. Foolish, though. "Mr. Olmstead, I've known a couple of killers who could be described that way, but it's a moot point. Boone said he did the deed and as far as I'm concerned, that's the end of it. While I appreciate your generous offer—I'm sure Jimmy has filled you in on our price structure—I've been out of my office too long."

"James told me how much you charge but he also told me that business was slow during August and that you're having someone else cover for you. So why don't we handle it this way. It's Thursday, right? Stay through the weekend, and if you haven't come up with anything to help Mr. Boone by Monday noon, I won't try to talk you out of driving back to Scottsdale. In effect, you would only be staying one more business day." Almost as an afterthought, he added, "I'm well aware that you charge double for weekend work, and I have no trouble with that. If need be, I'll pay you in advance."

My opinion of Olmstead rose again. He might be stuffy and stubborn, but he sure valued his friends.

And he'd raised Jimmy.

Softening, I said, "Tell you what, Mr. Olmstead. I need to make a couple of calls to check on some things. After that, I'll get back to you. What do you say?"

"I'll be waiting by the phone." He rang off.

Before I called Jean Begay back in Phoenix, I did some thinking. Leilani had told me about Sunset Trails' money troubles, which is why Tosches had smelled blood in the water. Those money troubles would now increase, because a murder on ranch grounds was bound to scare off tourists. Yet Olmstead was ready to shell out thousands to defend an admittedly guilty man.

Nevertheless, I punched in Jean Begay's Phoenix number. After she told me everything was copacetic and that she'd taken care of the few calls that had come in from Desert Investigations' clients, we bid amiable goodbyes. Then I called my favorite foster mother, my ninth, and asked if she'd stop by the Desert Investigations office during her weekly trip into Scottsdale.

"I just want to make certain everything's okay," I explained. "No vandals, no taggers, no homeless encampments in the parking lot."

"Happy to do it for you, sweetie," Madeline said. "I'm driving over to Arizona Art Supply tomorrow and I'll swing by your office on the way. Want me to dust, clean, scrub the toilet?"

"Don't be silly."

She laughed. "I knew you'd say that, it's the only reason I offered. You know I'd rather be dead and stuffed in a taxidermy museum."

I spent the next few minutes listening to her as she discussed the critics' reaction to her recent one-man show. Mostly, she said, the reviews had been positive, but according to two critics, her allegiance to abstract expressionism—as well as to painting itself—was passé.

When I commiserated, she said, "They're the same nincompoops who raved over that fool who had a camera lens implanted in the back of his head and was streaming the images live over the Internet. To them, stunts are art. But what the hell. My show's almost completely sold out, and you know what they say—living well is the best revenge. Looks like I'll clear enough to buy that new hybrid car I've been eying. Well, gotta go, sweetie. When you called I was cleaning brushes and I'd better finish before they stiffen up. Give me a call as soon as you get back and we'll go out for lunch. I've found a scrumptious Indian vegetarian restaurant on Scottsdale Road, and it'll be my treat."

"American Indian or India Indian?"

"India Indian, and hotter than hell. It'll turn your blond hair red."

Thank God for Madeline. No matter how stressed I felt, she always soothed me. "How does Tuesday sound? I'll surely be back by then."

She agreed and we rang off.

Keeping my promise, I called Olmstead. "I'm yours, but only until noon Monday. Have Jimmy draw up the contract."

"He already did, Miss Jones."

Sometimes I suspect Jimmy knows me better than I know myself.

As I was about to submit to the jail's metal detector so I could visit Gabriel Boone, someone called my name. Turning around, I saw Sheriff Alcott hurrying toward me through the lobby.

"What can I do for you, Sheriff?"

He gestured toward the hallway that led to his office. "We need to talk."

Once his office door closed behind us, he rifled through the papers on his desk until he found what he was looking for, and jerked it out of the stack. Even from across his desk, I could see the Walapai County Crime Lab header.

After clearing his throat, he said, "I'm not going to try and cushion this, so here it is. The ballistics lab just faxed over the results on that slug you dug out of the desert. It matches the bullet that killed Kimama Olmstead."

Whatever I'd been expecting, it wasn't this. "But Kimama's murder happened months ago, and from what I've been told, most people believe it was connected to her activities in Victims of Uranium Mining. Why would her killer target me?"

He waggled a finger at me, like I was a dog that'd piddled on his rug. "Don't be too certain the shooter is the same. Yes, we now know that the same carbine was used for both you and Kimama Olmstead, but firearms can change hands, and frequently do. To prove my point, we matched the striations on the bullet in Donohue's killing to one taken from a four-year-old girl wounded fifteen years ago in a home invasion in Detroit."

Which meant that the pistol that fired the fatal Donohue bullet had either changed hands or its owner liked to travel. "Was anyone from Walapai Flats in Detroit during that time?"

"We're checking. As for the common belief that Mrs. Olmstead's killing was connected to that anti-mining group, that's mere conjecture. For all we know, the killing might have been a domestic."

"A domestic? What the hell are you getting at? Ted wouldn't dream of…"

"I said could have been, not was." Up to that point, he'd remained standing, but now he sat down and took a deep breath. "Let's talk about the timeline. Last Friday, Ike Donohue is murdered—by a different firearm, by the way—and we pick up Ted Olmstead as a material witness. This action brings his brother James riding to the rescue all the way from Scottsdale. Fine, no problem, I'm all for brotherly love. But no sooner does Mr. Sisiwan arrive than he starts questioning the good citizens of Walapai Flats and scaring the bejesus out of them, so we're forced to pick him up, too. Now we've got two Olmsteads in jail, which doesn't go over great with their father, who, before this happened, I was proud to call my friend. A couple of days later, you show up. Being a trained investigator, you ask many of the same questions Mr. Sisiwan asked, but with considerably more finesse. What happens then? Someone with access to the Kimama Olmstead murder weapon starts shooting at you. Before the dust settles, there's another murder, only this time the victim isn't a political activist; it's Roger Tosches, the richest man in the county. There you have it. In the space of one year, we have four shootings, three of them fatals, from two different weapons. Are you following me?"

I nodded.

"Miss Jones, my advice to you and your partner is to reacquaint yourself with the lovely town of Scottsdale."

"In other words, get out of Dodge."

He gave me a thin smile. "There's nothing to be gained by staying here. Whether we have one shooter or two or even three, the Walapai Flats County Sheriff's office is better equipped to handle an investigation like this. You and your partner are only muddying the waters, and God knows they're already muddy enough."

My smile was no more genuine than his. "While I always like to cooperate with law enforcement officials, there's a problem."

"Which is?"

"Hank Olmstead hired me to work on behalf of Gabriel Boone. In fact, I was on my way to talk to him when you flagged me down."

"You're in way over your head, Miss Jones."

I stood up to leave. "It won't be the first time."

Chapter Twenty

Gabe couldn't understand why the detention officer had brought him back to the interview room. He'd already given his statement to the detectives; he'd talked and talked to that pudgy attorney Hank Olmstead sent along, so what now? He was tired of talking. He'd said what he'd said and that was the end of it. He didn't much like the shackles they put on him every time they shuffled him out of his cell, either. What did they think a broken-down old cook was gonna do with those arthritic hands of his, twist off some kid deputy's head?

Baffled by the craziness of it all, he leaned back in his chair and began counting the fly specks on the ceiling. He'd reached fifty-seven when the door opened and a tall woman entered. She looked wrong in here, kinda reminded him of that line in *Stagecoach*, the movie that made the Duke a star: "She's like an angel in the jungle."

"Watch yourself with this one, Gabe," the Duke said, suddenly appearing behind her. He was still wearing that red double-breasted shirt. They didn't change clothes on the Other Side?

"I'm not worried," Gabe replied.

The woman looked confused for a moment, then said, "Well, I'm glad you're not worried, Mr. Boone." Her voice was a mixture of songbird and steel. "My name's Lena Jones and I'm a private investigator. Hank Olmstead hired me to help you."

He started to laugh, but the Duke cautioned him that would be rude, and it didn't do to be rude to a woman. Besides, Gabe thought, this Jones girl was a pretty thing, with green eyes and long yellow hair almost the same color as his Abby's back in the days when she was trying to look like Doris Day. He struggled to his feet. Shackled or not, he always stood when a lady entered the room. "Mighty pleased to meet you, Miss Jones, but you're wasting your time. Like I told them detectives, I surely did kill that man."

Her sad smile tore at his heart. Oh, yes, she was good-looking, all right. But no one, not even this Jones girl, could be as pure pretty as Abby.

"Sit back down, Mr. Boone. We need to talk."

Tough girl. Good breeding there. With horses, dogs, and women. "I'm always happy to talk to a lovely lady like yourself, Miss Jones."

The Duke nodded his approval. "You've got that spot on, Gabe. Blood always tells, and this filly is proof of that."

Miss Jones reached down into a backpack-sized purse and pulled out a notebook and pen. When she looked back up at him, her pretty smile was gone. "While I'm well aware that you've confessed to killing Ike Donohue, I want you to tell me how you did it and why. Give me as many details as you can remember."

Remembering. Ah, yes, that was the problem. Wasn't it always? He looked over to the Duke for inspiration, but the Duke picked that moment to vanish. Probably on his way to help someone else, so Gabe was on his own. But that was okay. He had rehearsed his speech so many times he knew it by heart.

He gave her an apologetic smile. "Well, now, Miss Jones, I already answered them same questions as best I could for them detectives who talked to me. They videotaped the whole thing. Me, in the movies! Ain't that a stitch? Anyways, them detectives had me write it all down on a yellow pad of paper, too, and when I was finished, I signed my John Hancock to the whole thing. I'm guessing they'll give you a copy if you ask nice. Maybe even a copy of the tape."

"I won't be able to get my hands on those materials for a while. Since Mr. Olmstead has already forked over a big check to your new attorney, why don't you make it worth his while by telling me what I need to know? Specifically, why did you shoot Mr. Donohue? Oh, and while you're at it, tell me about the firearm you used, whether it was a rifle or a handgun."

The interview room was air-conditioned, but it felt like the thing wasn't even running because sweat started dripping down his body. He hoped he wasn't stinking up the place. Not that the law would care, but he didn't want to offend this pretty girl. She sure didn't stink. Smelled like lilacs and soap, she did. There'd been a touch of lilac in Abby's Evening in Paris perfume, too, and he'd always been a sucker for lilacs.

Mindful of his language, he said, "You know, Miss Jones, when you get to be my age, your memory starts going, just like your hearing. I told that to the detectives, and they gave me a bad time about it, but what can you expect, 'cause the ages of both them boys together don't add up to mine. They don't know the first thing about getting old. I'll tell you what I told them, that the only thing I can remember is followin' that Donohue fellow up to Sunset Point, shooting him, then kicking his body over the ledge. That's pretty much it."

"You do remember what firearm you used, don't you?"

"Can't help you there, either. Might a been that old hunting rifle I've had since God was a pup, might a been that pistol I won in a poker game over in Sparks, Nevada. All I can remember is a big bang, then Donohue falling down."

"Where do you keep your firearms?"

No wedding ring on her left hand. What was wrong with men today, letting a fine woman like that get away? Were they blind or just plain stupid? To ease a heart that had to be lonely, he gentled his voice like he'd do with a skittish mare. "Well, Miss Jones, I keep my guns in my room, in the barn, sometimes in my truck. It all depends on what I'm gonna do during the day. Like most of them boys out at the ranch, I like to do me a little target shooting from time to time."

"Where are your firearms now?"

Talk about a one-track mind. Abby'd been like that, too, never letting him get away with anything. Knowing what she was like, he'd always behaved himself around his sweet girl, 'cause if he didn't, he'd never hear the end of it. That was a woman's job, wasn't it, keeping her man walking the straight and narrow. Once Abby was gone, look what had happened to him. If it hadn't been for the Duke setting him on the right path...Well, Hank Olmstead came in for some of the credit, too. He'd never forget what that man did for him—gave him a chance for redemption and he sure wasn't about to blow it.

He smiled real sweet-like. "Hmmm. Where are my firearms now? You know, that's a mighty good question. I kinda remember leaving them out there in the desert after I shot Mr. Donohue, but I don't know exactly where that was 'cause it was dark and ou know how things look around here when it gets dark. Can't see a thing."

"I've had some experience with that. Are you sure you can't remember anything else?"

"Hate to disappoint you again, ma'am, but nope. Oh, there's that conversation I had with the Duke that night, of course. I always remember talking with him."

"The Duke?"

"John Wayne. The Hollywood actor. He drops by regular to see how I'm doin'."

She gave him a slit-eyed stare. "How does that work, Mr. Boone? I was under the impression that John Wayne died some time in the seventies."

"The Duke stopped breathing the air of this Earth on Friday, June 11, 1979, at 5:35 p.m. But that don't mean he ain't still walking around, visiting with his friends, giving them the advice they need. Sometimes advice they don't think they need."

"What kind of advice has the long-dead John Wayne been giving you, Mr. Boone?"

He could tell she didn't believe him and he didn't much care. "Oh, that a man's gotta sit tall in the saddle, be a stayer not a quitter. Words to live by."

She scribbled something in her notebook. He wasn't all that good at reading upside down, but it looked like "crazy" was one of the words. Having been called crazy more than a few times in his life, it didn't bother him.

When she spoke again, her voice had changed. Now she sounded like she was talking to some addle-brained kid. "Did John Wayne tell you to kill Mr. Donohue?"

He looked up at the ceiling. The fly specks hadn't gone away. There even seemed to be more of them. When he looked back down, he repeated the same answer he'd given the detectives. "The Duke would never tell somebody to do that, not without just cause, anyway. When I killed Mr. Donohue, I did it for my own good reasons. You see, people as old as me, we collect grudges. Let's say, for the sake of argument, that Mr. Donohue once kicked Blue, my dog. Bet if a man kicked your dog, you'd shoot him, too."

"I don't have a dog."

"Your cat, then."

"No cat, no ferret, no goldfish." She gave a deep sigh, the same kind Abby used to give him when he'd done something she didn't much like. "Mr. Boone, you didn't kill Ike Donohue, did you?"

Gabe didn't answer right away, just studied the beauty of her. The blond hair, the green eyes, the back as straight and strong as that of a good horse. A woman a man should value, not lie to. But sometimes a lie was truer than the truth.

Crossing what was left of his fingers under the table where she couldn't see them, he said, "Miss Jones, I killed that man as sure as you and me is sitting here enjoying the kind hospitality of the Walapai County Jail."

Chapter Twenty-one

Gabe Boone was the worst liar I'd ever met.

As a detention officer escorted me back to the lobby, I understood why Hank Olmstead had hired me to help the poor old thing. I doubted if he was capable of killing anyone other than by accident, and he'd "confessed" for the sole purpose of springing Ted Olmstead from jail. In a way, it was almost gallant.

Didn't Boone realize that if he stuck with his lame story he'd wind up spending what little time he had left in prison? It might provide him with three hots and a cot, but the prison gangs would eat him alive. However, his compromised mental state gave me hope. The man was in the full grip of dementia, possibly Alzheimer's, and might be sentenced to a mental health facility. Not the best of all possible worlds, necessarily, but better than prison.

I stood there in the jail's reception area for a few minutes, trying to figure out whom to call first. Olmstead and Jimmy would still be celebrating Ted's release from jail, and I didn't want to interrupt their fun. Tomorrow morning would be soon enough. Same for Anderson Behar, Boone's new attorney.

Feeling more optimistic, I walked across the street to Ma's Kitchen and ordered a meatloaf sandwich and fries to go. While waiting for my takeout, I looked into the dining section and saw Olivia Eames sitting at a deuce, pushing a salad around on her plate. When I waved, she motioned me over.

Now that I was closer, I saw how depressed she looked. "Salad no good?" I asked, then promptly regretted it. The too-thin reporter displayed all the symptoms of anorexia, and discussing food with anorexics was never wise.

"It's delicious, but I'm not as hungry as I thought," she answered.

"Happens to all of us at one time or another. Say, while you were collecting information for your Black Basin story, did you come across any mention of Gabriel Boone?"

"The cook who confessed to murdering Ike Donohue? There's no connection that I know of. When I heard about the confession, I did try to get in to see him but they wouldn't let me. As soon as I'm through eating, I'm going to camp out on their doorstep until they grant me an interview. I'm the press, for God's sake! They have to let me in."

There's nothing like watching a reporter sensing a story in the making; she looked like a wolf smelling prey. Maybe she thought she could somehow connect Donohue's murder to Tosches', and by extension, to the Black Basin Mine.

"Is it true the man's in his eighties?" she asked.

When I nodded, she vented an obscenity that drew frowns from nearby diners. Oblivious, she said, "So now we've got an octogenarian sitting in a jail cell, confessing to murder. Jesus, what a mess."

"You can say that ag…" Before I could finish, Tara, the cute waitress who had a crush on Jimmy, came over with my to-go order, so I bade Olivia goodbye and followed Tara to the cash register.

When I arrived back at the Covered Wagons, I discovered that while I'd muted the television before driving over to the jail, I'd forgotten to turn it off. The John Wayne marathon continued in full bore. *True Grit* had finished and now an older, more exhausted-looking Wayne was shooting up a saloon that reminded me of the motel's restaurant. Had the Covered Wagon's decorator used the saloon as a model? Amused by their similarity, I unwrapped my takeout, un-muted the TV, and climbed onto the bed for a little light entertainment.

A few minutes later, Wayne took a bullet. Then another. And another. Shot full of holes, the weary warrior collapsed behind the bar and died. After the credits rolled, the marathon's host said, "As we've just seen in *The Shootist*, J.B. Books, the character played by John Wayne, was dying of prostate cancer, which is why he'd provoked that final shootout. In real life, Wayne himself was dying of cancer, and *The Shootist* turned out to be the last movie he starred in. You can see by his appearance that he wasn't feeling well."

The host's expression grew more serious. "Three years later, in January of 1979, after being in constant pain for months, Wayne went into the hospital for a gallstone operation. Instead of gallstones, the surgeons discovered that the lung cancer he thought he'd licked back in 1964 had metastasized to his stomach. They removed his stomach, but five days later, tests came back showing he also had cancer in his lymph nodes and intestines. John Wayne died six months later, mourned by millions of fans."

Having suffered my allotment of gloom and doom for the day, I grabbed the remote and was about to change the channel when the next thing the host said froze my hand.

"This brings us to *The Conqueror,* said to be the worst film Wayne ever made because with his rugged Western looks and swagger, he was simply unbelievable as Genghis Khan. *The Conqueror* was filmed in 1954 in Snow Canyon, a recreational area outside of St. George, Utah. This is the movie so many of Wayne's fans believe was responsible for his death. Of the two hundred and twenty Hollywood actors and crew members who worked on that Utah set, ninety-one contracted cancer. Most died, including John Wayne, Susan Hayward, Agnes Moorehead, Pedro Armendariz, and director Dick Powell. Why? The prevailing theory is that they died because three years before filming began on *The Conqueror*, the U.S. military started above-ground nuclear testing at the Nevada Test Site, ninety miles southwest of the film set."

I frowned. Yes, I'd heard about the A-bomb testing. Who hadn't? It had even been mentioned in one of my high school history textbooks. How could the tests be connected with all those deaths, especially Wayne's? From what I'd heard, Wayne had been a heavy smoker and drinker, habits that seldom contributed to a long life.

The TV host's next words cleared up my confusion. "Because of the prevailing western winds, the fallout from numerous nuclear bombs—many bigger than the bomb that destroyed Hiroshima—blew straight into Snow Canyon. The tests turned the picturesque canyon we saw in the movie into a radioactive hotspot the film crew was subjected to for thirteen weeks. To make matters worse, Howard Hughes, who bankrolled the film, had sixty tons of the red-tinted Snow Canyon dirt shipped back to Hollywood so that any retakes necessary would match the scenes shot on location."

He paused, then added, "And now, ladies and gentlemen, here is *The Conqueror*—infamous as 'the movie that killed John Wayne.' "

A bite of meatloaf tumbled out of my mouth and onto my lap.

Snow Canyon was less than sixty miles from Walapai Flats.

Brushing the wayward meatloaf onto the floor, I jumped off the bed and ran to my laptop.

Ten minutes later I was punching in Olivia's cell phone number.

"You were raised in this area," I said, the second she picked up. "Walapai Flats received nuclear fallout from the Nevada Test Site, didn't it?"

There was such a long silence that I thought the call had dropped, but then she said, "Well, well. So somebody finally broke the code of silence. Who was it? Earl Two Horses? He always was the wild card."

"Code of silence? What are you talking about?"

"Don't tell me you haven't noticed how people clam up when...Wait a minute." On the other end of the line I heard a man's voice, then Olivia's again. When she came back on, she sounded excited. "I just received permission to see that Boone guy for fifteen minutes, and it's going down right now. Gotta go, but I promise to call you back as soon as I'm done."

Dial tone.

I went back to my laptop, typing in BOMB+NEVADA TEST SITE. In the next half-hour I learned that between 1951 and 1992, the U.S. government detonated more than nine hundred nuclear bombs at Yucca Flat and Frenchman Flat, two of the main locations on the Nevada Test Site. The John Wayne marathon host had understated their power: some of those nukes were nearly *five times* the size of those dropped on Hiroshima and Nagasaki at the end of Second World War.

The radioactive fallout spread all over the U.S.—as far away as New York's Central Park—but Nevada, Arizona, Utah, and Colorado received the largest doses. The result was an enormous cancer cluster centered in the American Southwest. Those radiation-caused cancers included male and female breast cancer, leukemia, multiple myeloma, and lymphoma. Thyroid cancer was a big killer, but so were cancers of the pharynx, small intestine, ovaries, pancreas, salivary glands, lungs, esophagus, stomach, brain, bladder, kidney, bile ducts, liver, colon, and gall bladder. The exact numbers of deaths resulting from the bomb tests was not known, but was estimated to be in the hundreds of thousands. In 1977, the National Cancer Institute released a report estimating that fallout-related deaths from thyroid cancer alone totaled as many as seventy-five thousand.

I gasped. My high school history textbook hadn't mentioned deaths.

As I continued to read, I learned that on July 5, 1957, the Army drove more than 3,200 young American soldiers into the blast zone and exploded an atom bomb right over their heads. At seventy-four kilotons, the nuke represented the largest atmospheric test ever conducted within the continental United States. The government wanted to find out what effects eleven million Curies of iodine-131 would have on them. They found out, all right. Many of the men—some as young as nineteen—developed cancer. The bomb sterilized others on the spot.

When Olivia called me back a few minutes later, I'd calmed down enough to at least speak. "Let me tell you what I've discovered." Hating the tremor in my voice, I ranted about immorality of using uninformed Americans as radiation test subjects until my throat was raw. "When Saddam Hussein gassed and killed five thousand Kurds, our government called him a murderer. But the U.S. government killed at least a hundred thousand more of our own people!"

Olivia didn't sound all that steady, herself. "Sucks, doesn't it? Look, how would you like to get away from Walapai Flats for a couple of hours. I'm leaving for Silver Ridge in a few minutes to get some final information for a story I'm writing. It'd be nice to have you along for company."

"The Black Basin Mine story?"

"Not exactly, but in a way, there is a distant connection."

As emotionally exhausted as I felt, the idea of taking a drive to Silver Ridge didn't appeal to me. "I appreciate the offer, but before I got waylaid with all this radiation stuff, I was going to make some phone calls on behalf of Gabriel Boone. In fact, I'd better get started right now, because…"

"Lena, you'll learn more about Gabe by going to Silver Ridge with me than by hanging around your motel room."

Her use of the man's nickname made it like they'd already become fast friends. While Boone had been cordial to me, he'd been less than forthcoming, certainly not hail-fellow-well-met. That alone made me change my mind.

"Pick you up in ten minutes," she said.

I started to give her the name of my motel and the room number, but she stopped me in mid-sentence. "You're not the only one who knows how to check people out, Lena. Covered Wagons, room 217, right?"

"Can't hide anything from a reporter, can I?"

"Not for long."

Olivia seemed edgy during the drive to Silver Ridge, and I wondered if she had another migraine coming on. If so, I hoped she'd have enough sense to pull over and let me drive her back to Walapai Flats. But when I brought it up, she waved my concern away.

"I'll be fine. Thanks for the offer, though. If this damned headache continues, I might take you up on it after the meeting."

We traveled in silence the rest of the way, and by the time we arrived in Silver Ridge, the last vestiges of the usual spectacular sunset had been swallowed up by indigo.

I'd always liked the small mining town. Settled by Mormon pioneers in the mid-eighteen sixties, many of their original homes still stood, lending it a Victorian flavor that has been erased from Southwestern towns which concentrated on expansion instead of quality of life. As we twisted and turned along the broad, shaded streets, I appreciated the curlicued porches, the carefully-tended rose gardens, the perfectly maintained picket fences. It was like entering another, more charming, century. Given the town's bucolic charm, I couldn't help but wonder why Olivia had traded it for the more frenetic demands of Boston and New York. Maybe she liked the adrenalin rush the cities offered.

"Here we are," she announced, pulling into a Methodist church parking lot. Newer than most of the surrounding buildings, the church had made an attempt to blend with them by using a facade of weathered red brick and sparkling white trim.

"You brought me all the way up here to save my soul?" I said, as we exited her Explorer.

"I'm not sure the local Methodists are into that 'saving' stuff, but they've provided the room free of charge."

As we reached the side door, a church van pulled up, disgorging several passengers. One of them, a middle-aged woman sporting a jaunty red turban on her head, saw Olivia and waved.

Olivia waved back. "That's my cousin Edith." she explained. "Other members of the Eames clan may be inside. At least, the ones who are left."

"Left?"

"Look and listen." She started picking at her lip again.

We followed the van passengers down a dimly-lit hallway and into a carpeted parlor. Like most church parlors, the room was furnished with a mishmash of furniture. Flowered sofas, velveteen sofas, leather sofas—all different colors. Even though the room had no windows, lamps displaying the styles of at least four decades lent the room a cheery glow. Completing this picture of ecumenical benevolence, a painting of Jesus smiled down from a peach-toned wall as a white dove hovered over his head. Beneath it, Olivia's cousin climbed to the lectern. The flowered dress she wore would have better fit a woman three sizes larger, a pattern repeated over and over in the room, where other men and women with little or no hair were dressed in loose clothing that suggested sudden weight loss.

They were dying.

Chapter Twenty-two

As my nose adjusted to the sharp medicinal odors that warred for supremacy in the large parlor, I studied the crowd more carefully. While some stood on Death's doorstep, others appeared to be in radiant health. They all sat silently, holding yellowing photographs that displayed gaunt people, many of them children, attached to IVs. I recognized the elderly woman sitting in a damaged wheelchair near the door. At the demonstration, she'd been holding a sign that said 'Hasn't Walapai County Suffered Enough?' Tonight she held no picket sign, just a photograph that was the double of the one on Gabe Boone's bedside table.

"Is she related to Boone?" I whispered to Olivia.

"By marriage," she whispered back. "She's Elena Morehouse, Abby Boone's kid sister. "That's Abby in the photograph. Remember, I told you you'd learn more about Gabe here than anywhere else. These people are called Downwinders, Lena, because they all lived downwind of the Nevada Test Site. They…" She was interrupted by a rapping from the podium.

"This support meeting of the Tri-State Downwinders will now come to order," Olivia's cousin said. "We'll start by going around the room, giving our names, our diagnosis or the diagnosis of our loved ones, and where our appeal against the federal government now stands. But before we do that, let me issue a warning." Her thin face bloomed into a smile. "Keep it clean, folks. The press is with us today. My cousin Olivia, a big-shot journalist, has traveled all the way from New York to hear our stories. Olivia, wave hello to these nice folks."

Olivia waved. They waved back. Several blew kisses.

Then they prayed. Not being a big proponent of public prayer, I held my silence while they wove their way through the Lord's Prayer. As soon as they reached the "Amen" part, an elderly man in the first row introduced himself as Bill Nash, a native of Silver Ridge. Holding some sort of electronic buzzer to his throat to help him talk, he rasped in a metallic monotone, "My oncologist says it's spread to my…"

Before he could finish his sentence, the door opened and Earl Two Horses, Monty Carson, and "Ma" and Tara from Ma's Kitchen walked in. With them was an Indian woman I'd never seen before. From her Asian features and the darkness of her skin, I guessed she was Paiute.

Once they took seats in the rear of the room, Nash began again. He said that as a young man, he'd been a member of the Army unit used as guinea pigs during the bomb testing. The blast, located less than two thousand feet from his unprotected unit, caused the series of cancers he'd fought for decades.

"Me and Myra, we woulda liked kids, but the bomb sterilized me," he buzzed. "Maybe that was the whole point of the testing, maybe the government decided there was too many Americans running around and they needed to start sterilizing us. Or murdering us, like they did so many of my buddies. Well, it takes a lot to kill ol' Nash. Doctors been lopping off pieces of me for years, but now my larynx cancer's spread to my brain. Barring a miracle, my oncologist gives me a couple more months. The Feds offered me a fifty-thousand-dollar payout, said that was all I was going to get, so Myra made me accept it."

A low murmur around the room as others tendered their sympathies.

The next person, a former sheep rancher, spoke up. In his case, his sheep had died first, followed a year later by his younger brother, then his mother. Now it was his turn. Unlike Nash, he refused to have anything to do with the government's offer of fifty thousand dollars.

"With me, it's stomach cancer," the man growled. "My wife's down with thyroid cancer. You folks know I'm not one for crowds, but Evie's too sick to come out tonight, so here I am, flying the family flag. You wanna know what we told them government flunkies? We told them they could take their blood money and stick it where the sun don't shine. Hell, that wouldn't even pay for Evie's pain-killers, let alone her chemo, which ain't working anyway. Damn government scientists owe us a sight more than they're offering, using decent Americans for lab rats! Fifty million's more like it, and even then, it ain't enough."

For the next hour, I heard more versions of the same sad stories. Those who weren't dying spoke of loved ones who had. Some survivors, but far from all, had been offered fifty thousand dollars in compensation from the U.S. government, the maximum individual payout. Some took it, others chose to litigate. Still others described claims denied, having been told by federal attorneys that their cancers hadn't been caused by the tests, they'd just been "unlucky."

A young woman who wore neither wig nor scarf on her bald head said her claim had been turned down. "Before 1951, when the bombing began, no woman in my family had died of breast cancer," she explained, brandishing photographs of smiling women. "Since then, we've lost at least three women in each generation to breast cancer. My grandmother and three great-aunts; my mother and her two sisters. One of my sisters died last year, the other's in the hospital right now getting chemo. As for me, I've got Stage IV breast cancer. It's spread to my spine, but I'm a woman of faith and I can take anything God chooses to give me. But my daughter..." Her voice caught. Recovering, she said, "Lily's only four, but she's already..."

When she lost it again, the young man sitting with her pulled her back down to her seat, then stood up himself. "What my wife wants to say is that we're worried about Lily. She's been losing weight. The doctors haven't found anything yet, but they're still doing tests. And as for my wife, the government said we can't prove the cancer in her family was caused by the testing."

Three generations dead, another possibly dying.

The cumulative effect of these peoples' stories felt like being flayed alive. Just when I thought I couldn't take any more, Earl Two Horses spoke up.

His normally placid face was tight with anger. "You know the Paiute's story. My people are all Downwinders. That fallout blew over our land, killing us until there's hardly anyone left."

Earl held up a picture of a young man on horseback, dressed like a Mongol warrior. He made a more convincing Mongol than the Caucasian standing next to him: John Wayne, wearing heavy "Asian" makeup. "This is my grandfather. He was one of the three hundred Paiute extras on that cursed movie, *The Conqueror*. A few months after the movie finished filming and John Wayne and the other film people went home, the Paiute extras started getting sick. They were hunters, and besides getting dosed with radioactivity in Snow Canyon, they'd been eating the deer and the rabbit and all the other game that'd been contaminated during the tests. Most died. The skin fell away from their bones until there was hardly anything left to bury. The government didn't care, and our deaths aren't even listed in those articles you White folks keep quoting."

He made a sweeping gesture around the room, "Right now everyone's all up in arms over what happened in Japan, with the fallout from those nuclear reactors at Fukushima. But we got, what, ten times that amount almost every month for sixty years! Nobody bothered to get up in arms over the Paiute, did they? The Feds didn't even bother to track what happened to us. I guess they figured Indians didn't count. Nothing new there, right? And think about this. What happened to the people in Fukushima was an accident, but our government nuked us on purpose!

"When the attorneys finally got involved and the government started making those famous fifty-thousand-dollar payouts, the Feds made sure the Paiute didn't get a dime. In order to get the money, those government goons demanded that our widows and children prove they were residents of the United States. Residents! We Paiutes, people who have lived on this land for thousands of years! Most of our parents and grandparents were nomads and hunters, not office workers. They didn't have birth certificates, they didn't have Social Security records, they didn't have employment records, they didn't have deeds, they didn't have anything like that. And since they couldn't prove who they were, they were declared ineligible!"

The Paiute woman with him reached up and tugged at his arm, but Earl refused to sit down. "The government wasn't through hurting the Indians, either. This is my mother. Naiomi Two Horses. Her husband—my father—died of lung cancer after handling the yellow cake at the old Moccasin Peak Uranium Mine. Now my brother is about to go to work at the Black Basin, which is owned by the same man who managed Moccasin Peak. My brother needs to feed his family, but how long will it be before he dies, too?"

Naiomi Two Horses, aided now by the much stronger Monty, finally succeeded in hauling Earl back into his chair. Only then did I notice the photograph Monty was clutching; a young woman in a fifties-style dress. I wondered how many close family members he'd lost to the fallout.

Now it was Elena Morehouse's turn. Holding her photograph of Abby Boone high, she described her older sister and the hell she'd gone through after suffering through six miscarriages, then esophageal cancer.

"We figured she got that throat cancer from eating the vegetables from her own kitchen garden or drinking the water from her well," she said. "Whenever there was testing, the gardens were covered with radioactive ash, but the man the Atomic Energy Commission sent out to talk to folks guaranteed it was harmless, that all anybody had to do was rinse the dust off. He even swore that the water hadn't been contaminated!" She closed her eyes for a moment. "Earl, I'm sorry for what you and your people went through, but my sister suffered, too. So did her husband. When Abby died, Gabe just plain lost his mind."

After several more horror stories and a vow to keep pressuring the government to make payment commensurate with their suffering, the meeting broke up. A few people stayed behind to chat with friends, but the Walapai Flats contingent left after saying their farewells. Olivia exchanged some private words with her cousin, then joined me as I hurried out the door eager to breathe non-medicinal air.

"Jesus, Olivia," I said, as we walked toward her car. "How can you stand working on stories like this?"

"The same way you can stand doing what you do. You put aside your feelings and do what has to be done; otherwise you're no good to anyone."

Strong talk, but she'd chewed her lip until it bled.

In front of us twin girls of around eight skipped over to a row of rosebushes bordering the parking lot. With a mischievous giggle, the bald twin snapped off a deep red bloom while the other, her hair combed into blond ringlets, frowned in disapproval. "That's not your rosebush," she admonished.

"Nope, it's God's," her thieving sister answered, burying her nose in the petals. "And he created roses for us to enjoy." Her face was a map of profound joy.

I waited until we climbed in her car before I said, "Those girls. I didn't see them in the meeting."

"The children were being taken care of in the nursery by volunteers. Most of the kids believe they're going to be fine, which is why their parents didn't want them in the meeting."

"But they…" I motioned to the bald girl. "She wasn't around when the tests were being conducted."

"Her great-grandparents were."

"Are you saying that the nuclear tests caused genetic mutations?"

"Some people think it did, but the government's fighting that all the way, and their lawyers are the best money can buy."

"Boone's sister-in-law said that the government claimed the radioactive ash and water were safe. After what happened at Hiroshima and Nagasaki, they had to know better."

Olivia's jaw clenched. "The Atomic Energy Commission certainly knew better, but they were determined to test anyway. When the cattle, sheep, and deer died and then people started getting sick, the AEC flew out some low-level flunky from Washington to calm everybody down. He held meetings in the high school auditorium here in Silver Ridge, and convinced the locals everything was fine." She shrugged. "Why would they doubt him? He represented the U.S. government, didn't he?"

"Jesus."

She gave me a grim smile. "Jesus didn't have anything to do with it."

By unspoken agreement, we said nothing more about the meeting during the drive back to Walapai Flats, but it was obvious Olivia's headache had become worse. When I reminded her I was willing to drive, she shook her head.

"What are you going to do, take me home, then hitchhike back from Sunset Canyon Lakes?" she said. "I'll be fine."

I offered to let her stay the night in my motel room so she could dose herself to sleep, but she declined that offer, too.

"Thanks, but I can't afford the down time. I've got a deadline to meet."

When we pulled up in front of the Covered Wagons Inn, I breathed a sigh of relief. But as I climbed out of the Explorer into the inky night, Olivia slid down the car window and called out, "Lena! Have that hunky partner of yours run a search on Ike Donohue, if he hasn't already. Look for Donohue's tie-in with a man named Gerald Heber."

"Who's Gerald Heber?" And where had I heard that name before?

The motel's neon sign blinked blue on her face, making her look ghostlier than usual. "You'll find out."

With that, she drove away.

It was almost eleven, but after what I'd seen and heard at the Downwinders meeting, sleep was out of the question. Who was Heber and what was his connection to Ike Donohue? I paced around my motel room, fighting the temptation to call Jimmy regardless of the hour, to tell him what I'd seen and heard to share my outrage. I finally calmed down enough to realize that just because my night was ruined didn't mean I should ruin his, too. Vacillating between rage and depression, I logged back onto the Internet for the second time in a day, a record for me.

Typing Ike Donohue+Gerald Heber into Google, I found nothing. Frustrated, I sat there, cursing my limited Net skills. Trying again, I dismissed the Donohue/Heber tie-in and simply typed in Gerald Heber and was rewarded with seventy-two hits. Among them, I found a car salesman, a dentist, a dairy farmer, two real estate salesmen, and an ex-con blogging about the dire state of America's prisons. I was making my way through various businessmen touting their wares when my eye was drawn to another blog, this one posted by a Dr. Paul D. Howell, a physics professor at Oklahoma State University. Howell, musing about the strange turns life can take, wrote that he'd planned to become a rock drummer until he won top prize in a science fair competition held at his Arlington, Virginia high school. The man who'd bankrolled the competition was named Gerald Heber.

"I owe my career to him," Howell blogged, "but not, thank God, my ethics."

Since Arlington was a suburb of Washington, D.C., I narrowed the search to GERALD HEBER+WASHINGTON, D.C. Howell's snipe about ethics—or the lack thereof—was probably the remnants of some old grudge, but it was the best lead I'd found so far. When my search led me to a brief that ran September 2, 1965, on B-2 of the *Washington Post*, I struck pay dirt.

The article, so short it wasn't even by-lined, mentioned Gerald Heber's retirement from the Atomic Energy Commission. This particular Heber had been lauded for "his unique service to the United States of America during troubled times." However, the article made no mention of Ike Donohue, and a connection between the two still seemed unlikely. Heber had worked for the government, Donohue in the private sector. Further distancing the men were their ages. If the *Washington Post*'s Heber had retired in 1965 at the age of sixty-five, by now he was probably pushing up daisies in a cemetery somewhere.

What they say about Internet addiction is true. Once you're on, it's hard to get off. Following the trail of this particular Heber, I kept scrolling though the AEC+Heber hits until I found a longer piece.

A feature article titled *Nuking Nevada,* written by Alonzo Ertes and printed in the *Nevada Sentinel* on May 3, 1978, detailed the effects of radioactive fallout during above-ground atomic testing in the fifties and sixties.

> "Thanks to the efforts of Gerald Heber, the AEC's public relations officer, the AEC was able to hide the dangers of the Nevada bomb testing for decades. They spoon-fed Heber misleading information, which he softened even further until the radioactive ash that was falling across the U.S. looked as pure as Christmas snow. Heber even took to the airwaves, calling scientists who warned against the tests "non-informed alarmists" at best, and "Commie sympathizers" at worst.
>
> Believing Heber's reassurances, farmers in Utah brushed the radioactive ash off their tomatoes and shipped them to the stores. Arizona ranchers allowed their beef cattle to graze on radioactive land and drink radiation-polluted water. Nevada mothers gave their children milk from radioactive dairy cows. When Heber—now retired—was questioned about his role in the thousands of radiation-related deaths that followed decades of nuclear fallout in the U.S., he staunchly defended his work.

```
"Ancient history," Heber said. "That
all happened at the height of the Cold
War, and in every war there's going
to be collateral damage. If those
hayseeds had an ounce of patriotism
in their bones, they'd stop all their
whining and get down on their knees
to thank God and the U.S. government
for saving them from the Commies."
```

I remembered the hairless women at the Downwinders meeting, the men relying on oxygen tanks to breathe, the anguished parents clinging to photographs of long-dead children. Hayseeds. I read on.

```
Heber even defended the choice of
Nevada for the testing of 928 nuclear
bombs.
   "Where else was the government going
to test those weapons? That area was the
least populated section of the coun-
try," he said. "No one lived out there,
other than ranchers and Indians."
```

Remembering where Ike Donohue had lived before retiring to Arizona, I went back to Google and typed in HEBER+DURHAM, NORTH CAROLINA. Only one hit popped up, but it was a doozy.

On February 12, 1970, the *Durham Republic* reported that Gerald Heber had been hired as a consultant by the Cook & Creighton Tobacco Company, based in Durham, North Carolina. His duties were to format a new public relations policy to combat the advertising limitations recently imposed by the federal government on all tobacco products.

Public relations. Cook & Creighton Tobacco Company.

Where Ike Donohue once worked.

The man whose job it had been to convince the Southwest that nuclear fallout was harmless had been hired by a tobacco company to convince the world that cigarettes and chewing tobacco were harmless. Looking at the timeline, I realized that Heber had probably taught Donohue everything he knew about telling lies and about how to ignore the moral ramifications of those lies. Together, the two men were at least partially implicated in the diseases and deaths of untold numbers of smokers.

Now I remembered where I'd heard Heber's name before—from Nancy Donohue. She'd discovered that before her husband's murder, he'd placed a call to his old boss. "Some were to people he knew when he was married to Claudia, like that troll Gerald Heber. I wound up talking to the granddaughter. Old Heber'd been dead for years."

I looked at my watch. It was midnight, but damned be the hour. I picked up my cell phone and punched in Nancy Donohue's number. When she answered, she didn't sound sleepy at all, just slightly drunk.

"Oh, it's you, Jones. What the hell do you want?"

Following her example, I skipped the social pleasantries. "Did your husband ever work with a man named Gerald Heber?"

A catarrhal bark, probably a laugh. "Talk about a blast from the past! Why do you want to know about old Gerald?"

"I take it, then, your husband did work with him."

"Of course he did. Gerald was Ike's boss. When Gerald left C&C, Ike was promoted to head of the public relations department. But I repeat, why do you want to know about that old bastard and what business is it of yours, anyway?" In the background, I heard ice cubes rattling against glass.

"Mrs. Donohue, aren't you in the least curious about who shot your husband? Or why?"

A slurp, then a satisfied smacking of lips. "What difference does it make? As you so succinctly pointed out the last time we talked, Ike was dying anyway."

She slammed the phone down.

So there it was. The Atomic Energy Commission had hired Gerald Heber to lie for them. It had been his job—and the sonofabitch did it exceedingly well—to convince people that nuclear fallout posed a no larger safety risk than dewdrops on apples.

As a result, thousands of people—perhaps hundreds of thousands—had died.

Among them, Gabriel Boone's wife.

After that discovery, I knew sleep was a long way off, so I pulled my iPod out of my carry-all and brought up John Lee Hooker's "Will the Circle Be Unbroken," the bootlegged version with my father playing guitar. It had been surreptitiously recorded in some blues bar near where we'd once lived and although my father's name—whatever it was—did not appear on the credits, I recognized his voice and style, remembered his open, loving face. I hit REPEAT and listened to him until I drifted off…

I was back in the mine, but this time my father, not my mother, held my hand. For some reason, my mother had refused to attend the ceremony; she was too sick, she said, to see the surprise Abraham had prepared for us.

The mine was lit by torches. Incense filled the air. Abraham swept by, followed by his acolytes. He wore his priestly robes, and the light of God shone down upon him.

"Those who follow the Lord, draw nigh!" he commanded, his voice that of the angels.

My father, suddenly tense, tried to hold me back, but I was four years old and curious, so I wiggled out of his arms and moved forward with the rest of Abraham's flock. Hands pushed me along until I reached the front and saw the stone altar Abraham had prepared. On it lay a boy of about my age, dressed in nothing but a breechclout. He was smiling. Everyone was. Abraham's smile was brightest of them all.

"How do we show our love for the Lord?" Abraham asked his flock.

"By following his bidding!" his flock chorused.

"Does the Lord demand sacrifice?"

His flock responded, "The Lord demands sacrifice!"

"What does the Lord tell us to sacrifice?"

"Our firstborn!"

In the back, I heard my father scream my name until he was drowned out by the chants of the flock. "We do as the Lord bade us!" a hundred voices sang. Only then did I notice the knife in Abraham's upraised hand. Before I could tell him to stop, he plunged it into the boy's chest.

"Oh, great are the works of the Lord!" Abraham cried, as blood rolled down the sides of the altar to pool on the floor of the mine.

"Great are the works of the Lord!" the flock responded.

Confused, I ran back to my father. "I don't understand, Daddy. Why isn't the little boy getting up?"

My father couldn't answer, because blood was pouring from his own mouth.

Chapter Twenty-three

When the sirens woke me, the clock on my nightstand was flashing 6:03. a.m.

Not that I'd been sound asleep to begin with. After I'd awoken from that first nightmare and thrown my iPod across the room, the rest of the night was broken by short, sharp dreams about little girls with crumbling bones, Paiutes with melted faces, women keening over fresh graves. For once, my dreams about Abraham seemed gentle in comparison.

The continuing racket outside sounded like the entire Walapai County Sheriff's Department had been activated. Tumbling from the bed to the window, I pulled back the blinds to pinpoint the source of the racket. All I could see was the pool and one bath-robed tourist hunched over a steaming mug. He didn't look alarmed, and when the sirens faded into the distance, I closed the blinds and trudged to the bathroom.

The hot shower revived me somewhat, and once I brewed some coffee in the room's one-cup coffee maker, I felt almost human. As I sipped, I punched in Jimmy's cell phone number; he'd always been an early bird.

"Boone's legal situation just got worse," I told him.

"Speak up. I can't hear you."

No wonder. The background noise—people laughing, dishes and silverware rattling and clanking—made him almost unintelligible, too. "Where are you? Ma's Kitchen?"

"What?"

When I repeated myself, only louder, he shouted back. "Yeah! Ma's! I'm almost finished with breakfast, but if you want to talk, I'll hang around!"

This was no conversation to be conducted around nosey diners, many of whom wouldn't want the area's tragic history aired in a crowded restaurant. "Not Ma's!" I screamed. "Meet me at the park! In a half hour!"

"Meet you where?"

"The park!"

"Did you say the park?"

"Yes!"

"Where in the park?"

"Same table as the other day!"

"In a half hour?"

"Yes, dammit!" Hoarse from yelling, I rang off.

This early in the morning, the Walapai Flats City Park was as deserted as I'd hoped it would be, and Jimmy and I had it to ourselves. No toddlers played in the sandbox, no starlings rioted in the waste cans. In between bites of the Danish I'd picked up on my way to the park, I told him about the Downwinder's meeting, then asked the question that had kept me up all night.

"You were raised in Walapai Flats, Jimmy, which means you had to know all about those damned bombs. Why didn't you tell me?"

He looked off into the sky, which was an innocent blue, its radioactivity long since vanished. "It wasn't relevant to the case."

The outrage I'd kept inside bubbled to the surface. "Are you serious? Chances are it has everything to do with the case."

"How could it? The testing ended years ago."

"Not the cancer cases!"

He didn't answer right way, and when he did, just mumbled, "You don't understand."

"Really? Try me."

Turning away from the sky and facing me, he said, "All right. Maybe I made a mistake. But not being from here, you don't know the cloud this community was living under and I don't just mean the radioactive kind. You've seen how the people make their living. Tourism. Yeah, I heard about the tests when I was a kid, and the problems the Downwinders were having, but talking about them was a forbidden subject around the dinner table, so…so I guess it all just got pushed to the back of my mind."

Now I was really getting mad. What good was a partner who withheld information that might be pertinent to a case? "Don't you try to tell me…"

"Look, most of the damage was done when we were still living in Salt Lake, and back then I was too young to grasp what was going on when the news started leaking out. When we moved down here, I was still a kid and still didn't really understand. Yes, I finally got it, but by then I'd become like everyone else around here—since there was nothing I could do about it I made myself forget. Once I moved to the Pima Reservation and took back my birth name, Dad was so angry he didn't exactly keep me apprised of local events—not even what was happening with the Downwinders and their lawsuits against the Feds. As for Ted, he and the other kids were busy with their own lives. Whenever we got together, that's what we talked about, our lives, not a series of bomb tests before most of us were born."

"But…"

He waved my objection away. "You've met my father. You know what he's like. We were drilled in silence on the subject and that's what we promised. Absolute silence. He reminded me of that when I came up here to help Ted."

I thought about that for a moment, his father's demands, Jimmy's own conflicted soul. "You can hardly stand to be in the same room with him, yet you remain loyal to him?"

"Loyalty is a way of life. If you choose it. Which I did."

I didn't understand and probably never would. Just as Jimmy would never understand how much my childhood had shaped me. After all, I couldn't even remember my own birth name, could I? In our different ways, we were both haunted.

Pushing away my own ghosts, I stretched out my hand and covered his with my own. "Still friends, Almost Brother?"

"Forever, Lena." He didn't move his hand away.

As if there'd been no rift between us, I continued telling him what I'd learned. "Apparently the government switched to underground testing in the early sixties, not that it helped all that much. Seems the ground around the test site was so pocked with mine shafts and naturally-occurring vents that the radioactive dust continued to shoot into the atmosphere. And onto the rest of the country. Especially Walapai Flats. It coated the damn place."

With a great show of busyness, Jimmy took a pen and notebook from his shirt pocket and began jotting down notes. "You've done a good job on the history, but when I get back to the motel, I'll see what else I can find. That's if you can trust me to."

Did I? Yes, I decided, I did. "I'd appreciate it. Dig especially deep on Gerald Heber, Donohue, Tosches, and the lovely Mia." I thought for a moment. "Even Earl Two Horses and Monty Carson, the farrier. They were both at the Downwinders meeting. Oh, and Ma, the restaurant owner. He was there, too, with Tara, that waitress who's sweet on you. Did you ever learn Ma's name?"

A smile. "Marcello Sabbatini. He's Tara's father."

I couldn't see frail little Tara shooting Donohue or Tosches, but to keep everything politically correct, I added her name to the list. "On the off-chance that Tosches' death is connected to the Downwinders, you might want to do more checking into Cole Laveen. He's the new partner in the Black Basin Mine, and now that Tosches is dead, he might take over. I checked him out online myself, but he looked so blameless it made me suspicious. Check out Katherine Dysart, too, and her husband Trent. Being from Boston, Trent probably didn't have a personal grudge against either Donohue or Tosches, but there is such a thing as a hired hit man. The guy's killed before, and maybe it wasn't as accidental as Katherine would like people to believe. Prison tends to make people worse, not better."

"Is that it?" He started to close the notebook.

"One more thing. Add Sheriff Wiley Alcott to the mix."

"You're kidding."

"How many Arizona sheriffs have you met who wear Rolexes and Armani suits?"

He raised his eyebrows. "Top of the list for him, then."

Because of the strain between us, I didn't tell Jimmy about the other person who needed to be looked at more carefully. Hating what I did for a living, I decided to have another word with Hank Olmstead.

But only after I visited Desert Investigations' new client.

Jails aren't the sanest of places, but today the Walapai County Complex was weirder than ever. The guard manning the metal detector looked spooked, and even the calm old deputy at the front desk was flipping nervously through his copy of *Urban Living*. When I told him I was there to see Gabriel Boone, he made the appropriate call, but as soon as he disconnected, he whispered, "Stop by and see me before you leave."

When Boone was ushered into the interview room, he looked peaceful. I didn't want to change that, but it was necessary. "Mr. Boone…"

"Call me Gabe, Miss Jones. Everyone does."

"Only if you call me Lena."

He frowned. "I'm not used to treating women so familiar."

"This is the twenty-first century, Mr. Boone."

"Pretty day out, isn't it, ah, Lena? There's a window real high up in the corridor between the cells and this room, so I was able to see out. Bright blue sky, a clear Arizona day. Makes a person glad to be alive. Were there any clouds at all? This time of year, we sometimes get a light afternoon shower. Makes the earth smell like it'd just been born. Isn't that right, Duke?" He looked to his left, and cocked his head, as if listening to a distant voice.

Growing uncomfortable, I rushed, "Yes, I love the desert after a rain, especially in August. It helps cool things off. Gabe, do you know Nancy Donohue, Ike Donohue's wife?"

His eyes flickered, but that was all. "Good woman with horses and dogs, lousy with people. Except her husband, a course. I felt bad about making her a widow, because she sure did love that piece of dirt she was married to."

If Nancy Donohue had loved her husband, it was news to me, but I let it slide. "In what way was he a piece of dirt?"

"Let me give you a little tip, Miss, uh, Lena. Never trust a man who always follows orders. A hired gun, that's all Donohue was. Standing up there in front of the TV cameras, swearing in front of God and everybody that the mine would be safe when he knew damned well how many Navajos died at Moccasin Peak. He was used to making bad men look good, just like his old boss could. That man…"

He broke off, and I knew why. It was too early in the interview to bring up Heber's name, so I skirted around it. "When you took that trip up to Salt Lake City for your grandniece's funeral, did you have car trouble?"

His face brightened. "Boy, did I! Let me tell you, finding a clutch for a sixty-seven Ford pickup takes some doing. Guy at the repair shop, Sam, he said I'd be better off junking it and buying something newer, but me and that truck, we've driven a lot of road together, so I told him to do his best. He got on the Internet and found a clutch in a junkyard over in Colorado Springs, and they sent it over. Amazing thing, that Internet, isn't it? Sam worked on the clutch some, and it turned out fine. Took a few days, though, so I had to find me a motel."

"Sounds like an expensive trip."

He looked to his left again and muttered something I couldn't hear, but I could guess who he was talking to. Or thought he was. "Gabe, is John Wayne in this room?"

"Sure is, and he's hanging onto every word you say. To answer your question, yeah, my trip cost a bit, but I had me money put aside. I don't go out drinking any more, and Mr. Olmstead pays me a good salary, plus throws in room and board, so the only thing left to spend some money on is Blue. Unlike a lot of people I know around here, Blue's hale and hearty, thank the stars. I used

to own his great-great—forget how many greats-grandpappy."
His eyes unfocused for a moment, as if remembering. "That first
Blue, he died way too young. Got sick. Real sick."

To keep him on track, I said, "Must be hard losing a pet. Still,
motel rooms and meals must have cost you quite a bit during
your trip. Didn't you have any relatives you could stay with up
in Salt Lake?"

He stopped looking to his left and met my eyes. "My
grandniece, she was the last of my family. She was born here
in town, moved to Salt Lake when she married. She had better
luck than her mother and sister did, made it all the way to
fifty-one."

"They must have died young. What'd your grandniece die
of?" I was edging closer to Heber now.

"Breast cancer."

"Is that what took her mother and sister, too?"

A nod. "Why do you want to know?"

"Does the name Gerald Heber mean anything to you?"

The breath went out of him in such a rush I was surprised
it didn't knock me down.

"Come again, Lena? My hearing's not so good these days."

There was nothing wrong with Gabe's hearing; he just wanted
time to formulate his answer. I played along by raising my voice.
"Are you familiar with the name Gerald Heber?"

"Why are you asking about Heber?"

"Tell me what you know about him."

Continuing to ignore the imaginary presence on his left,
he lowered his head and seemed to be studying something
under the table. I looked down and saw nothing, only that
the table was bolted to the floor. So was his chair. While it
wasn't an uncommon occurrence for men in lockup to start
tossing furniture around, such measures seemed incongruous
for a shackled man in his eighties. Then again, what did I
really know about him? During my last visit I hadn't believed
his murder confession, but after attending the Downwinder's

meeting, I wasn't so certain. And he was crazy, no doubt about that.

"Could you please answer my question, Gabe? I'm here to help you."

When he looked at me again, he was a changed man. His eyes narrowed and his lips pulled tight against his teeth. "Heber? All you need to know about Gerald Heber is that the liar is dead and burning in hell, but it didn't happen soon enough for me or my wife and my mother-in-law and my best friend and my grandniece and her mother and sister and all them other folks who died in Walapai County. Not to mention the animals. Now I'm through talking, Miss Jones."

"But Gabe, how can I help you if…?"

He didn't move or say another word until I signaled the nervy-looking detention officer to lead him and his imaginary friend back to his cell. Gabe delivered a polite goodbye, but he had trouble doing even that.

Gabe Boone had hated Gerald Heber enough to kill him, so now I had more work for Jimmy. When, exactly, did Heber die? And where? My own rough Internet search had found no obit for the man, or any other mention of him after he left Cook & Creighton Tobacco. Had he remained in North Carolina, or did he relocate to the Southwest, like so many retired people were doing in the Seventies? I was so deep in thought I forgot about the deputy at the front desk, but he waved me over as I came back into the lobby. From the open pages on his desk, I saw that he was still hung up on *Urban Living*.

"Does what you wanted to see me about have anything to do with those sirens that work me up this morning?" I asked. "More squabbling over the Black Basin Mine?"

Before he could answer, a detention officer carrying a big box of doughnuts entered the lobby. After handing a glazed to my guy, he continued on toward the sheriff's side of the complex. Until he was out of sight, the deputy fanned the pages of his magazine, finally landing on a color spread that featured a Manhattan penthouse, all steel and chrome.

"What do you think of this?" he asked.

"It's okay if you like that sort of thing. Me, I'm not into the industrial look. Who wants to come home from work to an apartment that looks like a factory?"

"People who never had to work in one, probably." He flipped the pages again. "So sirens roused you from your beauty sleep? I'll tell the boys to mute them from now on whenever they pass the Covered Wagons."

"That's neighborly of you."

"We here in Walapai Flats pride ourselves on being neighborly."

"So I've noticed."

"It's not necessarily because we feel warm and fuzzy all the time, but we have to take good care of our tourists or they won't come back with all their lovely money."

"I've noticed that, too."

He placed the doughnut carefully in his desk drawer. "As I was saying, Walapai Flats depends on the tourist trade, which is why what happened this morning is such a damned shame. The roadblock on Route 47's got everyone up in arms. People at the resort, they're all pissed off, so we're working on a detour through the desert. The people with four-wheel-drives, they'll be okay, but I don't know about the rest. That's some rugged country out there."

"Another bad accident?'

"In a manner of speaking. Seems…" He broke off when two much younger deputies walked by, their faces ashen. My guy waited until they disappeared down the corridor toward the sheriff's office, then he motioned me to lean in closer.

"What?" I whispered.

He looked down at *Urban Living* again. Almost without moving his lips, he muttered, "Don't tell anyone you heard it from me, but Deputy Stark got shot. He's laying out there dead in his cruiser, a bullet through his forehead. It happened some time last night, about a mile from the Lakes."

I felt more satisfaction than I should have. Regardless of his off-hours behavior, Stark was a law officer who'd presumably died in the line of duty. "Has there been an arrest?"

The deputy shook his head. "Not that I've heard. He wasn't the world's most popular guy."

I flashed back to Connie Stark's battered face and the frustration I'd noticed on Sheriff Alcott's. Monty's, too. "Why are you telling me all this?"

He closed his copy of *Urban Living*, then tossed it into the waste basket. "Because you tried to help Connie. She's my granddaughter."

As Blue, tail a-wag as usual, escorted me to the lodge, I saw Dusty helping ranch guests mount up on some bored-looking horses. Keeping my face averted, I was able to make it inside without being spotted. Luck stayed with me as I crossed the deserted reception area, I saw Hank Olmstead walking toward me, Ted in tow. Ted smiled broadly, but the look on Olmstead's face was less welcoming. He frowned when I requested a few moments alone.

"We're busy, Miss Jones. Can't you come back later?"

"If you want to help Gabriel Boone, you'll answer a few questions."

Ted clapped Olmstead on the shoulder. "That's okay, Dad. Dusty and I can handle things." Without waiting for an answer, he flashed me a big smile and left.

Still frowning, Olmstead turned on his heel and headed toward the office. Without being invited, I followed.

"How crazy is Gabe Boone?" I asked, as soon as we were seated. "Crazy enough for an insanity defense?"

"Mr. Boone is not mentally ill."

"He talks to a dead man."

"I talk to God. Does that make me crazy?"

On that one, I kept my opinion to myself. "Gabe says something, John Wayne answers. John Wayne says something, Gabe answers. A regular tête-à-tête. Is he on medication?"

Olmstead sat back in his big leather chair and crossed his arms in front of his chest. "Gabriel Boone is as sane as you or me."

As far as I was concerned, that cast doubt on us both. "He says he owes you a debt, Mr. Olmstead. Mind telling me what it is? It could be important to his defense."

For a moment I thought he'd retreat into his usual stodgy non-answers, but he didn't. "Mr. Boone endured some rough years after his wife died," he said. "Did you know that the land Sunset Trails sits on used to belong to him, and that our house out back is where he and his wife once lived? This was a cattle spread then, not a particularly successful one, but it did well enough to pay the bills and put a little aside until Abby Boone fell ill."

"Cancer, by any chance?"

His face became mulish. "The exact nature of her illness isn't relevant."

"Actually, it is. I know Abby Boone fell 'ill' after the government started testing their nukes in Nevada. And at Silver Ridge last night, I…"

"What were you doing in Silver Ridge?" he interrupted.

"Attending the Downwinders meeting with Olivia Eames. Gabe's sister-in-law was there, along with several people from Walapai Flats."

"Don't tell me you're hanging out with that reporter!"

"Well, yes."

"Stay away from her. She's does nothing but stir up trouble."

I don't like people telling me what or what not to do but I kept my tone civil, something I felt increasingly difficult to do around this man. "You know Olivia?"

"Well enough to know that she's determined to rake up a subject more wisely left alone."

"Like radioactive ranchland?"

I thought his eyes would pop out of his head in fury, but he grasped the edges of his desk and took a deep breath. "You see? People hear those old stories and jump to conclusions. But let me assure you that the land in and around Walapai Flats is perfectly safe and has been for years, or I would never have moved my family down here from Salt Lake City."

Hank Olmstead may have been arrogant and stiff-necked, but I believed him, because there was no doubt that he treasured his family above all else. "I hope you didn't rely on the Atomic Energy Commission's claim that the land was clean."

Like so many men of his age and religious beliefs, he didn't like his pronouncements argued with, and although he'd let go of the desk, his voice still crackled with anger when he replied, "I am not stupid, Miss Jones. After what transpired at Nevada Test Site, no one around here believed a word those folks said. In fact, the AEC's propensity for telling lies is one of the reasons it was eventually disbanded. To make certain the land was safe, I did exactly what every sensible rancher and homeowner in the quad-state area was doing and bought myself a Geiger counter and tested every square foot of this entire property before entering escrow. This county, along with the rest of Arizona, Nevada, Utah, and Colorado, is now perfectly safe, so I and the other members of the Walapai Flats Chamber of Commerce would appreciate it if you don't go around blabbing about the problems the area used to have."

"Because it would be bad for business?"

He grabbed onto the desk again. "Miss Jones, the economy in this part of the state is based on tourism. There is nothing to be gained by alarming people unnecessarily."

"Speaking of rocks that glow in the dark, how safe do you think the Black Basin Mine will be? Would you feel comfortable having one of your children work there?"

He looked relieved to have the conversation shift away from the bomb tests. "I have faith in Cole Laveen's leadership. Roger Tosches was all about the money, but Mr. Laveen remembers the human connection."

In a way, Olmstead had just described himself. A formal, forbidding man, but one with a heart. If he was right about Cole Laveen, workers at the Black Basin would fare better than had the Navajos at Moccasin Peak.

"About Tosches, someone told me…" I stopped, my attention caught by the sound of boots clomping down the hallway toward the office. *Oh, please. Not Dusty. Not now.*

The door opened to reveal a pudgy man wearing beat-up Western wear covered by a white apron. "Everything's clean and put away, Hank. After I take a break, I'll put together the lunch buffet, then work on dinner. Hope your guests like lasagna."

"I'm certain they'll like yours, Mr. Carola. And thank you so much for helping us out like this. You've been a Godsend."

"Always glad to do it for you, Hank. You've been mighty generous to me and mine." He closed the door and clomped away.

"Our substitute cook," Olmstead explained, unnecessarily. "Until Gabe comes back."

Dream on, I thought. That old man belonged some place where he couldn't hurt himself or others, but trying to convince Olmstead was a lost cause. "I'm glad you brought up Tosches," I said. "Word is, he'd been trying to buy Sunset Trails and you two had a heated argument over it."

He didn't bother with a denial. "That 'someone' being Leilani, no doubt. I wish my daughter hadn't been so free with private family information, but at twenty-two, she's still naive enough to trust everyone, including reporters and private investigators. Since she's already let the cat out of the bag, yes, Mr. Tosches was trying to buy Sunset Trails, and I'm sure she told you why he thought he could. Our financial difficulties, correct?" Without waiting for a reply, he continued. "Because of the economy, things were tight for a while, but we survived. During Mr. Tosches' last visit I thanked him for his offer but requested that he discontinue stopping by, that we here at the ranch needed to concentrate on our guests, not business discussions with him. Perhaps if he'd taken my advice he would still be alive."

As if realizing what he'd said, he backtracked. "Not that his death had anything to do with us."

Maybe. Maybe not. "Do you think he believed more uranium could be found on your land?"

A dry laugh. "He couldn't possibly be that foolish. As I said, before Jeanette and I purchased the ranch, I went over every inch of the place with a Geiger counter. There were no hot spots which might have indicated either fallout or uranium deposits. Mr. Tosches wanted to build another resort like Sunset Canyon Lakes, that's all. Now, not that this hasn't been an interesting digression, but I thought you wanted to talk about Gabriel Boone."

"Correct. You started to tell me why Gabe feels so indebted to you." Indebted enough to confess to a murder he didn't commit to get your son out of jail.

The story Olmstead told was a sad one. After Boone's wife died from esophageal cancer, the bank foreclosed on his ranch. He spent the next few years wrangling for other ranchers until his drinking problem became so serious he couldn't hold a job. "The property passed through several hands before my wife and I turned it into a guest ranch," he said. "We were doing fairly well, too, until Jeanette…" He swallowed. "But on June 12, 1996, the day Mr. Boone arrived at Sunset Trails…"

He turned away and pretended to sneeze, not before I saw a drop of moisture on his cheek.

"Gesundheit," I said, to help this proud man save face. But I also wondered why a busy man like Olmstead could remember the exact day a drifter had turned up at his ranch.

"Thank you." He grabbed a tissue and made a big deal out of blowing his nose.

"Go on."

He cleared his throat. "That day Mr. Boone was pretty much at the end of his tether. His clothes were in rags, he had the shakes, he could barely talk. He wanted a job, but there was no way I could use anyone in his condition. Still, I felt sorry for him so I sent him over to the wrangler's cookhouse for a square meal. One for his dog, too, although the blue-eyed thing looked a lot healthier than Mr. Boone."

He stared off into space.

I waited.

"About an hour later is when…Jeanette was in the family quarters out back, hanging up a picture. You've probably sneaked out there and seen our house, right?"

"Big fenced yard. Good idea, with such a big family and the Virgin River being so close by."

His mouth twisted. "It wasn't fenced then. Jeanette was careful, a pearl of great price. She always kept close watch on everyone, especially the kids with Down syndrome. One of her sisters was living with us to help out, so everything should have been fine. But when Jeanette…" He had to take a few more breaths before continuing. "When Jeanette had the heart attack, it was chaos. I was up here at the lodge, and Miguel, that's our second oldest, called me from the house and I ran back there, and the kids were crying and screaming, and her sister was doing chest compressions, but I could see there was nothing to be done, but I took over and tried for the longest time, but the Lord had already called her home."

After taking a big gulp of air, he fell silent for so long I had to prompt him, "I'm sorry for your loss, Mr. Olmstead, but what does this have to do with Gabriel Boone?"

He stood up. "Excuse me, but I need to get a drink of water. Would you like one?"

"I'm fine."

For the next few minutes I sat there alone, listening to pots rattle in the kitchen, beyond that, the sound of horses neighing. Floating over the musty smell of record books and old leather, I could smell garlic and oregano.

When Olmstead returned, his eyes and nose were noticeably red. Sitting down, he said, "Life is for the living, even amidst death. In our grief, we didn't remember that Leilani wasn't in the house. She'd always been highly intelligent, curious, and very active despite her leg, so we'd bought one of those big swing sets that had a slide, teeter totter, all the bells and whistles, just to keep her occupied. To make a long story short, while the rest of us were working on Jeanette, we forgot about Leilani. The children had been warned about the river, told to never to go there, but once she realized she wasn't being watched, she made a beeline for it." He gave me a sad look. "She was only five. You know how children are at that age."

"Tell them not to do something, and that's the first thing they do."

"Exactly. In that, I failed her. But Mr. Boone didn't."

"How so?"

"He'd finished eating at the cookhouse and was walking toward the road when he saw her playing on top of the riverbank. When she suddenly disappeared, he knew she'd fallen in. Taking no care for his own safety, he ran and jumped in after her. The current's strong at that spot, and he almost drowned saving my daughter's life. For that, I and my family will be eternally grateful to Mr. Boone."

I could see it in my mind. A broken-down old drunk carrying a load of grief no one should have to carry, showing up at his old homestead to beg for a job, and getting turned down. Free meal or not, many men would have been bitter enough to just walk away.

Not Gabe Boone.

I remembered his face, the one I'd seen in the interview room. Careworn. Noble.

Olmstead had answered only half my question. "I can see why you're indebted to Gabe, but why does he feel indebted to you?" Looked at from another angle, Gabe had a strong reason to resent the entire Olmstead clan, since they were living on the ranch he'd once owned.

Olmstead shrugged. "We took him in, helped him get straightened up, but that's what anyone in our situation would do. Once he was released from rehab..."

"Who paid for that?" A good rehab facility could run thousands of dollars per week, and the free state-run places had long waiting lists.

"We did, of course."

In other words, Hank Olmstead paid for it out of his own pocket.

Glossing over his extraordinary generosity, he continued,
"Once Mr. Boone felt better, we gave him a job and he's been
with us ever since. So you see, we're the ones who owe the debt,
not Mr. Boone. We lost Jeanette that day but Gabriel Boone
gave us back our Leilani."

The death of a peace officer brings out even more law enforcement than the death of a gazillionaire. On the way from the
ranch toward Sunset Canyon Lakes, I drove though a desert
literally carpeted with police cruisers. Hoping for some first-
hand information, I approached several officers but found none
willing to talk. Forced to mind my own business, I allowed
myself to be directed off the highway and onto a rough track
between two mesas. The detour, which was almost as rough as
the riding trail along the Virgin River, curved far away from the
actual crime scene.

Less than fifteen minutes after returning to the blacktop, I
knocked on Nancy Donohue's front door. When she answered,
she was surprisingly genial.

"Another bad penny turns up," she sniped. "Come on in,
Jones, but don't expect hors d'oeuvres. Coffee's all you're going
to get and that's only because Olivia made it."

The reporter was sitting on the floral sofa, her thin fingers
curled around a carafe.

I settled myself at the other end of the floral sofa and asked,
"Have either of you heard about Deputy Stark?"

Nancy, who'd plopped herself down on the overstuffed chair
across from us, responded only with a nasty smile, but Olivia
nodded. "I've already started checking to see if his death is connected to the Black Basin Mine. The kid who found the body
works here and is desperate for his fifteen minutes of fame, so
he told me all about it."

"Kid?" I realized then that I'd taken it for granted Monty
found the body. What did that say about the way my mind was
tracking?

"Danny Ross, a sometimes golf caddy," Olivia said. "Very photogenic, like all the help seems to be here, so I snapped a picture, just in case. He lives in Walapai Flats, said he comes over to caddy whenever he's needed. Which was this morning, happily."

"What'd he say?"

"Pretty much what you'd expect. He noticed Stark's cruiser sitting on the side of the road with its door open. When he stopped and looked inside, he saw Stark slumped across the passenger's side. He called 9-1-1. Not that it did any good."

"Good riddance to bad rubbish," Nancy chirped cheerfully, holding out a jar of generic coffee creamer. "Hope the pig suffered. Cream, anyone?"

"Black for me, thank you," Olivia looked more amused than shocked by Nancy's callousness.

"No cream for me, either," I said. "Nancy, you sound like you might have had a run-in with Deputy Stark."

The merry widow flashed big, yellow teeth. "Show me a woman in Walapai County who hasn't and I'll show you an agoraphobic who never leaves her house. Stark's one of the reasons I volunteer at Haven. I was never able to talk that poor wife of his into taking advantage of our safe house program, but what can you expect? It's impossible to help someone who's not aware she needs help. Might as well try to talk the sun out of setting in the west. All water under the bridge, now, eh? Too bad we don't know who shot the miserable sonofabitch. I'd like to send him a thank-you note." With a satisfied sigh she ladled three teaspoons of ersatz creamer into her coffee and stirred until it looked like floating cottage cheese.

"Him?" Olivia said, a twinkle in her dark eyes. "Why not a 'her'?"

"That's always possible," I said. Sometimes, although not often enough, victims fought back. The fact that Stark had been shot to death in his cruiser made me briefly wonder if this was Connie Stark's shopping day. If so, she'd have had access to the family sedan. She could have known his regular patrol route and decided to lie in wait.

The scenario was intriguing, but I put it aside and responded to something Nancy had just said. "You're a volunteer at Haven?"

"Why, of course." She took a sip of lumpy coffee. "You're not from around here, Jones, so you won't remember that awful case three years ago when one of the groundskeepers here beat his wife to death. Roger Tosches tried to make Ike write up some lying press release claiming it was an isolated incident, that the man was drunk and didn't know what he was doing. Hell, everyone knew he beat the poor woman on a regular basis. I told Ike that if he wrote that release he could start looking for a new wife, so that was the end of that. Not that it mattered. The thinking in town at the time was that if women were stupid enough to put up with beatings, they deserved what they got. Truth was, women usually have no place to go, and few have access to fire-arms, like the lovely Winchester Safari Express I owned at the time my first husband hit me."

Olivia pretended interest in the sofa's fading floral print. After I caught my breath, I said, "Would you mind explaining that, Nancy?"

"You mean Miss Nosey Nose hasn't already discovered that I shot my first husband?"

Olivia smiled serenely at a tapestry geranium.

"Yes, in the course of my investigation into your husband's death I did check up on you, but I took it for granted the incident involving your first husband was a hunting accident."

Nancy cackled, teeth flashing. "I went on the hunt for the bastard, all right, but I can assure you the shooting was no accident. Any man who messes with me deserves what he gets."

If Nancy Donohue hadn't had access to firearms, she could have bitten her first husband to death with those big, yellow teeth. Then I wondered—had Ike Donohue ever "messed" with her?

The conversation turned to idle chatter for a few minutes until Nancy, her blood lust not yet satiated, interjected, "I hear the cook at Sunset Trails confessed to Ike's murder. Does that make sense to either of you?"

Before attending the Downwinders meeting, I would have responded in the negative, but now I listened as Olivia sprang to Gabe Boone's defense.

"When I interviewed Mr. Boone, he couldn't even come up with a consistent motive," she said. "First he talked about your husband maybe kicking his dog, then he said something about not liking Ike's looks in the first place. Then he talked about those bomb tests several years back. Granted, there are a lot of hard feelings in this area about them, but he was obviously casting around for anything that would stick. His whole story was such garbage that when the interview was finished, I demanded to see Sheriff Alcott. Alcott agreed with me, but said that when someone comes in confessing to a crime, he pretty much has to hold them while checking out the story. He said…"

Nancy broke in. "Wait a minute, Olivia. What could the bomb tests have to do with anything? Ike wasn't involved with the loathsome things. When that crap started he was still toddling around in diapers."

"But Gerald Heber…" I began, before Nancy interrupted me, too.

"I'm tired of hearing about that government stooge!" she snapped. "He was Ike's boss once, showed him the tricks of the trade, and that was the end of their relationship."

"But there's a picture of Heber in your den, the man who looks like someone's jolly old uncle. He's shaking your husband's hand, and they look pretty friendly to me."

"Correction, there was a picture of him in there." Nancy jerked her head toward the den. "The den was Ike's, to do with as he pleased. We had an agreement; he didn't bitch about my crappy housekeeping and I didn't bitch about his den. I'm not saying he didn't have a case of hero worship for the loathsome little slug, who believe me, was nowhere near as jolly as he looked, although that friendly appearance of his came in handy, considering what he did for a living. But Ike most definitely had nothing to do with those bomb tests. If he had, I'd have shot him when I met him."

Then she dropped her own bomb. "You're not as good a snoop as you think you are, Jones, or you'd have discovered that my own mother was born in Walapai Flats. She died of thyroid cancer when I was thirteen, and that makes me a Downwinder. The only reason I wasn't at the meeting last night was because I spent the day making…making Ike's funeral arrangements. The medical examiner's releasing his…his body tomorrow."

With that, something strange happened to her face. The musculature crumpled, leaving the flesh to fall in on itself. Her mouth went slack, and for a moment, I thought she'd suffered a stroke.

Then she began to wail.

"Well, that was awful," I said to Olivia an hour later, as we stood on Nancy's patio. The sky was clear. Sage and river water scented the air. Vivid pink oleanders and coral bougainvillea bloomed gaily against a stucco wall. I wondered how long they would last now that their gardener had lost her mind.

"You think you know people, then find out you never had a clue," Olivia responded. Nancy's collapse had shaken her even more than it had me. The reporter's normally pale face was white and she kept rubbing at her forehead.

"Another migraine?" I asked.

"Normal headache. I'll muddle through."

"Want some Excedrin? I always carry it."

"Excedrin won't help this. You know, when I first met Nancy I thought she was a heartless bitch, thus the name of her book group. I also thought she despised her husband. Live and learn, eh? Earl once mentioned in passing that Nancy volunteered at Haven, but for some reason I never connected it to the woman actually having a heart." She took a hefty swig from the bottle of Jack Daniels she'd lifted from Nancy's bar, then held it toward me. "Want some?"

I declined. "You joined the Book Bitches to get closer to Ike Donohue, didn't you?"

She quit rubbing her forehead long enough to nod. "I hadn't come out of the closet as a journalist yet, and I had this idea that Nancy was so big-mouthed she might drop information about the Black Basin during the meetings. She never did. A week ago I came to the group early, and admitted everything. I expected her to throw me out of the house, but that didn't happen. She just laughed like it was the biggest joke she'd ever heard. Then she told me to make the coffee."

I watched a jet leave a contrail across the sky. It was headed south, toward Phoenix, maybe San Diego. Wherever it was going, I wished I was on it.

"Olivia, there's no book club meeting today. Why are you here?"

"Just visiting. Regardless of the way she talked, I grew to like the old bitch. Somehow I could see beyond her bullshit." She nodded her head toward the house where Nancy Donohue lay in a drugged sleep, then rubbed her forehead. "Like you said—awful."

When grief had finally penetrated Nancy's brittle shell, she'd broken down so badly that Olivia called Katherine Dysart, who in turn, called one of the doctors who lived in the community. The two of us had comforted her as best we could until he arrived with his bag of tricks. Once he'd given her a shot, we helped get her into bed.

After stroking a particularly vivid oleander blossom, Olivia said, "I used to laugh at Nancy's snarky remarks about her husband." She gulped down more Jack Daniels. "But she really loved him, didn't she?"

"Women do tend to love their husbands. Just like Connie Stark loved that psychopath she was married to."

"Never having been married, I wouldn't know."

Remembering that Olivia's fiancé had died on 9/11, I didn't respond. Instead, I asked, "Did you know about Nancy's mother?"

"Earl Two Horses told me that, too."

"Small world."

She looked up at the jet, which symbolized something different to her than it did me. She rubbed her head again. "Too small, sometimes."

Chapter Twenty-four

Despite her headache, Olivia promised the doctor she'd stay and watch over Nancy, so I left. But once I boarded a trolley to take me to the leasing office, I used my down time to consider what Nancy's emotional meltdown might have revealed about Mrs. Putney.

For almost three decades I'd resented Mrs. Putney for turning me back over to the foster care system, a move which eventuated in a disastrous placement with the monster who terrorized and raped me. To my nine-year-old mind, and even my adult one, Mrs. Putney had been cold to the point of frigidity, and although she took good care of my physical needs, she seldom said a kind word. She was quick to find fault, slow to praise. The only affection she ever showed had been toward Mr. Jinx, her blind, decrepit cat. Myself, I stayed away from Mr. Jinx. Foster children learn not to get attached to anyone, especially pets, because our "homes" were temporary; soon we'd be given a new placement, leaving everyone—human and animal—behind. This emotional caution paid off the morning I found Mr. Jinx dead in his basket. Liking animals, I felt a twinge of sorrow, but nothing like Mrs. Putney, who when kneeling over the cat's stiff body, began to wail. Her shrieks had sounded like Nancy Donohue's.

That night, while sneaking down to the kitchen for a cookie, I'd heard Mrs. Putney sobbing on the telephone. I didn't understand what she was saying then, but thanks to Nancy Donohue, I did now.

"I can't do it any more," she wept to the person on the other end of the line. "You have to come get her, find her a new place. If she stays any longer, I'll get attached, and I just can't take it. I just can't take it. Everything I love dies."

We seldom understand why people do the things they do, we just guess. We're usually wrong, because you can never really know another person. In the end, each of us is a mystery to others—even to ourselves.

In some ways, Mrs. Putney had been a lot like me.

Sitting on that trolley, winding through the whisper-quiet streets of Sunset Canyon Lakes, I wondered where Mrs. Putney was now and if her wounds, whatever they were, ever healed. As soon as this case was over, I'd give her a call. She deserved to know that I was all right. What she didn't deserve was to hear what had happened to me during my next placement.

After several stops, the trolley let me off in front of the leasing office where I found Katherine Dysart locking up, a couple of prospective timeshare buyers waiting for her at the curb. She promised to call me when she was free. As she ushered the couple to her BMW, I reflected on her fraught appearance. Though she was normally the essence of understated elegance, today the hem of her ecru silk dress hung unevenly and her blonde Gucci pumps were scuffed. Small things, but they made me wonder.

I stood in front of the leasing office for a moment, trying to figure out what to do next. My mind was made up when the gate to the community pool opened and Mia Tosches strolled out wearing what amounted to little more than three bandages. She had on dark sunglasses. To hide her tears?

"Sorry for your loss," I said, trying to sound like I meant it. After all, I'd been wrong about Nancy. And about so many other people in my life.

Mia took off her shades and threw me a clear-eyed, dazzling smile. "Join me for a drink? Now that the cops are through grilling me, you can have your turn."

Hard to pass up an offer like that.

Because of my profession and the city where I lived, I've been in many luxurious homes, but the Tosches' pied-à-terre stood out among them. The ostentatious thing appeared to be carved out of one humongous block of Carrara marble, making the floor and walls shimmer with an uncomfortable blue-white light. The furnishings did little to soften the glare. The twelve-foot-long matching leather sofas and Mercedes-sized chairs were white, the area rugs were white, the coffee table and end tables were white, the lamps were white, the flowers were white, even the enormous minimalist painting on one wall was white-on-white. It felt like I'd been teleported to the polar ice cap.

"Let's have some privacy here, please," Mia ordered, sending a cadre of white-dressed servants skittering away like albino cockroaches.

Once they were gone, she sauntered over to a wet bar the size of most people's living rooms. "I'm drinking gin today, what about you?"

"Fruit juice or a soft drink will do fine, thanks."

"Ah, because you're working."

"Something like that."

"You see me as a murder suspect, right?"

I shrugged, but I watched her movements carefully as she mixed my drink. I made up my mind to do little more than sniff at the reddish-orange concoction I wound up with. Mango and hemlock?

"Interesting you should describe yourself as a murder suspect," I said, after she'd settled herself uncomfortably close to me on the sofa, a long, tanned leg brushing against mine.

"Why not? Judging from the way the cops acted, they think I offed poor old Roger for his money or at the very least, paid someone to do it."

"Did you?"

"Wouldn't you like to know." Said with a twinkle.

"As a matter of fact, I would. You must realize I've been hired by Hank Olmstead to, ah, clarify things."

"Well, I didn't. Murder Roger, that is. I also didn't murder Kimama Olmstead or Ike Donohue, either. So there, you've got your official denials. As to Kimama, I might be able to help you there. But first, would you like to see my collection of sex toys?" Cat-like, she stretched out her long legs.

"No thanks, Mia. My life's complicated enough already."

"You're such a fuddy-duddy."

At that I had to laugh. No one had ever called me a fuddy-duddy before. "About Kimama. What do you know?"

"Roger wanted her dead, of course."

Having expected more, I was disappointed. "Of course."

"But he wouldn't do anything as foolish as kill her himself."

"From what I've heard, he wasn't a foolish man."

"However, he had acquaintances who, for the right sum of money, would be happy to accommodate him. This is only conjecture, you understand. I haven't aided or abetted anything. After the cops left, I sat around for a while, thinking. Putting two and two together, as they say. You know how much I love a mystery."

"Understood. No aiding and abetting."

"Sure you don't want to see my sex toys? They're quite exotic, much nicer that those run-of-the-mill things you get at those cheap erotic boutiques."

"Thanks for your kind offer, Mia, but I'm quite sure."

"A pity. We'd have been good together."

Her smile disappeared, and for the first time, I saw something that looked like sorrow on her perfect face. Not for her husband, certainly. She looked out the picture window at the end of the cold, cavernous room, across the emerald expanse of the golf course toward the tall orange and red mesas fronting a desert that stretched into what looked like eternity. We both knew the desert was on life support, thanks to men like her dead husband.

There was no more flirtation when she spoke again. "Back to our little murder mystery—or make that mysteries. Kimama managed to get the mine opening temporarily halted, and Roger was worried that she might be able to stretch the ban into years." Her eyes tracked away from the desert to the white-on-white painting. Hardened. "Roger picked that out. Detestable, isn't it?" When I didn't answer, she continued. "As I've said, before I went down to the pool this morning, I was thinking. Mostly about someone I saw at this house once, someone who had no business to be here. Just before Kimama was killed, I was on my way into Roger's office to discuss a trip we were taking to Monaco when I heard him and another man talking. Something he said made me stop outside the door and listen."

I waited. No point in rushing her.

She took a large drink of gin, cleared her throat. Her voice was hoarse when she continued. "Roger said to the other man, 'That bitch is messing everything up,' and I knew he wasn't talking about me, because I'd never done anything to 'mess everything up.' Whatever he wanted from me, he got." Anger flickered across her face, then disappeared as quickly as it had come. "He said, 'You have to help me out, Ronnie.' I couldn't hear much after that because they lowered their voices, so I came back into the living room. A few minutes later, Roger ushered Deputy Ronald Stark out the door. Stark was holding a thick envelope. And Roger looked very, very happy."

Deputy Smiley Face had probably taken extra pleasure in the hit because his target was a woman. "Why didn't you tell anyone this earlier?" I asked.

Mia gave me a disbelieving look. "A wife owes her husband some loyalty." Then the anger returned to her face. "But now that Roger's dead, I don't owe him anything. As soon as you leave, I'm going to call Sheriff Alcott and tell him about that conversation and that fat envelope. I—I really liked Kimama." Without waiting for my answer, she walked back over to the wet bar and poured herself more gin. She downed half of it, then poured some more.

After she'd returned to the sofa, I softened my voice. "Calling the sheriff is a good idea, Mia. By the way, have you heard what happened to Deputy Stark this morning?"

When she smiled, I felt chilled, and the room's glacial decor had nothing to do with it. "One of the pool boys, Eric, informed me. He was driving in to work this morning, and said a deputy at some roadblock told him all about it."

Other than the late, unlamented Detective Smiley Face, law officers tended to be a close-mouthed bunch, and I said so.

"The cop was Eric's cousin. You know how everyone in Walapai Flats is related. Given that, coupled with all the nuclear fallout they've had around here, it's a miracle they're not all walking around with two heads. Anyway, the cop told Eric, and when Eric got to the community pool, he told everyone there. I imagine all of Sunset Canyon Lakes knows about it now."

"Kimama's death took place when you and Roger were out of town, right?"

She nodded. "Out of the entire country, as a matter of fact. Roger was a careful man, except when it came to gambling. We flew to Monaco, where he dropped a quarter million at the gaming tables. I could have killed him." Her brief session of sadness vanquished by gin, her brittle smile returned. "But I didn't."

"Why should I believe you?"

"Because I had no motive. There was plenty left after that quarter million went down the drain. True, some of Roger's habits could be annoying, but as far as I was concerned, his good qualities outweighed the negative. He gave me everything I wanted—clothes, jewelry, cars, boats, and houses all over the ass end of creation. He was my gravy train, and the gravy never stopped flowing. I'll even miss him. When I remember to."

"With him gone you'll still have all that, plus freedom."

Her earlier brittleness returned. "Lena, Lena. You are so naive. I already had all the freedom a girl could wish for, plus the protection of a powerful man. It doesn't get any better than that."

"You didn't love him, did you?"

"Define love."

Well, there was a poser. What was love, anyway? Need? Compassion? A blind cat? Given my own history, the only thing I knew for sure about love was that it had the power to rip your heart out.

When I didn't answer, she nodded. "You see?"

Maybe I did. "Do you think your husband had Ike Donohue killed, too?" I doubted it, but I wanted to hear her take.

She shook her head. "Absolutely not. In fact, when Roger found out Ike had been killed, he got more emotional than I'd ever seen him. Ike had pulled his ass out of the fires many times. He even called Sheriff Alcott, demanding to be kept up to date on the investigation."

"What did the sheriff say to that?"

"I couldn't hear the other side of the conversation, but when Roger ended the call, he didn't sound happy."

Alcott hadn't mentioned anything about that phone call to me, but there was no reason he should have. Strictly speaking, it was none of my business.

"What will you do now? With your life, I mean. Will you stay on here?"

After a dainty sip at her gin, she answered, "Get rid of this god-awful mausoleum, for starters, then sell my interest in the mine to Cole Laveen. Oh, don't look so surprised. Of course Roger left everything to me. Who else was there? Parents dead, no ex-wives, no kids. Anyway, Cole will do a lot more good for this town than my husband ever did. After that, maybe I'll move to Napa. I've always wanted to own a vineyard, with some pretty little Arabian horses—not white—for me to ride while I inspect the plants. Plants? Or vines? Which is it? I'll have to read a book on wine-making first, won't I? But that's okay, because I love research. Or maybe I'll just travel. Amsterdam and Geneva are lovely at this time of year. So's Russia, and God knows I love those fierce Russian men. Ever had one?"

Amused despite my fuddy-duddyness, I shook my head.

"Too bad. You might find the experience enlightening. There's nothing to keep me in Walapai Flats any longer. I've already run through all the interesting people. The cowboys were fun." A wink. "So were the cowgirls."

"Mia, have you ever really loved anyone?" Other than, possibly, Kimama Olmstead.

She shrugged. "Just before I turned eighteen, my mother took me to a Phoenix psychiatrist who diagnosed me as having something called a 'narcissistic personality disorder.' He told her I was interested only in myself and unable to form emotional attachments. As far as I'm concerned, that describes most of the winners in this world, so big deal."

"I'll bet it felt like a big deal to your mother, having a daughter who couldn't love her back."

"If that psychiatrist was right, there was nothing I could do about it, was there? No matter who you are, you can't force someone to love you. Mother made out okay in the end. You should have seen the house I bought her as soon as Roger and I married. It's worth ten times as much as that Apache Junction hovel she used to own. Now she's living in Biltmore Estates, having the time of her life. Golf every day, parties every night, diamonds up her ass. Those're good enough substitutes for a kissy-huggy relationship, I imagine. Come to think of it, maybe I'll pull a Brad and Angie and adopt a few kids from some benighted Third World country to give her those grandchildren she's been pining for."

I wondered which would be worse for a child: starving in a mud hut or being raised by Mia.

"Remember that mystery game we played at the mixer?" I asked. "Let's play it for real now. If you didn't kill your husband, who do you think did?"

"Not Deputy Stark, that's for sure. Unless I'm wrong, Kimama wasn't the first dirty job he did for Roger. Stark wasn't the smartest guy in town, but I doubt he was stupid enough to derail his own gravy train. Anyone around here could have killed him, maybe even those folks in Kimama's group, Victims of Uranium Mining. Or…" Here she twinkled at me again. "How about Hank Olmstead? He loathed Roger, but was too 'Christian' to admit it. You know how men like that are, straight-laced and cold, but when they erupt, they're regular volcanoes. And in the words of the immortal Martha Stewart, that can be a good thing. I tried to hook up with him once, but he wasn't having any. Come to think of it, that Polynesian daughter of his is pretty cute, brace and all."

"Touch Leilani and Olmstead will kill you. So that's it, only two people comprise your list of suspects? Given your devious mind, I find that hard to believe."

"Since you insist, there's Cole Laveen, his business partner. He and Roger were always butting heads over proposed mine safety issues. As you know, Roger used to be sole owner, very bottom line oriented, and he never saw a problem he couldn't fix with a few well-worded press releases penned by the sublimely sleazy Ike Donohue. If the natives remained restless, he'd be able to bribe the mine inspectors into seeing things his way, like they did at Moccasin Peak. But when the newspapers raised a fuss about all those dead Navajos, he was forced to bring Cole on board as partner."

She took another trip to the wet bar. This time, instead of just filling up her own glass, she poured me some mango straight from the bottle. Flashing me a smile, she said, "This one's not poisoned."

Such a kidder.

Once back on the sofa, she said, "You know, Lena, Cole Laveen is a lot like you, a regular do-gooder. He insisted on keeping the Black Basin up to code instead, of faking it like Roger planned to, so profits won't be what they could have been. That's Laveen's problem now, not mine, because I'm divesting myself of the whole controversial mess. But here's another suspect for you. Trent, Katherine Dysart's ex-con husband. Roger fired him yesterday over some money that went missing from the resort's entertainment account. My husband was open-minded about a lot of things, but thievery wasn't one of them."

Yet he'd married a thief. "Did the police take Trent in for questioning?"

"They're probably working him over with a rubber hose as we speak."

"Sheriff Alcott isn't the rubber hose type."

"You'd be surprised." Her eyes danced, revealing that she knew more about Alcott than I did. My, my, what a busy girl she'd been.

"Back to Cole Laveen. Do you think he might grant me an interview?"

Although she looked disappointed that I didn't ask her to fill me in on her sexual adventures with the sheriff, she answered readily enough. "You can try. Watch out for that maid, though." She winked.

Cole Laveen's house was right down the Aleppo pine-shaded lane from Mia's, so within minutes I was pressing buttons on the intercom beside a sturdy wooden gate. When a woman's disembodied voice answered, I told her who I was and what I wanted. She didn't reply, but a courtyard full of dogs—they sounded like mastiffs—did. They bayed so loudly I thought I'd go deaf. Every now and then one would take a running leap at the gate, hit it with a thud, and the gate would creak and bow outward. Five minutes later, just as I was ready to take to my heels, the baying suddenly stopped.

"I brought the dogs in," Intercom Lady announced. "But be careful in case I missed one."

The gate slowly swung open. I walked though, trying not to reveal how surprised I was. *This* was the home of Roger Tosches' business partner?

After the forbidding gate, I'd been expecting another marble monstrosity like Mia's or at least one of those pseudo-Tudor McMansions which were so popular in non-Tudor Arizona. I certainly hadn't expected a modest tri-level that could have been hauled here by helicopter from some Wisconsin suburb. White siding. Green shutters. Slate roof. Two garden gnomes flanking a plain oak door.

The frumpy maid who opened the door was as dowdy as the house. Nowhere near as sleek as Mia's white-clad servants, she wore a stained apron and a plain housedress that had suffered through too many washings. Her gray hair looked like it had never been styled, just combed.

"Here to see his nibs, huh?" she asked, ushering me into a house that smelled of dog.

Apparently she hadn't attended Maid School, either "The dogs aren't anywhere around, are they?"

"Nah, I ran them into the back yard, not that you were in any real danger. They're all pretty much toothless by now, been with us since I don't know when." She turned away and yelled, "Hey, Cole! That detective woman's here to see ya!"

"Be right there!" a man yelled back.

The maid grabbed me by the arm and steered me into a living room that paid more attention to comfort than style. Brown tweed carpeting, overstuffed furniture covered with dog hair, walls that were almost invisible because of a photographic surplus of children and dogs.

I'd just taken my seat when Cole Laveen walked in. He was as pretty as his house, wearing pink-and-green checked golf pants and a yellow golf shirt at war with the remnants of his red Bozo-the-Clown hair. His smile flashed cheap dentures.

"Hey, Babs, why don't you make us some coffee?" he asked the maid.

"You want it, you make it yourself," she replied. "That damned Jack Russell pissed on the stairs again and I have to clean it up."

I was beginning to get it. The "maid" was actually Mrs. Laveen, hence Mia's warning. "I don't need anything, I'm fine."

Laveen gave me a penetrating glance that seemed out of kilter with his clownish appearance. "No, no, you look dehydrated. I'll get you some water. I never could figure out how to run that coffee machine."

He disappeared for a minute, then returned carrying a bottle of generically labeled water, no glass. "This okay?"

Gratefully, I took the bottle and twisted off the cap. When I looked around to see where to put it, Laveen grabbed the cap from me and put it in his pocket.

"You're here to talk about poor Roger, right?" he said, sitting across from me on a sofa that was even hairier than my chair. "Sad, what happened to him, but I can't say I'm surprised. He was totally insensitive to other people's needs. A person might be able to get away with that sort of thing in a large city, but in a small place like Walapai Flats, it creates unnecessary problems. And as I'm sure you've discovered—tell me if you haven't—Roger did have an unfortunate past."

"The Moccasin Peak Uranium Mine?"

"A total of twenty-seven deaths were ascribed to it, and every one of them could have been prevented. Men like Roger, they think they're being clever by cutting corners on safety, but in the long run, they cost their companies more money in lawsuits than if they'd instituted proper safety procedures in the first place."

Seemingly, Laveen was being open, but experience had taught me to be careful around such openness; it was often a mere diversion. "Then you attribute his death to his business practices?"

He attempted to smooth down his wiry red hair, but it sprang back up again. "Oh, well, I'm not going so far as to say that, but I'm not blind to the amount of animosity people around here felt for him. I found him difficult to work with, myself. That's why I felt some temptation when he approached me last week with the intent of buying back his shares now that the Black Basin looks well on track."

"Were you going to sell?"

"Hell, no, he wasn't!" This from Mrs. Laveen, apparently finished with her piddle-cleaning chores. "He planned to be a constant presence at that mine to make certain Roger didn't get up to his old tricks again." She sat down next to her husband and patted him on his thigh. "Isn't that right, Cole?"

He patted her thigh in return. "Now that we've retired here, Babs and I feel a responsibility to this community, so yes. We're even thinking of setting up a teen center to give the kids something to do besides get in trouble." He waved toward his photograph-covered wall. "We had six kids, and every one of them raised bloody hell in their teen years. It's a miracle none of them wound up in jail, isn't it, Babs?"

"I'd of killed them first." She scowled like she meant it, but she couldn't disguise the pride in her voice when adding, "Three doctors, two social workers, and an engineer. No lawyers, thank God."

He smiled fondly at her. "Babs was the line-drawer and she made sure the kids toed it. Me, I tend to let things go."

This couple was too good to be true. Or maybe not. Even in this cynical old world, miracles sometimes happened.

But usually not on my watch.

"Mrs. Laveen, do you have any theories about the person who killed Roger Tosches? Or Ike Donohue, for that matter."

She shook her frowsy gray head. "Don't know, don't care. If there's an Afterlife, the both of them are in big trouble."

When the trolley dropped me off in front of the leasing office, Katherine had returned. She was sitting behind her chrome and glass desk, drinking 7-Up straight from the can, oddly inelegant behavior for such an elegant woman.

"How'd the sales pitch go?" I asked.

"They weren't in a buying mood." She took a final chug of 7-Up, then tossed the empty can toward the waste basket. She missed, and the can rolled across the floor until it came to rest in the corner. She didn't bother picking it up. "Knowing you, you've already heard about Trent."

"From Mia Tosches. Is it true?"

"True that the police took him in for questioning, true that he embezzled money from the entertainment account, or true that he murdered Roger Tosches?"

"Whichever."

"He's my husband," she said, as if that was answer enough.

"Which means you're sticking by him regardless."

"You love who you love."

I thought about Dusty. About Warren. About the mother and father I only vaguely remembered but yearned for every day. Then I thought about Mia, and the way her brittleness had softened when she spoke Kimama Olmstead's name. Katherine was right: you love who you love. "True as that may be, Katherine, why would Trent embezzle money? Surely with your combined salaries and free housing, you were making enough to get by."

The silence, which I'd taken as a mere pause before answering, stretched so long that I filled it with another question. "Enough money to get by, that is, unless Trent picked up a drug habit while serving time, a common enough occurrence. Did that happen?"

Her continued silence provided my answer.

Due to the detour around Deputy Stark's murder scene, traffic along Route 47 moved slowly. I didn't mind, because it gave me time to think. When the traffic arced around one of the smaller mesas, I pulled away and bumped the Trailblazer to the side, where the view—unhindered by a mile-long line of vehicles—was breathtaking.

Stepping out of the car into the still-cool morning air, I could see an azure sky so pure it almost hurt. Fawn-colored desert. Soft green cacti. Red, orange, and purple mesas clawing toward the heavens.

The "nothing" the Atomic Energy Commission had seen fit to despoil.

Grateful that I was always equipped with running shoes and a canteen—and that Deputy Stark was no longer around to shoot at me—I began to jog. The very physicality of running clears the mind, and as I headed toward a mitten-shaped mesa, I reviewed everything I'd learned. The fact that people lie isn't always a drawback. Lies often point toward a greater truth.

Ike Donohue lied for a living, and in their own way, so did Roger Tosches and Ronnie Stark. Donohue lied for a paycheck, Tosches lied to open the Black Basin Mine, Stark lied about his brutality in order to keep his job. Money wasn't the only reason people lied. Out of shame, Ted Olmstead lied about his relationship with Mia. Stark's damaged wife lied from misguided loyalty.

Nancy Donohue lied about her true feelings for her husband. Gabe Boone lied to spring Ted from jail.

Silence could be a lie, too. In order to keep tourist dollars rolling in, every member of the Walapai Chamber of Commerce remained silent about the area's history of radioactive contamination. Mia Tosches, no fool, hadn't revealed her feelings for Kimama Olmstead to her husband. Trent Dysart's résumé didn't list theft, manslaughter, prison, or drug addiction. Hank Olmstead wasn't foolish enough to admit that he loved his children enough to kill for them.

Sunset Canyon Lakes was the biggest lie of all. A so-called "oasis" in the middle of the desert, it catered to the middle-aged and elderly, yet all the resort's employees were young and good-looking, from the pool boys to the trolley drivers and golf cart chauffeurs. I wondered how much they made on "tips."

By the time I jogged into the long shadow of the mesa, I understood what had been happening in Walapai Flats, and why. I only needed to check in with Jimmy before I took my findings to the authorities.

Since I'd called ahead, Jimmy was fully dressed by the time I made it to the Desert View, thus sparing me my blushes. Once we were seated at the card table, he proceeded with his show-and-tell, our earlier dust-up at the park apparently forgotten.

"Let's start with Sheriff Wiley Alcott." He tapped a few keys and a legal document popped up.

"What's that?" I asked.

"The will of Wiley George Alcott I, filed in Walapai County Circuit Court, August 24, 1995, leaving all his worldly goods to grandson Wiley George Alcott III, which included a six-hundred-dred-fifty acre tract the centerpiece of which was the Two Devils Silver Mine in Silver Ridge, plus a twenty-five room house; no, make that a mansion. The sheriff's rolling in it."

Piles of money might explain the sheriff's Rolex and Armani, but it raised a different question. "Why didn't Grandpa Alcott leave his fortune to his son, the sheriff's father?"

"Couldn't. Wiley George Alcott II died of thyroid cancer in 1981, the same disease that eventually killed Grandpa Alcott, and Grandpa's sister Alice. The radiation from the Nevada Test Site wiped out the sheriff's entire family."

Which might explain something else. "Alcott's been pretty friendly, considering the fact that I was encroaching on his turf."

"He was hoping you'd dig up dirt in areas where his own hands were tied. People tend to forget that sheriffs are elected officials. Politicians, as it were, and as I'm sure you realize, most politicians don't want to irritate the electorate. Looks to me like Alcott has big plans, possibly some day running for state attorney general. And before you ask, yes, he has a law degree."

It was all coming together. "Does he still own the Two Devils?"

"Sure does. The silver's pretty much gone, but he's leased out the acreage for rangeland. He's made very good investments, too, enough to send his oldest daughter to study art at the Sorbonne. That's in…"

"Paris," I interrupted. "*Plus ça change, plus c'est la même chose.*"

"A la-di-da way of saying times change, but not really." He tapped a few more keys. "Moving on. Regarding Gerald Heber, one-time liar for the Atomic Energy Commission, I came up with something intriguing. Take a look at this old police report."

On May 30, 1960, Heber accused Gabriel Boone of assault during a community meeting in Silver Ridge designed to dispel fears about the dangers of continued nuclear fallout. Heber had been assuring the residents of Walapai County that the spike in cancer cases was in no way connected to the nearby testing when Boone, who'd been in the audience, shouted, "Liar! You government people killed Edna and now you're killing Abby!" When Heber scoffed at the accusation, Boone leapt from his chair and knocked him to the ground. Boone was taken into custody, but released the next day on his own recognizance. Heber was treated for minor injuries at the Walapai County Hospital.

"Wow," was all I could say.

"Ditto on the wow, and check out this next item."

Another screen popped up, its format similar to the last, but this time it was a report from the Clark County, Nevada, sheriff's office. On November 21, 1979, hikers in the desert a few miles outside Las Vegas found the body of an elderly white male. He'd been shot in the head at close range. When deputies arrived on the scene, they identified the man as Gerald Heber. His wallet contained approximately three hundred dollars in twenties and fifties, and a full deck of credit cards. That wasn't all. Detectives found four hundred dollars in chips from the Desert Inn Casino in another pocket, so robbery was not considered a motive.

I took a deep breath. "When did Boone's wife die?"

"November 12, 1979."

Nine days after her death, Heber was murdered. "Was the killer ever caught?"

"The case remains open."

Maybe Gabe Boone wasn't the innocent I'd believed he was. Therapists tell us that the first stage of grief is denial, and the second stage is anger. Just how deep had his anger run?

"Boone couldn't have known Heber was in Las Vegas," I said, with relief.

Without saying a word, Jimmy brought up another screen to reveal a small article that had appeared in the November 19, 1979, edition of the *Las Vegas Sun*. It announced the winners of the Senior Division of the Ezra Stroughmeyer Cerebral Palsy Charity Golf Tournament on Sunday, November 18. The caption on the photo accompanying the article read, "Pictured is Gerald Heber, 79, receiving the first place prize, a gold-plated golf ball. Heber, who is staying at the Desert Inn through the end of the week, said, "This old man beat out kids as young as 66! I've still got it, world!"

Given Walapai Flats' proximity to Vegas, it was possible that Gabe Boone had somehow seen the article. While I'd taken my stroll along John Wayne Boulevard, I'd seen two news racks selling the *Sun*—one right in front of Ma's Kitchen. For a moment I was tempted to go over to the jail and grill Gabe. Then I remembered the suffering aided and abetted by Heber's lies and decided that whatever the truth was, I really didn't want to know.

"Ready to see what else I found out about Mia Tosches?" Jimmy asked, interrupting my dark thoughts.

"Don't tell me Mia murdered someone, too."

"If she did, no one's found the body. But our little wild child's full of surprises. County records list her as the founder and chief financial supporter of Haven, the local safe house for battered women. Not only that, but she's also a major contributor to an emergency shelter for abused children. What do you think of that?"

"I think somewhere down in Phoenix there's a psychiatrist who needs to brush up on his diagnostic skills."

Jimmy looked puzzled, but I didn't bother to enlighten him. "What about Tosches himself? Did you find anything else on him?"

"Only that he was in talks to buy out Laveen's share in the Black Basin."

"I have it on good authority that he got turned down." That is, if the Laveens had told me the truth.

The rest of Jimmy's research, deeper than anything I'd been able to carry out, revealed more surprises, many of them monetary. Earl Two Horses didn't own the Walapai Gas-N-Go; his Paiute mother did. She'd bought the gas station with the settlement she received after the cancer deaths at the Moccasin Peak Mine became public; her Navajo husband's name appeared on the list of the mine's victims.

Before relocating with Katherine to Sunset Canyon Lakes, Trent Dysart had been fired from a Boston area video store when the till kept coming up short after his late-night shift. Farrier Monty Carson had been in several barroom fights, once having had to fork over six thousand dollars in damages to the Dew Drop Inn, from which he was permanently barred. Pretty little Tara Sabbatini, Jimmy's favorite waitress, had been arrested three years earlier for shoplifting a purple thong at the Silver Ridge Wal-Mart, but she hadn't re-offended since she'd begun waitressing for her father Marcello—better known as "Ma." Ma had his own criminal history. He'd once served three days in the Walapai Flats lockup after pushing a diner's head into a plate of spaghetti marinara after the diner complained his pasta wasn't *al dente* enough.

The most intriguing information was the dirt Jimmy dug up on Ronald Stark. At the time of his death, the deputy— who pulled down a whopping thirty-four thousand dollars per annum—had been under investigation by the Walapai County Sheriff's Office for expenditure-versus-income irregularities. The investigation began when Sheriff Alcott discovered that Deputy Smiley Face owned four Mohave County rental properties; a 2011 Bayliner 195 Discovery power boat he'd bought outright three days after Kimama Olmstead's murder, and which he kept docked at Lake Mead; a brand new Harley-Davidson Ultra, also bought outright; and a 1964 Corvette Pro Street he garaged at the rental home he leased to Georgette Hansen, a pole dancer at the Lake Mead Triple X Gentleman's Club. The lease for the three-bedroom-four-bath-plus pool home was for one hundred a month; I guessed the rest was made up in services rendered.

Stark had been on the take from Roger Tosches for years. The fact that the two men had been shot to death within one day of each other was intriguing, and I was willing to bet the same handgun had killed both. Coincidences may exist, but no good investigator believes in them.

"I don't see anything about Cole and Barbara Laveen here," I said, after scrolling through the various rap sheets of felonies and misdemeanors accumulated by the good folk of Walapai Flats.

"That's because I found no dirt on them, unless you want to count the ticket Laveen was issued last September when he got caught parking crossways in a strip mall driveway while rescuing a stray dog hit by a car. He paid the fine, apologized, and went on his merry way."

Considering everything that had happened, all the deceit, all the deaths, I shouldn't have asked my next question, but I couldn't help myself. "What happened to the dog?"

"When Laveen left the scene, the dog was with him. He took it to the vet, paid for the necessary repair work, and adopted it. The dog's name is Bobo, kind of a Jack Russell terrier mix. Cute. It even has its own Facebook page. As do all the Laveen's other dogs."

"So Laveen's brush with the law doesn't count."

He chuckled. "Strict law and order types wouldn't agree with that assessment, but as another animal lover, I applaud his crime. Other than that one incident, I found nothing but awards and accolades from other businessmen, state senators, and the people who run the community centers and homeless shelters the Laveens are funding. All in all, they look as pure as the driven snow."

"Even snow gets pissed in."

"Invariably. But I couldn't find the pissing place."

I could; the Laveens' stairs.

Maybe some people really were saints. Maybe pigs could fly, too. I eased back in the uncomfortable motel room chair and smiled at my partner. "You've done a lot of work for one morning." Now it was time to ask him something I'd always been curious about, but hadn't wanted to bother him with. "This case has dug up many troubling issues. For instance, look what happened to the Paiute. The nukes decimated the tribe."

Jimmy shifted his eyes away, something he always did when trying to hide his feelings. He probably knew what I was going to ask, and didn't like it. "Your point being?"

"When I realized there might be a connection between Ike Donohue's murder and what went on sixty years ago, I began to wonder. Your people seem to always get the shaft."

Still not looking at me, he answered, "There's no 'seem' to it, Lena."

I thought about the East Coast Indians being sold to Caribbean slavers, the Indian Removal Act, the Trail of Tears, Wounded Knee…Four centuries of genocide, planned and unplanned, a history written in the rage on Earl Two Horses' face at the Downwinders meeting.

"Jimmy, don't you or any of your biological family ever lust for revenge?"

When he finally turned back to me, a faint smile had returned to his handsome face. "Almost Sister, if we Indians were the vengeful sort, not one white person would be safe from us. Instead, we oh so graciously invite you to visit our casinos."

"Vengeance enough, Almost Brother?" I smiled back.

"Time will tell. Uh, why haven't you asked what else I found on Olivia Eames?"

From his tone of voice, I knew the news wasn't going to be good. "What did she do, strangle a nun?"

"She's dying, Lena."

With my lame joke already leaving a bad taste in my mouth, I remembered Olivia's ghost-pale face, the bleeding sore on her lip, the amount of weight she'd lost since I'd first met her. The signs had all been there, but I'd chosen not to see them.

"What's wrong with her?" Although I could guess the answer.

"Stage Four breast cancer, Lena. Metastasized. She'd been undergoing chemo at Sloan Kettering in New York, but stopped last month because it was no longer working. That's when she flew out here to write her last story, then die on her home turf. I'm sorry. I know you like her."

Yes, I liked Olivia. Her journalistic vision. Her courage. And—recalling her tenderness with the grieving Nancy Donohue—her compassion.

The poet William Blake had it right when he'd written,

Every night and every morn,
Some to misery are born,
Every morn and every night,
Some are born to sweet delight.
Some are born to sweet delight,
Some are born to endless night.

Olivia might have experienced moments of sweet delight, but it seemed to me that overall, her life had been one of endless night. Born into a fallout-cursed family, she'd been gang-raped in New York City mere months before losing her lover on 9/11. Now this. I wondered how the woman remained sane, or if she still was.

Ignoring the lump in my throat, I said, "There's no way you could hack into hospital records."

"It took all night and half the morning, but I got into Admissions. Even you ought to know that with everything computerized these days, nothing's one hundred percent secure. Some sites just take longer to hack, that's all. As soon as Olivia arrived in Walapai Flats last month, she checked in with Dr. Amos Carrollton, an oncologist at Arizona-Northwest Medical Center. I couldn't make it into the hospital's pharmacy records, but considering how long she's been sick, it's my guess the doctor gave her a prescription for Fentanyl. You know what that is?"

"Medication for extreme pain, administered when morphine no longer works. It's applied in patch form, usually on the upper arm."

He nodded. "She was probably stoned at least half the time you talked to her. You never noticed?"

"Dilated or pinpoint pupils are the first things I check for during an interview, and I never saw anything like that with her." However, Olivia had been oddly nervy during our drive to Silver Ridge for the Downwinders meeting, picking at her lip, rubbing her forehead. Maybe she'd backed off the Fentanyl in order to make the trip. The fact that she continued working on the Black Basin story at the same time as the Downwinders story was testament to her toughness, but Jimmy was right; there was only so much pain a human being could bear. At some point Olivia would have to apply another Fentanyl patch or shoot up or take whatever the hell else she was using.

Then I remembered her behavior as we stood on Nancy Donohue's patio, the headache she'd admitted to, the bitter tone in her voice when she told me Excedrin couldn't help.

My leaving her to care for another suffering woman had been one lousy judgment call.

The drive to Sunset Canyon Lakes went faster this time, only partially because I was prepared for the detour. Although detectives and crime techs hadn't yet finished working the Stark crime scene, afternoon traffic was sparse. Before I'd left Jimmy's motel room, I'd tried to reach Olivia to tell her that I was on my way; my call went straight to voice mail. The same thing happened when I tried Nancy Donohue's phone. Frustrated, I'd called Information, but the operator informed me that Elizabeth Waide, Nancy's lavender-haired neighbor, had an unlisted number.

I hoped Olivia could hold off on her meds and Nancy would continue her drugged sleep for several more hours. As soon as I arrived, I would cross the street to Elizabeth's house and ask her to watch Nancy. Then I'd take Olivia back to her timeshare to drug away her own misery.

As it turned out, Olivia had been realistic about her physical limitations, and when Nancy Donohue's door opened, Elizabeth Waide stood facing me. With finger pressed to her lips, the loyal Book Bitch whispered, "Nancy's sleeping. If you need to talk to her, come back tomorrow."

I whispered back, "Where's Olivia?"

"Gone. She told me she needed some fresh air and was driving up to Sunset Point."

Sunset Point.

The place where Olivia had killed Ike Donohue.

Chapter Twenty-five

If the desert between Walapai Flats and the resort was beautiful, it paled next to the severe majesty of Sunset Point.

Red rock walls plunged toward a blue-green ribbon of water below, where the Virgin River wound its way toward the Colorado. Sixty years ago, the river had been despoiled by radioactive fallout, but now it flowed clean, delivering life-saving moisture to plants and wildlife that would otherwise be doomed. Above, a pair of red-tailed hawks floated in the hot updrafts, calling out to each other when they spied their scurrying prey below.

As I parked my Trailblazer behind Olivia's Explorer, I saw her sitting on the very rim of the canyon, watching the river's zigzag progress south.

"Thinking about jumping?" I approached, training my .38 on her back. You could never be too careful with murderers, however much you like them.

"Not yet," she answered, never taking her eyes off the river. "I've already filed the Black Basin story, and I'm several hours away from finishing the one on the Downwinders. Once I do…" she shrugged her bony shoulders. "I'd originally planned to jump, but maybe I'll shoot myself instead. It would be poetic justice, don't you think? Live by the gun, die by the gun?"

Her voice held a slight slur. Once she turned around to face me, I saw the dilation of her pupils. I also saw the .38 lying next to her, the weapon with which she'd killed Ike Donohue, Roger Tosches, and Deputy Ronald Stark.

I ignored it. "You can't write in your condition."

When she smiled, it was with the rictus of death. "I can once the Fentanyl wears off, which will be soon. Put your gun away, Lena. Neither of us is going to shoot the other."

She was right, so I holstered my handgun and sat beside her, dangling my feet over the ledge. I would have comforted her with a hug, but there's a limit to my risk-taking. The drop was more than twelve hundred feet straight down, except for the narrow ledge a few yards to our right where Donohue's body had prematurely come to rest.

"Gorgeous view," I said, apropos of nothing.

"If you're into rock and river. Myself, I prefer Snow Canyon. The terrain is gentler."

"The place where John Wayne filmed *The Conqueror*."

A wry smile. "Girlfriend's been doing her research. Did you also find out that during Wayne's last days he refused all pain medication? He wanted to be awake when Death came for him."

I shook my head.

"Most people don't know. He could do anything, that man, but John Wayne as a Mongol? Wasn't happening. I've seen all his movies, the Westerns, even the war films where he played the big hero. But he wasn't a war hero. That old man sitting in jail back in Walapai Flats, he's the real deal, a hero several times over. You know what he did?"

"He saved Leilani from drowning," I said.

"Before that. When he was serving in Korea, a sniper shot a man in his unit. Everyone else in the platoon took cover, but Gabe crawled over to him while the sniper was still firing. He dragged the man to cover, stopped the bleeding, and took care of him until the medics arrived. In the process, he got shot up pretty bad himself. They gave him a fist full of medals, but when his wife died the way she did, he threw them out. He felt betrayed by the very government he almost gave his life for. Now he's a hero all over again, taking the blame for a crime I committed just so Ted Olmstead would get released from jail." Another rictus smile. "He had no way of knowing that by Monday I'd have confessed anyway, so his heroism wasn't needed."

"You're not going to leave Gabe to rot in jail, are you?"

"Give me some credit, girlfriend. We talked about it and came up with a plan."

At my look of surprise, she laughed. It sounded genuine, if slightly druggy. "Oh, yes, when I found out Gabe had 'confessed,' I arranged that interview with him and offered to turn myself in immediately. He's not young and fit like Ted, might not bounce back, so I was afraid of what jail might do to him. But he insisted I wait until I finished my story on the Downwinders. He even volunteered to take the blame for everything, to go to prison for me, but I couldn't allow that. So we compromised. He'd stay in jail for a while longer, I'd make a videotape confessing to killing Donohue, Tosches, and Stark, then send it to Sheriff Alcott as soon as I filed my last story. But like I was saying about John Wayne. Turns out he *was* a hero, only a different kind. Hanging around without pain meds so he could look Death in the eye and tell him what a sonuvabitch he was. It takes true grit to endure that kind of torment, grit I don't have."

"Don't sell yourself short." Gesturing toward her gun, I asked, "Why don't you give that to me?"

"It's the only thing I have left of my fiancé. He gave it to me for protection after I'd been raped."

"It was a throw-down, right? A weapon he picked up at a crime scene and kept in case he needed it later. That's why it was matched to a bullet dug out of a four-year-old girl wounded during a Detroit home invasion. Thugs travel, and their guns with them."

"You're thorough, Lena, I'll give you that."

"So's Sheriff Alcott."

"Yeah, but he's held back by the kind of legalistic red tape you ignore, so he's not as fast, is he? He had a false confession and a mountain of evidence to sift through—cops need that stuff—but you focused on motive." That awful smile again. "Anyway, Gabe's and my plan was to leave a message on your voice mail telling you where I hid the videotape, but since you're here in the flesh, I might as well tell you now. It's at my timeshare, in my nightstand drawer, wrapped in a hand-written, signed confession."

"Give me the gun, Olivia," I repeated. "Since you're not going to use it."

She picked up the .38 and cradled it in her lap. "I'm not going to use it now, certainly not on you, but being a free-thinking woman I reserve the right to…Well, you know."

I did, and I didn't like it. For a moment, I was tempted to make a grab for the gun, but I decided that would be foolish. During the struggle, Olivia and I might both fall into the canyon. So I held back and changed the subject, mainly to keep her talking. Not that it was necessary, because I'd already figured out the truth.

Suddenly one of the red-tailed hawks dove down, vanishing below the rim of the canyon. Soon it rose again, a rabbit clutched in its talons. I turned my eyes away. The rabbit wasn't dead yet.

"Why did you kill Ike Donohue, Olivia?"

Drugged though she was, an expression of pain crossed her face. "If I'd known how much Nancy loved him, maybe I wouldn't have. To cause another woman that much anguish, it's…it's inexcusable. If I wind up in Hell, it'll be for hurting her, not for killing Ike."

Having suffered through the loss of her own love in such a horrible way, Olivia understood that kind of anguish all too well. But in her addled state, she was incapable of understanding the evil inherent in taking any human life. On second thought, killing in self-defense wasn't evil; killing to save someone else wasn't, either. But in Donohue's case…"I know you feel remorse, Olivia, but why did you do it in the first place? He had nothing to do with the nuclear testing."

Despite her drugs, despite her pain, the hardness returned to her face. "Like his mentor Gerald Heber, Donohue lied for a living, spending decades convincing people it was safe to smoke when he knew damned well it wasn't. And when he retired, did he stop? No, he turned around and lied about the Black Basin Mine, swearing to everyone it would be safe, all the time knowing that Tosches would run it the same way he'd run the Moccasin Peak Mine. Bringing in Cole Laveen was cosmetic, nothing more. When I found out that Tosches was trying to buy Laveen out, I knew the whole thing was ready to start all over again. All Donohue cared about was getting his blood money. Just like he did when he worked for Cook & Creighton Tobacco. In the end, he helped kill as many people as that government toady Gerald Heber. Maybe more."

Pointing out the obvious, I said, "Donohue developed lung cancer, so he was paying for his sins."

"Hoist on his own petard, as they say."

There'd been no surprise on her face. "You knew, didn't you, Olivia?"

She looked up at the sky. Nothing up there now but blue. In a voice so soft that I could hardly hear her over the rushing wind, she said, "Donohue and I had a nice little chat before I shot him. Poor foolish Nancy blurted out at one of the Book Bitches meetings that her husband didn't always come home at night, so one evening I followed him, just to see where he was going. I caught up to him when he parked up here. Despite Nancy's suspicions that he was seeing another woman, he was doing what we dying people tend to do, spending some quiet time looking up at the stars, thinking about how beautiful they are, cursing God, wondering why he had to be taken away from all that beauty so soon. Or maybe he was just getting his nerve up. Not everyone can die the John Wayne way, with true grit."

Her voice became knife sharp. "When he saw my gun he knew he was going to die sooner than he thought."

"He must have been terrified."

Both hawks suddenly emerged from the rim of the canyon and soared past us, a mere thirty feet away. The rabbit the larger hawk held in its talons had stopped struggling.

"Believe it or not, Donohue wasn't at all frightened," Olivia said. "He told me he welcomed death, told me about his diagnosis and what lay in wait for him. Know what he did then? He actually held out his arms so I'd have an unobstructed heart shot." Her face was impassive as she watched the hawks disappear into the canyon again. "Killing him was no more than assisted suicide."

"Just call you Jack Kevorkian, right?"

She tried to laugh, but her breath began to spasm, and she coughed so hard that I worried she might tumble off the ledge. Without thinking, I grabbed her and pulled her away.

Once she regained her breath, she checked to see if she still had her gun. She didn't. She gave me a look that was a mixture of annoyance and relief. "That was sneaky."

I shrugged.

Her face contorted in pain, but she gamely struggled against it. "Looks like the Fentanyl's wearing off," she said, her voice trembling. "You're going to let me get back to my Downwinders article, aren't you? Or are you going to drag me over to the jail?"

I didn't answer her question, just asked another of my own. "Why didn't you leave Donohue for the coyotes?"

"That's what I'd planned to do, but while we were talking, he told me how much he loved to sail, so I thought, why not? I said 'Bon voyage,' shot him, and rolled his body over the edge for a final trip. The dead saluting the dead, and all that. I was just too weak to get him out far enough, the poor shit, so he landed on that damned ledge. He…"

An increasing wind from the canyon took away her voice. Mine too. When the wind calmed, I asked, "What about Tosches, Olivia?"

Her eyes narrowed in anger. Or maybe it was pain. I could no longer tell the difference. "After Donohue, killing Roger Tosches was a piece of cake, especially since I was certain he'd paid someone to kill Kimama Olmstead. As soon as I heard about Tosches' early morning trips to Olmstead's ranch, I made plans to be at the turnoff next time he turned up. For four days in a row I parked my car behind the mesa and hiked over to the turnoff and hid in the bushes. Don't look so surprised, Lena.

Reporters learn to be patient. Yesterday Tosches finally showed, driving his look-at-me Mercedes."

"What if there'd been someone around?"

"Like I said, I'm patient. When I saw him make the turn, I stepped into the road. Boy, did he hit the brakes. Not so much as to keep from running me down, but because he was pissed off about the article he knew I was writing about the Black Basin and wanted to give me a piece of his mind. Instead…"

"Instead, you gave him piece of yours. Okay, I understand your reasons for killing Tosches—not that I agree with vigilantism, I don't. But why shoot Deputy Stark? He never did anything to you."

Olivia's eyes were red with pain by now, but not enough that I couldn't see a gleam of satisfaction. "Consider it a community service."

Chapter Twenty-six

Snow Canyon, Utah

"Right here on this little hill, that's where Curly and me watched the Duke make his movie," Gabe said, raising his voice so it could be heard above the hot wind that screamed along Snow Canyon. "Curly stood over there where that creosote bush is now, I stood right where you're standing, and the Duke and Miss Hayward and the rest of the actors, they was spread out all along the canyon floor. Nothing's changed."

Except for the deaths. And the fact that the former movie location of *The Conqueror* was no longer radioactive.

As I looked down across the narrow valley that had caused so much misery, I imagined its appearance sixty years ago. Red dirt. Interminable wind. Horses neighing. Animal hide yurts scattered along the canyon. Two hundred and twenty actors and crew, three hundred Paiute extras—all trying their best to make the American Southwest look like Mongolia.

The vivid blue sky vibrated against jaw-dropping cliffs of orange and white-banded sandstone, falls of black lava rock, and acres of green brush that looked surreal against the spectacular red earth. If there really was a Heaven, it looked like this.

"That Opening Day party at the Black Basin was something, wasn't it?" Gabe said. "All them people. All them flags. Guess it's gonna make them nuclear power people happy." There was no irony in his voice.

"Yeah, happy," I said. Until there was a meltdown.

On the way up to Snow Canyon, we'd stopped to see the fes-tivities. It looked like the entire population of Walapai Flats was in attendance. Red, white, and blue streamers were everywhere, attached to the fence, the earth-moving equipment, the stage, the cotton candy concession, the parked pickup trucks and horse trailers—even the people. There was hardly a person there who hadn't stuck a streamer or two to a hat or purse, or wrapped it around their torsos like beauty queen banners. Neither of the Laveens wore streamers; they didn't have to. They and their Jack Russell terrier were dressed entirely in outfits that matched the streamers. When the high school band played "God Bless America," everyone cried.

Especially Gabe.

As moving as it had been, Gabe and I hadn't waited until the end of the festivities. A man of his word, he'd promised to show me this beautiful canyon, this holy canyon, this poisoned canyon.

"Is it as beautiful as I said, girl?"

"You didn't exaggerate, Gabe."

The wind kicked up again, blowing red dust into our faces until we could hardly breathe, let alone speak, so we stood there without speaking, just listening to the wind scream against those other-worldly cliffs.

When the wind took a break, I said, "Olivia never told me Curly was her grandfather," I said, admiring his straight-backed stance on the crown of the hillock. Now that he was a free man, he looked years younger than his actual eighty-two. Regardless of his age, I was half in love with him.

He turned away from the canyon to face me, his eyes bright and clear. "Oh, Lena, that poor girl was in so much pain there at the end she'd stopped tripping down Memory Lane. She didn't even tell me he was her granddaddy until I looked into that bony face of hers and saw my old buddy. When I asked her, she admitted it, but said she never got to know him. Her father Hector was Curly's only kid, born two months before they started filming *The Conqueror.* That's why he needed the money so bad. Wrangling don't pay squat unless you're wrangling for movie folks."

"What happened to Hector?" As if I needed to ask.

"Died of thyroid cancer sometime back in the eighties. So'd Olivia's mother. Girl was raised by her Aunt Delores, and from what I hear, old Delores was crazy-mean. Maybe the radiation got at her, too, only it ate away her brain instead of her glands."

Olivia's family history might explain her actions, not that it excused them. But who was I to judge? Before I left her at Sunset Point, she let me know she'd discovered my secrets, too—that when I was nine years old, I'd been raped by a foster father, and that a few weeks later I'd lain in wait with a knife to take my revenge. A revenge that wasn't yet finished.

"You were just a kid," she'd said to me, pity in her pain-ravaged eyes. "You couldn't stab deep enough."

"It's the only thing I'm sorry about."

"Speaking as one vigilante to another, have you decided what you'll do when he gets released from prison next year?"

I didn't answer because I didn't know. What would I do to the man who'd not only raped me, but was discovered to have raped three other foster children as well? I only knew one thing for sure. When he walked through those prison gates, I'd be waiting for him. Whether I'd be holding a bigger, sharper knife remained an open question.

Gabe's voice broke into my dark thoughts. "That was a good thing you did, letting the girl go."

"What's good about letting a three-time murderer off the hook?"

"Lena, you just granted her a temporary stay of execution."

That was one way of looking at it. After Olivia promised she wouldn't murder anyone else, I left her at Sunset Point, uncertain if she could hold out long enough to finish her Downwinders story.

But she did.

As if he could read my mind, Gabe said, "Too bad she didn't live one more day so's she could see her story on the front page of the *New York Times*. She'd have been so proud."

"Sometimes pride in a job well done isn't a strong enough reason to stick around. Sometimes you just have to end it."

Olivia had ended it last night in a swan dive off Sunset Point, plunging twelve hundred feet into the pure water of the Virgin River. By the time a family from Milwaukee found the suicide note spiked onto her car's aerial, her body was long gone.

Olivia wasn't the first Downwinder to die, and she wouldn't be the last. Wherever she wound up, she wouldn't be alone. Waiting for her were those who had gone before: her doomed family and friends, the long lost people of Walapai County. And the other lost ones, too. The southern Paiute, the Navajo, the Hopi, the Havasupai, the Chemehuevi, the Hualapai, the Tonto, the Apache, and a dozen other tribes whose homes and hunting grounds lay in the path of the radioactive wind. But as Gerald Heber once said, hey, they were only Indians.

"She coulda wrote another story, the one about Stark," Gabe said, still admiring the once deadly canyon. "What's that funny name you gave him?"

"Detective Smiley Face. Yes, I imagine she would have enjoyed writing that. But it wasn't to be, Gabe. We do what we do."

"Maybe she knows anyway."

It was nice to imagine Olivia looking down from some lofty paradise, smiling at the detective who found the carbine that killed Kimama Olmstead. Stark had hidden the weapon in his storage shed after warning his cowed wife he'd beat her within an inch of her life if she ever went in there. He forgot to warn his daughter. When Sheriff Alcott arrived at Connie Stark's front door to inform her she was a widow, the little girl volunteered the information about the "secret toy" Daddy kept out back. Sheriff Alcott immediately obtained a search warrant for the house and surrounding property. After retrieving the carbine, Alcott and a deputy drove it straight to the crime lab. Three hours later it was matched to the bullet that killed Kimama.

And to the bullet that came within inches of killing me.

Yes, imagining Olivia seeing all that in print was pretty, but when you're dead, you're dead, and that's all there is to it.

"I don't believe in the afterlife, Gabe," I said, because he was a man it didn't do to lie to. "Or in the ghosts of dead movie stars."

He gave me his sweet smile and my heart turned over. "The Duke's kept me fine company all these years, Lena."

"They have medication for that."

"Anybody ever tell you you've got a smart mouth?" But his smile stayed where it was with no hint of strain.

I smiled back. "More people than you can count." Oh, it was too bad he wasn't several decades younger. Or I wasn't several decades older.

But either way, he'd still be in love with his Abby.

Just then a busload of tourists rumbled up the road toward us. It parked at the bottom of the hillock, right where John Wayne had swaggered up to Susan Hayward and drawled his lines. People clambered out looking like they'd come straight from Sunset Canyon Lakes. The men wore sandals with white socks that reached almost to their knees; the women wore stiletto heels. Few had the forethought to bring a hat to keep off the blinding sun. I wondered how many of them had heard about the nuclear testing.

As if reading my mind, Gabe said, "You can't undo what's been done, Lena. All you can do is live with it."

"You mean the bombs?"

After a long silence, he said, "That, too."

So he'd been thinking about something else. I knew better than to ask him what. "Maybe it's time we moseyed on back to Walapai Flats, Gabe."

"You got it, girl. And just in case I haven't said it enough, thank you for everything you did. For me, the Olmsteads. And for Olivia. May she…" He lowered his voice, and with the wind blasting along the canyon and throwing all that dust at us, I couldn't quite hear his words. A prayer, maybe?

With that, he gave the canyon one final look and started down the hillock. Before I followed I took one last look around. Blood red sand. Orange and white cliffs. Black lava fields. Green buffalo grass. Like Gabe said, Snow Canyon hadn't changed in sixty years. Maybe not in thousands. It would outlast us all.

Then I saw someone I hadn't noticed earlier. On the butte opposite us sat a tall man on a steel gray horse, not that rare a sight in this area. Like Walapai Flats, Snow Canyon was ringed with guest ranches. Just another wrangler, probably, one with an odd choice of wardrobe. The rider's shirt was unusual; red and double-breasted. I'd recently seen a shirt like his, but given everything that had happened in the past few days, I couldn't remember where.

As I stared at him, the man raised his hand and snapped off a salute. Uncertain what else to do, I saluted back.

The cowboy tipped his hat and rode away.

Author's Note

Between 1951 and 1992, 928 nuclear bombs were exploded at the Nevada Test Site—an average of two bombs per month for 41 years. The last aboveground test took place November 4, 1962. After that, all tests were conducted underground, which was supposedly safer. However, the surrounding desert floor was replete not only with mineshafts, but naturally-occurring air vents that continued to release radioactive material into the atmosphere.

Perhaps the most notorious of those domestic nuclear tests was the May 19, 1953, firing of the 32-kiloton bomb nicknamed "Dirty Harry," because of its devastating effects on the local flora and fauna—including human beings. Philip L. Fradkin notes in his excellent book, *Fallout,* that "ten minutes after the detonation, the rising cloud collided with the troposphere and spread out at the 42,000-foot level, while the bottom of the cloud held steady at 27,000 feet." The westerly winds being particularly strong that day, the fallout drifted all the way to the East Coast. Particularly hard hit, though, were the miners at the Groom Mine, located just a few miles downwind of the test site.

Southern Utah, especially Snow Canyon—and the set of John Wayne's film, *The Conqueror*—lay squarely in the fallout's path. As noted in this book, almost half of the cast, crew, and Paiute extras later developed various cancers. Many died, including Wayne.

Whenever a nuclear test was scheduled, the government told people living downwind of the testing area to simply stay indoors for a couple of hours after the blast, then they could resume their usual activities, including eating produce from their contaminated gardens. While researching this book, I spoke to a man and woman in St. George, Utah (they prefer their names not be used), who watched the tests from their porch. "The colors were beautiful," the woman told me. "When we knew there was a blast coming, some of us in town would even picnic out in the yard to see the sight. We'd been assured the tests were harmless." Her husband, a former military man, said, "We were in the middle of the Cold War. The government only did what they thought was necessary for our defense."

Dirty Harry didn't produce the only killer cloud to rain down radiation on an unsuspecting populace. The nuclear testing continued for another thirty-nine years, causing unaccountable damage to the fauna and flora of the Southwest. The animals died quickly. The people died more slowly; some are still dying.

During all the years of nuclear testing, the Atomic Energy Commission (AEC) denied the harmful effects of radiation fallout. In 1965, when the rising rate of cancer deaths in the area became obvious, the Public Health Service began a study of children in southern Utah. The findings were shocking. A large percentage of the children had developed thyroid nodules, frequent precursors to thyroid cancer. When the press got wind of the studies, government officials issued a press release that stated, "Exaggerated and unbalanced press accounts could hamper not only the government's nuclear testing program but also peaceful applications of nuclear energy." For years, government officials continued to insist that the thyroid nodules meant nothing, and that the rising cases of thyroid cancers and leukemia among children and adults meant nothing.

The government was lying. Officials were already well aware of the disastrous effects that radiation had on the Pacific atolls—as well as the people of Japan. Women were miscarrying hideously deformed fetuses. Children were dying from leukemia.

Thyroid cancers—easily linked to high doses of radiation—began appearing nine years after exposure, and continued to appear forty years after exposure.

The American Southwest had been poisoned.

Because government officials had set up such an effective smokescreen, the first claims against the U.S. government for knowingly and repeatedly exposing American citizens to the dangers of nuclear fallout did not get filed until 1979. Then, using the testimony of the people now identified as Downwinders, the lawsuits began winding their way through the court system. At one point, it appeared that the Downwinders would win their damage claims against the government, but these temporary triumphs were finally overturned in court by the application of Sovereign Immunity, based on an old English law concept which meant, "The King can do no wrong." In this case, the U.S. Government was King.

Finally, after the newspapers began describing what was going on in the Southwest—and the reason for it—the government struck a deal with some Downwinders. The U.S. would award $50,000 to any person who could prove that his or her illness had been caused by the testing; in return, that person would forego any further legal action. To apply for this $50,000 payoff, each claimant had to submit a 22-page application written in dense legalese, much of it indecipherable by even the brightest citizen. Most hard hit by the legalese forms were the cancer-stricken Paiute Indians, many of whom spoke only their native language. Thus, successful claims were kept to a minimum—possibly what the government had in mind all along. But despite the obstacles put in their path, the Downwinders and their children continue to pursue their cause.

It takes a lot of uranium to build 928 nuclear bombs.

Thousands of uranium mines were operating on the Navajo Reservation from the 1940s until the 1980s, when the bottom dropped out of the uranium market. At that point, many mine operators simply walked away from their mines, leaving the radioactive waste—mine tailings—to pollute the Reservation's drinking water. Contemporary studies report that 75% of the wells in the uranium mining areas continue to have dangerous levels of uranium, arsenic, or both. In a desert where water is scarce, this is a tragedy eclipsed only by what happened to the Navajo miners themselves.

While the mines were operating, Navajo miners developed lung cancers at twenty-eight times the rate of non-mining Navajos. Kidney, brain, and bone cancers increased, as did incidents of leukemia. Non-mining Navajos were also placed at risk. Dust from the mine tailings rose into the air, leading local officials to warn those living in mining areas not to go outside when the wind was blowing (which it usually does in Navajoland). Those warnings were useless. The radioactive particles blew onto the rangeland where the Navajos grazed their sheep, thus polluting the food supply. The problems with radioactive pollution became so severe that in 2005, the Navajo Nation outlawed uranium mining and processing on its reservation.

It also takes a lot of uranium to build and maintain America's nuclear power plants.

After 9/11, the wisdom of reliance on Middle Eastern oil was called into question, and the uranium market perked up again, this time not to build bombs but to feed the 104 nuclear reactors spread across the continental U.S. The fact that fully half of those reactors are more than thirty years old and rely upon outdated technology is not considered a problem, even in light of the events at the Fukushima, Japan, nuclear plants.

Old uranium mines in the Southwest reopened and new ones were proposed. To date, approximately 3,500 uranium mining claims are pending on U.S. Bureau of Land Management and U.S. Forest Service land. In 2008, it was disclosed that some of those proposed mines were close to one of American's greatest scenic wonders—the Grand Canyon. Because of uranium mining's unsavory history, the proposed mines immediately attracted controversy. Groups leery of mining so close to the Grand Canyon and the Colorado River included the U. S. Environmental Protection Agency, the Sierra Club, the Center for Biological Diversity, the Grand Canyon Trust, the Southern Nevada Water Authority, and the Metropolitan Water District of Southern California, which gets its water from the Colorado River.

Their concerns were not without foundation.

Before the Orphan Uranium Mine closed in 1969, it produced 4.3 million pounds of some of the purest uranium ever found in the U.S. But it also dumped radioactive materials into Horn Creek, which lies within the Grand Canyon, mere miles from popular Bright Angel Trail. Campers within the Canyon have been warned not to drink Horn Creek's water because of its high level of radioactivity. Horn Creek flows into the Colorado River.

Roger Clark, a spokesman for the Grand Canyon Trust, said, "It is a stellar example of why we can't just trust the industry to say that they will not contaminate the groundwater."

But in 2010 uranium mining began again, only ten miles north of Grand Canyon National Park. In support were the National Mining Association, the Bureau of Land Management, the Arizona Department of Environmental Quality, and both of Arizona's senators, John McCain and John Kyl.

As had happened sixty years earlier when the A-bomb testing began in the American Southwest, much flag-waving ensued.

In a paper submitted to the U.S. House Subcommittee on National Parks, Forests and Public Lands, research geologist Dr. Karen J. Wenrich wrote, "We are being held hostage by dependence on imported oil. This dependence has created wars. If we are truly patriotic, we will look away from the 'not in my backyard' approach and salute mining to promote clean energy and independence from other nations who currently supply our fuel. With energy independence, we might not be caught in international wars."

Sources

Books

Bombs in the Back Yard: Atomic Testing and American Politics, by A. Costandina Titus. University of Nevada Press.

Fallout: An American Nuclear Tragedy, by Philip L. Fradkin. University of Arizona Press.

In Mortal Hands: A Cautionary History of the Nuclear Age, by Stephanie Cooke. Black Inc.

John Wayne: The Man Behind the Myth, by Michael Munn. New American Library.

Refuge: An Unnatural History of Family and Place, by Terry Tempest Williams. Pantheon Books.

The Swords of Armageddon: U.S. Nuclear Weapons Development Since 1945, by Chuck Hansen. Chucklea Publications.

Under the Cloud: The Decades of Nuclear Testing, by Richard L. Miller, Two-Sixty Press.

Reports/Articles

A History of the Atomic Energy Commission, by Alice Buck. U.S. Department of Energy, DOE/ES-003. 1983.

Archives: Atomic Bomb Casualty Commission. Issues in Science and Technology, Spring 1997.

Atomic Bomb Casualty Commission: General Report, prepared by Paul S. Henshaw and Austin M. Brues. January 1947.

Dangerous Breach Suspected at Japan Nuclear Plant, by Jay Alabaster and Shino Yasa. Associated Press. March 25, 2011.

Estimating Thyroid Doses of I-131 Received by Americans from Nevada Atmospheric Nuclear Bomb Tests, a study by the National Cancer Institute.

Federal Plan to Close Land Won't End Uranium Mining Near Grand Canyon, by Tara Alatorre, Cronkite News Service, May 9, 2011.

Half of U.S. Nuclear Reactors Over 30 Years Old, CNNMoney. March 15, 2011.

Mines Still Threaten Colorado River, Foes Say, by Shaun McKinnon, Arizona Republic, August 11, 2008.

History of the Nevada Test Site and Nuclear Testing Background, by the National Cancer Institute/National Institute of Health

Navajos Ban Uranium Mining on Reservation, Associated Press. April 22, 2005.

Nuclear Testing and the Downwinders, by Janet Burton Seegmiller. http://historytogo.utah.gov/utah_chapters/utah_today/nucleartestingandthedownwinders.html

Official List of Announced Nevada Test Site Explosions. 1995.

Radiation Effects Research Foundation (ongoing nuclear studies and reports).

Radiological Effluents Released from U.S. Continental Tests, 1961 through 1992, DOE/NV-317 (Rev. 1) August 1996.

Radiation Exposure Compensation System: Claims to Date Summary of Claims Received by 06/11/2009.

United States Nuclear Tests, July 1945 through September 1992, DOE/NV-209 (Rev. 14). December 1994.

Uranium Mining in Arizona Breccia Pipes—Environmental, Economic, and Human Impact, by Dr. Karen J. Wenrich, Research Geologist. From the Legislative Hearing on H.R. 644—the Subcommittee on National Parks, Forests and Public Lands of the Committee on Natural Resources. July 21, 2009.

Uranium Mining in Region Resumes, by Cyndy Cole, Arizona Daily Sun. January 13, 2010.

Films

America's Atomic Bomb Tests: At Ground Zero, a documentary in four parts, filmed on location in Nevada. Contains live footage of some of the bomb tests. 1997.

Atomic Cafe (The), a collection of government films from the 1940s and 1950s designed to show that atomic testing—especially those at the Nevada Test Site—was harmless. Directed by Jayne Loader, Kevin Rafferty (a cousin of George W. Bush), with footage of Harry S. Truman and other proponents of domestic bomb testing. 1982.

Atomic Mom, a documentary filmed by M.T. Silvia. 2010

Blue Sky, directed by Tony Richardson, starring Jessica Lange, Tommy Lee Jones, and Powers Boothe. The lives of a military family sent to the test site. 1994.

The Conqueror, directed by Dick Powell, starring John Wayne and Susan Hayward. Wayne as Ghengis Khan, Hayward as his reluctant bride-to-be.1956.

Desert Bloom, directed by Eugene Corr, starring Jon Voight, JoBeth Williams, and Ellen Barkin. The story of a family living near the Nevada Test Site. 1986.

Nightbreaker, directed by Peter Markle, starring Martin Sheen, Emilio Estevez, and Lea Thompson. The story of the American servicemen who were used as guinea pigs during the atomic testing. 1989.